Leo Kessler is a familiar name to readers of war fiction. In addition to his numerous super-selling war series he is the author of several non-fiction works and of the screenplay *Breakthrough*. He lives in Germany.

Also by Leo Kessler

The *SS Assault Regiment Wotan* Series
SS PANZER BATTALION
DEATH'S HEAD
CLAWS OF STEEL
GUNS AT CASSINO
THE DEVIL'S SHIELD
HAMMER OF THE GODS
FORCED MARCH
BLOOD AND ICE
THE SAND PANTHERS
COUNTER-ATTACK
PANZER HUNT
SLAUGHTER GROUND
HELLFIRE
FLASHPOINT
CAULDRON OF BLOOD
SCHIRMER'S HEADHUNTERS
WHORES OF WAR

The *Stormtroop* Series
STORMTROOP
BLOOD MOUNTAIN
VALLEY OF THE ASSASSINS
RED ASSAULT
HIMMLER'S GOLD
FIRE OVER KABUL

The *Rommel* Series
GHOST DIVISION
MASSACRE

The *Otto Stahl* Series
OTTO'S PHONEY WAR
OTTO'S BLITZKRIEG!
OTTO AND THE REDS

The *Sea Wolves* Series
SINK THE SCHARNHORST
DEATH TO THE DEUTSCHLAND

Also:

As Klaus Konrad
The *Russian* Series
FIRST BLOOD
MARCH ON MOSCOW
FRONT SWINE

Leo Kessler

Whores of War

Wotan 17

Futura
Macdonald & Co
London & Sydney

A Futura Book

First published in Great Britain in 1982
by Futura Publications, a Division of
Macdonald & Co (Publishers) Ltd
London & Sydney

ISBN 0 7088 2237 1

Filmset, printed and bound in Great Britain by
Hazell Watson & Viney Ltd, Aylesbury, Bucks

Futura Publications
A Division of
Macdonald & Co (Publishers) Ltd
Maxwell House
74 Worship Street
London EC2A 2EN

WHORES OF WAR

THE RISE AND FALL OF SS ASSAULT BATTALION WOTAN, 1939–1945

'I swear to you, Adolf Hitler, as Führer and Reich Chancellor, loyalty and bravery. I vow to you and those you have named to command me obedience unto death. So help me God.'

Oath sworn by every new member of SS Assault Battalion Wotan from 1939 onwards.

AUTHOR'S NOTE

When I first started to chronicle the history of that grim band, with the dreaded silver death's head cap badge that made them feared throughout the western world forty years ago, my main source of information was the so-called 'Von Dodenburg Papers' found amongst the belongings of Obersturmbannführer Kuno von Dodenburg, the last commander of SS Assault Regiment Wotan, who died and was buried in a pauper's grave in Italian exile in 1952. At that time, it was believed that the records – the after-action reports, and so on – of the Sixth SS Panzer Army had been burned at the Czech-Austrian frontier just before SS General Sepp Dietrich surrendered what was left of his once élite force to the Americans in May 1945.

Now, to the surprise of historians of World War Two, those records have turned up again, interestingly enough, in Alexandria, Virginia, USA. How they got there is a mystery in itself, and one which will take some solving. Did the Americans, despite Eisenhower's much-vaunted 'crusade' against the Nazis in Europe in World War Two, keep the records of Hitler's most feared fighting force just in case they might themselves use that élite formation against the Russians in days to come? Or was it just the whim of some local commander that those documents, now yellowed and thin with age, were preserved for posterity? Undoubtedly some keen young historian, eager to make a reputation for himself – and gain a professorial chair in the process – will explain all in due course.

But for the time being, those documents, with their dry statistics and colourless military jargon, have enabled me to fill in many gaps in the six-year history of the élite of the

SS Assault Regiment Wotan, as it finally became in 1944. Here, then, for the very first time, is the full history of that 'black band' which was the scourge of Europe in World War Two. It is a story full of horror and written in blood; it is the story of the WHORES OF WAR . . .

L. K. Trier, 1981

1939

THE BLACK BAND

'A new man, the storm soldier, the élite of Central Europe. A completely new race, cunning, strong and packed with purpose . . . battle-proven, merciless both to himself and others.'

Ernst Junger, German soldier and poet

ONE

The torches flickered in the sudden wind as the great oaken door to the underground chamber was flung open by the black-clad giants of the escort. An icy blast, as if from the grave itself, struck the prisoner's harsh, cynical face. At the door the drummers started a long mournful roll on their kettledrums.

'Prisoner will advance!' barked the blond giant, with the gleaming silver skull on his cap and the silver runes of the SS on his collar.

SS Sturmbannführer Gaier, otherwise known as the Vulture, adjusted his monocle and, flanked by the giants, began to march down the long medieval corridor, his boots echoing and re-echoing hollowly down its recesses.

His monocle and his light-grey breeches with their cowhide inlet marked him clearly for what he was – a regular officer who had recently transferred from the Wehrmacht to the newly formed Armed SS. Promotion prospects were better in the Black Guards. The prisoner and his escort swung round a corridor. At the far end, in a Gothic vaulted chamber, huddled in their black greatcoats in the freezing cold of Wawelsburg Castle, where once the ancient Saxon kings of this region had been buried, sat the members of his court-martial. Wolff, Juttner, Dietrich, Berger – all the SS generals were present, and in their midst, looking exactly like the pale-faced ex-chicken farmer he had once been, sat the Reichsführer himself: Heinrich Himmler, the bespectacled head of the SS and the commander of the most feared police *apparat* in the whole world.

'Prisoner – *halt*!' the escort commanded, his breath fogging on the icy air of the underground chamber.

The Vulture halted.

Somewhere a phonograph was switched on. There came the brutal, precise crunch of steel-shod jackboots, then suddenly the chamber was filled with the hoarse, masculine chant of the SS:

'Clear the street, the SS marches,
The storm-columns stand at the ready.
They will take the road
From tyranny to freedom.
So we are all ready to give our all,
As did our fathers before us.
Let death be our battle companion,
We are the Black Band . . .'

The Vulture was not impressed. He never was by the vulgar, cheap, *petit-bourgeois* pretensions of the National Socialists. Nor did Himmler's cold stare through those silver-rimmed schoolmaster's glasses of his bother or frighten him. All this cheap play-acting – the underground chambers, the pitch torches, the black-clad generals looking like the members of the Inquisition, the brutal marching song – all this was completely foreign to his nature. Regular officers of the old Wehrmacht such as he found this melodramatic rubbish repugnant and unworthy of a true soldier, whose heart is stirred only by horses and promotion.

Yet all the same, as the singing gave way to the harsh stamping of the boots, as rank after rank of the black-clad giants goose-stepped past on some parade or other in far-off Berlin, the Vulture felt an icy finger of fear trace its way down the small of his back. His little quirk had got him into serious trouble this time – though why the National Socialists made such a fuss about the Greek vice was beyond him. Still, he had been caught *in flagrante*, and he knew Himmler's feelings on the subject. Unless Dietrich, the commander of the Adolf Hitler Bodyguard Regiment, the premier SS formation, put in a good word for him, he might well end up in one of the newly established concentration camps – or even worse . . .

Suddenly Major Geier, known as the Vulture on account of his name and his nose – a monstrous abomination which would have been laughable on another, less dangerous man, was afraid. Very afraid.

Himmler waited till the stamp of marching boots had died away, leaving the torch-lit underground chamber loud with their echo, then cleared his throat. 'Sturmbannführer Geier,' he said prissily, 'this court of honour of the Armed SS,' he extended a pale hand around the assembled generals, 'has found you guilty of a very serious charge.' He looked down suddenly at the oaken table, as if almost ashamed of what he was saying. 'A charge against the morals of a minor.'

General Dietrich, Hitler's old companion and Party bully-boy from the days before the Führer had taken over power, seized the opportunity to wink at the prisoner, while handsome General Wolff with his intelligent, wary eyes smiled encouragingly.

Geier felt hope and sneered to himself. *Minor*! The boy had probably been selling it behind the Lehrter Bahnhof* since he was six. At fourteen he was steeped in evil and every kind of sexual debauchery. Minor, indeed!

Himmler raised his head once more. 'Sturmbannführer Geier, your official duties since you transferred from the Wehrmacht to the Armed SS have been carried out in an exemplary manner. General Berger here,' he indicated the oldest officer present, the real organizer of the Armed SS, 'vouches for you, and states you have made an outstanding contribution to the preparation of our fine formations for the heavy tasks which lie ahead of them. Generals Wolff and Dietrich also pay tribute to your skilled staff work and organizational talent.'

Geier licked his lips. So he was getting the sweet-and-sour treatment, like Chink food. First the sweet, then the

* Mainline Berlin railway station.

sour to come. Suddenly he bridled. Why *should* he tamely submit to punishment? Why not spill the beans – let this pompous, pale-faced ass, who looked so damned solemn and moral, know just what kind of generals he had surrounded himself with. A bunch of civvies in a fancy uniform – that's what most of them were. Abruptly he was overcome by that icy, calculating, cold-blooded rage and determination which would make him such a formidable regimental commander in the battles to come.

But on this burningly hot July day of 1939, Germany's year of destiny, Sturmbannführer Geier did not need to give vent to his rage. Himmler, it transpired, could not afford to lose him, in spite of the gravity of the charge.

'. . . I am in no way condoning the heinous crime that you committed, Geier,' Himmler continued, pressing his fingertips together under his weak receding chin and trying to give the impression of great sagacity. 'It is an unnatural offence and one totally unworthy of an SS officer. However, as several of your commanders have spoken so highly of you and your talents, and in view of present circumstances, I have decided on the following.'

The Vulture tensed, screwing up his right eye to retain his monocle.

'One,' Himmler ticked the point off on his finger like a bank clerk making a tally, 'you will be henceforth reduced in rank from major to captain.'

The Vulture winced. It had taken him two hard years with the SS to make that promotion, and Geier dearly loved rank. It was his *raison d'être*.

'Two, you are to be posted away from the temptations of Berlin immediately – to a fighting unit in the provinces.'

A poignant, fleeting vision of those effete, slim male bodies with their powdered faces, plucked eyebrows and simpering smiles flashed before Geier's eyes. He was going to miss Berlin, that was for sure.

'You know from your duties with planning, Geier, that the Führer in his wisdom has finally decided to have a reckoning with those insolent slavic subhumans the Poles.

You will know also that he has given his own guard, the Adolf Hitler Bodyguard, the honour of leading the attack. At the spearhead of the Bodyguard will be SS Assault Regiment Wotan. You, *Captain* Geier, will command the First Company of that regiment.'

The Vulture hastily suppressed a sigh of relief. He was going to get away with it after all!

But Himmler was not finished with him yet. 'Let me say this one last thing, Geier,' he said softly, his face hollowed out to a death's head by the light of the flickering torches, the eyes behind the glasses momentarily concealed by some trick of the flame, so that Geier fancied he was looking at an eyeless skull. 'You will lead those men to victory, Geier, but you will *not* come back! You will die on the battlefield and restore your honour – for Folk, Fatherland and Führer. That is all, Geier. I do not wish to see you ever again.'

Blindly the Vulture stumbled back up that long, echoing stone chasm, and staggered outside into the hot sunshine, blinking his eyes until he could see the flat Westphalian plain spread out beneath the castle once again. His mind was racing. So he had not escaped after all. Himmler, the swine, had virtually *ordered* him to commit suicide. One thing was for sure: there would be no appeal against a sentence passed by the most feared man in Europe.

Thus it was that that July, Captain Geier first came to join SS Assault Regiment Wotan and prepare for his first campaign in a bloody war which would last six long years, and which few of the black-clad giants, the élite of the élite, would survive. He pushed the appalling memory of his sentence to the back of his mind as he studied his new command and its advantages and disadvantages. The men were magnificent: not one of them was under six foot, and each was blond and robust, with not even a single filling. They were fools of course; their sole desire was to die a hero's death for their beloved Führer. Their officers were little better; fanatics to a man, driven by the same melodramatic urge to die leading their men to glory on the battlefield.

As for the CO, he was married and had two children – a fatal mistake for a career officer – and was reported to read books on military tactics, a habit which the Vulture found almost as horrifying as the fact that he could bring himself to have sexual intercourse with a woman – indeed, his wife. In his view the man wasn't fit to command a platoon, never mind a whole battalion.

After a week at his new station, the Vulture concluded that the only man of the 800-strong battalion whom he could take into his confidence a little was the company sergeant-major, Metzger, a butcher by trade, appearance and inclination. This huge hulk of a man, who, like Geier, had come from the Wehrmacht and was known as 'the Butcher' by the men of the 1st Company, was a coward – perhaps the only one in the whole battalion. It was a weakness that the Vulture knew he could use to his own advantage. Promise the Butcher freedom from dangerous combat action, and in return the big NCO would use his network of junior NCOs as a kind of spy system, feeding Geier the information he needed to survive – and survive he would. How exactly he didn't know at the moment, but he *would*!

The idea which would save him from committing suicide at the head of his troops and which was to gain him the first high decoration awarded to an SS officer in the course of the war, came to him during the final planning conference for the attack on Poland. Dietrich, detailing the role the Bodyguard would play in his usual slow, plodding, Bavarian manner, had at last come to the actual details of the attack and the difficulties posed by the rivers the SS would have to cross in order to achieve the link-up between the 8th and 10th Armies. Suddenly the great idea flashed into Geier's mind, perfect, formed, unbeatable.

'. . . Gentlemen,' Dietrich was saying, 'the Polacks will try to hold us first on the river line of the Prosna – here.' He poked a finger at the map. 'Then around Bzura – here. We will not give them that opportunity. The tanks of Battalion Wotan will *swim* – the Polacks won't be expecting that. They're still dicking around with those cavalry nags of theirs. Then, and only then, will the panzer grenadiers go in to mop them up.' He smiled at them, his gold teeth flashing underneath the old-fashioned moustache which he affected. 'In other words, we'll reverse the usual tactic of infantry going in first to protect the armour. It'll catch them completely off their guard. We'll have the rivers before the Polacks have pulled their thumbs out of their thick Polack arses! Good, eh?'

Geier nodded, but he was no longer listening as Dietrich continued his briefing. Instead his mind was racing excitedly as he considered his bold plan. What if those tanks were *not* to catch the Poles off guard? What if the defenders were alerted in time to ready whatever anti-tank weapons they had? And what if a certain Captain Geier had to come to the rescue of the stalled tanks with his 1st Company, heroically sacrificing the lives of his giant panzer grenadiers in order to ensure that the offensive kept rolling?

Hauptsturmführer Geier was ready to commit his first act of base treachery against his own men in his blind search for survival and military success. It would not be the last before finally he died the terrible death that he deserved . . .

TWO

Thwack!

The first slug howled off the fir tree next to where the Vulture was standing, staring out into the gloom of this first dawn of the new war.

Somewhere behind him a whistle shrilled urgently, and an officer cried out in alarm.

The Vulture swung round in anger. 'What in three devils' name—'

The rest of his angry outburst was drowned by the sudden chatter of an ancient machine gun. From across the sullen, turgid flow of the river which divided German Silesia from Poland, slow, white tracer bullets started to fly in the direction of the men crouching in the bushes and reeds, gathering speed by the instant.

Next to Geier, a soldier clutched his throat, spat out a thick gob of bright scarlet blood, and pitched face-forward on the damp ground, dead.

The Butcher gasped. 'But they're firing at . . . *at us*!' His frightened voice was full of awed disbelief.

The Vulture slapped his riding cane angrily against his boot. On this burning hot dawn of 1st September, 1939, things were not going quite as he planned, for already he could hear the roar of the waiting Mark IIIs of the Bodyguard, as the tanks started to waddle down to the river like metal ducks, preparing for the crossing.

'Just for practice, Metzger, just for practice,' the Vulture sneered, and then, drawing his pistol, cried above the roar as the first wave of tanks hit the water, 'Take cover . . . at the double now! *Take cover*!'

Everywhere his men went to ground, while the tracer

whipped the air all around, howling off the metal sides of the Mark IIIs, which were now up to their turrets in water, readying for the steep, muddy bank on the opposite side.

Cursing, the Vulture watched, more angry than afraid, as the first tank started to fight the mud bank, its tracks racing wildly as it tried to maintain a hold, churning up a whirling wake of mud and pebbles behind it. He gripped the butt of his pistol until his knuckles turned white, hoping against hope that the tanks would fail to overcome the bank and his infantry could come gloriously to the rescue.

But it was not to be. Somehow, with his 300-horse-power engine howling, the driver frantically smashing his way through his dozen or so gears, the first Mark III made it and disappeared over the other side, machine gun chattering. Another followed, and another. Slowly, the wild small arms fire from the other side of the river started to die away, to be replaced by the steady, awesome *boom* of the heavy guns, the permanent background music to war, which was to become an integral part of the Vulture's life for the next four years. Angrily, he thrust his pistol back into his shoulder. He had missed his chance for glory this time. 'All right, you bunch of sad sacks,' he yelled above the thunder of the guns. 'Follow me . . . Into the water now! *Los-mir nach*!'

That first week of September, the Black Band fought its way ever forward. Under the blistering heat, they waded on through the tall fields of brilliant yellow sunflowers, meeting khaki-clad men with the Eagle of Poland on their caps and stalking them like avenging gunmen in a Hollywood western. Before them, the Stukas fell screaming from the sky like metal gulls, their sirens howling, deadly eggs falling from their ugly black bellies. The self-propelled guns thundered, and the monstrous mechanized juggernaut the world had never seen before swept all before it – for this was the Blitzkrieg!

Horses against tanks . . . The Polish cavalryman's long lance against the stubby cannon and machine guns of the Mark III . . . The tanks of the Bodyguard slaughtered the defiant riders by the thousand, piling up great walls of dead and dying horses and riders in the vast fields, once ablaze with the yellow of sunflowers and maize, now stained red with blood.

Within forty-eight hours the flower of the Polish cavalry had vanished, as had the antiquated Polish air force. The speed and ruthless efficiency of the Blitzkrieg brooked no opposition. As the victorious men of the Black Band swept down those dusty Polish roads, the carnage on both sides was indescribable, the butchery of enemy soldiers and civilians total. They lay stacked on both sides like piles of cordwood, the lead tanks nosing their way through mountains of fresh corpses.

On and on they ploughed, hardened now to the sight of the dead and dying, the smashed refugee carts, the blackened, wrecked vehicles, the screams and whinnies of the dying, mutilated horses (for there was no one left alive now to put them out of their misery). In their nostrils every yard of the way was the sweet, cloying stench of the bloated corpses, blackening in the burning autumn sun.

By the end of the first week of the campaign, the Polish army had been vanquished. All its mobile formations had been destroyed. Now, with the remnants of its thirty-five divisions shattered or caught in a vast pincer movement, the two armoured claws of the German Blitzkrieg began relentlessly and inexorably closing on the Polish capital, Warsaw itself. But just then the weather changed. The rains came, and the Polish steppe was changed into one vast quagmire. With the tanks bogged down, the Blitzkrieg ground to a halt, and from the front came the news that Captain Geier had been hoping for ever since the start of the campaign. The 36th Panzer Regiment and the 1st SS Battalion had been stopped at the Bzura River. His panzer grenadiers were urgently needed at the front. It was the chance he had been waiting for!

★

As if some unseen hand had thrown a gigantic power switch, the night sky across the river was rent by an enormous flash of brilliant light. For one long moment, there was only that great burning, ugly red light. No sound, just searing flame. Then in an instant the vengeful fury of that impossible booming noise swamped the survivors of the first attack, who were now crouching on their side of the Bzura. Next moment, the whole weight of the dug-in Polish artillery swamped the Bodyguard, making the very earth shake, thrashing the trees with a great howling wind.

In a flash the Polish smaller weapons joined in. Mortars belched obscenely. Machine guns chattered frenetically. Flak cannon, used in a ground role, screamed white-glowing death. To the east, on the other side of the river, the Poles hammered the positions of the hard-pressed SS mercilessly, while on the western bank, a fantastic pattern of stabs and forked jabs of scarlet flame erupted, interspersed with signal flares hushing into the glowing sky – desperate pleas for help, advice, God knows what, as the young blond giants of the Black Band died in their scores, trapped in their smoking pits.

General Dietrich, his ankle-length leather coat smeared with mud, a trickle of dried black blood zig-zagging down his worn face, cupped his hands around the Vulture's right ear. 'The Polack pigs have got us by the short hairs, Geier! The Thirty-Sixth hasn't got a damned tank left, and I've written off the 1st SS!' Dietrich's gold teeth glittered in the night. 'Geier – get us across that river and you can write your own ticket! I'll get you a drawerful of tin if you do!'

Seemingly unaffected by the carnage and chaos all around him, the Vulture smiled coldly. He had it! He was saved. Even Himmler wouldn't dare offend Dietrich, a member of the Blood Order* who had served the Führer

* Awarded to those who had shed their blood for the Nazi Party prior to 1933.

ever since the Twenties. 'Oberführer,' he shouted above the racket, 'the River Bzura is yours!'

The Vulture swung round and addressed his men, who were crouched in the steaming brown holes, surrounded by the dead of the 1st SS. 'First Company, SS Assault Battalion Wotan,' he screeched. '*To the attack*!'

Screaming hoarsely, carried away by fear and rage, the young men slithered and slipped down the river bank into the water. Impelled by some wild atavastic fury, they started to wade across, shrieking obscenely, the water ahead whipped and tormented by the slugs of the Polish machine-gunners. The sacrifice of the First Company had commenced.

Now it was dawn. The third onslaught was collapsing – a furious Vulture, bleeding from a gaping wound in his shoulder, could see that. On the far bank a dozen Wotan men running frantically for cover were caught by a burst of Polish machine-gun fire. It swept them from their feet, scything them down mercilessly, continuing to thresh their writhing, heaving bodies, until finally all were still.

Now the survivors started to stream back past the Vulture, their eyes wild and wide with shock, holding their bleeding wounds, moaning or screaming obscenely at the unbelievable horror of the martyrdom they had just undergone.

'God in heaven!' Dietrich gasped, choking on a gulp of cognac from his flask – his third that long, terrible night, 'they're not soldiers any more, Captain Geier . . . they're walking corpses!'

Dietrich's face contorted with horror. But the Vulture was totally unmoved. 'Sergeant-Major Metzger, set up a machine-gun one hundred metres to the rear, next to the clump of firs. Have no mercy,' he rapped. 'Shoot down any man of the First Company who attempts to pass you!'

The Butcher's face lit up. It was just the kind of task he sought to escape the slaughter of the First on the River

Bzura. He hurried off before Geier could change his mind, leaving the survivors to their fate.

Geier tried to tug out his pistol, his face twisted with pain. It was impossible. He let his blood-soaked arm drop. 'First Company,' he called, 'First Company – *follow me*!'

Groggily the survivors rose to their feet for the fourth time, staring blindly ahead. Already the Polish guns had commenced chattering once more, and tracer hissed across the river. Again the First Company waded into the corpse-littered water to brave the lethal white hail. The first rank fell back screaming into the boiling water, while the second one fought its way on through their shattered bodies, towards the churned-up mud of the opposite bank. The German dead lay everywhere, surrounded by the debris of war, as if some crazy surgeon had gone to work on them, using high explosive instead of a scalpel.

The Vulture clambered over a soldier lying in a pool of his own blood. The corpse stared upwards with accusing eyes, while the evil fat-bellied bluebottles crawled greedily over his waxen face. Unperturbed but gasping with pain, Geier heaved himself up the bank.

There was the Polish bunker. A low earth and log structure with sandbags for a roof, with two heavy old-fashioned machine-guns spitting fire from its slits.

The Vulture slithered back down to the survivors, a mere handful of them now, sheltering in dead ground, their eyes glazed with a strange dreamy sheen, their lips twitching constantly.

He tried to ignore their protests, but they were close to breaking point, he knew that. There was no time for subtle tactics. It would have to be a direct assault, come what may. 'Fix bayonets!' he rasped.

With hands that trembled violently, the survivors drew their gleaming bayonets and fastened them to the ends of their rifles, some of them keening like men who would soon go mad.

Geier, his face contorted with the almost unbearable

agony of his wounded shoulder, clawed his way up the muddy bank once more, the survivors following him. Suddenly they burst out into the open. Immediately the Poles turned their machine-guns on them. With the last of their energy, the men spurted forward, taking hits all the time, but leaving the dead crumpled behind them in the mud as they sprinted those last terrible hundred metres.

The rusting wire stopped them briefly. Wildly they fought the treacherous barbs, dancing and hopping like crazy men, as the Poles, only ten metres away, their faces scared white blobs in the dark apertures, raked the line back and forth with a hail of glowing death. Finally they were through, ten of them, with Geier, wounded now in the thigh, hobbling after them, screaming obscenities, physically willing his men to take the bunker.

Carried away by that mad heroism of the battlefield, in which all reason is cast aside, a young soldier, bareheaded, his shaven blond skull gleaming like a bright flag in the new sun, ran screaming straight at the slit, great lumps of flesh being torn off his body as he did so. For a moment he staggered, and Geier thought he would go down. But somehow he managed it. With the last of his dying strength he clawed the red-hot muzzle of the nearest machine-gun to his shattered chest, thus masking its fire.

The next instant his comrades were scrambling up onto the sandbag roof, clawing them away and flinging in their stick grenades with hands that were already dying . . .

An hour later, the five survivors of the First Company SS Assault Battalion Wotan began to clamber wearily up the opposite bank of the Bzura. They had silenced the opposition. The triumphant advance could continue.

The Vulture in the lead, limping badly, his helmet and monocle gone, raised his good arm in salute.

Dietrich staggered back a pace, as if the Vulture had struck him.

The Vulture did not notice. Weary and in pain as he was, his icy-blue eyes were filled with a look of triumph.

Behind him the survivors trailed on, painfully and in silence, like sleep-walkers haunted by some terrible, never-ending nightmare, leaving the battlefields to the dead . . .

THREE

'*Stillgestanden*!'

Two hundred pairs of new army boots crashed to attention in deafening unison. The troop train which had brought the new recruits to this remote border region began to draw away, puffing and chugging mightily. Lieutenant Schwarz reported to the officer from SS Assault Battalion Wotan who had come to receive them. 'Draft from Sennelager, sir. One officer, four NCOs and two hundred men, *sir*! . . . All present and correct, *sir*!'

First Lieutenant Kuno von Dodenburg, one of the few survivors of the Polish bloodbath, whose chest bore the black wound medal and the ribbon of the Iron Cross third class, acknowledged Schwarz's salute with the casual air of the veteran, a look of mild boredom on his intelligent, harshly handsome face.

'*Danke, Untersturmführer*!' he snapped and turned his attention to the draft, every one of them bronzed, fit and towering over the two officers. 'When we leave this station, we will sing. And when I say sing, I mean *sing*! I want the local yokels to know this isn't the army that's marching through their streets, it's the SS. In particular, the SS of Assault Battalion Wotan. Got it?'

'Got it!' two hundred eager young voices snapped back.

Schulze, the broad-faced comedian of the new draft, nudged his neighbour and said, in the broad accents of Hamburg's waterfront, 'Them dum-dums!' He indicated the open-mouthed peasants gaping at them from the doorways of their hovels. 'Look as if they've got to be told to come in out of the rain. Bet they don't even know what the SS is!'

'Silence there in the ranks!' Lieutenant Schwarz yelled. 'Prepare to march off!'

Lieutenant von Dodenburg, leaning casually against one of the pillars that held up the sagging station roof, sucked his teeth. So the Vulture had got his new batch of cannon-fodder. The question was: where was this fresh lot going to die?

'A song – *one, two, three*!' the draft's lead singer commanded, as they swung into the little town's main thoroughfare.

Two hundred lusty male voices crashed into the *Horst Wessel Lied*, the marching song of the Party. But for most part the undersized peasants in their shabby blue smocks who lined the pavements did not react. They merely gaped at the eager young giants who stamped past on the worn cobbles as if they were invaders from another planet.

'Look at 'em,' Schulze's neighbour sneered, 'yer can tell they don't like the SS. Half of 'em have got frog blood in them anyhow. That's why we're here, Schulze, to kick the frogs out of the Maginot Line o' theirs and to learn this lot of half-breeds what it means to be German.'

Schulze grinned and winked broadly at a pretty, dark-haired girl, who blushed and looked away hurriedly. 'Ner,' he sneered. 'The Führer hasn't sent Mrs Schulze's handsome son down here to fight. He wants him and his SS to put a nice length of prime German beef into the local lassies. We're not here to fight, we're here to —'

'One more word from you,' a harsh voice cut in, 'and I'll have yer name in my book quicker than you can pull yer filthy piece of salami out of a poxed-up pavement pounder!'

Schulze got a quick glimpse of a brick-red angry face set above a pair of mighty shoulders, adorned with the stars of a regimental sergeant-major. Then they were swinging around the corner, past the onion-towered Catholic church, advancing on the red-brick pile of the Adolf Hitler Barracks, their new home.

★

'Morning, soldiers!' Captain Geier yelled, in his thin rasping, high-pitched voice, as soon as Lieutenant von Dodenburg had reported to him.

'*Morgen, Hauptsturmführer*!' came back the traditional reply.

Geier, now recovered from the wound he had received in Poland, though still limping slightly, stroked his monstrous beak and took in the draft with a single hard look from his ice-blue, cold eyes. 'Stand at ease!' he commanded. He slapped his riding cane against his highly polished topboots. 'Soldiers, my name is Geier, which I am told aptly suits my appearance*.' He stroked his nose as if to emphasize his point, but no one laughed. Even Schulze sensed that he was in the presence of a dangerous, totally unpredictable man and that it wouldn't be wise to make an enemy of this particular officer.

'At present, as you can see, my rank is that of a captain, a very humble and low rank indeed.' The Vulture's voice was deceptively soft. 'But I do not intend to remain in that rank very long. If this war lasts the year, I will be a major by the end of it. My father was a general and *I* intend to be a general, too. *General* Geier, that is what I shall become, do you hear?' He pointed his cane almost accusingly at the new recruits. 'And you know how I shall do it?' He answered his own question in the thin, rasping, Prussian Army voice that all the regular Wehrmacht officers that von Dodenburg had ever known seemed to affect. 'I shall do it on your backs. And when you're looking at the potatoes from below, I shall do it on the backs of those who come after you.

'You have now joined the premier regiment of the Armed SS,' Geier continued. 'The battalion to which you belong from this moment onwards is the best within that regiment, and it goes without saying that the best company in that battalion is *my* company. Do you understand?' Geier's piercing, ice-blue eyes searched the ranks of the young giants for any sign of weakness or doubt, but he saw

* *Geier*=vulture

none. For the young men who faced him were the best that National Socialist Germany could produce: devoted followers of the Führer, men of fanatical, devoted loyalty, whose last six years in the Hitler Youth and the Work Service had been one long preparation for this proud moment when they could finally bear the bold white legend 'Adolf Hitler' on the arm of their field-grey uniform.

'I cannot tell you the details of your assignment here,' Geier went on. 'All I can tell you is that you'll only have a short time to prepare for it. But when we march west, I want those damned Tommies and Frogs to break the Olympic record for running – right back where they came from. I want you men of the First Company to work like the devil for me. I already have one medal, won for me by the men of the First Company who died in Poland.' He tapped his skinny chest with his cane. 'That's enough tin for the time being. But next time I want the Führer to cure my throatache.'*

Geier let his words sink in before continuing, 'I do not ask you to love me, soldiers. I do not ask you to respect me. All I ask from you is that you obey my orders with unquestioning obedience.' His icy gaze swept their ranks once more. 'And Holy God help you – common soldier, non-commissioned officer, or officer – if you fail to do that. I shall be merciless.' The Vulture's voice rose harshly. 'Soldiers, I welcome you to SS Assault Battalion Wotan!'

They trained mercilessly, as they always did in SS Assault Battalion Wotan. 'Train hard, fight soft' was the Battalion's motto; and in the six years of Wotan's existence, there was no other unit in the whole of the ten-million-strong Wehrmacht which prepared for the battlefield with the same ruthless, back-breaking efficiency.

'*Aufstehen*!'

Everywhere the gravel-voiced NCOs were shrilling their

* Knight's Cross of the Iron Cross would be the medal which would cure the Vulture's 'throatache'; the decoration was worn around the neck.

whistles and bellowing themselves red-faced in the winter morning air. '*Hands off cocks – on with socks!*'

Immediately the recruits started tumbling out of their wooden bunks. They had now been in the SS long enough to know it didn't pay to linger.

At the door of Schulze's hut, the duty NCO in his blue cotton tracksuit, whistle hanging around his neck, charge book at his hip, stared grimly as the shaven-headed recruits dropped to the gleaming waxed floor, squeaking as their naked feet touched its icy surface.

'*Ausziehen!*' he commanded.

Hurriedly they tugged their old-fashioned issue night-shirts over their heads and stood there naked, shivering in the icy draught from the open door.

Contemptuously the NCO mustered their giant, naked bodies. 'Bunc o' piss-pansies,' he snapped. 'Call yersen soldiers – I've shat better!'

For what seemed an age he kept the young men standing there, their faces blue with cold, their limbs trembling. Finally he called, '*Lueften!*'

Glad of the opportunity to move, the men scrambled to pull down the blackout shutters and open the big windows. More ice-cold air streamed in. Their teeth started to chatter.

'Sergeant,' the big broad-faced ex-docker from Hamburg called Schulze said, 'I think mine's gonna shrink right away in the blizzard that's coming from that door. Do you think I could report sick?' he added hopefully.

'You might, you might, Schulze,' the duty NCO said, without any change of expression. 'But I think I ought to warn you that the MO was on the piss last night. He's got a bad case of the shakes this morning. I, for one, wouldn't let him get at my outside plumbing in the shape he's in.' Suddenly his voice erupted into a thunderous roar that made the recruits quail and their faces turn white. '*Report sick, Schulze! You never report sick in SS Assault Battalion Wotan. When you go to see the MO, they carry you to him in a wooden box! Now, get outside, you horrible shower of shit . . . The Butcher is waiting for yer – and it don't pay to keep the Butcher waiting.'*

'My name's Butcher – butcher by trade, butcher by name, and butcher by inclination!' the huge, red-faced sergeant-major bellowed at the men of the First Company, now standing rigidly to attention in the centre of the square.

Schulze sighed to himself. The NCO was the one who had barked at him on their way to the barracks from the station. It seemed that all his young life he had been terrorized by men like Sergeant Metzger,* born sadists who were cowards at heart.' A little voice inside his head whispered, 'Now you've gone and landed yourself right up to yer hooter in shit again!'

The Butcher's rat-trap of a mouth snapped open again, and his voice roared across the parade ground, bouncing back off the walls two hundred metres away. 'Believe me, nothing, but nothing in this world, will give me greater pleasure than making forced-meat out of you bunch of wet sacks. Do you get that?'

Standing there, feet astride, hands planted on his hips, helmet perched on shaven skull, as if some God of War had planted him there to show these miserable, pale-faced recruits what a *real* soldier looked like, Metzger ran his gaze along the ranks of the draft. His eyes flicked from recruit to recruit with an almost audible click, looking for an open button, a helmet set at the wrong angle, an unpolished SS emblem, a dull belt buckle.

But on this particular wintry morning, he found nothing that would grant him an opportunity to give expression to one of his celebrated outbursts of temper. Reluctantly he got down to the business of the day. 'All right, then, you bunch of greenbeaks, we'll start crapping then. *Stand at ease!'*

Automatically their left feet shot out. The Butcher

* *Metzger*=Butcher.

placed his big paws behind his back and started to rock back and forth on his toes.

'*You* think you're soldiers, because you've been passed out of recruit training,' he commenced his little homily. 'You're wrong. You're a bunch of Christmas tree soldiers, a collection of slack arseholes, a rabble of chimney-sweeps run amok, a lot of rooting sows, a bucket of pavement pounders' puke. You are, in short,' he ended with his favourite phrase, '*a bunch of horseshit!*'

Out of the side of his mouth, Schulze whispered hoarsely to his neighbour, 'You know, comrade, I have a sneaking suspicion that that noncom don't *like* us overmuch . . .'

'Now, I know that it is my duty and that of my NCOs to attempt to turn a bunch of shit like you into something approaching soldiers.' He held up a big red paw, as if to ward off their protests. 'I know, I know! Nobody in his right mind would ever think such a thing possible, except perhaps for the Butcher.' He lowered his gaze momentarily. 'But I have promised the CO on his Bible that I'll try.' Suddenly his voice rose from mock-sentimentality to its true naked fury. 'And by heaven, arse and cloudburst, God and His Son protect anyone of you wet sacks who dare let me down. *'Cos I'll cut his cock off with a blunt razorblade! God help me, but I will* . . .'

Wotan's assault course was one kilometre long, and evidently the brainchild of some zealous follower of the Marquis de Sade. A narrow plank suspended ten metres above the ground, a drop into a nettle-filled ditch, its walls sheer mud; a twenty-metre crawl under knee-high barbed wire; a wooden-plank wall fifteen metres high; a terrifying lunge for mud-slippery ropes an arm's length away; a breath-catching plunge into an icy, fast-flowing stream, while weighed down by thirty kilos of equipment; a final five rounds rapid fire with the target swaying and trembling in front of exhausted, crazed eyes . . .

They did it once. They did it twice. They did it a third

time. Their knees were like rubber, their chests heaving like cracked bellows. More than one of the exhausted, sweat-lathered young giants was sobbing like a broken-hearted child.

The Butcher watched their efforts, his brick-red beefy face set in a look of utter contempt. 'Ten minutes,' he sneered, pressing the knob of his stop-watch. 'What do you think Wotan is – a shitting finishing school for high-born young ladies? This is an SS fighting unit. Great crap on the Christmas tree, even those wet sacks of the Second Company can complete the course in nine minutes, and everybody knows they're a bunch of warm brothers. Too much playing with yerselves at night, that's what it is. Five against one. The old one-handed widow.' He made a rapid obscene gesture with his big paw and guffawed.

'You know what his problem is, comrade?' Schulze said to his neighbour. 'It's his missus. They say she's got enough pepper in her pants to service the whole regiment, including the officers' horses. Trouble is, the Butcher ain't giving her enough salami.'

'Did you say something?' the Butcher barked.

'Yessir,' Schulze answered dutifully, a look of innocence on his broad face. 'I said, I think we aren't trying hard enough.'

The Butcher snorted, wondering whether he was being had. 'Well, at least one of you cardboard soldiers knows what I'm on about. All right, you horned oxen, let's do it again.'

Groggily, their eyes glazed with exhaustion, their heavy packs biting agonizingly into their skinny shoulders, they lined up to begin Wotan's assault course for the fourth time.

As October 1939 gave way to November, and the Western Allies, dug in behind the Maginot Line not fifty kilometres away, refused the Führer's generous offer of peace, the training of SS Assault Battalion intensified, becoming ever harder and more gruelling. More and more men were taken to the MO's office now, not only with the usual bruises, cuts and fractures, but also with gunshot wounds. For now, the Vulture had ordered that live ammunition would be used at all times during training. 'Get them used to shot and shell now, von Dodenburg,' he snapped at the latter, who had protested that the men of the draft were not ready for such drastic measures. 'They'll be dead soon enough. At least here we can kit them out in a nice wooden box,' he added cynically, screwing his monocle more firmly in his right eye, 'instead of tossing them in the nearest ditch on the battlefield. Live ammo it is, von Dodenburg!'

Men like the Butcher and Lieutenant Schwarz were in their element now – so long as they could remain safely behind the weapon firing the live ammunition.

'All right, you heroes,' the Butcher bellowed, his breath fogging the cold November morning air in a thick grey cloud. 'You don't want to live for ever, do yer? Now listen to this, you bunch of piss-pansies, and listen good. Those two storm-men,' he indicated two machine-gunners crouched some hundred metres apart behind their MG 34s, 'are gonna simulate a creeping barrage with tracer – *real live tracer!*' He emphasized the three words with genuine pleasure, enjoying the looks of fear which had flashed into the eyes of his listeners. 'Now, in action, you'd have to keep right up behind that barrage if you didn't want some perverted banana-sucker of a frog or buck-teethed Tommy to pop up from his trench as soon as it lifts and shoot the nuts off yer. Though I don't suppose that would worry a lot of nancy-boys like you. All the same, in order to make sure that you *do* keep right up with the barrage, Sergeant-Major Metzger will be manning that third MG back there *in person*, firing to your rear. And you shower of ape-turds better keep up, 'cos Sergeant-Major Metzger'll show no mercy.' He grinned evilly at the pale faces. 'All right, form a skirmish line and remember – *it's march or croak this morning!*'

The terrified men ran as if the devil himself were behind them, feeling the heat of the glowing white tracer as it zapped through the grey, misty air, while behind them, the Butcher lay full length on the tarpaulin and hammered away, aiming ever closer to their flying heels, taking a sadistic delight in their obvious fear, shouting, 'I bet the shit's trickling into yer dice-beakers this time, ain't it?'

To which a gasping, red-faced Schulze replied, 'Aw, go and stick the machine-gun up yer fat arse, you horned ox!'

Finally, blessedly, the tracer ceased and the exhausted recruits flopped, packs and all, face downwards on the white, frozen grass, the backs of their uniforms black with sweat, all energy spent.

It was thus that Lieutenant Schwarz found them. 'What kind of piggery is this, Sarnt-Major?' he demanded, in his rasping, incisive voice.

The Butcher, who had been enjoying a quiet smoke with the other two NCOs who had manned the machine guns, almost swallowed his cheap cigar in alarm. Hastily he stubbed it out, thrust out his enormous barrel chest and flung the undersized sallow-faced officer a tremendous salute. 'First Company, SS Assault Battalion Wotan on the assault course, *sir!*' he reported at the top of his voice, as if Schwarz were two hundred metres away instead of two. 'One hundred and seventy-two men present. Nothing to report, *sir!*'

Schwarz acknowledged the Butcher's salute, his face icy. 'Nothing to report, you say, Sarnt-Major.' He pointed his grey-gloved hand at the exhausted, sweating men sprawled out on the grass. 'And what do you call *that?*'

The Butcher tried to bluster, but Schwarz cut him short. 'An SS man is an *élite* soldier, Sergeant-Major. He can't afford to loll about like those chaps in the Wehrmacht. I'm afraid you're molly-coddling them – you're too soft on them. Now trot off to my car and get the box you'll find behind the seat, that's a good chap.'

Like an obedient recruit, glad to get out of the way before the matter developed any further, the burly NCO trotted off to carry out the lieutenant's order, while the latter passed the time by making the exhausted company do a few press-ups. Using the left hand only.

Schwarz ordered the company to form a circle around him, while a mystified Butcher opened the wooden packing-case with a grunt and a quick rip with his ham of a hand. Schwarz then bent down and pulled away the metal foil, taking out a small, dark object. 'This is a British Mills bomb, vintage 1916, captured in Poland last September. And *this*,' he touched the bright metal pin, 'is the firing-pin. Pull it out and the bomb will explode within four seconds.'

Calmly and deliberately, and obviously very pleased with himself, he proceeded to remove the pin, but keeping his hand around the lever it released.

'If I were to drop this little object now,' Schwarz continued, 'everyone of you within ten metres' range would be killed or severely wounded.' He let his words sink in, then went on: 'Now, I want you to all take ten paces to the rear.'

Mystified and not a little scared by the eerie grin on Schwarz's face, the men shuffled back the required distance. Schwarz waited patiently.

'In Bad Toelz, during cadet-training,' he continued, 'we used to play a little game. It was, perhaps, rather childish and silly, but it did separate the men from the boys, the brave from the cowards. It went something like this. We took a grenade and placed it on the crown of our helmets. So.' He suited the action to his words. Abruptly, the faces all around him blanched as the men guessed suddenly what the little officer was going to do next.

'Thereupon we released the pin.' Schwarz let go, and the lever went whining off into the distance, while the men ducked with fear. Schwarz seemed not to notice, but his voice was a little taut and strained as he continued. 'Now, you have three seconds left. The trick is to keep your head perfectly straight. If you tremble, you have no head left—'

The thick crump of an explosion drowned the rest of his words. Momentarily a jet of vicious red-yellow flame spurted from the top of his helmet. It went a sudden black. Then red-hot slivers of gleaming razor-sharp steel were slicing through the air in all directions and the men of the First Company were hurling themselves to the ground in mad confusion.

Schwarz, standing rigidly to attention in their midst, looked down at their sickly-white faces contemptuously. '*Soft tails*,' he sneered. 'Frightened by a little firework? Half of you look as if you've wet your knickers!'

He gave them a few seconds to get back to their feet again, then with an impatient sweep of his hand, knocked the remaining fragments from the scorched top of his helmet and turned to the Butcher, whose face was also drained of colour. 'Sergeant-Major,' he snapped, business-like again, 'I want you to issue grenades to the first twenty men and then stand them twenty metres apart.'

The Butcher rccovered himself quickly, and bellowed to the men in the front rank, 'You heard what the officer said. What's wrong with you? Have you been eating big beans or something? Get the lead out of your arses! You, you and you – pick up those grenades! Come on, now. *Los!*'

Reluctantly, the first men moved off to the wooden box to receive their deadly little eggs. But they were fated not to go through with the lethal exercise. Suddenly the cultured voice of First Lieutenant Kuno von Dodenburg broke into the proceedings.

'Lieutenant Schwarz,' he said softly, 'I wonder if I could speak to you for a moment?'

Schwarz turned, startled. There was no mistaking the icy rage written all over von Dodenburg's harshly handsome face. A vein ticked angrily at his temple, and a suddenly alarmed Schwarz could see that his senior officer was only controlling himself with the greatest of difficulty. '*Yessir!* At once, sir!' he stuttered.

Von Dodenburg turned and stalked away, with Schwarz trotting after him like a beaten cur.

Schulze breathed an audible sigh or relief and sat down abruptly. 'Buckets of blood,' he said in a shaken voice to no one in particular, 'the crap's really filled my boot this time, that it has!'

1940

THE GREAT DAYS

'Who dares wins'

The battalion motto of Wotan

ONE

'Gentlemen,' the Vulture announced, hardly able to contain his excitement, his ice-blue eyes gleaming, 'we have our orders at last! And they are better than I could possibly have hoped. There'll be a piece of tin in this one for all of you, believe you me.'

The Vulture strode over to the big trestle table and pulled back a grey Wehrmacht blanket, to reveal a balsa-wood model. '*Meine Herren*,' he barked triumphantly, screwing his monocle more firmly into his right eye, 'Fort Eben Emael. The most impregnable fortification in the whole of Europe – stronger than anything we have in our own West Wall, and naturally far better than the French Maginot Line!'

The officers of the First Company crowded closer to examine the detailed model of Belgium's key fortified area, which guarded the junction of the River Meuse and the Albert Canal and barred the way to the plain of Northern France. The heavy, awed silence that had fallen on the room as the magnitude of their task dawned on those present, was broken only by the steady tread of the sentry on the gravel path outside.

'According to Intelligence,' Captain Geier began, addressing his audience as if they were all cadets again back at Bad Toelz, 'Fort Eben Emael is constructed in a series of concrete-and-steel underground galleries. How deep they go, the Abwehr* people don't know. However, we *do* know that the gun turrets are protected by the thickest armour the Belgian armaments industry can provide, and that they are built to withstand the heaviest

* German Intelligence.

known bomb or artillery shell. In other words, the Fort is regarded by the experts as impregnable.' He let his words sink in, then chuckled – it was not a pleasant sound. 'But what the Belgians *don't* know is that we've got a secret weapon: our hollow explosive charges. The attaching of them is a problem for the engineers—'

'And *our* problem, sir?' von Dodenburg asked softly, not taking his eyes off the model of the Belgian fortification, which he knew had been thoroughly modernized in 1935 on account of its vital strategic value, and was expected to hold up any enemy indefinitely.

'General Student of the airborne division has been training a special force of parachute engineers for the last six months,' the Vulture replied. 'They have the task of making the initial attack on Eben Emael. Eighty men or so under the command of a certain Captain Witzig.'

'*Eighty men!*' the assembled officers echoed incredulously. 'To take *that* place?'

'Why, the garrison alone must number several hundreds,' von Dodenburg objected.

The Vulture nodded calmly. 'One thousand, two hundred, to be exact,' the Vulture said. 'With elements of the Belgian Seventh Infantry Division, the *Cyclistes Frontière* and the *Chasseurs Ardennais* – the best troops the Belgians have on the frontier – to the immediate front of the fortifications, here.' He glanced around their earnest young faces. 'But gentlemen, I'm surprised that you should doubt German ingenuity for one single moment! Everything has been taken care of. The Führer himself took a personal interest in this particular aspect of the march west. Apart from our hollow charges, we have another surprise up our sleeves. Captain Witzig is going to land with his men by glider *directly on top of Fort Eben Emael!*'

The Vulture could barely conceal his satisfaction at the look of surprise which sprang to their faces at his announcement. 'It will be their task to keep the garrison occupied, while Wotan advances towards them, makes the link-up and reduces the Fort's defences, so that the rest of the army can move into Belgium and from there into France itself.'

The Vulture had said the words without any emphasis, as if he were talking about a route march, an everyday training exercise. Yet von Dodenburg's quick appraisal of the model told him that the link-up would be anything but a walkover. The River Meuse would have to be crossed, and then the Albert Canal. After that came what looked like a medieval moat – and all this before they could even come within striking distance of the great Fort's bristling guns. To add to their problems, they would come under concentrated machine-gun fire from the pillboxes which were everywhere.

'Our line of march will take us from Maastricht,' the Vulture continued, 'over the Meuse via one of the three bridges – here, here or here. The village of Canne – here – will then be stormed by the Second Company.

'Thereafter, the CO Major Hartmann *had* decided that the Third Company would take over from us and the Second, and attack the key gun emplacements. As you can see from the model, they cover the whole length of the river and the canal. As long as they are in Belgian hands, a mass crossing of our forces is impossible. In essence, those emplacements are the key to the door of Belgium and Northern France. Unless we can seize them, we will fail.' The Vulture looked at his young officers without a trace of his usual cynicism. 'However, I have asked Major Hartmann if this company could have the honour of taking those emplacements. He has granted me that honour. I hope you will agree that I acted in your best interests.'

The officers clicked to attention, as if at an unspoken command. Von Dodenburg spoke for the rest. 'As the company officer, sir, may I say that we are indebted to you for your foresight. It will be a great honour for the panzer grenadiers. The men will appreciate it, I am sure.'

'*Danke, von Dodenburg*, I am certain you are right. Undoubtedly the men will be duly appreciative when they learn the honour which has been bestowed upon them. At first, I must admit, the battalion commander doubted whether the First Company would be up to it, but I assured him that we could do it. Now I must rely on you, gentlemen, and the men, to ensure that I am not proved a liar.' He grinned suddenly. 'After all, as I am sure you are well aware, I want to come out of this campaign with my major's insignia.'

There was no answering smile on their serious young faces; they were too busy contemplating their glorious death for the National Socialist creed and the Führer.

The Vulture stretched himself to his full height, screwing his monocle more firmly in his right eye. '*Meine Herren*,' he rasped in his best Prussian manner, 'you realize the importance of our task. If we fail, we hold up the whole advance of the Greater German Wehrmacht. In essence, the success of the whole campaign lies in our hands. And we have exactly thirty-six hours to complete our mission. *Heil Hitler!*'

They responded as he had calculated they would, with all the fervour of their youthful hearts. They were typical products of the National Socialist dream, with its loud effrontery, brown-shirted vulgarity and jackbooted cruelty. Soon Folk, Fatherland and Führer would demand their sacrifice in blood from them.

A long line of heavily-laden half-tracks started to rattle through the exit to the Adolf Hitler Kaserne for the last time. The blacked-out streets of the town were empty. As the metallic clatter of the tracks reverberated between the houses of the narrow medieval streets, not a single window or shutter was opened. Instead, the humble Catholic folk hurried to light a candle and kneel before their plain wooden crucifixes, to say a swift prayer for delivery, as if the Devil himself were passing.

SS Assault Battalion Wotan, the Black Band, were going to war once more.

TWO

The handful of bearded, begrimed paras who had survived the crash-landing on top of the Fort had set up a position between one of the wrecked DFS 230 gliders and a bunker, which they had succeeded in putting out of action with their hollow charges. Von Dodenburg, sweating and begrimed himself from the morning's fighting, had now reached them with the vanguard of the First Company. Whenever their own artillery or that of the Belgians fired at them, they fled into the captured bunker, but for the rest of the time they seemed to prefer to be outside in the open, in spite of the slugs whistling everywhere.

'It's spooky down there, sir,' explained the para sergeant, a giant of a man in a camouflaged smock. 'The men don't like it. If you listen carefully, you can hear the Belgies down below in the underground galleries – hundreds of the snail-eating shits.' He shrugged his enormous shoulders. 'It unnerves them. They prefer to be out in the open in spite of the danger.'

Von Dodenburg removed his helmet for a moment and wiped the sweat from the leather band. 'I suppose so. Have you tried to get into those galleries?' he asked.

'Not possible, Lieutenant. We've run out of hollow charges. All we've got are our machine pistols and rifles – and a handful of grenades.'

'Grenades . . .' von Dodenburg mused.

'We used them in batches of three to knock out the guns in the turret below,' the para NCO explained. 'The lads shinned along the gun barrels, hung them on the muzzles and got out of the way – fast!'

Von Dodenburg wasn't really listening. 'Come with me,

Sergeant,' he commanded. 'I want you to explain something to me.'

Crouched low, the two doubled towards the nearest gun turret. Together, they crouched in the captured bunker, ignoring the howl of the ricochets and the *thump-thump* of a big cannon in one of the more distant emplacements, while the NCO explained the position to him, tracing an outline of the Fort in the dust of the floor. 'Below us there, sir, is a gallery running in this direction, if I guess right. Two gun emplacements run off that gallery – the one I told you we knocked out before our hollow charges ran out, and the other one, which you can still hear firing.'

'That'll be thirty?'

The NCO nodded.

'Is there any way to get into that gun emplacement, Sergeant?' von Dodenburg asked suddenly. 'Sergeant, *I'm speaking to you!*' he added sharply. The NCO jerked his head. He had fallen asleep. 'Through the gun ports, possibly – if you had a charge.'

'How big a charge?'

'God,' the para noncom rubbed his filthy hand over his bearded face wearily, 'I just don't know.' His eyes flicked close again.

Von Dodenburg reached out and slapped him hard across the face. The para started up angrily, until his gaze took in the burning rage in the SS officer's eyes. 'A small one, sir. A bundle of four or five stick grenades might do it.'

Von Dodenburg forgot the sergeant and left him slumped against the wall of the bunker, snoring loudly. 'Five grenades,' he whispered to himself, 'just five grenades.' Slowly a plan began to form in his mind. By dawn he wanted to be in the gallery below, ready to start the task of knocking out the gun emplacements. He looked at the glowing green luminous dial of his watch. He had exactly ten hours left before the German Army started to cross the Meuse in force. If what was left of First Company SS

Assault Battalion Wotan didn't have the guns knocked out by then, the crossing would be a massacre . . .

'All right, von Dodenburg,' Schwarz whispered, his sallow face with its hook of a nose readily showing the strain of these last terrible hours of combat. His lips drew back in a wolfish crazy grimace. 'Everything's ready.'

The raiding party on the top of the Fort tensed, as von Dodenburg gave a final tug on the rough-and-ready rope they had fashioned from the seat-harnesses of the wrecked glider and checked if the grenades were tucked away safely in his belt. They were. 'All right, ready to go,' he whispered.

The men of the raiding party took the strain, while below, the white tracer stitched aimlessly across the darkness and the cannon thundered at an unseen enemy.

Rapidly Kuno started to sink out of sight. Ten metres . . . twenty . . . twenty-five . . . The wind seemed to have increased in strength. Hanging there like a fly on the great concrete face of the Fort, he felt it pluck and tug at his body. Thirty metres . . . He came to a sudden stop. The thin cord tied to his wrist was jerked hard. It was the agreed signal. He had reached the required depth. He must now be level with the upper gun turret, the one the paras had knocked out during their first surprise attack.

He took a deep breath and dared to look down. Far below was the faint silver sheen of the Albert Canal, crossed here and there by the icy white lights of the Fort's searchlights and the zig-zag morse of the tracer-fire. He swallowed hard; if he made a wrong move now, that's where he would find himself.

'All right, you bastard,' he said to himself angrily, '*swing!*'

Slowly, almost imperceptibly at first, the makeshift rope began to move back and forth along the face of the man-made cliff, creaking alarmingly. He started to gain momentum. Like a human pendulum his body swung across the sheer face, swinging to and fro in the darkness, while the battle continued to rage far below. As the arc grew larger and larger he began to strike the rough concrete with ever-increasing frequency. He gasped as his body was buffeted by the concrete, his knuckles skinned and bleeding, his elbows bruised and swelling, but he forced himself to continue, his teeth clenched together with pain. Somewhere – perhaps a mere ten metres to his right – the silent 75 mm cannon were protruding into the darkness. He must secure a hold on them. *He must!*

Up above him, the raiding party sweated, with Schulze taking the most strain, his eyes bulging with effort, his steel-shod heels digging in, as the pressure on his arm muscles and burning palms mounted with agonizing intensity. They could no longer see von Dodenburg swinging back and forth below, but they could hear him as he struck the concrete. What if some Belgie did too and started to come up from below to investigate? Von Dodenburg would be a sitting duck out there.

Far below, the gasping, almost exhausted young officer swung in a great arc through the wind, which now howled around him, grabbing at his battered, bleeding body, as if eager to pluck him from his fragile perch. Twice he struck his head against a piece of concrete, and red stars exploded in front of his eyes; only his helmet saved him from losing consciousness.

Then suddenly the first of the twin cannon loomed into view, its muzzle splayed open where the paras had exploded their charges. Relying completely on the men above, von Dodenburg dared to take both hands off the rope round his waist, and grabbed for it. His nails scraped against the cold metal. Next instant he was swaying off wildly and frighteningly in the opposite direction. He tried again, and again. To no avail. The tips of his nails were bleeding and blunt now, devoid of all feeling.

Clenching his teeth, knowing that the men above wouldn't be able to stand the strain much longer, he came in again, the wind whistling past him with almost gale-force. He held his hands ready. The muzzle loomed. Stretching his arms to their fullest extent, straining with every fibre of his body, he lunged for it. His hands caught . . . slipped . . . caught again. A nail gave. An electric shock of sheer agony shot up his arm. He bit his bottom lip to repress the scream that welled up inside him. But he held on. With the last of his strength he heaved himself on top of the great cannon and hung there like a sack, gasping frantically, his unseeing eyes staring down numbly at the silver gleam of the Albert Canal far below. He had done it!

Once the raiding party had assembled in the abandoned gun turret, Schwarz took the lead. The little sallow-faced lieutenant seemed utterly fearless. But to the still groggy von Dodenburg, there was something almost crazy about the risks he took. Twice he led them past occupied posts, the crack of light below the doors and the low murmur of tired voices clearly indicating that the Belgian soldiers inside were awake. But neither time did he show fear. Instead, he simply grinned, his eyes blank, his teeth bared in an animal grimace. Once a dark shape shot out in front of them in the poorly-lit corridor, its size magnified enormously on the wall ahead by the light of Schwarz's torch. The officer didn't even seem to notice. His eyes empty of any expression, dark and unfathomable, his face covered with blood and grime, he led them deeper and deeper into the heart of the great Fort, the only sound that of their own boots, muffled now by socks, and the steady throb of the air-conditioning like the beat of some monstrous heart.

Suddenly Schwarz switched off his torch. '*Against the wall,*' he hissed urgently. '*Someone's coming!*'

Hearts beating frantically, they pressed themselves against the damp, dripping concrete, their eyes transfixed by the swinging arcs of light coming closer and closer.

'No firing,' von Dodenburg whispered.

Hurriedly, Schulze slipped on his celebrated 'Hamburg Equalizer', a set of brass knuckles which had seen much active service in Hamburg's waterfront bars in the old days. At his side, face wolfish and mad in the gloom, Schwarz crouched, bayonet at the ready.

A great shadow swung round the bend. And another. They preceded their owners like silent, black giants. Von Dodenburg gave a little sigh of relief. There were only two of them.

'*Ici . . . là bas*,' Schwarz called in his best French.

The first Belgian soldier, a corporal, turned off his torch, startled, as if he feared to blind the man crouching there. '*Quoi?*' he began, but before he could continue, Schwarz darted forward and slid the bayonet in between his ribs, right to the heart. The Belgian's mouth shot open in a dying gasp, and Schwarz's dirty paw clamped over it. Chuckling crazily, he lowered the Belgian, his knees buckling beneath him, to the floor.

At that same moment, Schulze's brass knuckles flashed. The Belgian howled with pain as they struck him a tremendous blow on the jaw – but he didn't go down. Schulze grabbed the back of the soldier's helmet and pulled hard. The helmet slid down, its strap falling around the Belgian's skinny throat. Schulze's knee shot into the small of his back, while with one hand he tugged at the helmet, forcing the strap deep into the soldier's throat, reducing his scream to a sudden strangled groan. Desperately the Belgian's hand clawed at the strap and tried to break Schulze's killing hold. Wriggling frantically, his eyes bulging in an ecstasy of fear, he flung himself from side to side. But there was no breaking that terrible vice-like grip. Slowly Schulze garrotted him to death, his knees buckling, as gently, almost tenderly, Schulze lowered him to the ground. 'The poor bastard's dead,' he said, and then suddenly he was leaning against the wall, retching and vomiting, as if he would never stop.

The others had no such scruples. They hurriedly began to loot the dead bodies in search of precious cigarettes. In their haste, they failed to notice the third man who, having stopped around the bend in the corridor, now slipped away fearfully and noiselessly, to report the presence of these bloody begrimed invaders in the heart of Fort Eben Emael.

They had been discovered!

Now they were deep in the heart of the Fort. The chatter of the machine-guns and the persistent *thump-thump* of the cannon above them were muted by depth, whereas the clatter of the Fort's machinery was getting louder by the instant. They couldn't be far off the fortification's control centre. Von Dodenburg, who had taken over from Schwarz once more, held up his hand, pointing to a ladder directly in front of them, clamped to the dripping wall, next to the legend DÉFENSE DE FUMER. On both sides of the ladder were open-doored lifts like the 'Our Fathers'* of the kind used in Northern Germany. 'Shell hoists going down from the ammo magazine to the gun turret,' he explained softly.

'Let's get the bastards,' Schulze snorted, first off the mark.

'How?'

Sculze grinned. 'Every time a machine stopped at the docks the lads got a coffee break. And on Monday morning, sir, after a night on the piss in the Reeperbahn the machines stopped a lot, I can tell yer. It's as easy as shitting in yer slipper. Look, everybody grab a handful of that cement dirt and follow me.' He suited his actions to his words and, mystified, the others did the same. Leaning forward, Schulze dropped the cement dirt down inside the polished metal runner at each side of the hoist. 'Come on,' he urged, 'put plenty in there. We'll need a lot to do it. Pity we ain't got some sugar. I could knock the engine out with it in zero comma nothing seconds.'

Slowly but surely, the hoist started to grind to a halt. Schulze winked happily at von Dodenburg. 'Now what do

* Slang name for a commonly used, open-faced office lift.

you say to that, sir? Ain't that a neat piece of industrial sabotage?'

'Damn terrorist!' von Dodenburg joked. 'Think I ought to report you to the gents of the Gestapo if we ever get out of this place alive! All right, you big rogue, you've given your star performance. Let's get on with the rough stuff.' He gripped his machine pistol aggressively. 'That gun turret down there has got to be knocked out next – and then we'll find the control centre.'

They ran down the tunnel until they came to the stairs. At the bottom there was another tunnel, dripping with moisture, its concrete walls covered with nitre. As they ran along the slippery duckboards, twice the Butcher – older and more ungainly than the rest – fell. No one helped him up. Now the young men knew him for the coward he was.

Suddenly the tunnel curved to the right sharply. Von Dodenburg, in the lead, stopped just in time. A great steel door stood in front of them, sharp white light cutting into the dim yellow of the tunnel. 'Emplacement number forty-six,' he whispered.

As if to emphasize his words, there was a thunderous crash from behind the door. Although massively thick, it trembled as if it were made of matchwood. The next instant the tunnel was flooded with thick yellow smoke that tore at their lungs. A monstrous clanging noise followed that made them grab for their ears to keep their eardrums from being shattered by the blast. Von Dodenburg felt as if his skull was going to split apart at any moment. He staggered violently against the wall and supported himself there, coughing and retching, the tears streaming down his dirty cheeks.

Not so Schwarz. 'Cover me,' he rasped . . . 'I'm going in!'

Without hesitating, he levelled his machine pistol and crashed the door with his booted foot. Surprisingly, it swung open. Inside the gunners, their heads protected by asbestos flash guards under their helmets, were grouped around the hoist, gesticulating angrily to one another.

Obviously they were puzzled and angry at its failure to deliver fresh ammunition.

Schwarz crept inside. A fat noncom with the yellow face of a soldier who had been in the fortress artillery too long, swung round. He saw the crazy man in the ragged field-grey crouched there. His hand flashed to his pistol holster. Too late. Schwarz pressed his trigger. The sergeant reeled back against the concrete, bloody button holes suddenly stitched across the front of his khaki uniform. He gasped and began to slither downwards, trailing scarlet blood on the wall after him.

Schwarz fired again, swinging from left to right, the turret ringing with the chatter of the machine pistol. The artillery-men were galvanized momentarily into frenzied action, before they fell to the floor in crazed confusion – dead for the most part before they hit it. In a matter of seconds it was all over. Schwarz had massacred the Belgians before one of them could fire a shot.

It was thus that von Dodenburg found him, crouched above the heap of corpses, machine pistol still at the ready, as if he half expected them to rise once more. He was cackling maniacally, eyes bulging widely from their sockets, saliva running unheeded from the corner of his slack mouth.

'Holy strawsack,' Schulze gasped, stopping short at the sight, 'he's gone combat-crazy. Schwarz has gone nuts!'

'*Schnauze!*' von Dodenburg snapped.

Almost tenderly, he placed his hands on the still-smoking machine pistol and forced its muzzle downwards. 'It's all right, Schwarz,' he said softly. 'All right . . .'

Schwarz shook his head hard. 'What's the matter?' he demanded. 'What are you doing with my weapon?'

'My dear Schwarz,' von Dodenburg said soothingly, while the other men stared at Schwarz's wild animal face in disbelief, 'it's quite all right.'

'Of course, it is,' Schwarz said harshly. 'What the hell are you talking about?' He trampled over the dead bodies to the breech and slapped the lever up to close it, not for one moment noticing that his feet rested on a dead Belgian with half his face shot off. 'We just took the place, didn't we? I don't know . . .'

Von Dodenburg turned away, unable to listen to Kurt Schwarz's rantings any longer. The little lieutenant was crazy, irrevocably crazy. The draft were paying the price in human suffering for the Vulture's ambition; and it would rise still higher before this terrible day was ended, he knew that.

THREE

Now inside the great Fort, the situation changed rapidly in a crazy kaleidoscope of sudden action and violent death.

The Belgians counter-attacked, catching von Dodenburg's party off guard just when they had succeeded in knocking out number thirty-six and spiking its guns. Advancing down one of the warren of underground chambers, the SS men ran right into the Belgians. The leading three SS men went reeling down, caught by their first burst. Von Dodenburg staggered against the wall, blood pouring from his shoulder.

Their progress suddenly halted, for a moment the SS men milled around in the loud echoing gloom, choking on the stink of burned explosive, not knowing what to do. But then a Belgian heavy machine-gun opened up, chattering like an angry woodpecker. The lead cut into them, bowling them along the corridor, legs and arms flailing in the horrible disjointedness of death. Schulze yelped angrily as a bullet whacked into his thigh. The Butcher, a neat hole drilled through his hand, stood in the middle of the panic-stricken mob, too frozen by fear to move.

Schulze shoved him to the ground and then, as abruptly as it had started, the machine-gun ceased firing and a hoarse voice called in excellent German, 'Submit! You haven't a chance. We'll give you five minutes to make up your minds.' Suddenly, strangely muffled, the voice added, 'And here's a sample of what's coming your way if you don't.'

A small round object sailed through the yellow smoke that flooded the corridor and struck the wall near the huddled survivors.

'Grenade!' someone screamed.

Frantically they flattened themselves. But the little egg didn't explode. Instead it just lay there, giving off a thick wet cloud of what looked like smoke.

Surprisingly enough the Butcher reacted first. With his good hand he flung it back at the Belgians. Next instant he started to retch and choke horribly.

Schulze flashed von Dodenburg, who was leaning weakly against the wall clutching his wounded shoulder, a look of horror on his face. '*Gas*,' he shrieked, even his nerve gone now. '*It's gas, sir!*'

Von Dodenburg felt a thrill of terror run through him. '*They wouldn't dare!*' he cried, hoping to reassure the panic-stricken men. But the faint smell of bitter almonds now assailing his notrils told him they would. 'Fit your masks!'

'I haven't got one!' someone screamed hysterically.

'Neither have I!'

'I've got a bottle of firewater in my container . . .'

The cries of alarm rang out on all sides. Just as they had done in the Polish campaign, the soldiers had started dumping all heavy equipment – including gas masks – once they had begun to fight.

'Piss on a piece of rag – your handkerchief, the tail of your shirt,' von Dodenburg cried, remembering what his father, the General, had told him about the primitive masks they had made in the trenches when the British had first used gas against the Prussian Foot Guards. 'Hold it to your mouths!' Forgetting his wound as yet another black, deadly egg came sailing towards him, he ripped open his flies and urinated on his handkerchief.

Everywhere the terrified survivors did the same, as more and more gas bombs started to whizz at them, releasing gas on all sides – in spite of the efforts of Schwarz, who kept attempting to throw them back, cackling crazily, as if this was simply a kind of mad game.

In spite of the improvised masks, the thick fumes began to creep into their lungs. Their feet disappeared in a thick fog of gas, creeping ever higher. Von Dodenburg started to gasp like an ancient asthmatic. Tears blinded him. He was choking. Crazily he ripped at his collar.

A man broke. Throwing down his rag, he ran, screaming, '*Surrender . . . Surrender!*' right into a burst of Belgian machine-gun fire. Clawing the air in his agony, as if climbing the rungs of an invisible ladder, he slowly sank to the ground. Another man fell to his knees, his mask askew, a thin pink foam of blood forming at his contorted mouth as he bit deep into his tongue. A moment later he disappeared into the killing fog.

Von Dodenburg grabbed at his throat, tossing his head back and forth, fighting for air. A great red darkness threatened to overcome him. Another few moments, he knew, and he would be gone.

'Hold on!' a well-known Prussian voice rasped into the last of his consciousness from far, far away.

Painfully he turned his head, as if it were worked by rusty springs.

The Vulture stood there, wreathed in the gas, his monocle steamed up, a bloodstained bandage round his head, his uniform in tatters. In his hand he held a flame-thrower. How he held it with his shattered shoulder, von Dodenburg neither knew nor cared, for behind him the door had been flung open and a great blast of cool, clean air was streaming in.

Von Dodenburg breathed it in in great greedy gasps, as the mixed force of paras and SS men thrust their way through with Geier at their head. They brooked no opposition, and the Vulture knew no mercy. Time was running out. There were only two hours left before the Wehrmacht attacked.

Geier pressed the trigger of the flame-thrower, and there was a sound like some great primeval monster drawing in a tremendous breath. Oil-tinged vicious-red flame wreathed the machine-gun. It glowed momentarily. The corridor echoed with the Belgians' screams. Some were caught immediately, shrivelled into charred pigmies. Others were trapped at the far end of the corridor, clawing each other frantically in their desperate unreasoning fear, trying to hide from that all-consuming flame, pleading with God for mercy. But there was no hiding-place nor merciful God on high, this terrible May day.

The Vulture pressed the trigger time and time again, until finally all that was left were glowing golden ashes and something which looked like the silhouettes of frantic midgets, fused for all time on the walls of Fort Eben Emael. Then and only then did the Vulture drop that terrible weapon from his nerveless fingers.

Now the end was near. Above them, on the top of the great fortification, the Belgians were still calling down their own artillery fire, picking off any remaining Germans like pesky field-grey flies. But the attackers were everywhere in the warren of passages and bunkers down below, fighting desperate battles in the glowing darkness, expecting no quarter and giving none. When an opponent went down, he was ruthlessly hacked to pieces with bayonets, trench knives, spades, or kicked and pounded into a lifeless pulp by cruel steel-shod military boots.

Everywhere there was the stench of fresh blood and explosive. Men were going mad in the darkness, running through the corridors, howling like crazed wolves before they were finally shot down. Others, scared beyond all reason, started to burrow anywhere – into stores, piles of ammunition, the storage tanks; clasping their hands over their ears, their eyes closed tightly like small children, attempting to escape this terrible underground nightmare. Now it was clear that the SS were winning. The spirit was going out of the Belgians. The fanaticism of the SS was paying off. They were prepared to pay the horrific butcher bill that the capture of the fort demanded, and still keep on fighting.

They raced down a corridor, mouthing hoarse, fearsome obscenities. The Belgians were waiting for them. A handful of SS men in the lead crumpled like deflated paper bags.

The second wave clambered over their writhing bodies, pelting straight at the defenders. Grenades whizzed back and forth. The corridor was loud with the screams and curses of frantic men. Red-hot shards of metal howled off the walls. Drunk with the bloodlust of battle, the field-grey giants closed with the smaller Belgians, stabbing and cutting their way through the barrier.

Schwarz, howling like a crazy dog, booted open the nearest door. Splay-legged, he sprayed the terrified soldiers crouching there, who fell like summer wheat before the harvester. A sniper's bullet struck him directly between the eyes and exploded there. His face seemed to slip down onto his chest like a molten red wax. He gave one long scream that seemed to go on for ever and ever, then he sank to the floor. The next instant, the wild men of Wotan were trampling over his inert body and into the next bunker.

They shot the gunners where they stood. Two shells were loaded into their cannon. A volunteer pulled the lanyard while the others hid behind the protection of the steel shield. With a tremendous roar, the great cannon, which would otherwise have slaughtered the army massing down below on the other side of the Albert Canal, exploded, filling the bunker with acrid, choking fumes, a neat split down its barrel.

When the smoke had cleared, the volunteer lay among the dead Belgians, bleeding from nose and ears, his arms reduced to two bleeding stumps. They left him, unconscious, to bleed to death.

Schulze hobbled at von Dodenburg's side, lobbing captured Belgian hand grenades as he went, his face as crazy as those of the rest. Together they burst into the last gun turret, where the gunners were already beginning to lay their piece on the mass of field-grey filling the shell-cratered fields beyond. But it was not to be. Their hands shot up at the first sight of the intruders, and suddenly the blood-rage went out of them.

With the last of their strength, Schulze and von Dodenburg disarmed the gunners, broke the firing pins of the cannon to make it impossible to fire and as their last energy drained out of them, slumped to the floor. For a few brief moments, friend and foe crouched there in a heavy silence, broken only by their harsh breathing, their heads bent or buried in their shaking hands, as if in defeat.

. . . And to the north, unseen by the handful of survivors who were all that was left of Captain Geier's First Company, the soldiers of General Reichenau's Sixth Army began to cross the canal: first a company, then a battalion. Each man feared that the great cannon of the Fort towering high above them might open up on them as they paddled their rubber dinghies across. But the cannon remained silent.

A regiment followed. The regiment became a division and the division a corps. Now as far as the eye could see, the flat, green, lush Belgian countryside was being swallowed up by a vast tide of field-grey. Fort Eben Emael was in German hands. The great triumphant dash into France could commence . . .

FOUR

Invincible, triumphant, unstoppable, SS Assault Battalion Wotan raced through France that glorious summer.

Now the survivors of the Battle of Fort Eben Emael had been reinforced by fresh young volunteers from the training camps back in the Reich, eager to win a decoration on the field of battle before the war was over. Before them they herded the battered remnants of the French Army, a mob of shattered, demoralized *poilus*, who usually surrendered at the first sight of the Wotan's tanks, while to their flank, the British fled to the coast like rats abandoning a sinking ship, racing for the safety of their island home, before they, too, were caught up in the great débâcle.

Hour after hour, day after day, week after week, the eager blond giants, their filthy field-grey uniforms now reeking of sweat and explosive, pushed ever forward through the smouldering countryside of *la belle France*, under the golden ball of a hot summer sun which shone every day without fail. The yellow of the uncut corn and the white of surrender were the predominant colours, for everywhere hung the symbol of France's decadence and defeat – flags, bedsheets, towels, tablecloths on cottages, farmhouses, churches, apartment blocks . . .

Occasionally the weary, bearded *poilus* turned and, under the command of hard-faced officers who threatened them with their pistols, tried to put up a token defence. But it was hopeless. Wotan's tanks swept aside the hastily improvised barricades of farm carts and abandoned vehicles as if they were made of match-wood. Their new and very impatient commander, the Vulture (for Major Hartmann, Wotan's first CO, had done him the favour of sticking his head out above the turret of his command tank, only to have it neatly drilled by an obliging French sniper) now urged them on with high-pitched, almost fevered cries. '*Tempo . . . tempo!* Smash the Frogs! Throw them into the sea! Wotan must be the first unit to reach the Channel! It'll mean the laurel leaves for me . . . On, you dogs of death! Do you want to live for ever? *Tempo!*'

'It's the champagne campaign!' a happy, drunken Schulze would cry from the deck of von Dodenburg's half-track, where he was recovering from his wound, reading looted French pornography and drinking *de luxe* French champagne by the bucketful. Occasionally he would lend a hand with the machine-gun, but not often; not for him Geier's almost hysterical desire to win the coveted laurel leaves to the Knight's Cross which the Führer had awarded him for taking Eben Emael. Schulze's sole concern was to keep permanently drunk while the going was good, for as he confided to anyone prepared to listen, 'Sup all the Champers you can, comrades. For when this little lot's over, it's back to neat beer for us poor old arse-haired stubble-hoppers!'

For the newly appointed Captain von Dodenburg, commander now of the First Company, the mad dash through France was a series of seemingly unrelated episodes – violent, tragic most of them (for the enemy), sometimes comic; but all of them confirming for him that nothing could stop the march of National Socialism, the creed of all that was good, vital, new, youthful in a continent that had allowed itself to sink into the decadent weariness of old age. Above all, the heady progress of the Bodyguard and in particular SS Assault Battalion Wotan, forced him time and time again to admire his young soldiers, now the veterans of the draft, and the greenbeaks who had come so readily to fill the gaps in their ranks. Where in the world could one find troops like them – bold young giants with such an unquenchable desire to fight and win?

How often did he see them sweep into the attack, driving

the miserable rabble in khaki or blue in front of them. Lyon, Vienne, Valence, Montelimar, Orange, the towns of the Rhône valley flashed by in Wotan's hectic dash for the Mediterranean and final victory. Now the British had fled, leaving the French to fight on alone.

'They'll never come back again, the Tommies,' the Vulture told him confidently, as they stood on some nameless crossroads under the olive trees in the south of France, observing the fleeing French to their front. 'They know what's good for them, the Tommies – they always have. They'll hang on to their precious Empire, and let us finish the Frogs and deal with the Russkis in our own time.' He dropped his binoculars and turned his face with that monstrous beak of a nose to the harshly handsome captain, his face grey with dust. 'With luck I'll make general yet – once the Greatest Captain of All Times,' he smiled cynically at the scornful name that the regular Wehrmacht gave to the Führer, 'attacks Mother Russia. All right, von Dodenburg, to the attack. Tomorrow I want to be at the sea!'

The French surrendered. An urgent order was sent to the Führer's beloved Bodyguard to attend the ceremony, which Hitler had designed to humiliate the French. From Nîmes on the Mediterranean, the survivors of Wotan, veterans and greenbeaks, were rushed through France, shaving, washing, changing into the new uniforms, pinning their newly won decorations to the fresh field-grey as they sped through the countryside, still littered with the débris of the recent campaign. An extra spur was the prospect of three days' leave in Paris, once the surrender ceremony at Compiègne was over.

It was a beautiful warm summer afternoon when the survivors of Wotan arrived at the Forest of Compiègne. The sun beat down on the ancient oaks, casting pleasant shadows on the glade where the sweating Wehrmacht engineers had finally managed to position the ancient *wagon-lit*, the tangible symbol of Germany's greatest and most bitter defeat.

At 3.15 pm precisely, the leader of the most powerful state in Europe arrived in his big black Mercedes, to a blare of trumpets and a roll of drums from the guard of honour drawn up by SS Assault Battalion Wotan. Behind him followed the cars carrying the Old Fighters of his revolutionary days, who had helped him achieve his great aim. At the head of this brilliant cavalcade of high-ranking officers and party leaders, Adolf Hitler strode into the glade, his step springy, his head raised in triumph, a happy smile on his face.

Standing rigidly to attention next to Geier, von Dodenburg felt a thrill of pride as the Führer paused at the great granite block which the French had erected here twenty-two years before. He read that infamous inscription, which von Dodenburg knew as if it had been branded on his heart by fire:

HERE ON THE ELEVENTH OF NOVEMBER 1918 SUCCUMBED THE CRIMINAL PRIDE OF THE GERMAN EMPIRE, VANQUISHED BY THE FREE PEOPLES WHICH IT TRIED TO ENSLAVE.

Von Dodenburg observed as, slowly and calculatingly, the Führer took a pace backwards. Hands on his hips, his shoulders arched, his booted feet planted wide apart he stared at the granite block with a look of infinite, magnificent contempt on his face. At that moment, the young captain knew he could never betray this leader, Germany's man of destiny. Come what may, he must follow him to the very end. Hitler passed on.

Major Geier stepped forward and drew his sword. It sparkled in the sunlight as he raised it to his head in salute.

'*Danke, Sturmbannführer*,' Hitler thanked him in his hoarse Austrian voice. For one long moment his dark magnetic gaze swept their bold young faces. To von Dodenburg, it seemed like an eternity. He felt the power of those eyes; they radiated an almost hypnotic force. Then the Führer's gaze softened, his eyes growing liquid and filling with tears. 'Only twenty left of your original company, Major Geier, I hear?' he asked in a broken voice.

'*Jawohl, mein Führer*,' Geier snapped back.

Hitler shook his head. 'My poor brave soldiers,' he whispered, almost to himself. 'Poor brave soldiers.'

Then the great man was gone.

Von Dodenburg could hardly repress a shudder of pride, delight, awe – a whole range of emotions he would never be able to define as long as he lived. All he knew was that for that fleeting instant he had glimpsed greatness, and that it had made everything worthwhile.

But time was running out once more. On the last day of August, 1940, while over the Channel the Luftwaffe fought desperately to conquer the perfidious English, the leave-men were suddenly recalled by chaindogs in heavily-armed patrols of at least ten men, who scoured the bars and brothels in search of them. Drunk or sober, they were tossed into the waiting trucks by the military policemen and sent on the long journey to the coast.

Von Dodenburg received his own company in the middle of a sudden rain shower from the Channel, while high overhead the British and German fighters curved to and fro in a vicious dogfight. His men didn't notice; they were all drunk, even the ones who had started out sober – thanks to Schulze, and his crony Matz, who had been given a whole case of cognac by the grateful whores of the brothel they had been patronizing the last four days.

Now, as the trucks rolled to a halt in the old barracks just outside Calais, they fell out of the vehicles, tumbling full length on the gleaming wet cobbles, singing drunkenly as they did so and giggling like schoolgirls as the regimental policemen hauled them to their feet.

Von Dodenburg frowned. The cover story that Geier had thought up for the recall was that Wotan would be used in the operation against England, which had already been secretly cancelled. As Geier and Von Dodenburg knew, Berlin had other plans for them.

Soon the trumpets would blare again, the drums roll, the harsh commands echo, and they would march once more: one thousand young men between eighteen and twenty-four, the élite of the élite, Young Germany, volunteers to a man, the Black Band which had conquered the west. But this time they would march in a different direction: eastwards, embarking on an impossible adventure the like of which had not been seen since the days of the Great Napoleon and his *Grande Armée* over a century or more before.

Kuno von Dodenburg shook off his mood of sudden despair. He strode forward through the bitter rain and took up his position in front of the drunks. 'First Company,' he barked, knowing instinctively that tragedy, perhaps ever disaster, loomed ahead, 'First Company . . . *attention*!'

Somehow the men managed to come to that position, and waited.

'First Company – *about turn*!'

Von Dodenburg took a last look at their honest young faces, flushed with drink and debauchery, yet somehow still innocent. 'First Company will advance . . . By the right . . . *Quick march*!'

They stumbled forward, heads bent under the rain like condemned men.

The good days were over.

1941

BARBAROSSA

'On the other side stands a population of 180 million, a mixture of races, whose very names are unpronounceable and whose physique is such that one can shoot them down without pity or compassion . . . When you, my men, fight in the east, you are carrying on the same struggle, against the same sub-humanity, the same inferior races, that at one time appeared under the name of Huns. Today they appear as Russians under the political banners of Bolshevism.'

Heinrich Himmler to his SS, 1941

ONE

For forty-eight hours now they had lain in the Polish wood, two kilometres from the river, plagued by flies and mosquitoes. During the day all movement had been forbidden by the Vulture and they had hidden under the trees playing cards, telling tales of past battles and women, or simply sleeping. Then, as soon the June sun went down, they were allowed to go to the stream to wash and shave before the ration-bearers came up, bearing the one warm meal of the day.

It would have been an idyllic existence, had it not been for the thought of what lay on the other side of that sluggish brown river. 'Like a Hitler Youth summer camp,' von Dodenburg said to Schulze, in an attempt at humour.

Schulze was unimpressed. 'I wouldn't know. I was in the Communist Youth Movement myself before 1933.' His big bronzed face serious, he added, 'Are we gonna have a crack at the Popovs over there?' He nodded in the general direction of the river and the frontier. 'Brest-Litovsk ain't far off, is it, sir? And that's in the Popovs' hands now.'

Von Dodenburg said nothing.

On the evening of 21st June, 1941, after the hot meal of the day had been served and the men were still belching happily and full-bellied with one litre of good pea soup and a thick pork sausage inside them, a message started to pass from platoon to platoon as they lounged in the trees. 'Battalion to fall in at twenty-two hundred hours in the large clearing. Battalion to fall in . . .' And from far away, even as the strange message circulated, there could be heard the rumble of armour – a lot of it.

It was dark when they assembled in the clearing.

Followed by his officers, the Vulture strode into the centre of the silent, now apprehensive men, and switched on the little blue light attached to his tunic. 'Battalion,' he rasped without ceremony, 'I shall now read you a message from the Führer.'

He held up the paper he was carrying, and read, 'Soldiers of the Eastern Front . . .'

'*Soldiers of the Eastern Front* . . .' The phrase was echoed in an excited whisper throughout the ranks of the young men. Watching, Von Dodenburg felt as if it had struck them an almost physical blow. So now they knew what lay ahead for Wotan.

'. . . At this moment, a build-up is in progress which has no equal in the history of the world. Allied with Finnish divisions, our comrades stand side by side with the victors of Narvik in the north to Bulgaria in the south. You stand on the Eastern Front. If this, the greatest front in world history, now goes into action, then it does so to create the necessary conditions for the final conclusion of this great war. Not only that, it will save the whole of European civilization and culture from the Jewish-Bolshevik curse. German soldiers! You are about to join battle, a hard and crucial battle. The destiny of Europe, the future of the German Reich, the existence of our nation, now lie in your hands alone. May the Almighty help us all in this titanic struggle.'

The Vulture broke off, his face illuminated by the little blue light. A heavy silence hung over the forest, broken only by the hoot of a distant owl. It was Germany's hour of destiny, and even the most unfeeling and thick-skinned of the one thousand young men assembled there knew it. A tremendous adventure lay before them, one that only a few of them would survive.

'Well, I'll go and piss up my sleeve, 'Schulze said, without enthusiasm.

No one laughed.

*

Soon it would be dawn. Already the darkness was beginning to break up to the east. Dawn came early in this part of the world.

Standing in the turret of his tank, von Dodenburg found himself constantly looking at the second-hand of his watch. Every minute he expected the Russians to open up with all they had and catch them completely exposed on the river bank. Surely they must have learned by now that a German army of three million men was about to attack them? But nothing happened. Perhaps they were waiting behind their machine-guns on the stork-legged wooden towers that marked their side of the river. Would the crossing of the River Bug be one great massacre?

The minutes slipped by. The green-glowing hands of his watch showed 3.15. A faint while light had begun to streak the horizon. Now he could make out the tense faces of his young soldiers, their eyes fixed as if with longing on the opposite bank. Just then he noticed that one of them wasn't wearing his helmet, and was on the point of ordering him to put it on . . . He never managed it.

Suddenly a great flash of evil white light rent the sky. Behind him, four hundred guns opened up with an earth-shaking, terrifying roar. Closer at hand, smaller weapons joined in. Mortars belched. Machine-guns chattered. Red, white and green tracer stitched a crazy hissing pattern across the water. In front of the tanks of Wotan, the infantry joined in with their rifles. From the Russian positions flares hushed urgently into the dawn sky as the new war drew its first, fierce, fiery breath.

In his turret, the Vulture stretched himself to his full height. 'Wotan will advance,' he cried. '*Los! Los!* Let's go!'

The turret flaps fell. Tank engines coughed and burst into life. Blue streams of smoke spurted from their exhausts. A metallic creak. A rumble of tracks. The first one moved off. A second followed. And a third. Hurriedly the infantry lining the bank cheered and scrambled out of the way. In long column, the metal monsters waddled to the water's edge.

The first one splashed into the water. Already the Soviet guns were beginning to thunder. Here and there the River Bug erupted into furious spouts of whirling white water. Tank after tank followed. On the opposite bank the Soviet infantry started to throw their rifles away and flee. Boldly the Mark IIIs began to plough towards Russian territory. The greatest battle in the history of war had commenced. Operation Barbarossa was under way.

TWO

The tanks moved towards the silent village like metal ducks waddling to a pond. Against the dawn sky, the little collection of straw-roofed *isbas* around the onion-towered church were outlined a stark black. But although the barrage was creeping steadily forward towards the Russian village, still there was no movement from it.

Von Dodenburg, standing upright in the turret of the command tank ran his glasses from one end of the little place to the other. Was it deserted? Or was his company heading for a trap?

Suddenly the radio crackled into excited action. 'Sunray . . . Sunray.' It was the Vulture – and he had spotted trouble. 'Bear left immediately . . . Do you read me, Honeybee? Do you read me? *Bear—*'

The rest of his words were drowned by the sudden harsh bark of an anti-tank cannon. Metal struck metal. There was a hollow boom. Next instant one of von Dodenburg's Mark IIIs reeled, as if suddenly struck by a hurricane. For a moment nothing seemed to happen. Then flame spurted an ugly scarlet into the dawn sky. Red hot splinters shot everywhere. A man reeled from the turret, dragging his almost severed leg behind him, to collapse in the yellow corn.

'*Urrah*!' With a hoarse roar, the Russian infantry in their earth-coloured smocks, bayonets gleaming in the first rays of the new sun, burst from their hiding place and rushed the line of German tanks.

Schulze, commanding the nearest Mark III, didn't hesitate. 'Carbide, you little ape-turd,' he yelled to Matz, ignoring the slugs howling off the turret, and kicked him savagely on the shoulder. Matz swung the right tiller bar back until they were rolling straight towards the Russians. The other tanks followed suit, smashing right into them and turning them into bloody paste. Over the network von Dodenburg heard someone gasp with horror and cry, 'Oh in God's name, look at that!'

Carried away by the excitement of battle, some of the drivers behind Schulze's tank, now heading straight for the village, were rolling up and down the lines of Russians, systematically crushing the infantry, their treads a bright red with the blood and gore of pulped limbs.

Just behind Schulze another Mark III took a direct hit and reeled to a stop, one trail flopping behind it like a severed limb. Immediately, Russians sprang out of the corn where they were hiding and swarmed over the stricken vehicle.

Schulze swung the turret machine-gun round and pressed the trigger. Men were swatted off the deck of the other tank like flies, but not before they had slaughtered its crew. 'Holy strawsack!' Schulze cried to Matz, dabbing his dripping brow. 'Matzi, this ain't gonna be like France. Those Popovs are crazy bastards. This is gonna be the tough—'

'—Enemy tanks one o'clock!' the Vulture's urgent bark cut into his words. 'Fire at will!'

Von Dodenburg swung his periscope round to the right. The squat, low shapes of six T34s had emerged from the cover of the village and were taking up the challenge.

'One o'clock!' he yelled at his sweating gunner – but the blond youth was already cranking the 75mm cannon round. Von Dodenburg grabbed an armour-piercing shell from the rack and thrust it into the open breech. The breech lever shot up with a clang. The gunner pressed his eye against the telescope. His fingers curled white around the firing bar. 'On target, sir!' he barked.

'*Fire*!' von Dodenburg roared above the racket.

He pulled the lever. The Mark III shuddered. The breech flew open. The ejected shell case clattered to the metal deck. Acrid smoke filled the turret. Hurriedly von Dodenburg activated the smoke-extractor keeping his eye glued to his own periscope as the white blob of the armour-piercing shell sped towards its target. It struck the steep front of the Soviet tank. The T34 reeled under the impact. The next instant the shell was bouncing off like a metal ping-pong ball and the T34 was coming on once more.

'Not the glacis plate, sir,' Schulze's excited voice crackled over the radio. 'Try the tracks, or the turret—'

His advice was cut short by the thunder of his own gun erupting. The AP shell clanged home just behind the nearest T34's rear sprocket. Schulze cheered as the enemy tank rolled to a stop and flames started to leap up greedily from the engine cowling. But the others kept on coming!

Von Dodenburg thrust another shell into the breech. His gunner pulled the bar back, his face pale and frightened now. The T34s were only three hundred metres away and coming straight for the command tank. The German tank shuddered. There was the hollow boom of metal striking metal. The T34 reeled to one side, starting to smoke immediately, white tracer bullets zig-zagging crazily into the burning sky as its ammo began to explode. The crew flung themselves out in mad haste, but they didn't get far. A machine-gun chattered and they slewed to a stop, dropping into the corn to be crushed under the tracks of the other T34s rolling straight for the command tank, which they had obviously identified from its many aerials.

'*Look out*!' von Dodenburg's driver screamed in sudden fear.

The young captain flung a glance to his right and caught a fleeting glimpse of a glowing white projectile hurrying straight at them. Instinctively he ducked. The tank shuddered violently. There was the frightening hiss of melting steel and suddenly the interior of the Mark III was full of the stench of burning cinders. Von Dodenburg waited for the end, watching horrified as the shell penetrated the turret, ran round the interior, making the metal glow a dull red, tracing a long furrow behind it like a finger through butter, before disappearing out of the other side – *without exploding*!

Von Dodenburg swallowed hard. With a hand that trembled violently he grabbed the gunner's shoulder. 'Get to it, man!' he cried. 'There are—' But he stopped short. The gunner had fallen back, sightless eyes staring into nothing. He was dead. He had died of shock.

That first long, bloody day of Operation Barbarossa, June 22nd, 1941, was for most of those in SS Assault Battalion Wotan a confused kaleidsocope of violent death and hectic activity, executed under a blazing, merciless sun.

Everywhere the Russians were in full retreat. As far as the eye could see on that limitless steppe, their villages and hamlets burned – set alight deliberately, in accordance with the Russian policy of not leaving anything behind for the hated Fritzes who had fallen on them so unexpectedly. Everywhere too, there were long columns of prisoners, hundreds, thousands, hundreds of thousands of them, shuffling back to the rear, gaze fixed miserably on the dusty ground, or begging piteously for water from the advancing Germans. But today the Germans were not giving Russians anything. For already the leading troops had begun to come across evidence of the brutality with which this new campaign would be fought.

A German soldier hung, crucified, from a telegraph pole, his body naked, with greedy bluebottles feasting on the bloody gore of what had once been his genitals; a kilometre further a burning village, where a dozen or so civilians lay sprawled dramatically in the dust, their hands tied together with barbed wire and the backs of their shaven skulls blown off; a woman, also dead, her skirt thrown up and her legs forced wide apart by the rapist who had killed her.

'They kill one of our men, and we kill a dozen of theirs in reprisal,' the Vulture announced as the men of Wotan stared numbly at the little massacre.

'I don't think,' von Dodenburg said slowly and carefully,

'that Germany should conduct the war like this, however brutal and sadistic the enemy might be.' He bent down and eased the woman's skirt down over her naked loins. 'We mustn't sink to the level of the savages, sir.'

The Vulture wiped the sweat from his dripping brow and prepared to swing himself back on his tank to continue the advance on Brest-Litovsk. 'My dear young friend. This is only the start. Before we have finished with Operation Barbarossa, I shouldn't be surprised if we're eating Popovs for breakfast - alive.' He waved his hand. 'Column will move on. *March*!'

The long convoy of tanks started to rumble once more towards the burning horizon.

By evening it was clear, however, that the Russians were putting up a determined resistance at Brest-Litovsk. The first indication that something was going wrong came when the second lieutenant of infantry came stumbling down towards the tanks, eyes wide and staring, a blood-stained bandage around his head, supporting himself with a stick. His cap had gone, and so had his revolver. He staggered past them, paying no need to their questions, weaving from side to side with a strange sort of mincing step, as if he were drunk. Then more men followed him - and more. All infantrymen, and all without their weapons, their eyes filled with that same wide, staring look as the lieutenant's.

'In three devils' name,' the Vulture exclaimed. 'They're the stubble-hoppers of the forty-fifth!'

'They look like the shitting walking dead to me,' Schulze whispered to Matz. 'Just look at 'em. They've had it. The clock's in the bucket for that lot.'

Wotan's tankers began to murmur. 'Things must be tough if the infantry have started to crack. Must be a bitch up there. The Popovs must have turned and made a stand. Now the wet fart's really hit the shithouse wall . . .'

'Be silent there, you dogs!' the Vulture cried finally in exasperation, his face crimson and glazed with sweat. 'Metzger, put out a picket line on both sides of the road back there, and arm the men with heavy machine-guns.

Anyone trying to cross the line after being warned – shoot them down. Mercilessly. Officer or man. I'll have no more of this type of disgraceful behaviour. And round up this rabble. Arm them with the weapons we've taken off the Russians.'

'*Sir*!' the Butcher sped away, happy to be excluded from whatever unpleasantness lay ahead.

The Vulture turned to his officers, 'Well, gentlemen, it seems as if the much-maligned SS will have to pick the Army's chestnuts out of the fire yet again.' He sprang on his command tank, monocle gleaming in the rays of that remorseless sun, and pointed his cane to the pyre of smoke rising slowly into the heavens. 'There it is, *meine Herren* – the key to Brest-Litovsk. And, I may add, big fat juicy headlines in the press back in the Reich – *promotion*!' He beamed down at their disapproving faces. 'Let us waste no more time . . . *To the attack*!'

Now it was the third day of Wotan's battle for the Citadel. To the immediate front of the eighteenth-century fortress, von Dodenburg had dug in what was left of his tanks, burying them in the rubble, using their 75mms as his artillery and the rest of the crew as infantry. They were now edging their way metre by metre through the shattered wasteland, ever closer to the battered main tower of the Citadel.

The Vulture himself made an appearance at von Dodenburg's sector of the line. As usual, he was unarmed save for a cane, and accompanied by an ashen-faced Sergeant-Major Metzger, who started violently every time a cannon fired. He ducked as a stream of Russian rockets hurtled skywards, trailing fiery-red flame after them. Next instant they crashed down on the German lines with a tremendous impact which made Mother Earth herself shudder violently. The Butcher choked back a sob of terror.

The Vulture, however, seemed completely unaffected. As the battle-grimed troopers stared at their CO and the

Vulture in awe, the two of them strolled along the front as if inspecting a peacetime parade. A sniper's bullet kicked up a spurt of rubble at the heels of the Vulture's gleaming riding boots. He slapped the side of his leg heartily with his cane. 'Awful bad shots these Popovs, what, von Dodenburg?'

Spontaneously a thin cheer went down the ragged line at the CO's coolness under fire. Even Schulze joined in.

The two officers passed into a ruined shed, with Metzger hastily clambering over the rubble to the rear towards a stout wall which offered protection from snipers.

Crouching there, von Dodenburg made his report. 'First Company, sir, one officer, one NCO and twenty men, five wounded. Fifty other ranks attached from the Forty-fifth Infantry. Three tanks still runners, five being used as dug-in artillery pieces, sir.'

'Thank you, von Dodenburg, you have done well. Now what's the situation here? Where's the fire?'

Von Dodenburg pointed through the shattered window, ignoring the sniper bullets running the length of the brick wall a mere five metres away, making little howling sounds as they ricocheted off. Two hundred metres away stood two concrete bunkers, the heat shimmering over their roofs in little blue waves. 'Those two damned anti-tank bunkers are causing all the trouble, sir. If we had some means of getting by them, we'd make short work of the Citadel – and that would be the end of Brest-Litovsk. I know I could blow them up if I could get close enough. One of my chaps has found some abandoned Popov satchel charges. But how to cover that two hundred metres?'

'Your three runners?'

'No can do, sir. The Popovs in those bunkers are well supplied with AP shells. My tanks would be cold meat the minute they broke cover.'

The Vulture absorbed the information, his long, ugly face pensive.

Suddenly a shout of alarm from von Dodenburg broke his thoughtful mood. 'Look out, sir! Incoming mail!'

There was the flat, dry crack of a Russian 57mm anti-tank cannon, and a solid white block of hurrying metal detached itself from the nearest bunker. It slammed into one of the abandoned streetcars near the shed with a resounding clang. The tram's signal bell rang merrily for a few moments.

'Close,' the Vulture commented, his voice shaking slightly, while behind the two officers, the Butcher felt the hot urine of fear flood his trousers. 'I see what you mean about those bunkers, but you're thin on the gound, von Dodenburg. Those broken wretches of the Forty-fifth are quite useless. You'll have to carry the bunkers with your chaps, few as they are.'

'But without armour, I can do—'

The Vulture held up his hand for silence. 'But you *do* have armour, my dear chap. Expendable armour, which even the Popovs won't be able to stop.'

Von Dodenburg looked at the Vulture as if he had just gone mad. 'But how . . .'

The Vulture pointed his cane at the trams. 'Those streetcars, von Dodenburg. They are your armour.'

For the next two hours the men of Wotan worked like crazy. Ignoring the solid shot which streaked through the tram shed at regular intervals, they filled the front of the two trams they had selected with whatever they could find in the way of protection: twisted steel girders, piles of fire buckets filled with sand, shattered wooden beams, even mattresses from the long vanished Russian crews' dormitory. Then, under the Vulture's command, they collected their own and the Russian dead and wedged the ghastly corpses in the seats as best they could, averting their faces and wiping their blood-streaked hands on the seats of their pants when they were finished. Finally they pushed a third car up to link up with the two already filled with corpses, and the Vulture went personally down its length, breaking the remaining windows with his cane until there was no glass left in them.

'Any of you men know how to drive one of these things?'

His question was greeted by a heavy silence, broken only by the moans of the wounded and the ever-present rumble of the permanent barrage, the eternal background music of war.

'Well, come on! Don't be like coy virgins holding your legs together! Speak up. There must be somebody!'

Reluctantly, Schulze raised his hand. 'I'll have a go, sir.'

'Excellent, Schulze. There'll be a piece of tin in it.'

'What about a nice bulletproof vest?' Schulze said sourly, but the Vulture, beaming with pleasure, had already hurried away to where the Forty-fifth Infantry survivors were dug in.

When he saw them, his smile vanished immediately. They were burnt out, he could see that; broken men, of no combat value whatsoever. They deserved what they were going to get.

'Now listen,' he said. 'My people will atack in the streetcar. I know you are tired; you have suffered severe casualties and have been here longer than we have. But I am doing nothing more than asking you to support us – that is all; a mere supporting role, with little or no danger for you.' He pointed his cane at a tall, bearded noncom. 'What's your name, Corporal?'

'Meier, sir.'

'Good then, Corporal Meier, you're in charge of your chaps.'

'Sir!'

'Once we're underway, I want you to take your people and cover our flanks. Don't take unnecessary risks. Just put a bit of pressure on the Ivans. My people will bear the brunt of the action. Is that clear, Meier?'

'Sir,' Meier barked, throwing out his chest smartly as if he were back on the parade ground. Obviously he was flattered by the Vulture's attention.

Geier turned away and murmured under his breath to

von Dodenburg, 'That man's a fool, but he'll serve his purpose. That sort was born to be used as cannon-fodder.'

Von Dodenburg looked worried. 'What do you mean sir?'

The Vulture smiled thinly, but his eyes remained icy. 'Do you really think I'm going to sacrifice what's left of the First Company? I shall need your experienced men to build up the new battalion once this business is over. When we start up that track, the Reds are going to fire at the leading tram. Once they discover their mistake – that they're shooting at dead men – what will be their reaction?' He answered his own question. 'They'll turn their attention to the only live men they can see: the cannon-fodder of the Forty-fifth.'

'But, sir,' von Dodenburg protested in horror. 'They're German after all. It'll be a massacre!'

'*Natürlich, mein lieber von Dodenburg*. Naturally,' the Vulture answered easily. 'What a naive young man you are!'

'All aboard who's coming aboard,' Schulze chortled, with the light-headed humour of exhaustion. 'This way for the ghost train. No fare on this one, comrades – and one-way tickets only!'

The Vulture took his place next to him, still armed only with his cane. 'All right, Corporal Meier, when the Ivans start popping away at us, you move out!'

'Sir!'

'All right, von Dodenburg, off we trot!'

Schulze whirled the twin brass handles of the driving controls in opposite directions. Above, there was a flash of blue sparks from the long rod connecting the tram with the overhead electric wires, and the streetcar shuddered in dismay. Up front, the dead bodies trembled frighteningly. A body fell clattering to the deck. Matz swallowed hard, and one of the Bavarians crossed himself and said a hasty prayer. Slowly the cars began moving out of the shed and began to gather speed. At the rear, Metzger took a last swig from his looted vodka bottle and flung it through the glassless window to shatter on the cobbles. In the same instant, the Soviet guns began to bark.

'All right, men,' Corporal Meier commanded, 'let's go.' Dutifully the cannon-fodder rose from their holes and hiding places and began to spread out on both sides of the road. The attack had commenced. The victims were ripe for the slaughter.

Tangles of telephone wires hung down from the shattered houses on both sides, as the trams rattled towards the bunkers. The houses were burning again and smoke was everywhere. A roof collapsed. Burning beams and shattered tiles rained down on the road. Swaying back and forth between the shaking houses, the trains rumbled onwards.

A shell slammed into the front of the first tram. It rocked like a ship at sea. Blue sparks flew from its steel wheels. For one alarming moment, von Dodenburg, holding on for dear life, thought it was going to overturn. That would spell disaster. But Schulze somehow managed to keep the vehicle on the track. The tram filled with acrid, choking dust; they kept on going.

Now more and more Russian guns were concentrating their fire on the advancing Germans, obviously rattled by this strange form of attack. Another AP shell rammed into the lead tram. A sudden stench of burnt flesh filled the air as flames started to leap from the leading tram car. Instinctively Schulze took his hands off the controls.

'Keep your flippers on the tillers!' the Vulture rapped and brought his cane down with a vicious thwack to emphasize his point. 'Keep going, man, or it'll be the end of us all!'

With the flames in front mounting ever higher and blinding them, the strange convoy of living and dead drew ever closer to the two key bunkers.

Suddenly the Russians spotted the cannon-fodder. A machine-gun burst into frenzied activity. A whole rank of the Forty-fifth disappeared, scythed down in an instant. The Vulture flung Corporal Meier an anxious glance through the swirling smoke. Would he and his men go to ground? No, they were keeping going – the fools!

Schulze watched as the corporal raced on, firing his machine pistol as he went, his men dropping like flies as they closed with the bunkers. Within seconds the attack of the Forty-fifth was over. All that remained was a handful of survivors, huddling fearfully in the smoking rubble. Among them was Corporal Meier, attempting to stuff his guts back into a great hole that had been ripped in his stomach, sobbing pitifully as he did so, dying on his feet.

'Remember his name, von Dodenburg,' the Vulture snapped, relieved to see that Meier and his men had served their purpose. 'He'll get a piece of tin for this, I'll see to that.'

'His widow, you mean – if he has one,' von Dodenburg replied bitterly. Helpless, he watched as Meier sank to his knees, head bent in defeat, entrails spilling out on to the ground, a loathsome pulsating snake of steaming grey.

Von Dodenburg's words were wasted on Geier, for now they were almost there. With a great resounding crash, the lead tram, completely ablaze now, slammed into the bunker.

In a confused rush, the SS troopers streamed out of the rear car, while the blazing tramcars in front of them effectively masked the Russian guns. Hand-grenades exploded on all sides. The cries of the wounded and the dying rose in a nightmarish cacophony and the air was filled with screams for help in German and Russian.

The SS men fought their way into the bunkers with spades, fists, claws. Von Dodenburg leaped over the body of a young blond trooper, his broken back twisted in agony. A potato-masher sailed over his shoulder and exploded among a group of Russians at the far end of the bunker, engulfing them in a ball of yellow fire. A Russian appeared to his right. He raised his tommy-gun. Von

Dodenburg was quicker. His machine pistol chattered at his hip. The Russian went down as if pole-axed.

All afternoon the battle of the bunkers raged. The men of Wotan were driven out of the second one three times by Soviet counter-attacks. The close combat was a nightmare. As the hours wore on, the streets became piled high with corpses, servered limbs, headless bodies, and streaked with trails of red gore where the wounded had dragged themselves away to die in the ruins.

But the Vulture refused to give up. His face blackened with powder burns, a patch of scarlet blood on his right shoulder, his helmet long gone, he led the survivors to the attack time and time again.

Finally it was over. The Russians surrendered, to be shot down mercilessly by the survivors, who then collapsed exhausted in the ruins. The Citadel was theirs. One day it would mean a regiment for Major Geier, as it had meant death for most of Captain von Dodenburg's First Company. But they were through. The great advance could continue.

When they moved out late that night, heading east yet again, the engineers were already bulldozing great holes in the rubble to bury the dead, Russian and German clinging together in one last embrace in the eternal darkness of the grave . . .

THREE

The days turned into weeks; the weeks months. On and on, they raced across the limitless plains of Russia. Nothing could stop them. Triumphant in the lead, SS Assault Battalion Wotan brooked no opposition.

Before them, the Russians fled in terror, but taking everything with them, even down to the last spent cartridge case. Nothing was allowed to fall into the hands of the Fritzes. Those Russians who refused to be evacuated or threatened to impede the headlong retreat eastwards were slaughtered mercilessly. Prisoners were massacred in huge numbers, mown down by machine-guns and set alight with gasoline. Those civilians who refused to abandon their homes were given the same treatment. For this was the policy of scorched earth which had defeated Napoleon's *Grande Armée* over a century before.

Still Wotan pressed on relentlessly, plunging deeper and deeper into this huge, cruel country, victorious yet awed by the many thousands of kilometres which now separated them from their homeland. Back in Germany, the Poison Dwarf, Minister of Propaganda Goebbels shrilled, 'Nothing, but nothing, can stop our Black Bands! They are invincible! They will sweep the world clean of the red plague! *Es lebe die Waffen SS . . . Es lebe SS Wotan*!'*

'Goebbels personally!' the Vulture chortled happily, when he heard the news from Dietrich over the radio. 'By all that is holy, the Führer will be talking of us next.' He rubbed his hands together happily. 'Those general's stars are getting a little closer every day, von Dodenburg. Thank God for Barbarossa!'

* Long live Wotan.

Soon they had left the steppe and found themselves fighting strange, lonely battles in the endless fir forests. No quarter was given and none was asked, for both sides knew what would happen to them if they were taken prisoner. Even their own wounded were shot by their comrades rather than allowed to fall into the hands of the other side. The wounded themselves pleaded desperately for the benison of the last bullet rather than *that*!

July gave way to August, and August to September. Now they were in the swamps, fighting the clinging mud that threaten to swallow up their tanks, the plagues of midges and flies that were everywhere, and a new hazard – partisans.

The Russian partisans shot and burnt and robbed – usually at night and from an ambush – fleeing before help could come. On 15th September, two ambulances bearing the day's wounded were sent to the rear to the casualty clearing centre. They never reached it. At dawn, both ambulances were found on a deserted road, bodies strewn about the surrounding countryside with their throats cut, pockets pulled inside out to indicate that the Russians hadn't hesitated to loot the dead. Worse was to come. The dead body of the front line Red Cross nurse who had accompanied them was found some distance away, completely naked, both her breasts sawn off and placed neatly on the ground next to her.

That morning, General Dietrich ordered action to be broken off at the front and a great sweep made of the surrounding woods. The partisans were to be eradicated, once and for all.

For once, the weary troops, unwashed, unshaven, emaciated and lousy for the most part, went looking for the killers with a will . . .

Now they had left the forests and the partisans, and swept on once again, racing across the steppe. Here they encountered villages whose inhabitants had not fled. Indeed, here the villagers had murdered their commissars, chased away the *kolkhoz* managers, breaking up the collective farms which they hated into individual plots of land and eagerly returning to the system which had prevailed before the Revolution. Here the invaders were welcomed by the local headmen, flanked by pretty girls in native dress who curtsied politely to the officers, faces wreathed in smiles, offering them the traditional bread, salt and vodka of friendship. Here the marauding Germans were regarded as liberators, come to free them from the Stalinist yoke after more than twenty years of slavery.

For the first time since the campaign had started, the men felt they could sleep easily at night, and for the first time they could talk to Russians, mingling with them in their cramped huts, crudely furnished for the most part with table and chairs, a cooking range, and usually an enormous, green-tiled oven that reached to the ceiling and on which the whole family slept in winter. Here the men of Wotan made their first, hesitant attempts to pick up a few words of the native language, larding their talk with '*palshalsta*', '*ponemayu*' and the old toast, '*nastrovya pan*'. They started to call each other 'little brother' in the Russian fashion, and in moments of danger would cross their foreheads and breasts in a mock-imitation of the Russian custom.

The 'liberated' Russians even went as far as to start turning over their local Jews to the men of the SS extermination squads. These had already begun to appear just behind the front, their purpose being to rid Soviet Russia of its many million Jews, thus taking up where the nineteenth-century czars had left off. '*Pogrom . . . pogrom*,' the Russians would chortle, as they herded their miserable Jewish prisoners in front of them, miming the actions of a firing-squad or drawing a finger across their throats.

That September, while driving back to General Dietrich's divisional HQ to pick up some orders for the Vulture, von Dodenburg came across a scene which brought home to him the change that had already taken place in Operation Barbarossa. For many in the SS, and naturally in the Wehrmacht too, Barbarossa had begun as a kind of crusade against the 'red pestilence'. From this day onwards, von Dodenburg knew that it had become a crime against humanity – one for which Germans would pay for a hundred years. After this day, he knew instinctively, Germany would have to fight for her life. And if she failed to win, then woe Germany.

A fat police lieutenant, wearing the same silver death's head and silver SS runes as he did, sat at the roadside. Above him, six bodies in civilian clothes swayed slightly as they dangled from the trees, faces crimson, tongues hanging out like pieces of dry shoe leather.

The corpses in themselves were nothing. Since they had marched into Russia three months before, von Dodenburg had seen more than enough of them.

It was the pile of bodies that lay in the ditch at the fat lieutenant's feet. There must have been half a hundred of them – all young women, strapping heavily-bosomed young girls for the most part, wearing the simple uniform of the Soviet Youth Movement, their white blouses as red with blood now as the jaunty little scarf they wore round their necks.

The fat lieutanant saw von Dodenburg halt his VW jeep and nodded a greeting. After firing a quick burst with his tommy-gun at one of the bodies which had appeared to move, he sauntered casually over to a stern-faced von Dodenburg, as if a pleasant chat might break the monotony of a long September afternoon.

'My people are down at the stream having a swim,' he said, after touching his pudgy hand to his cap by way of a salute. 'Thought I'd give them a break. It's not much of a life, this.' He indicated the bodies. 'I told them I'd look after the stiffs for a couple of hours. But please, forgive me. In this barbaric country one forgets the niceties so easily. Globke, Heinz Globke from Soltau.' He extended his hand.

Von Dodenburg didn't take it, but the fat police

lieutenant seemed not to notice the studied discourtesy. 'Wish I had a job like yours, Captain. All medals and glory. Bet the girls back in the Reich make a rare old fuss of you with all that tin on your chest.' He gave an icy-faced von Dodenburg a knowing smile. Police Lieutenant Heinz Globke from Soltau was obviously not a very perceptive man; he didn't see the storm signals.

'What did they do?' von Dodenburg rapped.

Globke shrugged his shoulders carelessly. 'Not much. Just happened to be commies, that's all – and women, of course.'

'Why women?'

'Breeders. Fine Russian milch-cows. Awful waste, too. You should have seen the lungs on most of 'em. You don't find our women with tits like that. Still, orders are orders. Reichsführer Himmler has ordered that all intelligentsia and communist womenfolk should be rubbed out, so as to stop them producing more of the same red ilk. So we rub 'em out.'

Behind him there was a soft groan.

The police officer turned with surprising speed. 'Got to attend to that one.' He strode back the way he had come and raised his tommy-gun, an expression of boredom on his good-humoured face.

Von Dodenburg didn't hesitate. He drew his pistol and fired almost without aiming. Heinz Globke gave a soft moan, flung up his arms and flopped face-forward into the heap of murdered girls.

It was just before they were due to leave the 'liberated' Russians. Schulze and Matz were busy using a burning candle to free their seams of the grey felt lice which infected them all, when they were interrupted by a strange question from their host, an ancient peasant with a wizened, clever face and a wispy white beard.

'Are you Germans planning to stay in Mother Russia very long?' he quavered from his position at the great tiled oven which reached to the dirty ceiling of the straw-thatched hut.

'Long?' Schulze paused in his work, and half a dozen grey lice fled across his hand to safety. 'I supposed so, little father.' He turned to his companion. 'What do you think, Matzi?'

'Yer. We'll stay until the Führer in his infinite wisdom decides otherwise. Why do you ask?'

By way of answer, the old man tittered, revealing his toothless gums.

Mildly, Matz laid down his candle. 'What are you laughing at, you silly old fart? You're gonna fall off the oven in a minute, if yer not careful.'

The old man laughed again and pointed a shaking finger at the great stove. 'It's you Germans who'll be needing an oven soon, if you're going to stay here much longer. You'll see . . .'

Matz looked at Schulze, and the latter returned his look. 'The old boy ain't got all his cups in his cupboard,' he said, picking up his candle again and listening happily to the crack of the scorched lice.

But for a long time the old man continued to cackle, repeating 'You'll see . . . You'll see . . .' until finally he dropped off to sleep again, with his ancient back pressed tight to the comforting warmth of the green tiles.

By October they had passed out of the territory of the 'liberated' Russians and were once again meeting empty villages; but now the ever-retreating Red Army no longer burnt them down to the ground, as they had done at the beginning of Operation Barbarossa. Instead they played a lethal game of cat and mouse with the invaders. Nothing was safe to touch in the villages, for the fleeing Russians had booby-trapped everything. The magnificent pistol apparently dropped in haste on the floor of an *isba* concealed a wire attached to a tremendous charge of high explosive. Kilos of cordite were hidden in harmless-looking samovars.

Vodka bottles were filled with acid. Wells were poisoned. Even the rope from which the bucket was suspended – a terrible temptation for hot, thirsty troopers – had explosives attached to it. Deadly danger lurked everywhere.

The men of Wotan began to grow nervous and apprehensive. At night the Vulture was forced to double their sentries, for strange rumours had begun to go the rounds – rumours of lone guards being mysteriously snatched from their posts during the hours of darkness, never to be seen again, or to be discovered later, horribly mutilated.

Even animals were used by their enemy in their attempt to injure and unnerve the invaders. Rabid dogs roamed the abandoned villages, foaming at the mouth, eyes blazing with madness, threatening to bite the Wotan troopers and infect them with their deadly disease. Harmless-looking sheep were found to have concealed explosive under their fleece, timed to go off immediately the animal was seized.

And then, as October gave way to the first week of November, there was the episode of the German sheep dogs.

Von Dodenburg's First Company was at point. Ahead of them, black smoke and raging flames billowed up from the horizon. That was nothing new. For days now the retreating Russians had been burning the stubble of the fields harvested in the previous months. Apart from that, however, there was little sign of activity; the advancing tanks, crawling over the immense steppe in an extended 'V', radios crackling, might almost have been on some peacetime manoeuvre. There was not an enemy soldier anywhere in sight.

Von Dodenburg, standing upright in his turret, scoured the ground immediately ahead. But it was empty: not even a heap of fresh brown soil to indicate an anti-tank mine buried in the steppe. It looked as if the Russians had run, leaving the country for them to do with as they wished.

Von Dodenburg frowned and pressed his throat-mike. 'Honeybee One to all,' he called.

There was a rumble of replies over the metallic crackle of static.

'Don't like it,' von Dodenburg continued. 'Wooden eye, stay awake!' he said, using the common German phrase, just in case some hidden Russian was monitoring this particular net. 'It's all too good to be true. Over and out.'

Another five minutes passed. The tanks rumbled forward, their commanders tense and apprehensive. As they stared at the burning, leaden sky, all of them knew instinctively that something was wrong. As von Dodenburg had just said, it was too good to be true. The Popovs were up to something. The question was, what?

It was Schulze who first spotted trouble. Draining the last of a bottle of looted vodka, he stared at the dog which crouched immediately ahead of him. There was something strange about the animal – he could see that at once. A normal dog would have been alarmed by the rumble of tracks, especially a country dog, as this one seemed to be. It should have turned tail and fled, bushy tail between its flying hind legs. Instead, this great brown creature lay there on its haunches, following the progress of the approaching tank with dark intelligent eyes, its ears lying flat against its skull, its damp gleaming muzzle sniffing the air.

Schulze pressed his throat-mike. 'Matzi,' he said, his voice soft and wary. 'See that hound?'

'Course I see it!' Matz began scornfully. 'Would I be in the shitting Armed SS—' He stopped short, the small hairs at the back of his skull rising alarmingly. The dog had risen and had begun to come towards them, crouched low and parting the grass carefully like one of its primitive wild ancestors, hunting some unsuspecting prey.

'Hey, Schulzi, I don't like the look of that cur. Better put a slug through it – just in case.'

Matz's urgent warning convinced Schulze: there *was* something wrong about this sinister brown creature. He dived for the other end of the turret, grabbed the handles of the machine-gun and with one practised move, cocked it.

Suddenly the dog moved, baring its yellow teeth savagely and diving forward – and an alarmed Schulze saw for the first time that it had a small pack on its back from which extended a metal prong.

'Great crab on the Christmas tree!' Schulze cried, as the dog swung to the back of the tank and began to try and scuttle underneath it. He swung the gun round and fired in the very same instant that the animal ducked its head under the fire-bucket hanging to the rear and tried to worm its way under the engine.

The burst hit the animal in the snout. Fur and gore flew. Suddenly the dog was lying there in the tank's wake, howling pitifully, its claws flailing the air crazily in its death agonies. But not for long. One moment later, as the prong struck the earth, the pack on its back exploded. There was a tremendous roar, a great flash of ugly yellow and red flame, and what was left of the killer-dog flew high into the air, splattering the back of the tank with red drops of blood.

Schulze choked a gasp of horror and pressed the throat-mike. Forgetting all radio procedure in his haste and horror, he cried, 'To all! Watch those shitting dogs! They're trained to creep under the tanks and set off an expl—'

The rest of his warning was drowned by a thick, muffled *crump* from the tank closest to his own. The Mark III rose six feet into the air and then thumped down again, both tracks bursting under the impact, thick white smoke streaming from its engine. A second later it was burning fiercely and its crew were pelting madly for their lives, as more and more of the killer dogs started bounding from the long grass, intent on wrecking the tanks.

What happened next was slaughter, pure and simple.

'Smoke . . . use your smoke dischargers!' von Dodenburg cried frantically over the radio. 'Blind them for a bit . . . Knock them off when they come through the smoke.' He grabbed the trigger and pressed it. The two smoke dischargers attached to the turret fired. Two bombs rose high into the air. A soft plop. Next instant, the area to the immediate front of the command tank was filled with thick, white billowing smoke and the dogs racing towards it halted, momentarily blinded.

Seconds later they started to grope their way through the fog, searching for some means to crawl underneath the tank as their Russian handlers had trained them to do. But now every member of the crew was waiting for them, even the driver. Dog after dog died in a merciless hail of fire.

Immediately the other tank crews adopted the same tactics. Dogs went down on all sides, their pitiful howls punctuated by the roar of an exploding tank, until finally the slaughter was over. Dead dogs sprawled everywhere on the burning steppe – and one fifth of von Dodenburg's company was destroyed or damaged.

Numbly von Dodenburg shook his head and watched a dog with crippled hind legs drag itself off to die somewhere on the steppe, making little yelps of agony as it went.

'*My God*,' he said saidly, '*what kind of war is this?*'

But to that overwhelming question there was no answer. The drive eastwards went on.

FOUR

'Moscow,' the Vulture rasped excitedly, his face crimson in the keen wind that whistled across the steppe beneath a leaden, ominous sky. '*We march on Moscow*!'

There was an excited murmur among the young officers sheltering behind the command tank, stamping their feet in the icy cold, eyes narrowed against the wind.

'Have you the details of Wotan's role, sir?' von Dodenburg broke in anxiously, taking his gaze from the threatening sky.

'Yes, and they are good, damned good!' The Vulture tugged at the end of his monstrous beak, which was already beginning to turn a strange dull white in the icy air. 'As always we are going to lead the attack at the head of the Division. God in heaven, von Dodenburg – don't look so glum! Don't you realize what an opportunity this will be for us? No one has taken Moscow since Napoleon back in 1812. Think of the glory, the decorations!' His eyes sparkled, although his monocle was beginning to mist over. 'Gentlemen,' he said confidently, when he saw his enthusiasm was not shared by his senior company commander, 'Wotan will celebrate Christmas Eve 1941 under the towers of the Kremlin. Christmas in Moscow, *meine Herren*!'

'*Christmas in Moscow*!' echoed the replacements who had filled the gaps in Wotan's ranks, their breath fogging the air. A moody von Dodenburg eyed the grey, lowering sky and kept his thoughts to himself.

On that first day of December the long column of tanks started to move out, leading the whole Bodyguard into the attack, twenty thousand young men, Germany's finest, determined to bring Operation Barbarossa to a successful conclusion and end the six-month-long campaign which had already cost the Reich half a million soldiers.

But right from the start things began to go wrong. Late that afternoon the grey skies opened up and a snowstorm the like of which none of them had ever seen before descended on them. An icy hundred-kilometre-an-hour wind, packed with great rolling white flakes, struck the column. In an instant the drivers were blinded behind their open ports and the commanders forced to hide behind the protection of their turrets, unable to keep their eyes open as that terrible wind buffeted them from side to side.

Hastily the tankers tried to keep going by tying handkerchieves over their mouths and slipping on their dust goggles. But they had proceeded a bare kilometre or so before their goggles were once more clogged with snow and the wind was dragging the very breath from their lungs. Almost at once icicles started to form at their nostrils.

Their eyebrows glittered with frost. Each fresh breath was only achieved with an effort of will, and the icy air stabbed their lungs like a sharp knife. They choked and gasped – and finally gave in. Everywhere the tanks rumbled to a stop, the men burying themselves in tarpaulins, extra blankets, anything that could keep them warm, jamming the accelerators to keep the engines roaring and the heat circulating.

Now Wotan – indeed, the whole of the Bodyguard – was stalled in an icy, snowbound waste; the most powerful armoured force in the whole world broken into scattered units, tiny groups of terror-stricken, awed men huddled behind the armour, listening to the howl of the wind outside as if it were some terrible Russian banshee come to snatch them away.

Hours passed. Now radio communications began to break down as batteries ran out. Gas started to give out too. The temperature began to fall inside the tanks. Relentlessly the snow poured down, the tanks disappearing under its heavy flakes. By the time night started to fall, the roads on which they had been advancing had vanished and the tanks were mere white humps dotting the snowy waste.

By midnight the storm had abated. Now the tankers ventured outside, forcing the snow off the turret hatches, shaking with cold, and staring, amazed, at a transformed world. The steppe had vanished, replaced by a wild, white waste that stretched as far as the eye could see in the hard bright gleam of a full moon which was now rising.

Von Dodenburg forced himself to step outside and set about trying to organize his column, although he would have much preferred to stay within the pathetic shelter afforded by the tank. He dropped down and ploughing knee-keep in snow from tank to tank, ordered their occupants to start shovelling their vehicles free and not to let the engines stop running on any account; in this cold they would never be able to start them again.

The men set to work, their fingers feeling like thick pork sausages, their feet and hands completely numb, great clouds of frozen breath fogging the air about their ears. Furiously they dug away the snow, pouring gasoline from the jerricans into the fillers to ensure that the engines didn't die for lack of fuel, while von Dodenburg tried to raise the rest of the battalion. It was impossible. His batteries were too weak, and the static was exceptionally bad; he concluded that it might have something to do with the storm. Frowning, he took stock of his surroundings, and his situation.

For once the First Company had not been leading the battalion. Bastian's Second Company, with the new Mark IVs with their heavier improved 75mm, had been at point. To his front, therefore, there were German troops; he was not advancing into the unknown. But where in three devils' name *was* he advancing?

He clambered up the slippery side of his command tank, its whole surface now sparkling with hoar frost, and stared to his front. The whole area seemed devoid of human habitation: there wasn't even a forest where his men could shelter – something unusual in Russia. Von Dodenburg knew that shelter was vital. He had already forgotten the great March on Moscow, at least for the time being. Today priority number one was to get his men under cover and feed them something warm.

Then he spotted it.

Far, far to the right there seemed to be a lighter, higher patch of white that might indicate a house – probably a large one, if it was visible from this distance.

He sucked his teeth thoughtfully and watched as the wind raised wild flurries of dancing snow, glittering like a cheap pre-war Christmas card. The Vulture would be furious if he broke away from the column without orders. But there was no Vulture present; he had to make his own decisions and take the consequences. He'd risk it. Cupping his hands around his wind-cracked mouth, he cried above the roar of tank engines, 'All right, hear this . . . We're moving on. I think I've seen a place where we can find shelter out of this damn cold for the night and cook some food. But I want everyone to be on his toes.'

'*Karbid* . . .' he shouted and clambered inside the turret to kick his driver on the right shoulder, the signal for advance. '*Roll 'em, drivers* . . .'

They were on their way again.

Two hours later the first tank began to nose its way up the long snow-bound drive of the house, past the old castellated lodge, its roof heavy with snow, but silent and sombre, as if it had been abandoned these many years. Steadily the leading Mark III churned along the avenue of snow-heavy trees, their long branches like white, clutching hands, swaying rhythmically in the wind.

The mansion was empty. The door broke easily under one hefty blow from Schulze's shoulder. Hurriedly the others crowded in behind him to get out of the terrible cold, while von Dodenburg organized a hasty defensive perimeter with his Mark IIIs. The atmosphere of the place was curiously hushed and airless, with the damp smell of fir and laurel thick in the nostrils of the awed soldiers as they stamped through the high-ceilinged empty rooms. The place looked as if it hadn't been lived in since the Revolution.

'What do you make of it, Schulzi?' Matz asked apprehensively, as they crept into a large, bare-boarded dining room. The ceiling here was so high that their torches were barely able to illuminate it.

'Not much, Matzi. But don't worry about it, little fart in a trance. The main thing is that we're out of that shitting freezing white stuff out there till morning.'

Sergeant Schulze didn't know it, but they would not be out of the 'shitting freezing white stuff' the following morning – nor for a whole terrible week. And when they finally did emerge, they would not be driving for Moscow, but running panic-stricken for their lives.

All through that night of the first great snowfall, the Soviet command used the great natural advantage – 'General Winter', as it was called gratefully by the barrel-chested generals of the Stavka* – to help break up the German assault on their capital.

Unlike the Germans, whose tanks stalled or became snowbound, their crews freezing, unable to use their engines or cannon for lack of special winter greases and clothing, the Russians were active, as if the great storm meant nothing to them. Countless patrols, often up to the strength of a whole regiment, set out that long night: on foot, on horseback, on skis and on motor-sledges; delaying, sabotaging, destroying the great German advance, breaking the German assault force into ever weaker groups of frightened, freezing men, cut off from their fellows by the snow. Each time, the Ivans would appear as if from

* Soviet High Command.

nowhere out of the whirling white gloom and disappear again before the Germans even had time to retaliate.

Nothing, however, was more vital to the bemedalled generals who ran Russia's war than to stop the élite formation of the Fritz army, the force most likely to succeed in breaking through in spite of all the horrific conditions. The Leibstandarte Adolf Hitler, the Bodyguard, had to be halted. For 'Old Leather Face' (as they called that wizened dictator in the Kremlin) had personally issued the order: '*Stop the SS*!'

Now, blazing log fires crackled in the great marble fireplaces. Even the wet branches from the snowbound trees outside burnt cheerfully, after being doused with cordite and gasoline. The air in the big high-ceilinged dining room was filled with the delicious odour of 'Old Man' stew and fried sauerkraut, while the half-frozen men stretching out their red fingers gratefully and greedily towards the blazing flames, licked their wind-cracked lips with eager anticipation.

Now all those not on sentry-duty finished off the last of the food, stoking up the fires and settling themselves down on the damp wooden floor to sleep, the flames casting strange, glowing shapes on the walls above them.

Von Dodenburg walked softly through the lofty rooms, checking on his men, who were now mostly snoring, and running his mind over the events of the day. He was a little worried about the fate of the Vulture and the remaining two companies of Wotan, but there was little he could do about it till morning, when he would try to resume radio contact.

In the end he turned in himself, after giving Metzger the first watch and responsibility for changing the sentries outside in the freezing steel coffins. Slowly sleep overcame him, the last sound to penetrate his conscious mind a strange hissing burr, which he attributed to the wind. Seconds later he was fast asleep.

The Butcher awoke with a start and the anxious, guilty knowledge that he had fallen asleep while on sentry duty – a crime punishable by death in the Armed SS. He licked his dry lips, blinked his eyes several times, and the big room swung into focus: the flames were still flickering in the grate, the men still huddled in their blankets on the floor, lying as motionless as if they were dead. The Butcher shivered; he mustn't go on thinking so morbidly – this place put the wind up him as it was. Suddenly he heard again the sound which had awakened him from his sleep: a strange sort of scratching sound, accompanied by a faint animal whimpering, like a dog makes when it is badly hurt.

He gulped and felt the small hairs at the back of his bull-like neck stand erect. God, it was enough to make a grown man fill his pants like some wet-tailed infant! With an effort he pulled himself together. After all, there were half a dozen well-armed, alert sentries in the tanks outside, thank God. There was nothing to be afraid of . . .

All the same, he loosened the flap of his pistol-holster.

Grabbing his torch, he stepped over the bodies of the sleeping men and went to investigate, as was his duty. With both hands he seized the big iron handle of the door, and pressed it down. The oaken door creaked and swung open. A beam of silver moonlight cut into the darkness of the interior. The Butcher gasped with horror as he saw what had caused the sound.

Lying in the snow was one of the sentries, his throat slashed from ear to ear like a gaping red mouth, his hands aready frozen into bloody claws, the snow behind him red with his blood.

'*Popovs*!' the Butcher screamed, high and hysterical, as the full realization of what must have happened to the dead sentry flashed terrifyingly into his mind. '*The Popovs are here! Stand to . . .*'

Suddenly a white-smocked figure on skis hissed from behind the nearest tank, wielding a stubby sub-machine-gun. A hail of slugs ripped sparks and stone fragments off the wall only metres from the Butcher's head. The Butcher darted back inside the door, slamming it shut with one mighty kick, as more and more of the white-clad ski troops hissed out of the silver night heading straight for the house.

In an instant all was crazed, frantic action within the big house, as the Soviet ski troops closed in on all four sides, firing as they came. A startled von Dodenburg rapped out orders to his men, so rudely woken from their slumbers.

'*Get to the windows . . . Throw those packs and bedrolls down as barricades . . . Make every shot count . . . Don't waste ammo, that fool over there . . . All the rest is in the vehicles . . .*'

Now, as the firefight started to break out in earnest and the angry snap-and-crack of slugs filled the air, Captain von Dodenburg, followed by Matz and Schulze – who as always in such emergencies had appointed themselves as their beloved CO's unofficial bodyguards – raced up the stairs three at a time to take stock of the situation.

It was bad. Von Dodenburg crouched next to a panting Schulze and peered out cautiously at the snowbound park below. The Popovs were everywhere. There was at least a battalion out there, well entrenched behind the tanks and inside the groves of laurel and fir. Further small groups lay out in the open, their snow-suits blending in perfectly with the white mass that covered the ground, sniping at the windows of the big house.

'They're round the back, too!' Matz gasped, skidding to a stop and dropping hastily to the floor as a sudden burst of bullets showered him with plaster and wood chippings. 'Hundreds of the little shits – Siberians by the look of 'em. Yellow-faced, slant-eyed buggers, the lot of them!'

Von Dodenburg groaned. The situation couldn't be worse – not only for him, but for the whole army. The Siberians were the élite of the Red Army and had been stationed in the Far East to meet any threat from Japan. If they were here, it meant that Stalin had brought his great million-strong Army of the Far East to oppose the German drive on Moscow.

'Holy strawsack,' Sergeant Schulze groaned, 'they've really got us with our hooters in the shit this time!'

'Perhaps,' von Dodenburg agreed, looking grim. 'We're heavily outnumbered, that's for sure. And you can be damn sure they'll have immobilized the Mark IIIs by now. They won't run the risk of our trying to recapture them. But you know what they say, Schulze – weeds don't die so easily. Wotan isn't finished yet. Come on, you big rogue, let's get down there and put some pepper into the defence. If we can hold them off for one night, who knows what the morrow might bring?'

Schulze wasn't convinced. 'If yer thinking that our lot'll break through to us tomorrow, sir,' he said glumly, 'I think you'd better have another think. Just look at the sky. It's full of violins!'

Von Dodenburg looked. Schulze was right: it *was* full of violins.

They were in for some more snow.

The snow streamed down in a relentless white curtain, as if God on high had determined that the war-torn landscape down below should be blotted out for good. For the frozen-faced, weary men peering out into the whirling white gloom for the first sign of an enemy attack, it was yet another misery to add to their already miserable existence.

It was now three days since first they had been surrounded by the Soviet ski troops and the snows had commenced. In spite of the weather, the Siberians had attacked time and time again with reckless bravery, before breaking up to regroup and attack once more. Now the ground outside was littered with white humps of snow concealing what had once been men. For all their losses, the attackers still outnumbered the defenders by four to one, and a worried von Dodenburg knew, too, that once the storm was over the Siberians would call up reinforcements, perhaps even dive-bombers, to blast them out of the bullet-pocked mansion.

On the first day they had made repeated attempts to raise the battalion on the radio, but their batteries had been fading alarmingly all the time. They had even resorted to the old trick of taking them out and renewing their waning power by heating them over the fire. But all they had heard was the crash and blare of Soviet military band music jamming the German broadcasts, and in between, the occasional terrified message in German demanding help, as whole battalions, then divisions, and finally corps signalled that they were being forced to retreat. At four o'clock that first day, a lucky sniper's bullet had put the radio out of action for good.

A weary von Dodenburg realized with a sense of impending doom that the Vulture would have written them off by now. Now it was *sauve qui peut* – and the Vulture would be running with the remnants of SS Assault Battalion – just like the rest of the Army which had set out so boldly to conquer Moscow only a few days ago.

The second day had been even worse. The Siberians had penetrated the house, not as von Dodenburg had expected they might by the basement, but by the roof. They had taken the defenders completely by surprise, swarming down the great ornamental staircase in their scores, squat yellow-faced figures firing from the hip, their slant-eyes blazing with excitement.

Schulze had rallied first. 'Get back, you shitting Siberian bastards!' he had roared, carried away by rage as SS men went down on all sides and it seemed that nothing could stop the attackers. Seizing the big MG 34, he had cradled it in his arms and opened fire, aiming right into the front rank of the Siberians.

The little men had gone down like ninepins, yelping with pain, bowling over their comrades who were crowding in behind them. In an instant their surprise attack had been halted. Von Dodenburg rallied his men at once. 'Follow me!' he cried, dashing forward to aid Schulze, treading unheedingly on the groaning bodies of the fallen as he did so.

Schulze's 'Hamburger Equalizer' flashed as he waded into the little Siberians, striking terrible blows to left and right, sending one of them flying high up into the air with a tremendous blow to his chin. Then the rest of the Wotan men were among them, cutting, slashing, hacking, carried away by that old atavistic bloodlust of men stretched by battle to the very limit.

It had been too much for the Siberians. They had fled back the way they had come, screeching in a strange high-pitched manner, jostling, clawing and fighting each other to get away from the terrible, glittering-eyed wrath of the crazed blond giants.

But still they retained control of the upper floor. In the end, to prevent any more of his men being killed, von Dodenburg ordered that a barricade should be built at the base of the grand staircase. Now, on this third day, a barrier of bodies, German and Siberian, sealed off the two floors, the corpses trembling uncannily at periodic intervals every time a Siberian popped around the corner above and poured a quick burst of fire downstairs.

On this third afternoon of siege, with the snow hissing down in straight sheets outside, muting even the occasional bursts of machine-gun fire and the krump of the grenades, von Dodenburg was a worried man. Soon the snow would stop – and that would mean the end for what was left of his company. Even if it didn't stop, the weary survivors couldn't last out much longer. Ammunition was low and their food was running out. This morning they had been forced to loot the bodies of the dead Siberians in search of something to eat, and had had to satisfy their gnawing hunger with a handful of oats, tiny pieces of stinking fish which seemed to be the Siberians' staple diet in combat, and a cupful of melted snow water. As Matz had moaned, 'Well, at least we won't run out of shitting snow the way that stuff's coming down!'

Von Dodenburg slumped down next to Schulze, who was busy examining the lining of his breadbag to check if there were any crumbs of *Kommissbrot** left there and finding to his disappointment that there weren't. 'Hard luck,' he sympathized with the crestfallen Hamburger.

Schulze forced a grin. 'Suppose the slant-eyes will feed us before they shoot us, sir, don't you think?'

Von Dodenburg returned the grin. 'It's a nice thought, Schulze . . . How are the men taking all this, do you think?'

'The boys – even the greenbeaks – are bearing up well. They know well enough what the slant-eyes'll do to them if they surrender.' Schulze's big face crumpled into a frown. 'The only thing is, there's no hope. The lads need to believe that there's still some way out of this damned trap.'

Von Dodenburg nodded. 'I know what you mean, Schulze. I've been racking my brains all afternoon to come up with something. We can't stay here much longer, as you well know. The question is – how to get out?'

'Well, they managed to get in, sir,' Schulze said, indicating the Siberians on the floor above them, 'and really caught us on the hop. Maybe we could play the same kind of trick on them.'

'I agree, but going out through the roof wouldn't help us very much, would it now? They'd still be waiting for us outside.'

Schulze grunted something, and then his eyes lit up. 'What about out through the basement? I've been in the cellars down below. The walls are metres thick, but there *is* a small exit window. I've got a couple of these cardboard soldiers armed with an MG posted down there, just in case the Siberians decide to try any funny business . . .'

Von Dodenburg shook his head, 'Same problem as before, Schulze. They'd be waiting for us. And I don't think even this kind of snow would cover our exit—' He broke off suddenly. 'But you've given me an idea, Schulze.'

'What, sir?'

In his eagerness, von Dodenburg didn't have time to

* Army issue hard-bread

answer. He sprang to his feet and was gone, racing down the stone stairs three at a time to the basement, leaving a bewildered Schulze to stare blankly after him.

'The house has sanitation,' von Dodenburg announced to the men grouped around. Outside, the whirling white flakes were still descending like silent tracer.

'That's nice to know,' Schulze said cheerfully. 'First house I've ever come across in the whole Workers' Paradise that ain't got a plop shithouse. But what's so important about it, sir?'

'Well, don't you see? In a house of this size there would have to be a flushing system capable of carrying away a great deal of – er – shit, to use your own delicate phrase.'

Schulze and the rest grinned dutifully, but they were still somewhat mystified as to why their CO should think it important.

'So, a flushing system of that kind would have needed a very large drainage pipe—'

'—Leading to a cess pit somewhere far enough away from the house,' continued Matz, who was always quicker off the mark than the rest, 'to prevent the delicate aristocratic nostrils of their lordships from being offended by the common odour of crap!'

'Exactly,' von Dodenburg agreed happily. 'And I've found it!'

'So?' Schulze said warily.

'So, assuming we can tunnel into that drainage pipe and it isn't blocked, we'll have found what we've been looking for all this day.'

'Yes, muttonhead,' Matz agreed, staring scornfully at Schulze. 'Well, come on, think it out, you thick shithead. The cesspit's got to be at least fifty metres – no, a hundred metres – away from the house. So if we can get into it – *and out of it* – we'll do so *behind* the slant-eyes. Get it?'

Schulze got it. They all did. New hope lit up their worn, emaciated faces, the old fervour springing back to their lacklustre eyes. Schulze grabbed for his entrenching tool, leaned up against the bullet-chipped wall. 'Just give the word, sir,' he snapped with all his old enthusiasm, 'and I'm ready to start shovelling shit from here back to good old Hamburg.'

Von Dodenburg looked down at them. 'Well then, you big rogue, prepare to start shovelling shit – *now!*'

All was silent now save for the hiss of the still-falling snow, and for once in this long week von Dodenburg was glad of it; it would muffle the noise as they made their escape. Cautiously, he peered out from the hole in the snow, thanking God for the clear, icy air after the stench of centuries below.

For nearly three days they had tunnelled down the old working, halted time and time again by falls of rubble and loose stone, and groaning as they removed the mighty flags that sealed off the old sewage pit. Here a man could only work for five minutes before being overcome by the fumes. Finally, gasping with the effort, their emaciated bodies racked with pain, they had managed to clear a narrow passage and had begun the last phase of their escape – the tunnel through the two metres of snow that rested above the old sewer. That they had accomplished too – though after two days without a bite to eat, nearly all of the diggers were by now at the end of their strength.

Von Dodenburg shivered as he thought of what lay before them this snowy December night, deep in the heart of Russia, so far away from their own lines. Their only strength lay in their weapons – and in the dedicated fanaticism of the Armed SS. It would have been easy to have accepted surrender and the inevitable death that would have followed, but he knew that for the men of Wotan, surrender was unthinkable. They could never give in.

'All right, men,' he whispered, 'you can start coming

out now. Come on, let's hurry it up . . . From now onwards, it's *march or croak!*'

March or croak. That indeed was the motto for the survivors of the First Company as they trailed across that vast white waste; weary, starving, hunched creatures of no significance in that cruel, remote country.

It was clear even to their starved, dulled minds that Germany had suffered a great defeat. For now they were passing through the graveyard of Germany's hopes; fields of snow littered with the débris of a beaten army – abandoned burnt-out trucks; discarded steel helmets, rifles, gas masks; tanks that had run out of fuel; cannon, their breech blocks smashed by sledge-hammers. Corpses. Corpses clad in field-grey, some almost buried by the drifting snow, others frozen solid, their faces white and sparkling with hoar frost, so stiff that the desperate troopers had to saw at their breadbags with their bayonets in order to get at the pathetic hunks of bread inside and smash them into rock-hard fragments with their rifle-butts. Only the bread kept them alive, making them forget the dull ache in their skinny guts and giving them the strength to overcome the nagging fear that the Cossacks would catch them before they reached the safety of their own lines – wherever they might be.

It was unearthly cold. The icy wind raced across the winter waste, lashing thousands of razor-sharp particles of snow against their sunken, grey faces. Weary shoulders bent under the strain, they stumbled their way across that never-ending white plain, driven only by the pride and iron discipline of the SS and a flickering, ever-weakening desire to stay alive.

With Von Dodenburg at the front, marching by compass, and Schulze and Matz at the rear, bullying, cajoling, pleading, threatening them, the breath pouring from their mouths like cigar smoke, they somehow managed to keep going.

On and on they staggered, all through that second week of December 1941, while two thousand kilometres away in the Reich, where people slept in soft warm beds and ate their fill, unsuspecting German civilians prepared for Christmas. Soon the war would be over, they told each other joyfully; soon 'the boys' would be coming home. Hopelessly misled about what had happened in Russia, they little knew that Operation Barbarossa had failed and that Germany would have to fight for four more long, terrible years.

Like automatons, the troopers pressed ever westwards, spurred on by the thought of pans full of frying eggs and homefries, mounds of good white bread, bubbling urns of hot coffee . . . Their eyes narrowed to slits in the terrible wind, their stomachs rumbling furiously, they plodded, hobbled, stumbled home.

On the fourth day of their escape, they started to leave the steppe behind and plod wearily up the snowy slope which led to the hills. Later, von Dodenburg realized that he should have known immediately that those hills would be *the* defensive position, but at the time his mind was too numb to think of anything but the simple task of putting one foot in front of the other, as they advanced like drunken old men up the incline.

Now they began to encounter more and more evidence of the great retreat; scattered, burnt-out abandoned trucks and tanks, and every now and then a ghastly tableau of bodies heaped indiscriminately together – a frozen hand, a bloody stump, a pair of eyes staring at the weary strangers as if in accusation. Once they came across a truckload of dead panzer grenadiers sitting bolt upright in their seats, like rotting cabbage stumps in an abandoned allotment. Further on, a bunch of infantry about to set up a machine-gun had been caught by a sudden barrage; their devotion to duty had been preserved by the freezing cold and could still be seen in their dramatic postures. A severed head stood by itself on the snow, like an abandoned football . . .

One by one they faltered to a stop and stood there,

swaying, as if they might collapse at any moment. But it was not the sight of these terrible bodies which halted them, nor the prospect, ghastly though it was, of looting them for food. No – it was the red flare that was now beginning to arc its way into the leaden, threatening sky above, trailing spluttering sparks behind it, colouring the snow a dull red.

An instant later it was followed by a green one.

The troopers gazed up, as if they had been granted a view into Paradise itself, their worn young faces crossed by a look of absolute wonder, their red-rimmed eyes a mixture of hope and disbelief. Slowly two great tears started to course down Schulze's exhausted, bearded face.

'It's the signal, sir,' he croaked, 'the signal . . .' He grabbed von Dodenburg's arm and shook it violently. 'Don't you fucking well understand? *The signal . . . THE SIGNAL!*'

Von Dodenburg looked at the big noncom like a man waking slowly from a deep sleep, unsure whether this was reality or he was still dreaming. He swallowed hard, while at his side Schulze started to howl like a crazy animal, the tears streaming down his honest face in ever-increasing profusion. 'Of course!' he whispered, his voice full of awe, 'the infantry signal for "advance and be recognized" . . . *Advance and be recognized!*' he blurted out the next instant, new hope streaming into his grey face. 'Up there . . . They must be our people . . .' He choked hard. 'We've reached the German lines! We're saved . . . We're saved, comrades . . . *We've done it!*'

1942

TIME OUT OF WAR

'Do yer know the *second* thing the soldier does when he goes home on leave to his old woman, comrades? I'll tell yer. *He takes off his pack!*'

The Sayings of Sergeant Schulze

ONE

This fine spring evening, the narrow streets of the great Rhenish city were filled with strollers: well-fed, well-dressed civilians. Only the drab field-grey of the soldiers reminded Major von Dodenburg, the new second-in-command of SS Assault Battalion Wotan, that there was a war on. Otherwise, the tragedy still taking place in far-off Russia seemed a million light-years away.

Handsome, lean, the bright bauble of the Knight's Cross of the Iron Cross hanging at his throat, Kuno von Dodenburg was much admired by the elegantly dressed women as they sipped their wine in the street cafés or indulged themselves with outsize portions of ice-cream topped with whipped cream. But although it was now a year since he had last enjoyed a woman, the tall major in his smart new uniform didn't return the interest. Somehow he felt like a stranger in this civilian world – indeed, a stranger in his own country.

Idly, without knowing why, he turned off Cologne's elegant Hansaring and began to stroll down the narrow street that led to the great Gothic cathedral and the clash and blare of a brass band. Automatically he acknowledged the salutes of the men in field-grey and the '*Heil Hitlers*' of the pompous golden pheasants in their polished jackboots, their chests covered with decorations from the old war. Here and there the walls of the tall apartment blocks were covered with garish posters announcing '*Better dead than red!*' and '*Shush, the enemy is listening!*' One depicted two handsome blond giants standing side by side at attention, beneath the legend '*The Armed SS needs Y-O-U!*'

Kuno von Dodenburg frowned. The poster reminded

him of everything he was trying to forget on this warm spring night in this pleasant old city: that soon the young recruits would once more begin flooding the barracks, ready again to be thrust into the greedy maw of that bloodstained Moloch waiting for them out there in Russia.

He emerged from the narrow street and blinked up at the great grey spires of the cathedral, eyes narrowed against the sun still sparkling on the Rhine beyond.

In the cobbled square beneath its west entrance, an army band played: the fat middle-aged bandsmen with their great red-and-black epaulettes thumping out one of those harsh Prussian marches that had once sent shivers down his spine. That had been before Russia, and the realization of what war was *really* about.

Von Dodenburg, pausing at the edge of the gay crowd, was unimpressed. But not so the civilians. They clapped their hands and tapped their feet, the men whistling along with the band. Dotted among the crowd were boys of the Hitler Youth in their grey shirts and black short pants, listening with eyes gleaming, as if the martial music filled them with the urge to die a glorious death on some remote battlefield. Von Dodenburg frowned. Few of them were more than fifteen or sixteen years old – boys in short pants; yet soon, they, too, would be called to that terrible war-machine, and they would be boys no more; they would be men – for the short time they would still live.

Coins rattled next to him and an educated, if mischievous voice said, 'Something for the Winterhilfe, Major?'

He turned, a little startled, and stared down.

A girl of perhaps sixteen stood there, shaking the collection box, her eyes bright, blue and eager. There was little of the schoolgirl about her. Beneath the short black skirt of the Hitler Maidens, her legs were brown and shapely, and her breasts were full, threatening to burst out of her tight white blouse. She shook her box once more and thrust her fine bosom up at him provocatively. 'Surely a handsome soldier like you has got *something* for me,

Major?' In her voice, there was now a husky note of unmistakable sexual promise.

Thus Kuno von Dodenburg met Heidi von Waldesdorf and learnt the facts of life in Hitler's Reich – that same Reich the Führer promised would last another thousand years. The spiritual education of Kuno von Dodenburg had commenced.

'Enjoy the war, for the peace will be terrible. That's what we're all saying this year,' Heidi said, with that outspoken cynicism of hers which von Dodenburg had never seen before in a girl of her age. 'This isn't 1939, you know, with patriotic speeches and hopes of great glory, Kuno. This is 1942, the year of the bombs and black marketeers. The war has grown old and corrupt.'

'So it would seem, if I'm to believe you, Heidi,' Kuno von Dodenburg said mildly, letting her talk; for she talked like a woman of twice her age.

Now he knew a great deal more about the girl. Her father was a senior officer in one of the many headquarters behind the Eastern Front; her mother, much younger, was what they had begun to call on the Home Front a 'green widow', one of those many wives of serving soldiers who amused herself with other men while their husbands fought and died at the front. 'And why not?' Heidi had commented cynically, after she had told him about her mother's liaisons. 'My father is probably doing the same in Russia.'

Heidi herself was still at school – nominally, at least – but she used her membership of the Hitler Maidens to absent herself from her classes, using the time to roam the streets of Cologne in search of whatever adventure the city had to offer. Somehow von Dodenburg suspected the adventures she found would be distinctly frowned upon by the man who had given his name to the movement to which she belonged.

'For you men at the front, life is simple,' she continued,

gazing out over the Rhine and its slow-moving barges. 'A matter of black and white. Kill or be killed.'

'I suppose so,' von Dodenburg humoured the girl, whom he had grown to like, in spite of the age difference between them.

'But here at home, things aren't black and white, but . . .' her pretty face creased in a frown, '. . . a kind of grey. Not simple at all.' She picked up a stone and tossed it into the water, as if reluctant to go on. 'Do you know they kill people here in Cologne, all the time?' She kept her gaze fixed on the water.

'*Kill* people? Who kills whom?'

'What does it matter?' She turned and looked at him defiantly, thrusting out her breasts provocatively. For the first time in a long while von Dodenburg felt desire. 'Let's forget it. Let's enjoy ourselves . . . My mother has gone away for a few days with a new friend. The house is mine, apart from the new Russian maid we've got from the East, and she can't understand a word of German.'

Von Dodenburg swallowed hard. She *was* only sixteen; perhaps he'd better think of other things. 'What were you saying before – about killing? Tell me, Heidi. You seem to think it's important.'

She pouted a little, obviously torn between imparting to him what she knew and her desire to have this handsome young SS officer make love to her. 'They kill Russians – prisoners of war – and they kill Germans; communists, social democrats, Jews . . .' She shrugged. 'They kill them all.'

He tugged her arm angrily. The conversation was getting out of hand. 'Who kills these people?' he rasped.

'We do,' she said simply.

'*We do?*'

'Yes – our policemen, the golden pheasants, the men who wear the same insignia as you do, Major.'

He looked at her, aghast. 'What do you mean?'

'It's very simple. Enemies of the state, parasites, Russians, Asiatic sub-humans – anyone who's no further use in our factories we take away and shoot in the woods outside Cologne. Naturally, we give them a taste of German culture first in the form of the camp; then we relieve them of their miserable existence. Once we were the nation of poets and writers, now we are the people of judges and hangmen.'*

'You mean the labour camps? I've heard of them,' said von Dodenburg, a little relieved. 'But surely they don't kill people there? They just attempt to make them see the error of their ways. Heidi, you've been listening to rumour-mongers.'

'Have I?' she said harshly. 'Look at this, then, and tell me if this is the work of a rumour-monger, my dear Major von Dodenburg.' So saying, she produced a photograph and handed it to him.

Von Dodenburg gasped with horror. The print was poor, blurred and grainy, as if some amateur might have developed it in his bathroom, but there was no mistaking the horrific scene depicted. Four men dressed in what appeared to be striped pyjamas and one woman, completely naked and skeletal, hung from a long wooden beam; their faces were contorted horribly, heads on one side, their tongues hanging out almost down to the tips of their chins, and what looked like chicken wire dug deep into their necks. Behind them, in the pose of the conquerors, were two middle-aged storm-men in black, hands placed on their hips, highly polished boots well apart, laughing as if this was one of the funniest sights they had ever seen.

'In three devils' name,' he croaked, 'where did you get this, Heidi?'

She shrugged carelessly. 'My dear lady mother has a variety of friends. One of them happens to be the commandant of the local labour camp, as you so delicately call them. In his cups last month he showed this one and others to my mother. I stole it—'

Heidi stopped short. Von Dodenburg was rising to his

* In German the phrase is, '*Volk der Dichter und Denker, jetzt Richter und Henker.*'

feet, his face pale. 'Kuno, I didn't mean it,' she cried, alarmed. 'Where are you going? *Kuno, please . . .*'

But already Major von Dodenburg was hurrying along the embankment, savagely pushing past anyone who stood in his way, head raised high, as if suddenly the sight of his fellow Germans sickened him.

That night he got swinishly drunk. Vaguely he remembered a woman. A woman in black. A big matrimonial bed with a crucifix on the wall above it. Next to it a picture of a young officer, the frame of the photo wreathed in black ribbon. 'Killed in Poland,' the widow giggled drunkenly. 'Iron Cross, Third Class. The next one at Dunkirk, Second Class . . . Two more in Greece and Russia, Iron Cross, First Class . . . And now you, my beautiful man. Knight's Cross as well . . . Isn't it all exciting? Everything gets better every day. *Long Live the Führer!*'

He remembered blundering drunkenly into the Vulture's room unannounced, surprising him over his photographs of naked boys, overruling his angry protest with a slurred, 'They're killing them in the camps! communists, social democrats, Jews . . . Russians,' he waved his hand with drunken vagueness. 'Everybody . . . and *we're* doing the killing . . . Now what do you say to that, Colonel shitting Geier?'

'Oh *that*,' the Vulture said easily, recovering his temper and swiftly slipping the well-thumbed photos back into the drawer. He valued von Dodenburg. He was the best of his commanders and would be of considerable help to him in getting those coveted general's stars; he would humour him. 'Yes, I know.'

'*You know!*' von Dodenburg exclaimed, so forcefully that he staggered and nearly fell over.

'Yes. I have known for some time. It is perfectly easy to understand. Our beloved Führer,' he added with a sneer, 'had planned it right from the start. You've seen what the extermination commandos did in Russia to the communists and Jews and rats of that ilk? Why shouldn't we do the same here in the homeland? I'm surprised we didn't start much earlier, in fact. I mean – the golden pheasants have been ranting for years about cleansing the Germanic race of these parasites . . .'

Von Dodenburg stood there, swaying, and looking down at the man seated there on the bed, tears suddenly streaming down his face. 'But they wore the same uniform as we do, the same insignia . . . They were SS men, Colonel.' There was a note of desperate pleading in his voice. 'The murderers were . . . *are . . . our comrades!*'

TWO

Sergeant Schulze lounged on his bunk, his stomach distended like a tethered barrage balloon. Inside it was a litre of good thick pea soup and an enormous piece of boiled pork sausage. He felt lazy, relaxed and happy with the world.

Outside, the Butcher was making 'sows' out of the new draft, doubling them back and forth across the square, ordering them to toss themselves into the specially prepared mudpits at the far end, and then making them hop the whole length of the parade ground with their rifles extended and held in one hand.

'That arsehole will rupture hissen if he goes on like that much longer,' said Schulze, and let rip a long pea-soup-inspired fart.

'Fart-cannon!' Corporal Matz said, without rancour. 'Do that once again and yer'll scorch yer skivvies.' Then he remembered what he had come to talk to his old running mate about. 'Know what? They're giving out at the battalion office that we're gonna be posted to France, just in case the Tommies want to play at Dunkirk agen. But can you see them sending Wotan to a cushy number like that – especially with those new Mark IVs they're shipping in to us? Ner, we're for the chop agen.'

Schulze yawned. 'Could be, Matzi, could be.' He was too full of sausage and soup to worry. 'Hey, toss us a fag. I'm out. And tell me what yer bin up to without me in Cologne these last three nights?'

Outside, the Butcher was bellowing furiously, 'Suck in those beer-guts, you bunch of cardboard soldiers, you! Tuck those candy-cracks tight! Feed yer flippers to yer legs! By God and all his Great Triangles, I'll make soldiers of you wet-tails yet!'

Matz's face brightened, and for a brief moment he forgot the appalling prospect of being posted back to Russia as soon as the greenbeaks were sufficiently trained. 'What have I bin up to!' he echoed in delight. 'Man, you don't know the half of it! I swear these Catholic women love the old salami like no one I've ever met before. Hell, I have to fight them off at night when I get off the bus.'

Schulze laughed uproariously, then stopped suddenly. He cocked his head to one side, listening intently. Then came the stamp of heavy nailed boots from outside, and more of the Butcher's bellowed commands.

'What's up?' Matz asked.

Suddenly a flickering pink light was reflected on Schulze's broad, honest face. Outside, the Butcher stopped shouting and the draft faltered to an awkward halt. In the silence the two NCOs could now make out the sound which had startled Schulze. It was the first thin wail of the air-raid siren – and it was coming from the direction of Cologne! Now more and more sirens took up the sound. Schulze sat up, his stomach forgotten, a worried look on his face now.

'Somehow, old friend,' he said slowly and seriously, 'I don't think you'll be getting off that six o'clock bus to Cologne tonight . . .'

The ancient city of Cologne was dying. First, the English had dropped incendiaries – in their thousands. Then the fire bombs had been followed by high explosive, the blast spreading the fire storm with frightening rapidity. Now both sides of the Rhine were alight, the spires of the great eight-hundred-year-old cathedral coloured an ugly crimson hue as the flames mounted higher and higher.

Even as the trucks of the Wotan screamed to a halt

just outside the main station and the awed greenbeaks started to tumble out, they could smell the sweet smell of charred flesh mingled with the more acrid bitter one of smoke.

Von Dodenburg shielded his eyes against the orange glare of the flames. Above his head the medieval timbered merchants' houses swayed back and forth in the clouds of smoke, as the flames ate them up greedily.

'Schulze, get the men to put their gas masks on! . . . All of you, don't stray off singly! Keep in pairs! Come on now, let's see what we can do!'

Scared as they were, the men needed no urging. Screams came from all sides, and the earth shook and trembled as fire-gutted buildings collapsed everywhere, slapping their faces with the hot blast wind, making them cough and choke. They broke up as ordered and in little groups doubled down the various side streets leading off from the square in front of the main station, leaping over the débris, dodging the falling masonry, crunching over glass-littered cobbles.

A group of amputees from the Russian front, pathetic, screaming creatures in blue-and-white striped pyjamas, crawling along on their stumps, pleaded for help before the fire storm consumed them. Horses bolted from a burning brewery, their manes on fire, their eyes wide with unreasoning fear, to be shot down in full gallop by a burst of machine-gun fire. A naked woman fled screaming, ripping the last of her clothes off as she ran, her body a mass of searing white flames as the phosphorous pellets imbedded in her skin burnt furiously . . .

Horror was piled on horror. This spring night, for the first time in the history of warfare, one thousand British bombers had launched the greatest raid the world had ever known. Cologne's defences had been swamped, and now the city was dying, the first of many of Germany's big cities to be devastated by the Allied onslaught. That night the men of Wotan were witnessing the commencement of the slaughter of the Third Reich.

Von Dodenburg was unaware of the historical importance of the raid as he raced through the burning streets, dodging death time and time again as buildings collapsed all around him. Now it was *sauve qui peut*. There could be no organized rescue attempt made in this chaos. The men would do their best, he knew that; but his thoughts were with one specific person – that bold-eyed girl imbued with a cynicism born of despair, Heidi von Waldesdorf. He had to save her if he could; for ever since her disclosure to him of what went on in the labour camps, he had divided his fellow countrymen into two groups: the murderers (to whom he knew he belonged himself) – who could not, *should* not survive the war because of what they had done; and the others, the innocent, or at least those who were not guilty – who had to survive what was to come. Heidi belonged to that second group. She must not die!

Skidding round the corner of the once-elegant street of late-nineteenth-century villas where she lived, von Dodenburg felt his heart miss a beat. Uprooted trees lay everywhere. Obviously a stick of HE bombs had straddled the street. Houses were ablaze, or reduced to smoking rubble at regular intervals, and the air was full of smoke. At the far end a wrecked fire-engine was burning furiously, its horses lying dead in their traces. Refugees, terror written across their faces, were scrambling for safety in all directions. He brushed by them and raced for number twelve, Heidi's house, his feet crunching over splintered glass.

The place had been hit well enough. The front of the roof had sagged in as if it had been made of soft rubber and most of the upper storey had gone, to reveal a bed teetering at the edge where the wall had once been. On it lay a naked woman with her legs raised and spread. Over her, also naked, crouched a headless horror, blown into eternity at the moment of supreme human pleasure.

Von Dodenburg swallowed hard, the green bitter bile threatening to choke him. It was Heidi's mother, all right – he recognized the long white-blonde hair which trailed from the pillow. Now the 'green widow' was dead, frozen as if for ever in this absurd, yet obscene position which made a mockery of all womankind – on her back, her legs in the air, revealing to the world that dark, secret patch.

But what of Heidi? Von Dodenburg pushed his shoulder against the sagging door. It gave, and he stumbled inside, choking on the acrid smell of smoke and explosive. '*Heidi!*' he croaked, blinking rapidly in the smoke, 'Heidi . . . Where are you? *Heidi?*'

He stumbled through the smoke-filled room, trying to force himself to be rational, to reason out where she might be. Outside, the sirens wailed and the bells clattered. Someone, a woman, was screaming hysterically '*If there were a God, he wouldn't allow this! If there were a . . .*'

He blundered over the débris to the stairs, pulled aside some smoking rubble and looked under them. The stairwell always provided the most solid cover in a house. But Heidi wasn't there. He whirled around. The cellar! Of course! Many of Cologne's houses were too close to the Rhine to have cellars, because of the risk of flooding. But not this street.

His eyes watering furiously, he blinked and coughed his way through the cluttered rooms, past the portraits of Heidi's stiff-collared eighteenth- and nineteenth-century ancestors.

He flung open the door to the cellar, and a shaft of yellow light slanted through the white, acrid smoke. 'Heidi!' he yelled once more.

'Kuno . . . Kuno, it's all right . . . I'm here,' Heidi's voice came from below.

His heart missed a beat. 'I'm coming!' he cried, and clattered furiously down the steps, ducking under the massive beams which had protected the cellar's roof against the bombs – those same bombs that the people of Cologne had been telling themselves for three years would never come.

She was sitting on the bottom of a double bunk, wearing an absurdly large steel helmet on her pretty curls, her face perfectly calm. Indeed, *too* calm. Von Dodenburg had seen that look often enough before in these last terrible years. He had seen it in the eyes of young soldiers who had already taken too much and would break if any more strain were placed upon them . . .

'Heidi – you're safe! Thank God!'

Suddenly she had sprung from her bed and flung her arms around him, pressing her young, firm body to his with the fervour and uninhibited commitment that only a very young woman can give.

'Kuno!'

In that candle-lit cellar, its walls glowing a dull purple from the fires raging outside, the screams of the trapped and dying muted but still audible, Kuno and Heidi forgot the world for a little while. Passionately, brutally, he kissed her, all inhibitions vanished, knowing only that she was safe and that this was the only moment they would ever have together; there would be no other. She responded wildly, with an abandon that he had not expected, pressing her slim young body against his, winding her arms around his neck tightly, passionately, as if she would never let go of him again.

Gasping crazily like two people drowning with love, they fell on the crude bunk. His eager tongue burrowed deep into her gaping mouth, his hand, that hard soldier's hand that had dealt out so much death in these last three years, gently tracing the soft silken line of her stocking. It found the naked flesh beneath. It delved further and further. Until finally those greedy, groping fingers found the wet softness beyond. Kuno von Dodenburg's heart gave a great leap.

Now the ruined city, the death all around, the war, Wotan – all were forgotten as the two of them writhed and heaved on the squeaking bunk in that ill-lit cellar on the night of May 29th, 1942. Nearby a house collapsed, setting the whole street shaking violently. Their sweating, naked young bodies were showered with tiny flakes of plaster. They did not notice. Their shadows, gigantically magnified by the yellow, wildly flickering flame of the candle, continued their frantic, doomed dance.

THREE

Kuno and Heidi met in the shadows of the great, echoing station hall for the last time. Matz's fears had proved groundless. The Bodyguard, and with it SS Assault Battalion Wotan, were not going to Russia, as he had suspected, but to France – just in case the Tommies invaded.

Heidi wore one of her mother's coats in order to make herself look older and not embarrass Kuno in front of his men, who were now lining up to enter to waiting troop train. But there had been no need. She already looked old beyond her years, and there were dark circles under her eyes, caused by more than these last days of hectic, furtive love-making in that half-ruined villa.

They stood there in silence, embracing each other, watching the typical wartime scene being played before them. The officious men of the RTO* striding briskly down the platform with their checkboards, looking smart and very soldierly – hardly surprising, since they never went to the front; the weeping womenfolk hanging desperately onto their men; the locomotive with its painted slogan '*Wheels roll for victory*', snorting steam as if impatient to be off. And the stern military policemen, carbines slung over their shoulders, watching and waiting, suspicion writ large in their unfeeling eyes.

For a while Heidi and Kuno clung to each other there in the shadows, exchanging the idle words customary on such occasions; but soon the Vulture shrilled his whistle and the reluctant soldiers began to sling their rifles and enter the trains.

Heidi pressed herself against him fervently. 'Don't go,'

* Army railway officials.

she pleaded, looking up at him, her eyes brimming with tears. 'Don't go, Kuno! They'll kill you in the end!'

He tried to force a smile as he disengaged himself gently from her arms. 'Don't be silly, Heidi,' he said softly. 'We're going to France. You know the old saying; there one lives, like God in France . . .'

Steam started to jet from the locomotive's boiler, shrouding the legs of the soldiers as if they were ghosts walking through a fog.

'But they'll kill you, Kuno. I know they will. Sooner or later . . .' Her voice faltered and she made an effort to contain herself as Kuno started to walk to the waiting train. 'Write,' she called after him. There seemed a new look in her eyes, as if she were gazing into eternity, all her tears suddenly exhausted.

'Of course I will. And you too – don't forget.'

'I will,' she promised. But even as she said the words, she knew she wouldn't. The affair was over.

Five minutes later the locomotive shuddered violently, its great steel wheels racing and sending up a shower of sparks. Steam jetted from the exhausts. Suddenly the sobbing women began to spring up and down, waving and shouting at the field-grey figures leaning dangerously out of the carriage windows. The train jerked, and then with a great groan, as if reluctant to depart, it began to move, slowly at first, but gathering speed by the instant. The women's cries redoubled, but already they were drowned by the clatter of the steel wheels as coach after coach filled with young men raced by. The chaindogs slung their carbines. The RTO men lowered their checkboards. It was over. Another batch of cannon-fodder was on its way. Now they could go home, put up their feet, drink their beer, make love to their women, do all the things ordinary men did on a spring evening.

A last flash of the twin red rear lights, and then the long troop train had disappeared from sight. The smoke descended from the echoing roof and the women trailed away as if through a grey mist.

Outside, Heidi von Waldesdorf spoke to the first soldier she met. They went on their way happily, linked arm in arm . . .

In France that glorious summer of 1942, they trained relentlessly, with the Vulture showing no mercy to his young giants. Their days were full of burning sun, tearing sea winds, hoarse, bellowed commands and backbreaking, unrelieved strain that had their lungs heaving, limbs trembling, vision fogged with fatigue. The unremitting torture was broken only by hastily-swallowed meals – but even here the Vulture never let up on his aim of turning these 'Christmas-tree soldiers' into the hardbitten, one hundred per cent killers he needed if he was to win his general's stars. Every so often their meals would be disturbed by sudden bursts of machine-gun fire, training grenades sailing through the open windows of the mess hall, the rattle of gas bells, air-raid warning sirens, a score of sudden alarms – all intended to remind the young giants with their lean, sunburnt faces that the war was ever-present.

Even the 'old heads' grumbled. 'Heaven, arse and earthquake!' said Schulze, 'that Vulture'll be the death of us!'

In August the Tommies returned to Europe after two years' absence, only to be slaughtered in their thousands at Dieppe. On the evening of 18th August, after the terrible blood-letting was over, an awed von Dodenburg stood with Field Marshal von Rundstedt and his staff on that beach of death, and viewed the slaughter in a profound silence, broken only by the soft whimpering of the last of the Canadian wounded not yet evacuated.

Nothing had escaped the defenders' withering fire – neither man nor machine. Everywhere lay the British dead, face downwards in the warm sand among the shattered tanks and landing craft. As far as the eye could see, the whole beach seemed carpeted with their khaki-clad bodies.

And everything was so dreadfully still. Nothing stirred except the sand flies buzzing above the corpses, and the pathetic, wilted hedge-roses which some of the Canadians had plucked to stick in their helmets as they had marched so bravely to their boats in England only a few short hours before.

Everyone had hung on the ancient Field Marshal's words as he inspected the battlefield, followed by his faithful adjutant Heinz, bearing a flask of cognac – the only thing that kept von Rundstedt going these days. For a long while his watery gaze remained fixed on a group of Tommies caught by a burst of fire in the act of setting up a machine-gun. One still lay propped up behind his Bren gun in the sand, peering along the barrel, his face set in an eloquent, passionate look of devotion to duty – even in death, with the sand flies crawling over the glassy, unseeing balls of his eyes. Next to him lay the loader, the curved magazine clutched in his claw of a hand, his lips drawn back in a grim smile that seemed to give his dead face an almost triumphant look.

Finally von Rundstedt spoke. 'It was an amateurish operation,' he summed up in his dry, ancient whisper. 'One would think they wanted it to fail right from the start.' For a moment his skinny frame seemed to shudder.

'Is anything the matter, Excellency?' the faithful Heinz enquired anxiously.

'No, Heinz, it is nothing.' Von Rundstedt smiled thinly, his fading eyes almost disappearing into a mass of wrinkles. 'A louse must have run over my grave. But I will tell you this, gentlemen,' he continued, raising his voice so that they could all hear, 'they will do it differently next time. And there *will* be a next time. Take it from me, the English gentlemen will return.'

He took a last look at the still sea, momentarily flushed a dramatic blood-red by the dying sun, and turned away without another word. His staff officers, suddenly depressed and apprehensive after the victory of this day, filed after him to the waiting cars.

The Vulture, his face streaked with the black powder burns of battle, looked after him scornfully. 'The man's too old, von Dodenburg,' he sneered. 'An old woman in flannel knickers. The English won't be back. They've made their token payment in blood to the Russians. Now they'll sit on their bottoms in that island of theirs, drinking their filthy tea and let the Ivans do the fighting for them out there in the East.' He shrugged carelessly and slapped his cane against his boot. 'Even if they did come back, the Frogs wouldn't support them. They're far too tame.'

But there, for once, Colonel Geier was wrong . . .

On the morning of 1st September, 1942, the crazy little Jewish adjutant Schwarz disappeared. At first there was no undue alarm at Battalion HQ; the officers had become accustomed to Schwarz's strange behaviour. He was often missing for hours on end, apparently wandering around in the old quarters of the towns around – Rouen, Arras, Amiens and the like.

But when Schwarz had been missing all day and hadn't turned up to supervise the weekly pay-day as was his duty as adjutant, the alarm was raised.

That night, the body of Lieutenant Schwarz was found floating in the canal near Amiens. The back of his head was smashed to pulp, as if it had been beaten with heavy sticks, and he had been emasculated. That much was obvious in the searing white light of the overhead arc lamps as they dragged his naked, battered body from the slimy water.

Even the Butcher was shocked, brutalized as he was. 'Good God,' he gasped, 'they shortened the poor devil's dick for good this time!' He turned away and started to retch into the green scum of the canal.

The murder of Lieutenant Schwarz in the back streets of Amiens was the first of several incidents that took place in Wotan's area that autumn. Two days later two troopers were knifed in a backstreet bar in Rouen. Four days after that a supply lorry was blown up by a mine on the secondary road leading to Bethune and half a dozen soldiers seriously injured. The following Sunday, a senior NCO was found dead in the empty bed of a local whore just outside Cambrai. He had been garrotted to death slowly and viciously, his eyes bulging from a crimson face, hard black blood caked around his nostrils and ears.

The realization that these were something more than isolated incidents came one week later.

Now that that battalion was fully trained, it was allowed to rest on Saturday afternoons and Sundays, and it had become the Vulture's custom to go out riding, taking with him a couple of his senior company commanders to discuss plans for the future. The company commanders hated the invitation and played cards beforehand to decide who should be given the unpleasant task.

Thus it was, on a dark, gloomy Saturday afternoon that a grumpy von Dodenburg found himself trotting unhappily down the long *pavé* secondary road to Le Cateau, half-listening to the Vulture as he expounded the military virtues of a secret new tank they were to receive in the coming year.

'The Tiger, as it is known, my dear von Dodenburg, will revolutionize tank warfare. It will live up to its rather melodramatic name, believe you me. Firstly the cannon. It's a high-velocity eighty-eight . . .'

Von Dodenburg let the words drone on, his eyes fixed on the flat, dripping, dreary French countryside, dotted here and there by a slag-heap or the big, clanking wheel of a pit-head. It was a grey place, and a grey time. The war seemed to have been going on for ever, and still there seemed no prospect of an end to the miserable business.

'The glacis plate,' the Vulture was saying, 'is virtually impregnable at one thousand metres. All studies so far have shown that we can knock out any known Allied tank with the Tiger at that range, whereas the Sherman and the Churchill would have to get within three hundred metres—'

Suddenly, a hundred metres to their right, the grey gloom surrounding a group of dark, dank, dripping firs was stabbed by a spurt of scarlet flame.

Von Dodenburg reacted quicker than his CO. He jabbed his elbow into the Vulture's back so that he gasped and crumpled forward in the same instant that the slugs from the machine pistol of the unknown assailant cut the air just where his head had been. Ramming his spurs immediately into the side of his mount, von Dodenburg cantered heavily over the ploughed field towards the trees. A figure broke from the undergrowth and began running towards the lane on the far side. Von Dodenburg spotted the dark Citroen waiting there, its frightened driver gunning his engine. He dug his spurs cruelly into the horse's flanks, and it charged on, flinging up huge clods of earth from its flying hooves.

Now he was gaining fast on the would-be assassin. He could see every detail of his skinny neck, thin frame clad in a cheap suit, hear his breath coming in frightened, hectic gasps as he fled before his pursuer. In a minute he would have him. But it wasn't to be. Suddenly his horse stumbled. Desperately, he tried to retain his hold. The horse whinnied furiously and went down. Next moment von Dodenburg found himself flying over its head. He hit the ground with a thud. The last thing he remembered before he blacked out was the Vulture firing a whole magazine from his pistol at the assailant, and the squeal of protesting tyres as the car accelerated down the narrow Norman lane to escape . . .

The sun shone brilliantly for late September, the Norman fields suddenly surprisingly green and lush once more. The air was heavy with the smell of dung and the rotting apples which lay everywhere in the orchards surrounding the village.

The men in the silent tanks waited for the signal, peering out of their hiding places at the fat French dairy cows cropping the grass in the fields beyond the orchards. The village itself, grey and squat around the spire of the Gothic church, like a medieval fortress, was silent, and there was no sign of life. But the blue smoke of wood fires trailing into the air here and there indicated that *someone* was in the low stone houses . . .

Von Dodenburg, in command of the left wing of Wotan, frowned at this peaceful pastoral scene. It wouldn't remain peaceful much longer. The French Deuxième Bureau, which worked closely with the Gestapo in such matters, had informed the authorities that it was from this remote hamlet that the terrorists, supported by British air-drops, had attacked the Wotan. Now the Commanding General of the Army of Occupation in Northern France had given his approval to the reprisal. Apparently the Führer had spoken personally with Marshal Pétain of the Vichy Government* about the matter, and the aged Hero of Verdun had given his approval. According to the Vulture, he had said in Vichy that 'all good Frenchmen actively want France to be rid of communists, Jews and criminals of that nature'. The Germans had been given his fullest co-operation.

Now it was Wotan's task to carry out that reprisal. Von Dodenburg had tried to talk the Vulture out of it, maintaining that the task could be carried out equally well by one of the security battalions. But the Vulture had been adamant. 'My God, von Dodenburg,' he had exploded, 'I don't know where you have left your mind these days! Don't you see? The Führer will be informed personally of our success in this mission. Unit titles and officers will be named. Publicity, newspaper, headlines, radio broadcasts – it'll all catch the eye of the Führer! *That's* the sort of stuff that makes generals these days, von Dodenburg, not having your fool head blown off in some Godforsaken corner of Russia!'

Now von Dodenburg waited, and worried. It seemed to him wrong that a fighting unit should be involved, that

* Head of the government set up in 1940 to rule the southern, unoccupied half of France.

such duties put his men on the same level as 'writing desk' killers* in Berlin. They brutalized them, encouraging them to kill without feeling, without thought, like robots who didn't care who they slaughtered or why.

A red flare hushed into the bright sky. Below a cow shied and began to lumber across the nearest field, udders swinging clumsily.

'The signal, sir!' his gunner cried.

Von Dodenburg opened his mouth to say something, but suddenly the air was thick as if with bees. Tiny red flames streaked in between the apple trees, sending the leaves raining down in green fury, pinging off the sides of the tanks and fetching chips of stone off the walls.

'Holy strawsack, sir!' the driver's voice came from below. 'They're firing back!'

'What did you expect them to do?' yelled von Dodenburg. 'Turn over on their backs like a family dog and let you slit their bellies? *Karbid!*'

'Yes sir!' the driver rapped, and started the engine.

Everywhere the other drivers were doing the same. Suddenly the air was full of blue fumes, and slowly the tanks began to lumber out of their hiding places, breaking the apple trees down in front of them like sticks of matchwood.

Now automatics blazed from the huddled collection of barns and houses, and von Dodenburg could hear the *wheep-wheep* of slugs howling off the sides of his turret. Hurriedly he slid below and pulled the hatch closed. The bullets were too close for comfort. The last thing he wanted was to get his turnip shot off by some rural hayseed of a *franc-tireur*. Swiftly he pressed his throat-mike. 'Sunray Two to all – button-up . . . Do you read me? Sunray Two to all – button up at once. The air's too full of iron. Out!'

Turret lids clanged down everywhere as the tank commanders took cover. They knew that standing upright they made a beautiful target for snipers, and 'old heads' from

* German phrase for those who committed murder by signing a warrant at a desk remote from the actual spot where the killing would take place.

Russia also knew that partisans hidden in the upper storeys of houses had a nasty habit of dropping grenades down into open turrets.

They rumbled on. Von Dodenburg, peaked cap shoved to the back of his cropped blond head, peered through the turret periscope, swinging his gleaming glass from left to right, while below him his second gunner hammered away with the machine-gun, sending tracer racing towards the nearest barn like gleaming ping-pong balls. Yet so far the partisans still hadn't broken and started to flee to the western side of the village as planned.

'It will be like a shoot, von Dodenburg,' the Vulture had explained earlier. 'You will drive them out of the village with your tanks like a lot of silly rabbits. I will be waiting for them at the other side with the panzer grenadiers. I'm not risking any unnecessary casualties by involving my infantry within the village itself. The Führer will be watching this operation. I want him to know that Wotan carried it out with the minimum of casualties. There has been far too much criticism already of our high casualty rate from those crimson-striped rear échelon stallions in Berlin. In short, you *drive*, I *shoot*, von Dodenburg.'

Von Dodenburg took his eyes from the periscope for a moment. 'Gunner,' he snapped above the roar of the grinding tracks and the chatter of the machine-gun.

'Sir!'

'Give that barn at two o'clock just in front of the church a round of HE. Let's see if we can scare them into the open.'

'Sir!' the gunner replied happily, glad to have something to do. For him the operation so far had been boring. For someone like himself, protected by millimetres of best Krupp steel, this was a cushy number, as easy as falling off a log. What could a Frog civvie armed with an ancient hunting rifle do against him in his Mark IV?

Metal clanged as he swung open the breech and Von Dodenburg slapped the arm-high 75mm shell into his waiting hands. The gunner slid it home. The breech lever snapped closed. The gunner pressed his right eye against the telescope, his hand tightening around the firing lever. The barn loomed up in the gleaming calibrated glass of the sight, white puffs of rifle smoke coming from it. Behind the stone structure rose the tower of the medieval Gothic church. The gunner sighed. He'd dearly love to put a shell through that – he'd never yet shot at a church steeple. Yes, it *was* tempting. He concentrated on the barn, forgetting the steeple. He'd put the HE to the right of the door. With a bit of luck, the wall would be breeched and the door come flying off with the blast. It would look very dramatic. He prepared to fire . . .

So engrossed was the gunner in his task that he failed to notice the little man carrying what looked like a golf bag over his skinny shoulder, who now rose from the dip in the ground to his right. Suddenly he had shrugged the 'bag' off his shoulders and dropped it to the ground, to rest it on the foot that protruded from the clumsy apparatus. He pressed the awkward padded shoulder-rest into the hollow formed by his right shoulder, chin and neck. The Englishman had told him if he didn't pull it well in, he could have his neck snapped by the force of the explosion. He sighted, and in the very same instant fired.

The Englishman had been right to warn him. A flash, a tremendous howl, and next moment the little man found himself lying on his back in a ditch – which turned out to be very fortunate for him, since he would be the only male from the village who would survive the events of the day. Dazed and bewildered, he lay there gasping, ears still ringing with the tremendous hollow boom, followed a second later by the crackle of sudden flame and the screams of the trapped men . . .

'Blast and triple blast it!' cried von Dodenburg, exasperated beyond all measure, as he dragged the dying gunner, the last survivor, from his steadily burning Mark IV, while the other tanks waddled on through the grass and into the village.

Forgetting the gunner, he turned to the driver, a large-limbed youth now covered with splashes of bright blood. His left trouser leg was torn and revealed the lacerated flesh, pulpy and glistening red like fresh meat. He sniffed. At least this one would live.

Mentally cursing the Vulture for risking his men's lives when he could have let a security battalion do the job for him, he concentrated on the task of getting the man's trousers slit open and the wound bandaged.

Next to him as he worked, the gunner died quietly – without a moan, not even a last groan, as if he felt it a breach of military courtesy to disturb an officer while he was engaged on another task. Von Dodenburg finished and sat down, empty of all emotion.

Not a hundred metres away, the skinny little Frenchman, unknown to the slumped blond officer, crawled to safety; he would live to tell his story forty years later as an old man, fat with too much good Norman camembert and calvados.

Von Dodenburg stared at the dead gunner. The big youth seemed suddenly pathetic, lying in this Norman field so from home, broken like a large doll. He would have to write to the boy's mother, if he had one. But what would he tell her? That her beloved son, aged – what? eighteen perhaps? – had died in the corner of a field outside a foreign village whose very name he had not known, so that a certain Colonel Geier could carry out an obscure mission against a handful of civilians in order to gain those precious general's stars . . . Could he tell her *that?*

Suddenly Kuno von Dodenburg felt very, very old. He raised himself to his feet and began to stumble after the rest. The bed-pan plumbers would be following up soon. They would find the wounded driver and take care of him. For once it was good to be alone.

*

Heedless of his own safety, von Dodenburg trudged through the French village, its single cobbled street covered with the mud churned up by the tracks of the vanished tanks. A body lay squashed in the road, pressed into the *pavé* by the force of the tanks rumbling over it. At the street corner a burst of fire from a tank had caught one of the *franc-tireurs* as he had attempted to flee on an ancient motorbike. Now he crouched there over the wide handlebars, cap pulled down well over his forehead, eyes contorted, over-large and hideous behind his goggles. Von Dodenburg gave a shiver and felt a cold finger trace its way down his spine. His heart began to beat louder. There was something nightmarish about this abandoned village. He quickened his pace and swung round the corner.

He stopped dead.

A woman stood there, swaying alarmingly, one side of her raven-black hair stained a dull purple with blood, a sten gun held loosely in her hands.

For what seemed an age, the two of them stared at each other, the German major and the French partisan. Then slowly, very slowly, she started to raise the little machine pistol. Major von Dodenburg made no move. He knew the woman was wounded; he could see how her knees sagged as if she might collapse at any moment. But he did not attempt to grab for his pistol. Somehow he didn't care any more. He might as well die here as anywhere. He raised his head and waited for death at the hands of this pale-faced beauty, whose chest heaved hard as if she had just run a great race.

Her finger curled around the trigger. At that distance he could see the knuckles whiten. He waited for the end, completely calm and resigned now . . .

But Major Kuno von Dodenburg was not fated to die just yet.

The French girl pressed the trigger. There was a dull click. The magazine was empty. She let it drop helplessly and stood hanging there, despair and hopelessness written all over her face.

For a long while the two of them didn't move, just stood there like characters in a nineteenth-century melodrama, frozen at the end of an act. Then von Dodenburg took a step forward and, with odd formality for him, touched his hand to his cap. '*M'selle*,' he said in his best French, 'you'd better come with me.'

Without a word she accompanied him to where the sound of the firing was growing ever louder. They were shooting the prisoners. They would shoot her, too. She had been taken near the scene of the action with a weapon in her hand. There was no hope for her. She knew it, and so did Kuno von Dodenburg. But he didn't care. When she had first confronted him he had wanted to die. But he hadn't. Now, with the clatter of the machine-guns, the pleas for mercy, the agonized screams already ringing in his ears, he was being forced to make an irrevocable decision. And he made it. The spiritual education which had begun with his affair with Heidi von Waldesdorf that spring was over.

They turned a corner together, and von Dodenburg beckoned to the soldier lounging there, watching the sweating firing squad at work. 'Hey, you,' he barked sharply, his voice revealing nothing. 'Here's another one of them. Put her over with the rest for execution!'

'*Jawohl*,' the soldier rasped and, grabbing the girl, started pushing her towards the rest.

Kuno von Dodenburg had joined the murderers.

1943

THE TIGERS ARE BURNING!

'Soldiers of the Reich! This day you are to take part in an offensive of such importance that the whole future of the war may depend on its outcome. More than anything else, your victory will show the whole world that resistance to the power of the German Army is hopeless.'

Adolf Hitler, July 5th, 1943.

ONE

'What a hell of a time to go and get yersen shitting well knocked off!' Sergeant Schulze grumbled, as he drooped over the turret of his Tiger, staring at the silent, endless Russian steppe in front of him. 'Midday in the middle of the month of July. At least it's cooler in a dawn attack.'

Von Dodenburg, standing next to him, licked his parched lips and pushing back his helmet, wiped the sweat off his streaming forehead. 'My dear thick Schulze, the Ivans are accustomed to us attacking at dawn. This time we're going to jump off late afternoon. Catch 'em on the hop.'

'Perhaps,' Schulze said gloomily. He had no faith in the great new offensive, in spite of the pep-talks and the propaganda the officers had been pumping into the battalion ever since they had been alerted for action. Thirty-three divisions . . . Nine hundred thousand men . . . Ten thousand guns . . . Two thousand seven hundred tanks and assault guns . . . Two thousand four hundred aircraft, and all the rest of it. He wondered.

Von Dodenburg wondered, too, although he knew that covering this fifty kilometres of front held by Hoth's Fourth Panzer Army there were the Third Panzer Division, the Eleventh Panzer, the Sixth, the Nineteenth, and the Seventh, *plus* the Bodyguard, to which Wotan belonged, the SS Death's Head, SS Reich and Greater Germany. Here, indeed, was the cream of the SS, prepared to spearhead the greatest tank attack in history, which would break through the Russian front in the south and drive to its objective, Kursk, where it would meet the northern arm of the mighty pincer move and surround a Soviet army of one and a half million men. If Hitler's plan worked, then it could well mean the end of the Red Army. Still, von Dodenburg wondered.

Tension was growing, and in the waiting turrets the commanders started to glance at their wrist-watches with ever-increasing frequency. Zero hour was not far away now.

'*Ten minutes to go!*' the Vulture's harsh voice rasped over the radio.

The grenadiers started to slide on their combat packs, sticking extra grenades into their boots and slinging their machine pistols across their chests. Standing on the decks of the Tigers, the tank-men took a final pee into the high yellow corn which had concealed them since the day before. Officers flung a last glance at their notes.

'First Company ready . . .'

'Second Company ready . . .'

Now the reports began to crackle across the airways, already badly distorted by the large number of sets operating in such a small area.

'*Roll em!*' the Vulture commanded.

Hastily the drivers pressed their starters. Everywhere there were thick, asthmatic coughs like old men trying to clear their chests in the early morning. Thin blue smoke started to stream out of the Tigers' exhausts. With a frightening roar, the first engine burst into ear-slitting life. Another and another followed suit. Abruptly the July afternoon was hideous with noise.

Frantically the panzer grenadiers in their camouflaged smocks clambered onto the decks of the huge tanks, like a crowd of school kids boarding an excursion bus, afraid of being left behind. Slowly, the huge armoured mass began to move to the start line, crushing the yellow carpet of corn beneath their mighty tracks as they did so.

On the stroke of two, there was an earth-shaking roar behind them, and the sky split apart in red fury. The new noise drowned that of the tanks into insignificance. With a hoarse, exultant scream, the whole weight of the SS

Panzerkorps sped over their heads, tearing into the Soviet lines on the horizon and bursting with a tremendous, ear-splitting crash. The thunder of the softening-up barrage increased by the second as flight after flight of shells streamed over the helmeted heads of the awed grenadiers, letting out a monstrous, never-ending baleful scream. The scream rose in fury and became a shriek, elemental, awe-inspiring, terrifying. Before the eyes of the gaping deafened soldiers, the first Soviet line of defence disappeared. Now the whole horizon was burning fiercely.

The heavy artillery moved onto the second line. Now the electric six-barrelled mortars took over. From their positions two hundred metres behind the Wotan positions, the gunners pressed their firing mechanisms. There was a sound like someone hitting the bass notes of a piano. A grating noise followed, like that of a diamond being run along glass. Suddenly the burning air in front of the tanks was full of dark clusters of heavy canopies, bearing fierce red angry flames behind them. With a series of tremendous crashes they started to land among the Soviet hedgehogs.

This was it!

Von Dodenburg tensed and waited for the signal to advance. The mortar men would keep the survivors of the first bombardment in their holes until the tankloads of panzer grenadiers were in among them, ready to mop up.

'*Advance!*' the Vulture's harsh rasp came across the air.

Automatically von Dodenburg pressed both intercom and radio buttons. 'Forward – First Company!' he commanded. 'Gunners, prepare to fire smoke once the barrage lifts!'

The great tanks started to lumber forward, cutting great swathes through the corn. The Battle of Kursk had commenced.

The Tigers breasted the rise. In front of them the Ivans' front line was ablaze. Angry blue flames flickered everywhere and thick black smoke billowed skywards. Still the mortars pounded the Russian hedgehogs. Staring through his periscope at the awesome destruction, von Dodenburg felt sure that no one could live in that hell.

A sudden shock wave penetrated the turret, and he sucked in his breath hastily. He felt as if something had just scorched his tonsils. A zinc-white light blazed to his right. A wild tearing ripped the air apart with a noise like a huge sheet of canvas being torn. A Soviet shell zipped by so close that the whole sixty-ton tank trembled. Suddenly his right ear went deaf. He banged his right earphone with the flat of his hand angrily. A flurry of twigs and leaves descended upon the deck, momentarily turning everything a startling green in front of von Dodenburg's eyes.

'Sir,' the second gunner screamed, 'Lieutenant Kunze's been hit!'

Von Dodenburg swung his periscope round. To his left, Kunze's tank had come to an abrupt stop, the loud gong-like noise it was giving off becoming a roar. A colossal smoke ring was rising from its turret, staggering off into the corn, a lone survivor fell to the earth, his body wreathed in flames. Suddenly a tremendous pillar of fire belched from the turret. Next moment the sixty-ton monster disintegrated in an explosion that made von Dodenburg's Tiger tremble as if struck by a raging whirlwind.

A great rage overcame von Dodenburg. Kunze had been all of eighteen years of age. Within the first five minutes of his first action he was dead, horribly burned to death.

'*Popovs!*' he screamed, sighting the first T34 emerging from the smoke to his right, its long, hooded cannon searching from left to right like the snout of some primeval monster seeking its prey. 'Gunner, traverse right . . . Two o'clock . . . Three hundred metres . . . *On!*'

Hastily the sweating, half-naked gunner swung the great 88mm cannon round.

Von Dodenburg threw a quick look at the T34. It was neatly dissected by the crosswires of the periscope. '*Fire!*' he bellowed, in the same moment that the unknown Russian spotted them and swung his cannon round.

The Germans were quicker off the mark. Von Dodenburg pulled the firing bar, automatically opening his mouth against the blast. The Tiger shuddered. It reared back on its sprockets. Acrid yellow smoke filled the turret. The blast slapped von Dodenburg's shocked face. The breech opened. A smoking yellow shell-case came clattering onto the metal floor. With his left hand von Dodenburg loaded a new round. With his right he pressed the smoke extractor.

'Fire again . . . brew the bastard up!' he screamed above the noise.

The smoke cleared. The T34 had stopped. Slowly, terribly slowly, the Russian gunner tried to swing his gun round, as if he were already slumped dying over his breech. Von Dodenburg's young gunner didn't give him a chance. The 88mm erupted in full fury once more. The T34 reared up like a live thing, its right track flapping out behind it like a metal whip. Suddenly the turret lurched forward, smoke pouring from it and the gun.

A man wriggled out of the escape hatch below the stricken T34 and frantically tried to run for cover in the corn. A dozen machine-guns chattered mercilessly. His black-charred hands clawed the air. Next second he flopped flat on his face in the corn. On the turret another Russian raised his hands in surrender, but the SS knew no mercy this terrible afternoon. Again the machine-guns ripped into hectic activity. The Russian's body disappeared into a pulped, gory welter, as if someone had just run it through a gigantic mincing-machine.

'*Hot shit!*' Sergeant Schulze's excited voice came crackling over the air. 'We're really shafting the Popovs today, ain't we, sir?'

But von Dodenburg had no time to reply, for now the burning horizon to his front was suddenly packed with T34s crawling forward with grim determination to do battle. Now it was kill or be killed . . .

All that long afternoon they fought the T34s. The Soviets

seemed to have an inexhaustible supply of the tanks. Everywhere their wrecked hulks burned furiously, destroyed by those terrible 88mm cannon. Yet every time von Dodenburg thought he had fought his way through them, a new wave came rattling in out of the blood-red ball of the July sun to fight once more.

Now his gunner was lathered with sweat and black-faced from powder flashes, trembling in every limb, and Von Dodenburg could see the small hairs at the back of his neck standing erect in fearful anticipation, as he fired and fired like an automaton, his eyes large and white-rimmed with terror in the dark, glowing compartment. Now the whole world was this steel box. Their faces were scorched as the great cannon slapped back over and over again, choking them with its fumes, littering the deck with shell cases so that they fought up to their knees in them.

Now they could hardly move from their padded shelf-like seats. Von Dodenburg could feel the sweat pouring down his chest and back in rivulets to collect at his belt. His brain raced. He couldn't shake off his unreasoning, harrowing anxiety. He knew that they couldn't avoid being hit for much longer. Behind him in the corn lay half his company, already blazing or crippled. Why should his luck hold out so long? At every explosion close by, his whole frame would contract with tense expectation, waiting for steel to slam against the turret and bore its way inside in a white-hot fury, ready to shred them to pieces.

At last, just when von Dodenburg had given up all hope of breaking down the resistance of the T34s, they were rolling straight for the Soviet ground positions.

Now all was confused, frenetic action. The air was filled with the hysterical howl of the Soviet Stalin Organs, as their gunners brought down fire on their own bunkers in order to stop the hated Fritzes. Machine-guns chattered. Tracer, red, white and green, zipped back and forth in electric frenzy.

Suddenly the network was crackling with cries for help, confusion, orders, counter-orders, screams of unbearable pain. '*Two machine-guns hitting me from left flank . . . All my grenadiers casualties . . . Send up stretcher-bearers at once . . . Like an ice-rink with blood on the deck . . . Bailing out, bailing out NOW . . . Get those shitting recovery men up here at the shitting double . . . Out here in the open with a broken track . . . Driver severely wounded, gunner dead . . . HELP!*'

Von Dodenburg's ears buzzed with the crackle and confusion of the battle, his eyes wild, wide and staring at the lunar landscape now emerging from the smoke to his front: huge steaming brown shell-holes; trees stripped white of their bark, their boughs hanging like shattered limbs; the dead sprawled everywhere like bundles of carelessly abandoned rags.

Now lead started to patter against the thick steel sides of the turret like heavy tropical rain. A flame-thrower tank went into action to his right to knock out the machine-gun nest. It hissed. Evil blue flame licked around the bunker until its wall glowed a dull purple and the paint bubbled like molten toffee. Suddenly the machine-guns stopped firing.

Two T34s came rumbling from a grove of burning trees. In their haste and fear they slammed into each other. A second later, a lucky shot slammed into first the one and then the other, tearing great gleaming silver holes in their sides. No one bailed out.

'Spread out . . . In three devils' name, *spread out!*' von Dodenburg screamed frantically over the radio to the handful of survivors of his command.

Not a moment too soon. A Soviet 57mm anti-tank cannon, concealed in what looked like a barn, poked its long, sinister barrel through the door and opened up at point-blank range. Von Dodenburg could see the white blur of the AP shell hurrying towards him. '*Gunner*,' he barked, 'target—'

But the terrified gunner beat him to it, firing without even aiming. At that range he couldn't miss. The gun disappeared in a bursting ball of angry flame, the crew flailing through the air, dropping limbs as they hurtled round and round.

Below, the driver wrenched at the steering. Von Dodenburg lurched forward, his face slamming against the interior of the tank. Salty blood filled his mouth, but he had no time to worry about it. The shell hissed past them, but another danger had already presented itself in this terrible battle for the bunker line. A soldier in an earth-coloured smock was running towards the tank, two oddly-shaped metallic objects in his hands.

'Hollow charges . . . Sticky bombs!' von Dodenburg shrieked. 'Get him!'

The lower gunner knew the threat posed by a magnetic bomb stuck to the Tiger's side. His gun chattered. The bomber screamed. Next instant he disappeared beneath the tank's metal track to be flung out the other side like so many pieces of chopped beef.

A T34 driver panicked and teetered on the edge of a ridge, exposing the soft underbelly of the tank. To von Dodenburg peering through his periscope it seemed that the metal stomach filled the whole world; he could see every rivet, every mud-clogged, petrol-stained bolt. The gunner fired instinctively. The T34 rose high into the air and dropped on its back, tracks still racing, like an up-ended beetle waving its legs.

Now Russian infantry came streaming from their bunkers – whether to surrender or to fight, the battle-crazed tankers neither knew nor cared. A dozen machine-guns concentrated their fire, and the Russians went down in huge, screaming heaps, falling like crazy ninepins to pile high and block the exits. As the tanks rolled by, commanders lobbed grenades to either side as if they were distributing rose petals, then roared on.

For five long minutes more, the fight for the first line went on in all its blood-frenzied chaos: the muzzle flashes, the scrunch of metal against metal, the gong-like boom of the tank guns, the howl of the ricochets, the great whoosh of fuel tanks exploding as another Tiger died in a great black funeral pyre of oily black smoke. Twice von Dodenburg heard death rapping on the side of his tank like the beak of some monstrous black raven, as shells careened off, leaving a momentary glow of red behind; and twice the young major felt his lower limbs turn to water and told himself he couldn't go on much longer. And then, abruptly, the fight seemed to go out of the Russians. The surviving T34s turned in wild wakes of showering mud and pebbles and began to flee to the rear, churning great red waves through their own infantry in their haste to escape the terrible wrath of the blond giants in field-grey.

Everywhere the tankers cheered. Von Dodenburg could hear the crackle over the air and breathed out a deep sigh of relief as more and more of the Russian infantry started to throw down their weapons and raise their hands in surrender. A minute later the horizon to the east was burning like a blast furnace, as the Stalin Organs to the rear of the Russian line started a counter-barrage to cover the escape of their armour.

Hastily von Dodenburg pressed his throat mike. 'All units,' he rapped hastily, '*retire . . . Retire!*'

'A German soldier never gives up ground,' an angry young voice thundered in his earphones.

'You'll be telling me next that babies are found under cabbage leaves,' Schulze shouted. 'Get yer arse outa here before the Popovs slice off yer eggs with a blunt bayonet . . .'

That was sufficient for the survivors, the handful who were left. Spinning their tanks round, churning up the earth madly as they did so, the drivers left the battlefield to the dead and the dying.

The first day of the Battle of Kursk was over.

TWO

All was tense confusion in the laager that the survivors of the day's battle had set up in the Russian positions as the infantry streamed forward through their lines to consolidate the gains of the day, jumping at every fresh burst of Soviet gunfire.

The wounded were being brought back all the time: dozens of them, smashed and blood-splattered, faces black with smoke and oil, while the artificers and mechanics bustled about their task of trying to get the tanks ready for the morrow's battle.

Down by the bunkers they were shooting Russian officers, making them kneel and bend their heads to have their shaven skulls shattered in a flurry of blood and gore, while their soldiers watched, their slavic faces impassive.

Von Dodenburg shook his head. Even the greenbeaks who had only joined the battalion a few weeks ago were now completely brutalized; they *all* were. None of them would be much use in polite society after the war, if there were ever such a thing again. Wearily he walked over to where the Vulture, his face black, was directing a small group of mechanics trying to clean out the inside of a shot-up Tiger prior to repairing it. They had been using a small foot-pump to swill out the interior and a stream of blood and water had been spurting out of the drainage holes. But now, for some reason, the stream had stopped.

'Well?' the Vulture barked at the corporal in charge of the crew. 'What are you going to do about it, man?'

The mechanic gulped. 'She took a direct hit with a 75mm, sir,' he began, and pointed to the gleaming silver hole skewered neatly through the Tiger's turret. 'All the crew bought it, and—'

'You're downright scared, aren't you?' the Vulture cut him short, with a contemptuous sneer. 'Here, let me have a look.' Impatiently, he pushed the man aside and clambered inside the blackened turret.

For a few moments the crew and von Dodenburg could hear him rummaging around inside the wrecked tank, and then the pink water started to run out of the drainage holes once more. A moment later the Vulture appeared at the turret, his beak of a nose wrinkled in disgust. 'Like a piggery in there,' he choked, and held up the object that had blocked the drain. With a sudden hot spasm of nausea, von Dodenburg recognized it for what it was. The thing that the Vulture was holding up by the hair was the severed head of Corporal Dehn of his own company.

Almost casually, the Vulture tossed the head aside and the crew at the pump ducked hastily as the gruesome thing sailed by. The Vulture wiped his hands on the seat of his breeches. 'Get on with it. We've got exactly seven hours to first light.' He nodded to von Dodenburg. 'Come with me, Major, I want to fill you in.'

Briskly, as if this was all in a day's work, he strode off to the tent that had been put up for him, followed by von Dodenburg. Behind them, the sightless eyes of Corporal Dehn, lying in the scuffed dust of the battlefield, stared into a darkening sky.

'We've done quite well, all things considered,' the Vulture said. Von Dodenburg tried to forget the hideous scene he had just witnessed and concentrate on the Vulture's words. 'Obviously we caught the Ivans with their knickers down. They assumed, according to those warm brothers back there in Intelligence, that we would launch a main attack in the north. We've smashed one of their Red Guard divisions and put to flight at least two rifle brigades.'

'Our casualties, sir?' von Dodenburg asked, knowing they had to be high.

'We've got about twenty runners left at the moment, but those idle mechanics might get another ten on the road by dawn. Corps have promised me replacement crews for ten vehicles, at all events.'

'I meant *human* casualties, sir?' von Dodenburg persisted.

'Oh those,' the Vulture shrugged easily. 'Perhaps thirty per cent. The bed-pan plumbers haven't got round to giving me the totals yet, and that fool Sergeant-Major Metzger is a bundle of nerves – gone absolutely to pieces. Can hardly hold a pencil, never mind count the casualties.'

Von Dodenburg nodded gloomily. It was as he had expected. Casualties had to be high when a unit attacked a fixed line such as the one they had captured today. 'And the morrow, sir?'

'The Soviet second line, von Dodenburg, of course.'

'That'll mean more casualties.'

'Of course, of course! You can't make an omelette without breaking eggs, you know. But think of the honour.' The Vulture rubbed his skinny claws together happily. 'This time it will definitely mean a regiment for us, von Dodenburg. We have been disappointed before, I know. Last year, for example. But not after this. 1943 – *Regiment* Wotan.' The Vulture smiled, which he rarely did, for his yellow false teeth were ill-fitting and tended to bulge out of his mouth. '1944 – SS *Division* Wotan, commanded by no less than *General* Geier . . .' He shook his head fondly. 'It is a pleasant thought, von Dodenburg. A very pleasant one indeed. It gives me new hope and new courage on days like this. Yes, my dear young friend,' he said expansively, 'a year from now and it could well be SS Division Wotan, led by its brilliant commander, General Geier . . .'

But events were already taking place far away to the south which would ensure that one year on, the Vulture would be dead and what was left of the Wotan would be running for their lives . . .

★

The advance ground on. Borne up by tremendous high spirits in spite of their great losses, the men of the Armed SS carried everything before them. Each new day, the Soviets flung in fresh divisions, corps, even armies. But still they couldn't stop the Black Band.

Now, in an area not much bigger than Greater New York City, nearly three million men and ten thousand tanks were involved in the greatest tank battle the world had ever seen. Their racing tracks ate up the burning steppe: driving, fighting, driving, fighting – ever onwards, and always leaving more young giants lying there in the burnt grass never to rise again; and more blazing Tigers, soon to serve as rusting red coffins for the hopelessly mangled bodies within. Nothing, it seemed, could ever stop these bold young men, eager for glory, for they had sworn a personal oath to die for Adolf Hitler. '*March or croak* . . .' It was the order of the day.

On and on it went. Each dawn the battle commenced once again and raged all day, until the steppe was dotted with burning hulks and littered with dead. No one had the slightest idea which side was getting the worst of it until evening, when the fighting would start to peter out, leaving the silver-grey grass stained with oil and blood and the sky jet-coloured with the smoke of the belching fires, and both sides retired to count up their losses . . .

Now it was the sixth day of the great battle. Another dawn with the great blood-red ball of the July sun sliding over the horizon, glowing on the glacis plates of the waiting tanks, their crews smoking silently, reflectively, like men who know they have a hard day's work ahead of them.

Von Dodenburg had recovered his nerve again. To left and right as far as the eye could see, were the tanks of the SS Corps. Today they would drive to the south-east of Kursk. By evening, with luck, they might even link up with the armour of the pincer coming down from the north. Then perhaps the bloody business would be over.

He tossed away his cigarette. Even if the Popovs outnumbered them ten to one, could they stop the élite of Germany's armour, manned by the best soldiers in the world, each a convinced believer in the holy creed of National Socialism, Europe's last hope against the creeping evil of Communism? He doubted it strongly.

Slowly Wotan started to form up under the Vulture's command, rumbling forward at ten kilometres an hour, the drivers squinting against the glare of the sun. But the steppe to their front remained empty and uncannily quiet. Now they started to catch themselves breathing more quickly, their bodies tensed for that first brazen flash and howl of metal tearing the morning apart.

The minutes ticked by. The sun rose a little higher, flushing the faces of the tank commanders, proud and upright in their turrets.

A flare hissed in the morning sky ahead of them, and hung there for what seemed an eternity, sending out showers of silver sparks into the azure before it died and descended to the steppe like a fallen angel. Von Dodenburg pressed his throat mike. 'Attention all units,' he said, his voice kept purposefully low and unemotional. 'Prepare for action!'

In his ears as he spoke he could hear the crackle of many other radios giving the same command, '*Prepare for action . . . Prepare for action . . . Prepare . . .*'

A hiss. A sound as if some enormous monster were drawing a fiery breath. The horizon trembled and trembled again. A great ripping sound. Red lights rippled the length of the horizon to their right. Suddenly white burning blobs were flying towards them, gathering speed by the second.

'*Anti-tank fire!*' the Vulture screamed. '*Deploy—*'

The rest of his warning was drowned by the awesome, echoing clang and boom of metal striking metal. A Mark IV close to von Dodenburg reared up on its sprockets like a bucking bronco in a western rodeo and came to a sudden halt, smoke pouring from its engine. No one got out.

In an instant, solid armour-piercing shot was flying

everywhere and the air was full of the stench of cordite, scorched metal and charred human flesh. German tanks were being hit on all sides. In a matter of seconds a score of them were burning fiercely.

The Tigers fought back, the gunners traversing left and right, turning the wheels furiously, eyes glued to their telescopes, jerking their firing bars as soon as they spotted their target. Now the Russians started to take casualties. Gun after gun was hit, disintegrating in a ball of glowing red fire, their crews vanishing momentarily to reappear as a collection of bloody bits and pieces like offal outside a butcher's shop.

Now the Tigers were right in among the cunningly concealed anti-tank guns. A duel commenced at impossibly short range, threatening even the Tigers with their tremendously thick frontal armour.

Schulze, at point for the First Company, spotted the nest of three A/T cannon just as they blazed into action. All three shells struck the Tiger of the one-armed commander of the Third Company at point-blank range. The Tiger skidded to a stop and reeled violently, as if punched by a great metal fist, white smoke streaming from its engines.

They turned their attention on Schulze's racing monster. A whooshing rush of air. That well-remembered, awesome whiplash which made the small hairs on the back of Schulze's head stand on end. The first solid shot hushed by his tank like a bat out of hell. Schulze jabbed his elbow viciously into the side of the mesmerized gunner. 'Fire, you arse with ears. *Fire!*'

As Schulze's long overhanging 88mm roared into action, von Dodenburg, metres away, yelled into his mike, 'Hartmann . . . Find me a bit of dead ground. I want to tackle the bastards hull-down!'

'*D'accord*,' yelled back the driver, an ex-Legionnaire with a crime sheet as long as his arm. Wiping the sweat off his brow, he raised his head, revealing the tattoed line across his neck and the old legend, '*Slit here.*' Then he spotted his opportunity.

Without hesitation, he charged straight into the thick, white smoke coming from the crippled tank of the 3rd Company Commander, which shielded them a little from the A/T nest. Just when it seemed the two monsters would collide, Hartmann swung sharply to the right, sending up a shower of mud and pebbles. Immediately he ran up the whole range of the Tiger's forward gears, desperately taking the sixty-ton tank up to top speed, for now her whole right flank was exposed to the Soviet cannon. Shells howled towards the racing Tiger. But the sudden charge had unnerved the Soviet gunners. Before they could range in correctly, the Tiger sailed into the air and disappeared with a crash into a slight depression, ramming her nose deep into the life-saving earth.

'First class, Hartmann!' von Dodenburg yelled, as the gunner swung the deadly cannon round to take up the challenge.

'Don't bother about the tin, sir. The frogs gave me a whole kitbag full of the stuff,' Hartmann replied coolly. 'I'll settle for an immediate transfer to the paymaster branch.'

Von Dodenburg laughed, then concentrated on the task in hand. Infuriated that the Germans had escaped the fate the gunners had reserved for them, the Russians had started pounding the earth in front of the half-buried Tiger with solid shot. *Thump . . . Thump . . . Thump . . .* The shells struck the ground with an iron punch, flinging up pebbles and earth and half-blinding the men in the quaking, trembling tank. But the gunner was not rattled. Already he had become a veteran over these last few terrible days. Aiming carefully, he pulled the firing bar. The long gun erupted. The Tiger shook appallingly. The first high explosive shell crashed into the steppe fifty metres in front of the nest.

'Short,' von Dodenburg cried angrily. 'For God's sake, man, hit the bastard!'

The sweating gunner flushed and said, 'But, sir—'

His protest was drowned by the chatter of Hartmann's machine-gun. Vicious white tracer zipped flatly across the burning steppe and slammed right into the fleeing crew of the anti-tank gun. The one shot had been close enough for them. The first three were bowled over. The fourth dropped to the ground, feigning death.

Hartmann waited. '*Alors maintenant, sale con!*' he said to himself through gritted teeth, as the Russian rose again and attempted to make a break for it. '*Vive le Légion!*' He pressed the trigger again. The fleeing Russian was ripped apart before he had gone five metres.

Now Schulze thrust his way through the burning fog to help his CO, bellowing with fury. '*Matzi*,' he screamed over the mike, '*shit me no more! Go straight for the cunts!*'

Matzi thrust home his gears. Schulze took over the cannon himself. Now they were on a collision course with the two remaining A/T cannon. Shells howled off their thick frontal armour, and Schulze was blinded by searing flame as the Tiger rocked from side to side over the shell-pitted ground. Eyes narrowed to slits, he pulled the firing bar. Shrapnel flew everywhere to their immediate front and pattered against the shields of the 57mms. On one, the left tyre burst and the cannon sank to one side. The crew panicked. It was just the opportunity Hartmann in von Dodenburg's tank was waiting for. His machine-gun chattered frantically once more. Eight hundred slugs a minute sliced through the burning air, and the Ivans went down in a screaming bundle of flailing, bullet-shredded limbs.

'Excellent . . . Excellent,' rasped a familar voice into von Dodenburg's earphones. It was the Vulture, his voice as calm as if he were on some training exercise on the Westphalian plain, instead of a confused life-and-death battle for survival. 'The Popovs' fire was good at the beginning, but they're getting rattled now. Keep after them, von Dodenburg . . . Good hunting!'

'*Good hunting!*' von Dodenburg sneered when the air

went dead. 'What in three devils' name does he think this *is*?'

Hartmann backed out of the depression. Now the survivors of the charges against the anti-tank line were rumbling through the shattered Russian positions, forming up into great extended battle Vs once more, confident that they had broken the back of the Soviet resistance.

Now they began to ascend a long slope, spotted here and there with patches of white smoke from the enemy smoke dischargers, which were now clearing rapidly. Then at last they were through it and once more bathed in bright red sunshine, which outlined everything in stark, terrifying clarity to their front.

Hartmann gasped and whispered, '*Merde!*'

Matzi missed a gear and said in a faint voice, 'I think I've pissed myself!'

'Great flying buckets of shit,' Schulze breathed, 'willya get a load of that!'

The advancing SS men stared ahead in disbelief; for what they saw frightened them more than anything they had ever seen before in three years of total war: from one side of the horizon to the other, a solid mass of Soviet tanks, hundreds, no – *thousands* – of them, slowly rolling forward to do battle.

Von Dodenburg suddenly felt more afraid than he had ever been in his whole life. This *had* to be the end. They would never be able to break through that amount of armour. It was impossible.

Slowly, inexorably, the two great steel masses began to close in on each other . . .

Now it was furnace hot, the glare of the sun cutting the eye like a sharp knife. Above the halted Tigers the sky was smoke-coloured, menacing, the sun glittering through it like a copper coin. The men waited and sweated, the identification panels draped over the front of their tanks, huge arrows drawn on the parched grass, pointing directly to the hundreds of waiting Soviet tanks, poised on the heights above. If the tank hunters came in time, Rudel's skilled killers, they *might* have a chance of breaking through. Now everyone kept looking at his watch. The Russians wouldn't wait for ever.

Suddenly to the west, the sky was broken by a series of black dots and the faint sound of airplane motors could be heard. All eyes shot in that direction. 'There they are!' Schulze cried, pointing upwards. 'Here they come,' the men of Wotan took up the cry, clambering onto the burning decks of their Tigers to get a better view. Up on the Soviet-held heights, urgent flares began to sail into the air.

Like evil black hawks, the Stukas came roaring in over the cheering German lines. They were Rudel's tank busters, all right. The one-legged colonel's men had arrived on time! For a moment or two they hovered over the burning plain below, each plane picking out its prey, ignoring the white tracer that started to curve upwards through the burning sky towards them. Rudel waggled his bent-hawk wings once, twice, three times. It was the signal.

The first flight of three peeled off. In an instant they had pitched themselves out of the sky, sirens howling hideously, hurtling downwards as if they would never stop. The Soviet flak went into action. On all sides puffballs of cotton-white smoke erupted, but Colonel Rudel, the Luftwaffe's leading ace, was undeterred. He pressed home his attack, until, just when it seemed that nothing could stop him smashing right into the ground at four hundred kilometres an hour, he levelled out. The plane seemed to stand in mid-air. Myriad little black bombs fell from its white belly. The earth around the tanks on the heights vomited fire and T34s disappeared in smoke and flame on all sides. As Rudel and his flight soared high into the sky in triumph, they left behind them a dozen burning Russian tanks. On the Tigers the troopers shrieked with joy.

Now the next flight came hurtling down through the

flak – and the next. The air between the Russians and the Germans below became a thick, choking fog of yellow steppe-dust and dense, oily smoke. The whole battlefield rang with the monstrous din, as if an enormous brass gong was being beaten at regular intervals, through which the troopers could faintly hear the tortured cries of the Russian wounded.

As suddenly as it had started, the air attack ceased. The flak fired a few more shots, but as the Stukas soared high into the air, their firing stopped too. The attack was over. Now they could count the cost.

But the one-legged tank buster ace Rudel was not finished with the Russians yet. His next wing came flying in from the West: eighteen Henschel 129s, spread out in the strangest formation that the watching troopers had ever seen; not the usual flying V, but a long line extending right across the sky, the planes flying unusually slowly.

Suddenly the troopers gasped. One of the Henschels staggered in the sky, hit by machine-gun fire from the ground. Thick white smoke started to pour from its starboard engine. Vainly the pilot tried to hold the crippled plane in the sky, while the wing formed into another strange formation, like the three prongs of an enormous hayfork. Suddenly it burst into a gigantic ball of flame. In an instant it shattered into a million pieces, débris raining to the ground below. But the rest flew steadily on into the attack.

Suddenly their cannon started to thump. Their undercarriages down acting as a brake slowing them even more, the planes hovered in the sky pouring 20mm shells at the Russians. T34 after T34 brewed up. Panic-stricken Russian crews abandoned their vehicles even before they were hit. Time and time again the Henschels came at tree-top height, weaving and twisting crazily, trailing white fumes behind them as they tried to dodge the Soviet flak, before pulling up into the sky in a back-breaking climb to start all over again. The watching SS men cheered themselves hoarse in their admiration for these brave pilots.

But now the Red Air Force had been alerted. Fat-bellied Yak fighters by the score came zooming in from the east. Machine-guns blazed, cannon chattered, and the sky was criss-crossed from end to end by vapour trails and the white morse of tracer. But the Henschels were no match for the Yaks, although their pilots were superior and used every opportunity their slower speed offered them.

Now the Henschels started to pay the price in blood for their earlier success – and the butcher bill was high. A stricken Henschel, white smoke pouring from its bullet-riddled engine, glycol jetting out in a furious cream spray, came screaming down to where the tanks of Wotan lay. It hit the ground, sprang a good thirty metres in the air, slapped down again, both wings snapping off like twigs, and braked to a halt in a huge cloud of dust. Amazingly, the pilot emerged, with a twisted grin on his deathly-white face. Tottering up to von Dodenburg on india-rubber legs, he saluted, asked for a Schnapps and fainted clean away before he could be given the drink.

The pilot, however, was one of the lucky few. His comrades were not so fortunate. The Yak pilots knocked them out of the air one by one, executing flashy barrel rolls afterwards, following the screeching aircraft down, riddling the parachutes of those who attempted to escape with machine-gun fire, so that in the end the survivors fled, sticking to tree-top level in a vain effort to protect themselves.

Schulze spat drily in the dust, watching as the dust and smoke began to clear once more over the heights to reveal the enemy positions. The Ivans had been hurt, he could see that. Colonel Rudel's men had knocked out scores of their tanks, and they were now burning everywhere on the parched, blackened steppe. But behind them waited hundreds more: black, squat and impassive, their long cannon swinging round once more to face the waiting Germans.

'Shit,' he cursed. 'I've blinked my glassy orbs twice, Matzi, but the Ivan swine still haven't gone away.

Grimly, Matzi nodded his head.

'Attention, all commanders,' the Vulture's voice crackled over the air. 'Prepare to move out, gentlemen. *Meine Herren*, I wish you luck.' For the first time in the four years he had known the Vulture, von Dodenburg sensed a note of emotion in his voice. It was as bad as that, he told himself. 'And good shooting . . . *Move out!*'

'*Good shooting!*' Schulze snorted, as Matz let out the clutch and the Tiger started to lumber forward. 'We'll need more than good shooting up there today.' He stared gloomily at the massed ranks of Soviet tanks on the heights.

'Hell, you don't want to live for ever, do you, Schulzi?' Matz said over the intercom. '*I* don't.'

'Stop that chatter,' von Dodenburg said sternly over the radio net. 'Keep it clear for important instructions.'

'Yes sir,' Schulze answered promptly, and from below Matz grumbled, ' "Crap," said the King, and a thousand arses bent and took the strain, for in those days the word of the King was law . . .'

But no one was listening to Matz's grumbles now. All eyes were concentrated on the hundred or so Russian tanks advancing on what was left of Wotan.

Von Dodenburg saw that they were buttoned up now, and ready for battle. Twisting his periscope, he flung a glance to left and right. The Vulture had done well with the surviving runners. He had taken the remnants of the Second Company, which had been badly hit by the anti-tank guns, and given them the advantage of some shallow ground where they could take up the hull-down position, if necessary. The Third had been given a more mobile role on the opposite flank, while his own First held the centre with the Tigers, relying on the strength of their frontal armour to withstand any concentrated Russian artillery fire. Their defence was excellent. All the same, the number of Soviet tanks advancing on them was awesome. Even in his wildest dreams he had never imagined that the Russians had so *many* tanks; they were outnumbered by at least six to one.

Now the Russians' pace started to quicken, and for lack of wireless communication the Russian commanders began wagging their little coloured flags. The T34s bounced up and down on their excellent Christie suspension. Now they were streaking along on a collision course with the waiting Germans. They had to be doing at least fifty kilometres an hour. The distance between them and Wotan narrowed rapidly. *Seven hundred . . . Six hundred . . . Five hundred and fifty . . .*

'Surely, we *must* open fire?' von Dodenburg began urgently.

'You may open fire now, gentlemen,' the Vulture broke in, quite unemotionally. 'Fire at will!'

They needed no urging. The whole horizon was blotted out by the jolting, bouncing racing monsters. In a minute they would be completely overrun.

'*Damn* it – *Fire!*' von Dodenbury roared frantically.

All of von Dodenburg's six lone Tigers holding the centre fired at once. All six shots were hits. To their immediate front a whole squad of T34s came to an abrupt halt, flames shooting from them. But the rest were still rattling on. Now the sweating gunners began to fire all out, knowing that as soon as they let up, the T34s would swamp them. In a flash the ground ahead was littered with burning hulks, their crews sprawled out dead in a circle of charred grass or lying slumped over the turret. But despite their heavy losses, there seemed no end to them. Relentless, regardless of cost, they rumbled ever closer.

The first Tiger was hit, Outflanking what was left of the First Company, a T34 sneaked to the rear of the sixty-ton monster and sent a 75mm shell right into its engine. No one bailed out.

'Close up . . . *Close up!*' von Dodenburg screamed urgently, 'unless you want the Popovs to put a steel shaft up your arses!'

Hurriedly the two Tigers holding the flanks reversed

closer to the remaining three German tanks, guns pumping away as they did so. Too late! Three T34s pounced on the Tiger to the left, coming in from front and both flanks. 75mm shells smashed it back and forth, skewering great gleaming silver holes all along its length. Metal lava erupted. The first tongue of flame licked up from the engine cowling, then another and another. But von Dodenburg had no time for the stricken Tiger. The crew would have to look out for themselves.

Five further T34s had broken away from the main force now and were racing through the drifting smoke after the first three.

'Everybody . . . Everybody,' von Dodenburg screamed, 'concentrate on those T34s to the left flank!' . . . Gunner, see that one with the officer waving the flags?' Von Dodenburg thought fast: if they knocked out the commander, there was a good chance the rest of the Russians would lose heart. Soviet troops were hopeless when it came to making decisions for themselves.

'Sir!' The gunner swung the long gun round and fired. The tracer guide missed the command tank by metres.

Von Dodenburg groaned: The Russian disappeared into the swirling smoke and suddenly von Dodenburg found himself swamped by fire from all sides. Now they were fighting for their very lives.

The dispatch rider slewed his dust-covered bike round dramatically and dropped it in the dust. Ducking low, he doubled towards the command vehicle. With the butt of his Schmeisser he hammered against the metal side of the Tiger, while shells howled above his head and machine-guns chattered. 'For Chrissake, open up!' he screamed in a paroxysm of fear, as more and more Soviet tanks loomed up out of the smoke. '*Open up!*'

Finally he was heard. The Vulture thrust his head up out of the cupola. 'What is it?' he yelled above the hideous din.

The DR cupped his hands above his mouth. 'Message from Division, sir!'

'Give it me.'

Hastily the Vulture's eyes flew across the scribbled words, while an ashen Metzger, trembling at every limb, watched anxiously. Slowly a thin smile began to grow on the Vulture's cruel thin lips, a smile that broadened and broadened so that his yellow false teeth bulged from his mouth as if they might pop out at any moment.

'What is it, sir?' Metzger gasped in wonder, as the Tiger rocked under the impact of a fresh explosion nearby.

'What is it? I'll tell you, my dear Metzger. We shall live to fight again. We have been ordered to break off the battle and withdraw – *immediately!*'

Tears of relief flooded Metzger's frightened red-rimmed eyes. 'Oh, thank God! Thank God for that, sir!'

'Yes, Metzger,' the Vulture said fervently. 'I knew I wasn't fated to die in this arsehole of the world . . . I'll make those general's stars yet.' The Vulture grabbed his mike. 'To all,' he cried urgently. 'To all. Make smoke . . . Make smoke now . . . *We're pulling back!*'

The panic-stricken young commanders, their nerve broken now, needed no encouragement. The Ivans were almost upon them. In a matter of minutes it would all be over and they would be swamped by that steel sea. All along the line of the survivors, the black smoke containers hissed into the air and exploded with soft plops. Thick white clouds of smoke began to billow upwards. Revving madly, the drivers started to reverse, the gunners firing as they went.

Wotan had been beaten. They were pulling back.

The Tiger bounced and came to a sudden stop. Down below, Hartmann screamed shrilly. 'It's Deschner, sir! He's been hit. The top of his head has come off!'

For a moment von Dodenburg seemed unable to digest the news. His head rang like a bell. The turret was filled with a strange echoing sound that refused to die. Suddenly he saw the thick white smoke streaming in from the engine compartment and he knew what had happened. 'Bale out . . . Bale out,' he commanded, choking and coughing in the acrid fumes.

The stalled Tiger was shaken by another tremendous explosion close by. Dark blue flames began to creep up through the instrument panel. Von Dodenburg bent down and peered into the driving compartment.

Deschner, the co-driver, was still crouched at his machine-gun as if about to fire, but where his head had been there was nothing but a gory red stump. His head swung back and forth gently, on the earphones to which it was still attached. Von Dodenburg felt himself choked with vomit. As Hartmann wriggled out of his hatch, he dropped over the side of the turret, half-expecting to be riddled by gunfire as he did so. But his luck still held out. The smoke covered their escape.

Schulze loomed up, his helmet gone, blood running down the side of his face. Matz, unconscious, lay slung over his shoulder like a toy soldier. The little corporal's face was a lead-grey; one of his legs was hanging on by a few shreds of flesh. Again von Dodenburg felt sickened.

Hartmann came up, taking off his pistol belt and dropping it at von Dodenburg's feet. 'I've had enough,' he yelled above the racket. 'A noseful up to here . . . I'm buggering off!'

'But that's desertion!'

'I've deserted before, and I'll shittingly well desert now. Don't you see?' The ex-Legionnaire's eyes bulged from his head with rage. 'We've had it . . . *Germany's lost the fucking war! The Ivans have beaten us!*'

Frantically von Dodenburg fumbled for his pistol as more and more battered survivors grouped themselves around the strange little scene being played out in the middle of the greatest tank battle in history.

'Hartmann,' he gasped. 'You must be out of your head,

man! This is only one battle. Germany isn't finished by a long—'

Suddenly Major von Dodenburg groaned, the words dying on his lips. What felt like a brick wall fell on the back of his head. The burning horizon tilted, righted itself and tilted again. The whites of his eyes swung upwards, sightless. He gasped harshly. Slowly but surely, his legs started to splay out beneath him and then he was submerged by the roaring red darkness.

And in far-away Moscow that night, the long impatient queues of skinny, pale-faced civilians formed, kopecks in their hands, jostling and pushing each other to get a copy of the vital newspapers which told of victory. For there it was, splashed in exultant bold red letters across the title page. It read, with truth for once:

THE TIGERS ARE BURNING!

THREE

'Where are we going, sir? I ask you, where are we going in this year of 1943? Eh? Answer my question, if you can.'

Von Dodenburg winced slightly under the barrage of words coming from the old man. His head wound still ached, although the bed-pan plumbers back in Berlin had assured him he would be fit for duty by Christmas again.

'What do you mean, where are we going, Father?'

'Have you lost your wits, boy?' his father snapped. 'I know the Armed SS isn't renowned for its brains, but I thought anyone with a modicum of intelligence would understand what I meant.' He glared at his son, pale and handsome in his best uniform, the tunic heavy with decorations, a snowy-white bandage wrapped romantically around his head. 'I *mean*, what are we going to do about the situation in Russia, sir?'

'I'm afraid I'm just a simple front swine, sir. All I can tell you is that we're holding them out there – just,' von Dodenburg said, a little hopelessly.

'But how long can you continue to hold them, Kuno? I fought the Russkis in the First War. They're easy enough to kill, God knows, the poor devils. But there are always more of them – and more. In the end they just swamped us by their sheer numbers. And they'll do the same to your vaunted Greatest Captain of All Times,' he added with a sneer, using the contemptuous name the older generation of German officers reserved for the Führer.

'Yes, the numbers they certainly have,' Kuno agreed glumly, thinking of those massed T34s which had slaughtered Wotan back in the summer.

Kuno's father gestured emphatically. 'The time has

come to make peace with the Allies before it's too late. The Anglo-Americans have already got a foothold in Italy. Sooner or later they'll be landing in France. If not this year, then the next. When they do, it'll be too late. Once they commence beating us in the field, then they won't *want* to talk. Then they'll stick to this foolish Unconditional Surrender business which that provincial dolt Roosevelt has forced on Churchill. It'll be the end of Germany! We'll be neatly divided up among the victors, you mark my words.' He paused for a moment and added gloomily, 'This place here, which has housed the von Dodenburgs for nearly a thousand years, will be Slavic again – that's if it's still standing by the time the Russkis get here.'

Von Dodenburg forced a smile. 'I don't think the situation is as black as you picture it, Father,' he said. 'Our army in France is in excellent shape, and the Russians won't attack again this winter. The spring will bring a complete change in our fortunes. Besides, there are always the secret revenge weapons the Führer has promised us for 1944.'

'Rubbish!' the old man snorted. 'Secret weapons – opium for the people! A sop to keep the civvies at the top factory benches working for final victory. There will be *no* secret weapons, and *no* final victory.' The old man looked keenly at Kuno from beneath his bristling white eyebrows, the blue eyes very clear for a man of his age – and very challenging. 'You know we've got to get rid of him, don't you?' he said, his voice unusually quiet.

'Get rid of whom, Father?' Kuno asked, bewildered.

'Hitler, of course,' the old man answered.

Von Dodenburg's mouth dropped open in shocked surprise. Finally he spoke. 'But how do you mean, get rid of the Führer, Father?'

'I don't know, Kuno – not exactly. All I know is that he won't go of his own accord, and that if he doesn't go soon, Germany will be ruined. It'll be too late.' As he spoke, he kept his keen gaze fixed on his son all the time, as if he were trying to read his thoughts; find out what was going on behind that pale, shocked, handsome face.

'But if you—' Hastily, Kuno changed tack. 'But if any attempt to remove the Führer were made without his approval, that would mean—'

The old man beat him to it, his voice harsh. 'Treason. Of *course* it would. Naturally we know that.'

'*We?*'

'Yes, there's a group of us, mostly generals, but also a few civvies – politicians and the like in the old days before 1933.' He paused.

'And? Well, go on, Father.'

'What else is there to say?'

Von Dodenburg looked at his father incredulously. 'But do you really know what you're saying, Father?'

'Of course I do, Kuno! The thatch on my cottage,' he touched his hair, 'may be white, but I'm not completely ga-ga, you know. I'm well aware of the danger of our undertaking.'

'But, Father,' Kuno protested hotly, 'I shouldn't even be listening to this madness! I'm a serving officer of the Armed SS. You can't be seriously considering . . .' He found he couldn't complete the sentence; the thought was simply too monstrous.

Solemnly his father nodded his white head. 'We are, Kuno . . . We are. 1944 will be a year of decision for me, for our family, for Germany. Perhaps even for the world.' He gazed out at the sad flakes of snow drifting down beyond the window of the study, his face hollowed out to a sombre death's head by the unnatural white light. 'Those of us who care must risk all, even our lives, to save what is left of our poor country – before it's too late.' He said the words as if to himself.

Slowly, very slowly, Kuno von Dodenburg rose to his feet. 'Father.' He spoke softly, his gaze veiled, revealing nothing of the emotional turmoil taking place within him, for he knew he would never see his father again. He was committed to the side of the murderers; there was no way back for him. His father still believed there was hope for Germany. 'I must go back to Berlin.'

His father opened his mouth quickly, as if to make an angry retort, but when he spoke his voice was restrained, impassive. 'Then you must go, Kuno.'

They didn't shake hands as the horse-drawn sledge, driven by the only servant, drew up, bells jingling merrily, at the big oak door. Instead, his father turned, head bowed, the unseen tears trickling down his thin, haughty face. He had lost his only surviving son. He, too, knew instinctively that he wouldn't see him again. Once more, as so often in the past, the von Dodenburgs had made a terrible sacrifice for their Fatherland.

Slowly the hiss of the sledges and the jingle of the old nag's bells died away in the distance, and the old man was left alone in that dark study, alone with the sad snowflakes, the steady, regular sound of the old grandfather clock ticking away with grim metallic inexorability, and his sombre thought for the future . . .

1944

THE YEAR OF DECISION

'Buy combs, lads! There's gonna be lousy times ahead!'

The Sayings of Sergeant Schulze, 1944

ONE

The fat Italian woman in the rusty black dress and thick woollen stockings was busy cutting up the pasta into long strips like grey tapeworms. At the open fire, her witch-like mother stoked the blaze with olive-wood, cackling crazily all the time.

Matz produced the two tins of Old Man from his pack and gave them to the fat woman. 'There you are,' he said generously, following the meat with a handful of cigarettes. 'Any wine? *Vino?*'

The *padrone* produced a big two-litre bottle as if by magic and handed it to Matz.

The little man put it to his lips, but Schulze snatched it from him just as he was about to drink. 'Hey, don't yer know yer manners, yer little arse with ears? Rank hath its privileges, yer know.' And with that he took a tremendous swig, while an apprehensive Matz watched his Adam's apple bobbing up and down. Finally Schulze gasped and deigned to hand the Chianti over.

Schulze walked to the little window – most of the glass had been shattered during the fighting – and peered out at their objective.

Beyond the twin cypresses, the Italian countryside lay flooded in the warm light of the evening. Away on the horizon, hill upon hill lay revealed in that radiance, each topped with a tumbledown ancient village or castle, like something out of a fairy story. Except that in the middle ground there was the silver sheen of the river, and on the other side were the Americans – the enemy.

Ever since January 1st, Wotan had been perched on Peak 555 in this god-forsaken corner of the Italian countryside, holding it against anything the Allies had been able to throw at them; for the Vulture knew that if Peak 555 fell, then the road to Rome would be open. Time and time again the SS troopers, serving as infantry, had held off enemy attacks. Tommies, Frogs, Polacks – they'd thrown them all back. Now it was the turn of the Amis. Soon they'd be coming across the Rapido River down there. The question was, *when* exactly? That was why he and Matz were out on this NCOs' patrol. Because when the Amis started their crossing, the Vulture intended to prepare a warm welcome for them. As he had told von Dodenburg in Schulze's presence, 'I intend to see that those young gentlemen from the New World are given a reception they'll never forget.' So saying, he had chuckled evilly and rubbed his hands greedily.

Presently the meal started – roast sparrows and young peas, followed by a strange lump of meat that was supposed to be hare, but might well have been cat, all washed down with generous helpings of red wine. '*Prima della guerra era bella, bellissima*,' the *padrone* was saying, shaking his head, face sombre, '*e sempre la miseria*.' Opposite him the toothless old crone who was his mother cackled all the while, the juice from the strange meat trickling down her skinny pointed chin.

'*Eh la guerra – quando finira?*' the *padrone* continued.

'I don't know,' Schulze stuttered, as outside the first flashes of the new evening's artillery bombardment appeared; for the Amis had been softening up Wotan's positions on Peak 555 for six days now.

'*Ancora . . . ancora*,' the *padrone* insisted, indicating the strange meat. '*Oggi festa . . . molto . . . molto*.'

Just at that moment, a heavy boot crashed against the door and sent it flying open.

'Okay,' a harsh voice commanded, 'reach for the sky! Get those mitts up – *schnell!*'

'Holy strawsack!' Matz stuttered, dropping his fork and thrusting up his hands, his mouth still full of meat. '*Amis!*'

Schulze turned his head in the direction of the door. In

the fading light he could make out half a dozen big men in dirty khaki uniforms, laden with grenades, tommy-guns, fighting knives and in one case a looted sword; their faces were grim and intent. Slowly he began to raise his hands. So after all that, he was now a prisoner of war. Nearly five years of continuous fighting in a dozen countries in three continents, against white, black, brown and yellow men – and he, Sergeant Schulze, had been taken prisoner, with his mouth full of roasted cat. He had certainly been caught with his knickers well and truly down.

'By rights,' the big sergeant in charge of the American patrol grumbled, as they plodded down to the boat waiting on this side of the Rapido, 'we should blow your goddamn heads off. You're SS, so that means you're killers. You deserve it. But Intelligence needs you guys, so I guess we won't shoot you – just yet.' He drew his fat forefinger across his neck, as if he were slitting a throat, and added in broken German to make his meaning quite clear: '*Später . . . Mak kaput*.'

The expression on Schulze's face didn't change; he was still struggling to come to terms with his horrifying new predicament.

Their captors shoved them into the little assault boat and, using the butts of their tommy-guns as paddles, started to propel it across the Rapido towards the other boats on the opposite bank. Preoccupied as he was with his gloomy thoughts, Schulze could now see that the Amis would be crossing in force soon. Everywhere there were piles of ammunition and supplies on the bank, with dirty white tapes leading into the water itself, marking out the lanes the attacking soldiers would use. Further on, among the reeds and stunted olive trees, he could see, too, the little bivouacs of the waiting soldiers, with here and there the tiny flicker of a cooking fire. His trained eye told him that the American attack across the Rapido was perhaps only a matter of hours away. He ground his teeth with frustration and anger; he was a fool to have gone and got himself captured – and all for the sake of a bit of warm food.

The big sergeant pushed him up the muddy bank towards the flickering lights, and suddenly the two begrimed prisoners in their dirty, mud-splattered field-grey found themselves surrounded by big men in sloppy khaki uniforms, licking ice-cream or eating sandwiches of pure white bread – food the like of which the two bewildered prisoners hadn't seen this many a year.

'Christ! Did you see that, Schulzi?' Matz gasped, as he watched a soldier casually toss away a half-eaten chocolate bar into the mud. 'Ice-cream, white bread and as much chocolate as you can eat – and all us heroes get is shitting Old Man and roof-hare. I think I'm gonna volunteer for this lot. At least you die with a full gut in the Ami Army.'

'Knock it off,' the NCO in charge of the patrol snarled. 'Save your breath for the Big Yid.'

'Big Yid?' Schulze asked, catching and understanding that much English. '*Wer ist*–'

'*Ich bin es!*' a harsh voice barked out. Schulze turned, startled by the perfect German, to be confronted by a swarthy-faced American who towered above him, his dark eyes above the beak of a nose set in a look of infinite evil and cunning. He was gently slapping a rubber hose against the palm of his left hand, which was the size of a small steam-shovel. 'Kay, bring the Krauts in here,' he commanded.

He turned and walked into his tent. Schulze and Matz were shoved in behind him, blinking suddenly in the brilliant hissing white light of the lantern which rested on the trestle table.

The Big Yid sat down on the wooden chair, thrust his muddy boots on the table and stared up at them, still gently slapping that rubber hose against the palm of his hand. 'You know why they call me the Big Yid?' he asked in a deceptively soft voice. 'I'll tell yer. Because I'm a Jew, and I'm big, and I'm mean – awful mean! Nobody likes me. These Texans, they all hate kikes. And I like nobody, 'cos I'm mean. Now I'm gonna ask you Krauts three little questions, and I want the answers to those three simple little questions, and I want 'em damn smart. *Do you understand?*' His voice rose, his swarthy face suddenly crimson, a vein ticking furiously at his right temple, as he brought the cosh down hard against the palm of his hand.

Matzi jumped, startled, and Schulze felt an icy finger of fear tracing its way down the small of his back. The small hairs suddenly stood erect on his shaven skull. The Big Yid was trouble, bad trouble – there was no mistaking that.

'We're SS,' he said, trying to keep his voice steady. 'You should know what we're like. You'll get nothing out of us.'

The Big Yid shook his head from side to side and clapped his big hand to his right cheek. '*Oi veh!*' he said in imitation of the stage Jew. 'Big, tough SS men, eh? Strong and silent? Rather-die-than-talk types?' He leaned forward, his dark eyes blazing furiously, menace written all over his face. 'Listen, you Kraut shit, you'll be begging me to let you talk before I've finished with you. You'll be singing like a shitting yellow canary bird. Now, here are the questions and let's have the answers to them quick, 'cos I want to hit the hay before we go across at dawn. Now, one: what's the strength of the centre of your perimeter on the Peak? Two: where's your artillery located? Three: which is the stronger of your two flanks?'

'Sir, I'll stake my professional reputation on it,' von Dodenburg said vehemently, staring at the Vulture's ugly red face in the flickering light of the candle which illuminated the command dugout, 'those two rogues, Schulze and Matz, have run straight into the Amis. They're too smart to have done anything foolish. The Amis were – and are – about to jump off, and Schulze and Matz have bumped right into them.'

The Vulture puffed at his cigar, brow creased in a worried frown. Outside, the bombardment was increasing in fury, and he could feel the earth of Peak 555 shiver beneath him. 'I am inclined to believe you are right, von Dodenburg,' he said at last. 'All indications are that their attack can't be far off now.' He sucked his big, ugly teeth. 'All the same, if we mistime Operation Left Hook your battalion could get itself shot up for nothing down there on the Rapido.'

'It's a chance I'm prepared to take, sir,' von Dodenburg said stoutly.

A huge American 155mm shell landed nearby and the ground beneath their feet shimmied alarmingly. A grey rain of soil came down on the ration case which served the Vulture as a table. Von Dodenburg noted that his hands trembled as he puffed on his cigar. The month they had spent fighting for this damn hillside was getting to even the Vulture. The knowledge made von Dodenburg press his case.

'Sir,' he said urgently, as the Vulture regained control of himself, 'we can't afford to allow the Amis to start digging in on the Peak itself. We're too thin on the ground, and the men have suffered too much to tolerate that kind of slogging match. We must stop them at the river.'

The Vulture knew that if von Dodenburg's bold plan misfired, the forces left on Peak 555 would be too weak to hold an American attack in divisional strength – but he had no choice but to give in. 'All right, von Dodenburg. Put Operation Left Hook into action. But I warn you: do it quick and efficiently. If you fail, it will mean that I will never get those general's stars.'

Von Dodenburg rose to his feet and looked down at his commander. 'Sir,' he said in controlled fury, 'for five years now, Wotan has fought, bled and died for the sake of *your* promotion. We've brought you up from the rank of humble captain to that of full colonel, and we've paid an enormous butcher's bill to do so. *Now for God's sake, shut up about those goddamned general's stars, or I'll . . .*' His hand flashed down to his pistol, while the Vulture stared up at him, his face suddenly blanched with fear and shock.

But just then von Dodenburg's shoulders slumped, all his rage spent. Without another word, he brushed aside the blanket that covered the entrance to the dugout and went out into the glowing darkness, leaving the Vulture sitting there alone in the light of that flickering candle . . .

'Nobble him – *now!*' von Dodenburg hissed.

The dark shadows detached themselves from the bushes which lined the American-held side of the Rapido. Crouched low, they darted forward. The American sentry, a stark black silhouette against the glowing night sky, never knew what hit him. One trooper slammed into the back of his knees, the other grabbed his helmet and pulled it down so that the strap dug deep into his throat, cutting off his cry of alarm. Next instant the two of them had him down in the mud, writhing and heaving desperately, as they cold-bloodedly garrotted him to death.

Von Dodenburg concentrated on the task ahead. Three companies of his First Battalion were already in position on the bank behind him, heavy machine-guns and mortars dug in ready to give the Amis a hot reception once they started crossing the Rapido. Now, with his remaining company – 'the blowtorch boys', as they called themselves in the brutal unfeeling jargon of the veterans they had become – he was going to put the left hook into action: the desperate and bold feint which would start the Amis crossing the river to their death.

'All clear,' he whispered. 'Let's move out!'

Cautiously, the fifty or so remaining men of the company began to crawl up the muddy bank, the riflemen in front, the 'blowtorch boys' with their clumsy, round packs to the middle, the machine-gunners lugging their heavy weapons to the rear.

Now the main Ami lines were only a couple of hundred metres away. In spite of the bombardment, the men crawling through the glowing darkness could hear the chatter of many voices. And there was a regular slapping sound coming from a lighted tent to the rear that von Dodenburg couldn't quite identify.

At they crawled closer and closer to the unsuspecting Americans, they fanned out automatically, with the 'blow-torch boys' in the centre, covered by the riflemen, and the machine-gunners, who would cover their retreat, falling behind and setting up their positions fifty metres from the river bank. Now they were a mere hundred metres away. At this distance von Dodenburg could even smell the Amis: there was a scent of freshly washed bodies in the air – bodies accustomed to perfumed toilet soap, so unlike the foul-smelling men of Wotan, who hadn't had a proper wash with decent soap for weeks. He wrinkled his nose up with pleasure at the sudden smell. Then he raised his bell-nosed signal pistol. '*One . . . Two . . . Three . . .*' As he counted off the seconds to himself, heart beating like a trip-hammer, he prayed fervently that nothing would go wrong. Unless they achieved total surprise, they'd be sitting ducks, at the mercy of an entire American division.

He pressed the trigger. A soft plop. A shower of fiery red sparks, climbing in a graceful arc into the sky. *Crack!* The green signal flare exploded in a burst of unreal, eerily glowing light.

'*Wotan!*' The battle-cry of the regiment went up lustily from half a hundred throats as they stormed forward at the surprised Americans, machine-pistols chattering in angry fury, the blowtorch boys already preparing their terrible weapons for action.

The sudden attack threw the Texans into a panic. Suddenly men were going down everywhere, as scarlet, angry flame stabbed the night and tracer zipped into the massed ranks of the Amis. Screams, howls of agony, panic-stricken orders and counter-orders went up on all sides. Running men blundered into the tents. Others scattered to the river and flung themselves into it in shallow dives, to writhe and heave in the boiling water as the German bullets ripped their bodies apart.

A hefty sergeant, with big shoulders bent forward like

an American football player making a touch-down, rushed the line of cheering troopers, firing his tommy-gun from the hip as he did so. Von Dodenburg let him have a quick burst into the stomach. He careened round, still firing, spraying the burning sky with bullets.

Now the blowtorch boys were within range. They pressed the triggers of their terrible weapons. The flame-throwers hissed, and long streaks of evil blue flame spurted towards the Americans, curling around their huddled bodies. In an instant the night air was full of their hideous screaming, and the air was thick with the smell of burning human flesh. Then the flame had vanished leaving scores of Amis fused upright, or in the crouching position, blue flames crackling the length of their shrunken, charred bodies, their fingers like black claws raised to protect their hideously burnt faces.

But the men of Wotan had no mercy. They all knew just how pathetically small this attacking force was. If the Amis ever recovered now, they would be slaughtered in their turn. The flame-throwers roared and hissed again, wreathing all before them in terrible, all-consuming blue flame, as the blowtorch boys raced forward, screaming their chilling battle-cry over and over again.

'*Wotan . . . Wotan . . . Wotan . . .*'

Schulze wiped the last drops of water from his face. They had just flung another bucket of water over him to bring him round after their latest attempt to make him talk.

Suddenly everything swung into focus once more. Matz crumpled on the floor beside him, the NCO with the tin pail, and in the centre of the tent, the Big Yid standing with his powerful legs apart . . .

Yet there was something different about the scene since he had passed out – Schulze knew there was. But what *was* it? From far, far away there came a faint but familiar shout. Suddenly the NCO dropped the bucket and at the entrance to the tent the two others grabbed for their pistols. Schulze shook his head. Then the full impact of that wonderful cry smote his ears.

'*Wotan . . . Wotan . . . Wotan . . .*'

It was the regiment!

He struggled to his feet, trying to forget the terrible burning ache in his limbs. He drew his breath and wished he hadn't. The pain stabbed through him like the blade of a sharp knife. The Big Yid backed off. 'Stay where you are, you Kraut bast—'

He never finished his sentence. With all his strength, Schulze had dived forward and slammed his head right into the big officer's stomach. He gasped, staggered back against the tent pole and went down, submerging them all in the falling canvas.

TWO

The Texans had attacked and attacked again, surprised and angry at the bold attack on their positions. Throughout the last week of January 1944, they had attempted to break through the Wotan lining the opposite bank of the Rapido.

They took enormous casualties, but still they kept on coming. Day after day, their assault boats would appear, nosing their way out of the smoke screen on the opposite bank, nudging through the twisted wrecks of other boats and between the burning tanks, edging the bodies to one side, as if they were working their way through a carpet of khaki. Then their troops would disembark, only to run into a terrible barrage that would rip their ranks apart and send the few survivors reeling back the way they had come, shocked and half-drowned, some numb, some screaming hysterically. Back on the other side they would throw their weapons away and pound the mud with their fists like men who find life unbearable, to be forced back into the attack once more by senior officers wielding pistols and sticks.

But in the end the big men from the Lone Star State did it, walking across a thick carpet of their own dead on the other side, stumbling through the rusting wire and the minefields, fighting for every metre of churned-up lunar landscape, carried forward by some atavistic fury, elemental and coldly burning, animated only by one desire before they died: to kill the Krauts who had inflicted this slaughter on them.

Then it had been von Dodenburg's men who had snapped. They had rushed out of their holes as if only too eager to die, grateful to be released at last from the unbearable claustrophobia. Armed with bayonets, entrenching tools, spades, anything with which they could hack, gouge, slice, they had raced forward to where the khaki-clad Texans were bogged down in the last line of wire.

The line broke up now into a series of desperate hand-to-hand fights, with the men of Wotan grunting like animals as they fought, and yelling terrible obscenities at their adversaries while the battle swayed back and forth, until finally they had staggered back to their holes, chests heaving, faces ashen and sickened, all energy drained out of their skinny bodies. Behind them the churned-up mud was littered with the khaki-clad, terribly mutilated bodies of the Texans.

In the end the men had been too exhausted to hold the Texans any longer. During the hours of darkness on January 31st, 1944, the survivors had abandoned the positions they had fought so hard to hold, stealing away like thieves in the night and leaving the Rapido to the Americans.

But the Amis had been fought to a standstill. They had been replaced by the Tommies. For days on end the Liri Valley had quaked with the roar of big guns as the Tommies pounded Peak 555. From end to end the angry red flames had blinked like enormous blast furnaces as the enemy poured fire onto the mountain.

The men of Wotan had huddled at the bottom of their pits as the whole mountainside had swayed and heaved, like a ship running before a great storm. Foxholes had collapsed. Bleeding, screaming men had fought the smoking soil, scratching at it with bleeding fingertips in their hysteria before finally being submerged and choked to death. Bunkers were hit, filled instantly with dead and dying men who drowned in their own blood. The casualties had been enormous.

Every night fresh cannon-fodder was pushed into the line, callow young men straight from the training depots back in the Reich, who died before they even knew the names of their commanders. One minute a second-lieutenant straight from Bad Toelz Cadet School would be standing upright to set an example to this cowering veterans. Next instant, he would be squatting helplessly, watching the blood jet in bright scarlet streams from his severed limbs. A handful of seventeen-year-olds panicked beyond all reason, broke ranks and willingly rushed into the massed enemy fire, dying with happy smiles on their contorted faces, released from this booming endless misery for good.

Sikhs, New Zealanders, Tommies – they had all come, paid their debt in blood, and gone. But there had always been new ones to take their place. Frogs and Algerians, Rajputs and Maoris, Ghurkas and Grenadiers. It seemed as if men were being summoned from every corner of the earth to be sacrificed to the greedy, bloodstained maw of this Moloch.

Now even the nerves of the veterans were beginning to break. One frosty morning in February, two of the old corporals who had been with Wotan since the beginning were found shattered and dead, bound together in a last embrace in their shattered foxhole, chests ripped apart by stick grenades they had clasped to them in their final attempt to escape this horror. Each new dawn now brought cases of suicide – men who had removed their right boot and foot-rag, curled their big toe around the trigger of their rifle, and wedged the muzzle into their mouth. Others risked death at the hands of the public executioner with his dreaded axe, by giving themselves self-inflicted wounds.

The Vulture's nerve had finally gone. Most of the day he was drunk, smoking cigar after cigar, rarely venturing out of the hole he shared with his signaller, even to perform his natural functions. Much of his time he spent sending off radio messages to anyone he thought might help him in the Reich, demanding that he, Geier, and a selected cadre of Wotan's officers and NCOs should be evacuated to reform the Regiment before it was too late. Now all thought of those general's stars which had been his reason for living for so many years had vanished. After five years of total war, the Commander of Wotan, Nazi Germany's most élite formation, the once-nerveless Colonel Geier, had reached breaking-point . . .

That month, the Butcher, who had survived so long by cowardice and treachery, finally met his end – at the hands of two Moroccans, who slit his throat as part of their debt to *la belle France*, which had offered them a few sous a day and as much plunder as they could carry in their packs in return for the privilege of dying here in this remote country. The two North African irregulars slit the big SS man's throat with neat, deliberate, unhurried calm. The dead ex-butcher's boy couldn't have done a better job himself.

Peak 555 became a graveyard for the young men of the Wotan. The foxholes were heaped with their dead. At night, when survivors prowling the area in search of food stepped on the bodies, the gas escaped from their bloated bellies so that they appeared to give out strange, eerie cries. Rats the size of cats feasted off the dead and grew fat. The wounded were handed pistols to fight them off, and if they fell asleep they awoke to find the loathsome creatures gnawing at their fingers, toes, noses . . .

Now the whole perimeter was heavy with the sickly sweet odour of putrefaction for there were no drugs or bandages left. Ammunition started to run out, and at night there were ever-smaller bearer parties bringing fresh supplies. The entire German front in Italy was breaking down. Water was fetched from green-scummed ponds filled with rotting corpses. Food was looted from the dead bodies of the Tommies who covered the hillside below. Peak 555 had become a hell on earth; and all the time the enemy attacked and attacked again, one great amorphous khaki mass, intent only on wiping the handful of men in field-grey off the face of the earth.

On April 20th, 1944, the day on which civilians back in

the Reich celebrated the Führer's Birthday, the Vulture called together his last 'O-Group'.* It was a pathetic affair, for out of the forty officers who had climbed that peak four or more months before, only four now survived: the Vulture himself; his loathsome police spy, Lieutenant Kriecher, nicknamed the 'Creeper'; von Dodenburg, and another 'retread' from the old days, Captain Schwartz, a one-armed veteran of 1939.

'*Meine Herren*,' the Vulture commenced, as he always had done ever since von Dodenburg had first known him as a young lieutenant, back in what seemed now another age. But the voice had long lost its harsh, confident Prussian rasp; now it was weak and wavering. 'I – we – have to make a decision.'

A mortar bomb landed close by. The bunker in which they sat shook, and the candle, flickering wildly, cast enormous grotesque shadows on the dirt walls. The Vulture's eyes filled with fear. For a moment he couldn't go on, until Schwartz, massaging his wooden arm as if he could still feel pain in it, said calmly, 'You were saying, sir?'

'We must evacuate the peak . . . It has no military value any more. Monte Cassino to our rear will fall any day now, and the Allies will advance to Rome.'

He had expected little protest from his officers, and none came. They all knew that the only reason they were sacrificing their lives here was because the Führer hated giving up terrain – however worthless.

'The problem is, of course,' the Vulture continued, 'the wounded. Then, there are our numbers . . .' His voice trailed away and the others stared at him, as outside the machine-gunners hammered short rationed bursts at the attacking Poles. In between them they could distinctly hear cries in Polish. 'You see,' the Vulture faltered, 'we can't *all* come out.'

Schwartz stopped rubbing his arm. Von Dodenburg

* Officers' conference

stared at him, while the fat-faced 'Creeper' lowered his cunning eyes to the ground.

'Not all of us?' Schwartz broke the silence. 'Then can I volunteer to stay behind with the rearguard? I'm not much good with my one flipper, but . . .' He gave the Vulture the stout, staunch smile of the loyal soldier that he was.

'It is not matter of a rearguard, Schwartz,' the Vulture said hesitantly. 'You see, I only have the C-in-C's permission to take a *cadre* out. They will then be taken to the Homeland to form a new Battle Group Wotan with this summer's intake of seventeen-year-olds into the SS. I will select that cadre, who will be picked up by the C-in-C's personal liaison planes in an hour's time. They'll land just behind this position. That is why it should be held to the last, and—'

Von Dodenburg held up his hand for silence. 'Two liaison planes? That means only about twelve men. You mean you're going to abandon a hundred loyal soldiers and the same number of wounded? Just leave them like that, without a thought—'

'I shall be taking *you*, naturally, my dear Major,' the Vulture interrupted hastily, his face blanched with fear at the look in the younger officer's eyes. 'Oh, surely you know how much I have always valued your services?'

'Take me, Colonel! Please take me, Colonel Geier!' the Creeper shrieked, grabbing the Vulture's claw in his own chubby, damp paws.

The Vulture pushed him away, as von Dodenburg rose to his feet slowly, deliberately, his hand falling to his pistol. Hastily the Vulture did the same.

For a long moment there was no sound, save that of the machine-guns outside and the Creeper's muted sobbing. Now the two of them knew it was the parting of the ways; that parting that had been inevitable ever since that day in 1939 when von Dodenburg had first joined SS Assault Battalion Wotan. For five years they had fought side by side, bound together not by ideals but by their common loyalty to Wotan. Now for von Dodenburg that bond was broken at last. The Vulture had shown irrevocably just how little that loyalty meant to him; his first loyalty was to himself and his own overweening ambition.

'You are a traitor, Colonel Geier,' von Dodenburg hissed, fumbling with the flap of his pistol. 'You will betray everything and everybody in order to save your own skin and further your own petty interests. I have known it all along. I should have shot you years ago. You are a parasite of the worst kind—'

'Don't be a damned fool, von Dodenburg!' the Vulture cried, his eyes fixed on the other's pistol. 'Don't you understand? I'm doing this for Germany, trying to save her from the people who will drag her down for another thousand years. A few of us *must* reach the Homeland, cost what it may—'

The words died on his lips as, coldly, von Dodenburg cocked his pistol. Schwartz drew a sharp breath. The Vulture backed off, his whole body trembling as if with a violent fever. His hands flew to his face. 'Von Dodenburg, I beseech you . . . Don't do anything foolish.'

'I'll help you, Colonel, if you'll only take me with you!' the Creeper screamed, and flung himself forward at von Dodenburg.

Instinctively Kuno pressed the trigger.

The Vulture gave a great shriek. At that close range the slug slammed him hard against the dirt wall. He looked down, his eyes suddenly full of disbelief as he saw the great, gaping hole among all those decorations for which he had sacrificed so many young men's lives.

'Colonel! Colonel!' the Creeper cried, in a paroxysm of abject fear as he clutched the dying man's cold hand. 'It was all a mistake! Take me with you.'

Feebly, the Vulture pushed him away and began to slide down the wall. 'Stars . . . General's stars,' he whispered throatily, the black blood trickling from the side of his cruel little mouth. 'Stars . . .'

The Vulture was dead.

*

What was left of SS Assault Regiment Wotan broke out of the circle of enemy troops besieging Peak 555 on the night of June 1st, 1944, under their new commander Colonel von Dodenburg. The C-in-C had radioed him permission to sneak out a select party, leaving the rest to hold out till 'the last man and the last bullet.' Twice von Dodenburg had refused; in the end he had smashed the last surviving radio and made his own decision.

Now they stumbled and slithered down the mountainside, through the débris-littered valleys, taking their wounded with them, each man hanging onto the belt of the man in front, kept on their feet solely by the desire to escape and by von Dodenburg's inspired leadership.

Behind them, the snap and crackle of small arms fire grew fainter and fainter, to merge finally into the steady rumble of the heavy guns pounding Monte Cassino, now ringed with flames which symbolized for von Dodenburg the end of Germany's hopes in Italy.

The Cassino front was finished. Soon the Allies would be storming towards Rome. And from there? Who knew? But one thing *was* certain; Wotan would never be wasted again. Wherever and whenever the élite of the SS went into action, he, Kuno von Dodenburg, would ensure that they would be employed only in the decisive battles. Never again would their precious lives be thrown away at the whim of the men in Berlin. 'If we are to dig our own graves,' he whispered to himself through gritted teeth more than once, that long night, 'then we shall decide for ourselves where they will be sited . . .'

Before dawn they had reached the German lines and were forming up in the grey morning light behind the Italian barn which housed the CP of the regiment holding this sector of the new line.

Von Dodenburg, weary and bloodstained, gazed ruefully at the men of his command: for Germany's élite, they looked a sorry lot.

He licked his lips and cried '*Hab acht!*'

The men clicked to attention, bodies suddenly rigid, eyes fixed on the horizon.

A German infantry major looked at him as if he had suddenly gone crazy. 'But Colonel, there are trucks on the way to pick up your men. Most of them are wounded . . .'

But Colonel von Dodenburg wasn't listening. 'SS Assault Regiment Wotan,' he commanded in a cracked voice, 'right . . . *turn!*'

The hundred or so men who could still walk swung round.

'*Forward march!*'

While the infantry gaped at them as if they were clean out of their minds, the survivors of Wotan started to limp behind their two remaining officers.

'A song . . . One, two, three!' the lead singer commanded, and as one, the Wotan burst into that proud, bold song of the good years:

> *'Clear the street, the SS marches,*
> *The storm columns stand at the ready.*
> *They will take the road . . .*
> *Let death be our battle companion,*
> *We are the Black Band . . .'*

Slowly, almost reluctantly, the infantry major came to attention and brought his hand to his cap in salute, a look of wonder, admiration and disbelief on his young face. 'Gentlemen,' he said to his staff, as the scarecrows of the Wotan passed from sight, leaving behind them only the echo of their singing, and the stamp of their boots, 'there goes the Armed SS . . .'

THREE

'Traitors one and all . . . The scum of the earth . . . Folk-parasites . . . The dregs of German society, for whom there can be only one penalty – *death!*'

Sitting there in the anonymous darkness of a freezing cold cinema, von Dodenburg watched, horrified, as Chief Prosecutor Rudolf Freisler, dressed in his black robes with the swastika on his breast, worked himself up to a mad frenzy, eyes gleaming crazily, the spittle dripping from his cruel, narrow mouth.

The trial of the 'July criminals', as the men who had attempted to kill the Führer four months before had become known, was now being publicly shown throughout the Reich as a stern warning to the waverers and defeatists. Its message was simple: nothing could change the course of German history; the Führer was invincible; those who raised their hand against him, even in this moment of great crisis, would be punished by the supreme penalty.

The cameras shifted from Freisler's mad face and focused on the court, which was filled with solemn civilians and enthusiastic soldiers, evidently hand-picked by the 'Poison Dwarf', Dr Goebbels, to demonstrate that the nation was really one hundred per cent behind the Führer. Slowly the cameras turned from that solid National Socialist audience to the broad corridor in the middle of the court which led down to the cells.

Two fat, middle-aged Schupos led a procession of elderly men in shabby civilian clothes who were now filing up from below. The cameras zoomed in closer, and there they were; the conspirators who had placed a bomb in the conference room at the Führer's East Prussian HQ that fateful July

20th. Civilians, some of them former captains of industry and prominent politicians; soldiers and sailors, some heroes of the fighting of the early part of the war; but now all broken men, in ill-fitting clothes, their false teeth and belts removed to prevent them attempting suicide, shuffling forward to face that merciless public prosecutor.

Anger ran through the crowded provincial cinema. 'Traitors,' people muttered. 'Shoot the lot of 'em! . . . Shooting's too good for swine like that . . .'

Kuno von Dodenburg caught his breath. Goerdeler, the chief civilian in the plot, had just filed past. Behind him came Colonel-General Beck, half-concealing the next man, who stood ramrod straight and head held proudly erect despite his seventy-five years.

'*Father*,' gasped von Dodenburg.

Now the prisoners were lined up in front of the feared Freisler, some with heads bowed as if in shame, others seemingly oblivious to their surroundings, staring straight ahead. All had their skinny hands manacled in front of them like common criminals.

The harsh, excited voice of the newsreel commentator now took over from Freisler. 'There they are, folk-comrades, the criminals of the July Plot. Degenerates, opportunists, defeatists to a man – concerned only with their own safety, unthinking of the fate of this proud, precious Reich of ours, which will, as our Führer Adolf Hitler has promised, undoubtedly last for another thousand years . . .'

Blinded with tears, von Dodenburg stared for a few last, fleeting seconds at his father's stern, lean, soldierly face. He had been tortured to make him confess, he could see that – they all had. But there was no shame on his features. He was the same proud von Dodenburg he had always been, aware of his lineage and his family's record of service to the crown of Prussia and to those masters who had followed the Hohenzollerns. Now, soon, they would take him away, to be impaled on a butcher's hook, to hang there in the Gestapo cellars like a side of beef, waiting to be slowly garrotted to death with a thin piece of chicken wire while the cameras whirled, recording his death agonies for the Führer. For that was the fate of the first batch of 'July criminals' whom Freisler had sentenced to death.

Just then the screen went blank. A series of flickering numbers – and suddenly they were in the East, with the sounds of the artillery and rattle of tank tracks submerged in the triumphant tones of a military march and a bombastic voice crying, 'Once again on the Eastern Front, our victorious soldiers of the Greater German Army advance against the Bolshevik hordes . . .'

Kuno von Dodenburg had had enough of the *Deutsche Tonende Wochenschau.** 'Excuse me,' he said throatily to his neighbour, a middle-aged civilian in Party brown, wrapped, like most of the audience, in blankets to keep out the biting cold of the unheated cinema. 'Could you let me pass, please?'

'But Folk-Comrade, not in the middle of the news,' the fat Party man began – but then he caught a glimpse of that hard, lean face above the Knight's Cross and the silver jagged runes of the SS. Embarrassed, he rose hastily, his blankets dropping to the floor.

It wasn't *fair*, von Dodenburg told himself, as he staggered blindly through the silent streets, past the rows of houses wrecked during the latest bombing attacks by the Americans and the RAF. Not only had his father served Germany loyally and well, but so had all the von Dodenburgs before him. Hadn't he, Kuno von Dodenburg – even though he no longer believed in Final Victory – brought the remnants of the Wotan and the 'Baby Division', Panzermeyer's Twelfth SS, 'the Hitler Youth', out of the inferno of Normandy and safely back to the Reich? And then fought the Amis to a standstill at Aachen, in order to give Germany a chance to prepare for the Allied invasion of the Homeland? Indeed, he and his brave men had done so well that the Amis had been stopped in their tracks and the Reich was now prepared not merely to

* German newsreel.

defend the frontier, but to go over to the offensive: the Führer was now contemplating a great drive for Antwerp which would split the Allied forces in two and change the course of the war decisively in Germany's favour.

Yet his father, foolish old conservative that he was, an old man with not a single political idea worth five pfennigs in his wooden soldier's head, was now going to suffer the ultimate penalty – all because his love for Germany had led him to take part in this absurd plot to kill the Führer. Von Dodenburg stopped and hammered his fist in rage against the brick wall, which bore the new legend of December 1944; '*Victory or Siberia.*' But the wall was as cold, unyielding and unfeeling as the winter night in this remote frontier township.

Von Dodenburg calmed himself and wiped the last tears from his eyes. Above him, the stars shone down with cold, silver hardness, while the searchlights cut through the blackness, poking their hard white fingers into the clouds. Somewhere up there were the 'terror bombers', which had been coming now for over a year, day after day, night after night, transforming Germany into a stone wasteland, desolate and ruined.

Suddenly Kuno von Dodenburg knew what he must do this evening. There were only forty-eight hours left before his regiment moved into the line for the start of the great western offensive. Before then he needed the boon of oblivion that alcohol afforded, and he needed a woman. My God, how he needed a woman! He had to feel something soft and loving, however faked that loving might be. Tonight of all nights, he must find forgetfulness . . .

The room swayed drunkenly before Kuno von Dodenburg's eyes. Peering through the smoke-filled atmosphere, he beamed happily at the pianist in the corner, who for some reason suddenly seemed to have acquired two heads.

'The Tommies are getting extravagant,' said the bespectacled war correspondent at his side, as the sirens finished wailing. 'That's two raids in one night.'

The girl said nothing.

The guns began to thunder now. Everywhere in the large cellar, the bottles and glasses which littered the wet tables started to tremble, the lights flickering wildly. In the corner, the fat whore with the dyed-blonde hair who ran the after-hours establishment, slipped slowly but inevitably from her chair, either fast asleep or dead drunk, revealing a quantity of plump white thigh and a mass of frilled black underwear.

The cellar swayed violently as the first salvo of bombs hit the ground. Plaster came raining down and some of the whores who were still sober screamed. The pianist ducked behind his instrument, which hummed as if ten pianists had struck chords on it simultaneously. A chilly draught came whistling in from somewhere.

Von Dodenburg looked dreamily at the girl, oblivious to the panic that was beginning to develop all around as the first acrid smoke started to stream in. 'You got a place?' he asked drunkenly.

She nodded. She was a thin girl with a sharp face and no breasts to speak off. She was twenty-one, and while he had been sober he recalled her telling him that her husband had been killed in Russia in '43. 'Now I whore – for money,' she had added bluntly; without aggression, indeed without any emotion whatsoever – simply as a statement of fact. Now she rose to her feet, slung her gas mask, picked up her bag containing food, money, water and clothes for forty-eight hours, as all the women's bags did these days, and grabbed his arm to prevent him from falling, 'Come on, before the panic starts.'

Outside night had been transformed into day once again, a burning orange scene that could well have come straight from hell itself.

They staggered through the night, the girl leading the drunken SS colonel by the hand, coughing and choking in the foul air, crunching over glass and débris, past an Army car crushed and compressed against a wall as if it had been put through a gigantic baling machine.

They turned a corner. The houses there were still standing, but their facades had gone, exposing the interiors in all their domestic intimacy; tablecloths on the tables, the feather beds turned back, clocks ticking in the background against the roar of the bombs, the crackle of the flames and the sound of the firemen below, sloshing through the ponds of water gushing from the ruptured water mains.

Colonel von Dodenburg giggled drunkenly and pointed to the sign painted on the wall:

> GIVE ME FIVE YEARS AND YOU WILL NOT RECOGNIZE GERMANY AGAIN!
>
> *Adolf Hitler, 1933*

Laughing weakly, clutching his stomach with his one free hand, Kuno allowed himself to be dragged down into the safety of the girl's cellar.

Now he was half sober. The bombing had gone on for too long and the screams had been too terrible for him to remain in the happy state of total drunkenness for long. By the flickering light of the candles, he stared at the girl, and she stared back at him while the cellar rocked and swayed under the impact of the explosions.

On impulse, forgetting his own needs and desire for forgetfulness, he reached across the bare wooden table and took her hand. It was icy cold. 'Don't be frightened,' he said softly. 'At the front, they always say you never hear the one that croaks you.'

'They're dying everywhere in the cellars now,' she said, her voice hardly audible. 'Old men, women, children, babies. Not armed soldiers, just defenceless civilians.'

Another bomb dropped close by and the cellar shook violently. Dust rained down. Her face turned a sudden deathly grey. He didn't seem to notice. 'We'll pay them back a thousandfold, the swine,' he said, iron in his voice again.

'Pay them back? How can you pay them back? By killing them, too? Must we all end up as corpses? Will nobody be left of the human race?' Her bottom lip trembled badly. Soon she would cry, and that would finish everything.

'Don't talk,' he rapped harshly. 'There's been too much damned talk! No more of it!' He grabbed her hand cruelly and pulled her body to his.

Almost brutally he took her, thrusting her back across the wooden table, forcing her legs apart, ignoring the little cries she made at the back of her throat, whether in protest or pleasure he neither knew nor cared. The frantic, panting, sweating, all-consuming act of love began, while all around them the world shuddered, trembled and finally died . . .

As she watched him dress, saw the dull purple wounds that marked his lean white body, she knew that he was a man marked by death. All the township buzzed with the rumours of the great new offensive; why else would the élite of the élite be here, the Wotan? Yes, the SS were marching westwards once again after four long years. And in the forefront would be the young man who now straightened up in front of her, raising his hand to his cap with its silver death's head insignia, in a kind of last salute.

Somehow that face with its haggard eyes, its lines and ridges around them, the topography of fear, exhaustion, grief – that face moved her, jerked her out of her mood of despair, made her want to shake him, force him to face up to the world in which they lived, this dying, decadent 'New Germany'. Made her long to scream to him to run while there was still time to save himself.

'Colonel,' she said, 'I once knew a man like you a long time ago. He was brave and fearless too, a patriot.' She lowered her voice. 'He died in '43 in another great attack that was to end the war and bring ultimate victory. I loved him a great deal.' Then, almost as an afterthought, 'He expected to die for his Fatherland too. Do you?'

'No,' Kuno said slowly, as if he were giving the question some thought, 'I do not expect to die . . . Now I must go. Thank you.'

'Thank *you*,' she said, with all her old, hopeless cynicism. The fool would go to his inevitable fate; all her desire to help him had gone as quickly as it had come. She didn't look up as he went through the door into the burning dawn . . .

FOUR

A shadow darted from behind one of the little stone peasant houses above the bridge, held by the retreating Americans, 'All clear, Major,' he reported to the hard-faced SS officer, the whites of his eyes gleaming against his soot-blackened face. 'The Tommies have really hit the hay down there. I swear I could hear 'em sawing wood!'

Harsch, von Dodenburg's second-in-command, turned to the young Colonel. 'Any further orders, Obersturmbannführer?'

Von Dodenburg shook his head. Everything was working splendidly. This was the third day of the great offensive westwards and already Wotan was in sight of their first objective, the bridge across the River Meuse at Huy. If they could take and hold that bridge, the whole mass of the 6th SS Panzer Army would cross it and dash for the great Allied supply port of Antwerp. Once that was taken and the Americans were cut off from their British allies, all of whose supplies came through Antwerp, then Germany would be able to negotiate a peace in the West from a position of strength. Suddenly the young colonel standing there in the December dawn realized the magnitude of the task ahead of them. This morning he might well decide the fate of Germany!

Harsch, who commanded the Regiment's panzer grenadiers, took a last look at the grey ghosts waiting to follow up his assault infantry down to the vital bridge; then he commanded softly, as if unwilling to break the dawn stillness, '*Los! Worwärts!*'

The young grenadiers, their side-arms muffled in the sacking they had found in the abandoned cottages on both sides of the steep road that led down to the Belgian township, moved from the cover of the houses. Immediately, they were struck by the icy blast of the wind, knifing across the snowbound countryside. In their thin uniforms, the seventeen- and eighteen-year-olds who now made up Wotan shivered violently. But still they gripped their machine pistols and stick grenades firmly, faces set and resolute. Like grey timber-wolves stealing from a winter forest, they began to advance down the silent street.

Harsch could now just make out the gothic outline of a church and the great grey bulk of the medieval citadel to the left of the all-important bridge. Things were going well. The Tommies hadn't spotted them yet. His lips curled contemptuously. What careless cardboard soldiers the English were!

Now the bridge started to loom up ever larger out of the icy dawn gloom.

To the right a bonfire soaked in petrol exploded with a sudden *woosh*. The grenadiers stopped, their faces a frightened crimson. '*Who the sodding hell goes there?*' an angry, scared voice called in English. '*On the double!*' someone yelled harshly. Whistles shrilled. Orders were shouted. There was the sound of heavy nailed boots running over the icy cobbles. White tracer suddenly cut through the air.

'*Mir nach!*' Harsch yelled.

Now the bridge was only a hundred metres away. Suddenly Harsch was possessed by the crazy fantasy that once he had crossed it, all would be well; the bridge at Huy was his path to safety. He *had* to get across it.

A terrified face in a soup-bowl helmet loomed up out of the mist. A Tommy! Harsh's machine-pistol chattered. The Tommy went down as if pole-axed.

In a matter of moments the men in khaki and those in the camouflaged smocks of the SS were struggling in close combat all over the entrance to the bridge, swaying back and forth as they fought to the death, skidding and slipping like ice-skaters on the bloody cobbles. On all sides screams, frightened cries, pleas for help rose – and above them all the first throaty coughs of tank engines being started in the cold December air.

To Harsch's front there were both Germans and English tangled in a confused mêlée, but the hard-faced major had no time for such considerations now. He *had* to have that bridge!

'When I throw,' he cried to the grenadiers crouched behind him, waving his grenades, 'straight in men . . . just like Blücher!' He grunted and lobbed first one and then the other grenade. *'Now!'*

With a cheer, the grenadiers charged, as the twin explosions rent the air, stumbling and stepping over the writhing bodies of friend and foe alike. A Tommy staggered up from the smoking wreckage of a gunpit. Harsch fired from the hip. The Tommy's hands fanned the air wildly, and he fell back among the dead and dying. Another Tommy ran for the officer leading the charge, wielding a long old-fashioned bayonet. Harsch beat him to it. He jammed his Schmeisser against the bayonet, parried, and before the Tommy could react, smashed the Schmeisser like an iron whip across his face. The man reeled back, his face a red, oozing mess.

'*Los . . . Los! . . .*' Harsch gasped. Nothing could stop them now. 'We're nearly there, Grenadiers . . . *Wotan!*'

'*Wotan . . . Wotan . . . Wotan!*' Half a hundred eager young voices took up the old battle-cry.

They plunged into the smoke of battle. The noise of the first Churchills advancing on the bridge from the other side of the Meuse was getting louder by the instant. They were only metres away from the bridge now.

A group of frantic-fingered Tommies emerged from the fog of war, struggling to set up a bren-gun. Behind them, a bare-headed old man, perhaps a senior officer, cursed. In his hand he held a strange, bell-barrelled brass pistol. The clank of the Churchills was getting frighteningly close. Harsch pressed the trigger of his Schmeisser. The men around the machine-gun were cut to pieces as the slugs tore into them at short range, whirling them round, arms flailing, until they flopped to the ground, bodies twitching crazily.

Still the man with the strange pistol didn't move. He remained standing there, legs spread apart. The first ugly hulk of a tank loomed up out of the mist. 'Damned old fool!' Harsch cried, carried away by a burning excitement. He pressed the trigger of his pistol and a hail of slugs rippled along the cobbles at the Englishman's feet. Violent little purple sparks erupted all around him. Still the Englishman didn't flee.

'Smoke!' Harsch cried desperately. 'Blind that Churchill!'

Behind him a young grenadier tugged a smoke grenade from his belt and hurriedly lobbed it. It explodded just in front of the Churchill. Thick white smoke began to billow up at once. The blinded driver braked, to halt right across the bridge, blocking it effectively for the moment.

Harsch grinned in triumph. The bridge was virtually his. Still the old bare-headed Englishman didn't move. In spite of the smoke, Harsch could see him quite clearly; the clipped, old-fashioned moustache, the grey hair, the stern, soldierly face. He raised his machine-pistol. Almost pleasurably, confident now that nothing could stop him capturing the bridge, he took first pressure, trying to control the wild beating of his heart. Second pressure.

Nothing happened.

He pressed again.

Again nothing!

Ten metres away the old Tommy raised his strange pistol, and at last Harsch recognized it for what it was.

'Kill him!' he screamed in an ecstasy of fear. '*Kill him*—'

The desperate cry died on his lips. The Englishman fired. A blinding white light exploded right in front of him. He screamed shrilly as the searing flame ate into his face. Screaming wildly, he staggered back, clawing at his empty eye sockets, frantically trying to extinguish the agonizing pain as his face started to burn with phosphorus. But there was no hope. Major Harsch sank to his knees on the cobbles, his head burning furiously, his features disintegrating like red molten wax; and then he was down, and the surviving panzer grenadiers, who had come so close to capturing the bridge at Huy, were racing back the way they had come . . .

A thin, watery sun slid over the grey winter horizon, tried to struggle higher, failed and lay there, as if beaten by the bitter greyness of this December morning.

The bridge was silent now. To left and right, behind the bodies sprawled out extravagantly on the cobbles, the Churchills waited, buttoned down, the eyes of their commanders tensely glued to their periscopes, the gunners poised anxiously behind their guns, which were pointed up the hill the way the Germans must come.

Time passed leadenly. All was frightened expectation. In the houses, the infantry cocked and re-cocked their weapons, as if they wanted to be quite sure they'd fire first time. Behind them in the grey medieval town above the Meuse, a clock started to strike the hour of eight but broke off at the stroke of four. Perhaps some frightened *curé* or verger had stopped it lest it draw attention to his precious church; for even the civilians huddled in their cellars knew that the battle had to start soon. Then the slaughter would commence again.

On the roof of the eighteenth-century brick factory overlooking the vital bridge, the heavily moustached Tank Corps brigadier, surveying the opposite bank with his glasses, grunted angrily as he was interrupted in his observations by an officer bearing a message. He read it through and stuffed it deep into the pocket of his grey tank overall. 'Damn and blast!' he snorted, moustaches fluttering.

'What is it, sir?' asked his aide, a delicate young man with woman's hands.

'Monty in his infinite wisdom has just signalled that we're to move out of our positions and take on the Boche up there on the slope, Charles. God knows what he's thinking of.' He sighed. 'Well, His Master's voice has spoken and I suppose we'll have to bark. All right, Charles, order the chaps to move out.'

The delicate young man opened his mouth to protest, but the brigadier cut him short. 'I know, I know, Charles. The chaps are windy about facing up to those Hun Tigers and Panthers. Our Shermans are no match for them. But we might catch them with their knickers down at close range. That way we *might* have a chance of seeing them off.'

'Yes sir,' the delicate young man answered, and went off to do as he was ordered. He knew full well that they didn't have a chance in hell, but as an old Etonian he was far too polite to tell the Brig. that.

Schulze had led Wotan's point so far in a captured Sherman – an old trick aimed to persuade the enemy that friends were approaching. Now he was moving cautiously down the slippery, battle-littered slope, with Matz down below, sweating over the controls. They roared round a tight bend, Matz fighting the tiller bars. Schulze gasped. Right to his front was a long line of other Shermans and Churchills, crossing the bridge and beginning to advance up the incline.

Schulze reacted first. 'Churchill at two o'clock, Matzi!' he yelled, to warn his driver. He pressed his eye to the firing telescope and waited.

The first Churchill filled the round gleaming circle of calibrated glass. In an instant the cross-wires centered squarely on the joint between the deck and turret of the squat English tank – its weakest spot. Schulze pulled the firing bar.

The Sherman shuddered violently. Smoke flooded the compartment. One hundred metres away the Churchill reeled back, as if punched by a giant fist, and slammed into the nearest wall, bricks raining down on its smoking turret.

'You've got the Tommy bastard!' Matz yelled triumphantly. 'You've got—'

'Hold yer piss!' Schulze cried, seeing the danger from the next Churchill, nosing its way past the wreck. 'Bash us through that house at eight o'clock! Smartish!'

In the same moment that the Churchill fired, sending a hurtling white six-pounder shell racing towards the lone Sherman, Matz smashed the tank into the house. Bricks showered down upon it. They crashed through what might have been a drawing room. A french window loomed up. Instinctively Schulze closed his eyes. With a crash of breaking glass they were through it and churning their way through an ornamental garden, scattering snow, soil and ornamental flower vases in a crazy, ruined wake behind them. A moment later the roof of the house they had just left collapsed in a shower of red tiles. Then they were gone, twisting and turning crazily through the maze of little alleys behind the main bridge road, leaving the battle behind them.

'All right, this is the drill,' von Dodenburg rasped through his throat mike, his voice kept purposely unemotional. 'We're going to slog it out with them. If we can't take the bridge, at least we'll hold them until the rest of the Sixth Panzer reaches us.' Even as he said the words, von Dodenburg knew that Dietrich's boys would never link up with them now. The sun was shining again, and that meant the dreaded Allied *jabos*.* Dietrich's tanks wouldn't have a chance in hell against the Allied rocket-firing tank-killers. 'Numbers three and four will take up position to the left of the road . . . Number two will join me to the right. Over and out.'

* Fighter-bombers.

He waited a moment and pressed the throat-mike again. 'Half-track, do you read me?'

'Sir,' the signaller answered.

'Try to raise Sixth Panzer. Tell them our situation.' He hesitated an instant. 'If we don't make it, signal the rest of the Regiment to beat it back the way we came. Over and out.'

An instant later they were rolling forward through the black billowing smoke from below, and into the attack.

The driver drove his tank straight at the nearest house. The sixty-ton monster crashed into its wall, buckled it and brought down the roof, virtually burying the Tiger, so that only its feared long, hooded cannon was visible. On both sides of the road, the other tanks did the same.

The first enemy Churchill spun into sight. Desperately its driver fought for control on the slippery, treacherous cobbles. 'Not yet,' von Dodenburg hissed warningly, as he felt the gunner tense at his side in the icy compartment. 'There'll be plenty more of them to come yet.'

Slowly the lead tank advanced towards them, gun swinging from left to right warily, like an animal trying to scent its prey, followed by more and more of the grey, clanking monsters, rolling unsuspectingly into the trap which had been laid for them.

At the critical moment von Dodenburg laid his hand almost casually on the shoulder of the tense young gunner, who was all of seventeen. 'One round, AP, lead tank . . . One round, understand? No more. Then switch immediately to number six. We're going to bottle them in.'

The young gunner, his face lathered with sweat in spite of the cold, followed the lead Churchill, while von Dodenburg rapped out his orders to the other tanks in the ambush.

Now the Churchill was only two hundred metres away. Von Dodenburg had a clear view of the bedrolls, extra jerricans of fuel, and spare track that littered its deck. He squeezed the gunner's shoulder hard. '*Now!*'

Von Dodenburg pressed his right eye against the periscope. There were ten Tommy tanks labouring up the slope now. Suddenly the horizon trembled before the glass. Something white and burning tore from his panzer. A howling wind swept down the road in its wake, dragging the fallen leaves with it. The lead tank shuddered violently. White smoke erupted from its turret, flames crackling the length of its deck.

'*Number six!*' von Dodenburg yelled, thrusting home a fresh shell into the steaming open breech.

Shoulders hunched, the sweating gunner swung his long piece round with frenzied fingers. He grunted and tugged. Again the 88mm erupted. A shell shot forth, acting as a signal for the rest to join in.

In moments everything was wild, breathless chaos. On both sides of the stalled English column, tanks and houses were burning as the Germans slammed home shell after shell. Two Churchills trying to escape the trap collided with a hollow boom of metal striking metal, sending up a fiery rain of sparks. A gas tank exploded. Scarlet flame rent the greyness. A huge mushroom of smoke started to ascend heavenwards. Men fled in all directions, carried away by a crazy panic. Machine-guns chattered. Tracer zipped back and forth in burning fury. Everywhere men fell, tanks burnt.

'By the great whore of Buxtehude,' von Dodenburg's gunner breathed in enraptured awe, 'today we slaughter the Tommies!'

Crazily Matz steered the Sherman in and out of the maze of backstreets. There were Tommies everywhere. Slugs pattered off the steel hull of the tank like heavy tropical raindrops on a tinplate roof. Up above, Schulze, like a man possessed, swept the turret gun back and forth, carried away by the blood-lust of battle, gasping like a man in the throes of sexual ecstasy as he hosed the enemy ranks.

They crashed through a greenhouse, careened off a stone wall, then stormed down an alley so narrow that Matz could hear the stones gouge the sides of the tank. Across a square they rumbled, slugs howling off the turret, men firing furiously from every upper-storey window, and into a parallel street. Mills bombs rained down them like evil black eggs, bouncing off the deck and exploding harmlessly, if frighteningly, on both sides of the road. A barrier. They crashed through, throwing splintered wood and wire to left and right, and raced round a corner. Matz hit the brakes. Schulze yelled as he was pitched headfirst into the front of the turret, his mouth full of the salty taste of warm blood.

To their immediate front was a solid line of English six-pounder anti-tank guns.

Schulze and Matz saw them in the same instant. Immediately Schulze pulled the trigger of the smoke discharger and white smoke exploded to their front. Desperately Matz tried to start the stalled engine. To no avail! Schulze screamed as a shell slammed into the Sherman, rocking it back on its bogies. 'Out . . .' he yelled. '*Out – now!*'

The survivors wriggled out of the escape hatches, leaving the dead behind, as the greedy little blue flames spurted up everywhere inside the stricken vehicle and yet another shell hurtled towards them.

They pelted to the cover of the nearest house, Schulze in the lead, machine-gun fire ripping up the cobbles about their flying heels. 'Keep going . . . keep going . . .' The words faltered on Schulze's lips and he came to a ragged halt, big chest heaving.

Matz was falling – it couldn't be true. But it was. Matz, his old running-mate, had been hit. He was clawing the air as he fell, fighting to stay upright, blood gushing from a line of dark holes which had suddenly appeared the length of his little body.

'*Matzi!*' he screamed. '*Matzi!*'

'Piss off,' Matzi gasped through gritted teeth, down on his knees now. 'Piss off and let me fucking well . . . croak . . . in peace.'

He hit the cobbles with a fearful whack.

*

Charles, the adjutant, his helmet gone, his once-elegant uniform oil-stained and bloody, pushed his way through the staff officers grouped around the brigadier. 'Sir! Sir!' he gasped with quite un-Etonian urgency. 'They're massacring us on the hill! We ran straight into a trap!'

The brigadier looked down at the pale-faced, delicate young man. 'I say,' he said in his most affected Sandhurst accent, 'don't you salute your senior officer when you want to speak to him, Charles? I know we aren't exactly the Guards in this brigade, but there *are* certain proprieties which ought to be observed, don't you think? Even in this horrid business, what?' He stared down shrewdly at the young officer. He knew damn well what a ham actor he was, but he also knew the show was necessary. He had seen it all before – in France, the Desert, Normandy. Once you let things get out of hand, the panic spread to everyone – officers and other ranks – like a dread infectious disease. It had to be stopped right at the start.

The delicate young officer gave a parody of a salute, the blood dripping down his right arm. His head was bare – quite irregular, but the brigadier wasn't going to quibble now. 'Sir, as far as I can judge, the Boche have knocked out eight of our tanks. They're sited in the houses on both sides of the road in the hull-down position, and they've got what's left of our poor chaps trapped. As soon as they attempt to move, the Boche brew them up in short order.'

The Brigadier kept up the pretence. 'Bad show, what?' He looked around his officers' worried faces, and forced a smile – though secretly he had never felt less like smiling. 'Not to worry, chaps. We'll manage. Charles, your chaps will make smoke and withdraw the best they can. I'll push a troop of anti-tank guns up the slope to give them some cover. In the meantime I want as many PIAT* men as we can muster up there at the double. They can infiltrate the houses and work their way up the slope.' He flung a quick glance at the sky, which had become grey, leaden and threatening once more. 'Once it starts to snow and visibility

* One-man anti-tank bazooka.

goes, we're going to take those bloody Jerry panzers one by one, if it's the last thing we do!'

The three of them crouched fearfully in the cellar, Schulze's hand pressed over Matz's mouth, heads cocked to one side as the heavy boots of the Tommy infantry passed by. Gently then, Schulze took his bloody paw from his friend's mouth.

Matz was dying. The little man's breath was coming in harsh, shallow gasps and slowly his tongue was beginning to curl back in his blood-filled mouth.

Schulze whipped out his bayonet and clamped it in his friend's mouth, then lowered the teeth upon the blade. It was a primitive but effective means of stopping him from choking. He looked down at Matz's blood-filled trousers, the wooden leg sticking through the torn knee of the right leg.

With surprising gentleness for such a big man, he began to turn Matz. The latter's eyes flickered a moment, but didn't open. He was too far gone.

'Oh, my God!' Schulze gasped as he saw the condition of Matz's lower back. The skinny white buttocks were swamped with dark red blood. 'Haemorrhage . . . internal haemorrhage!'

But Schulze took the bayonet from between his friend's teeth and asked, 'Matzi, can you hear me? How do you feel, old friend?' The tears were streaming down his begrimed, weary face now.

'Like . . . like shit,' Matz gasped, not opening his eyes.

Schulze pulled down the sleeve of his tunic and wiped away the greasy sweat from Matz's forehead. 'You've been hit in the guts, Matzi,' he said, staring down hopelessly at Matz's ashen-grey face, the tears trickling down his cheeks unheeded.

'Bin . . . hit before worse . . . Remember that time back in '41 near Kiev?' He broke off suddenly, his nose pinched and white, his eyelashes flickering repeatedly.

Schulze knew the signs; he'd seen them often enough these last five years. 'Matzi!' he cried harshly. 'Open your eyes! Do you hear me, you little arse-with-ears? *Open yer shitting eyes!*' His voice rose to a scream. 'Sergeant Matz, I *order* you—'

He stopped short. Matz's head had flopped to one side, his mouth gaping wide, his limbs suddenly limp. Matz, the indestructable, was dead.

Now it was snowing hard at Huy, just as the brigadier had predicted. Coming straight from Siberia, the fist-sized flakes covered the dead sprawled on the slope and the shot-up hulks of the Churchills in a matter of minutes. Almost instantly, visibility was reduced to fifty metres and the world became a howling, white-whirling wilderness. Now the PIAT men, led by the brigadier armed solely with his cane, were everywhere, swarming silently through the wrecked houses, drawing ever closer to the German tanks.

Von Dodenburg quickly recognized the dangerous position he was in. Without protecting infantry, his tanks were sitting ducks. They had to prepare to move out at once. 'Driver,' he croaked, his voice hoarse with smoke, 'start up – let's get ready to move immediately.' He jammed his shoulder against the hatch-cover and forced it open, sending the litter of bricks and rubble on top of it slithering to the ground.

Gratefully he breathed in the cold, refreshing December air and then, narrowing his eyes against the flying snow, peered into the gloom, machine-pistol gripped firmly in his hands. He could see nothing, yet he could hear the soft squelch of heavy boots in the new snow. The Tommies were out there somewhere. But where?

Across the street, scarlet flame stabbed the white gloom and Number Four sprang into view. By the violent light of the exploding bomb, he could see the stricken tank's track flop backwards in the snow and the crew, faces bloody and blackened by powder, sprawl out of their stricken vehicle.

The snow closed again. But von Dodenburg had seen enough. The Tommies were already among them with their bazookas.

'Driver,' he cried over the throat-mike. 'Back out! Back out now!'

The sixty-ton tank lurched out of the rubble. A Tommy ran out of a nearby garden. Scarlet flame sliced the white gloom. A dark object wobbled towards the Tiger, gathering speed at a tremendous rate. *'Left!'* von Dodenburg shrieked. *'On the road!'*

The Tiger lurched forward. Von Dodenburg grabbed hold. The move upset the Tommies. A good dozen bombs struck the Tiger's thick steel hide at an angle, ricocheting off without causing damage. The big tank careened to the right, throwing up a great white wake of flying snow. Now they began the ascent on the steep, slithery road, von Dodenburg firing wild bursts of tracer to left and right. But the Tommies were everywhere, yelling and cheering, pressing home their attack as the three Tigers ground up the hill at an agonizingly slow ten kilometres an hour.

'Driver, for God's sake, give her more speed!' von Dodenburg pleaded, as another salvo of anti-tank bombs hurtled towards the lone survivors.

'I can't, sir . . . I can't,' the driver yelled back, his voice full of fear, as they were struck again and the Tiger reeled under the impact.

Von Dodenburg bit his lip in despair. They'd never survive this one, he knew. Already dark figures were slipping through the snow-storm on both sides, long clumsy objects held in their hands: the tank killers. Again and again he fired bursts into the houses on both sides, the tracer cutting the air like angry red hornets, but always there were more of the killers, creeping closer and closer until even the thick armour of the Tiger offered no protection.

Now the Tommies concentrated on Number Two. Horrified, von Dodenburg watched as a good twenty bombs went winging their way towards the cumbersome crawling steel monster, at less than twenty metres' range. The Tiger reeled visibly under the impact. For an instant it seemed as if it might weather that whirlwind of flying steel. But no. There was a tremendous explosion. Von Dodenburg shut his eyes. When he opened them again there was nothing left of Number Two save a great patch of charred melting snow and two boogie wheels crazily wending their way down the ascent.

Now he was for it. 'Listen, driver,' he said, trying to keep his voice calm as he sprayed the Tommies advancing through the flying snow for the kill, 'when I say "go", I want you to swing her round and head straight for the Tommies back there.'

'*What?*'

'Don't blather – do as I say. Swing her round and then get ready to bail out. All right? *Go!*'

The driver spun the controls and the sixty-ton tank whipped round deftly on the slick surface of the hill. Thrusting home low gear, the driver accelerated. The Tiger started to gather speed by the instant.

'*Get out!*' von Dodenburg yelled urgently. He pulled off his mike, grabbed his machine-pistol and dived over the side of the turret, hitting the snow and rolling over, watching man after man of his crew do the same as the abandoned Tiger rumbled on.

Suddenly the Tommies saw it coming. Screaming warnings to each other, they scattered wildly, diving for the verges. Most of them were young men; they avoided the metal monster easily. Not so the brigadier, hampered by middle-age and heavy overalls. The Tiger struck him a glancing blow. He went down screaming. The right track passed right over him, churning his body to a bloody paste, scattering pieces of gore as it rumbled on.

Von Dodenburg rose to his feet. They had a few minutes' respite before the Tommies regrouped. 'Come on – down that side street!' he gasped.

'No, sir, over here! Quick!'

He spun round, startled, hardly able to believe his ears,

and blinked his eyes, trying to penetrate the whirling flurry of snowflakes. Below, the Tommies were beginning to collect themselves once more. There was the snapping of a sten-gun. Suddenly a well-known face loomed up out of the white gloom.

'Schulze!' he cried. '*You?*'

'Of course, sir. Who did you think it was – *Father Christmas*?'

Ten minutes later the survivors of the dramatic battle for the bridge at Huy were gathered shivering in the snow at the top of the hill. Of those who had gone into the attack that dawn, only a mere handful now remained.

'Now, get this, and get it good,' Schulze was lecturing the young men. 'From now onwards, lads, it's every man's hand agen us. If we're ever gonna get back to the Homeland, it's got to be march or croak. Get it? – *Marschieren oder krepieren!*'

But von Dodenburg, though standing there with the rest, wasn't listening. He was staring down towards the bridge.

Soon the spot would become simply a map reference on some staff officer's map – and the men of Wotan who had fought there and had passed into history, would never know that at that obscure little bridge at the Belgian township of Huy, the Thousand Year Empire of Adolf Hitler had finally crumbled for good.

'*Marschieren oder krepieren*,' Schulze growled through the snow. '*Also los, Männer!*'

In a long line, skinny shoulders bent in defeat, the survivors started to plough through the snow the way they had come.

Von Dodenburg hesitated only a fraction of a second, then he, too, joined the column without a second look. He would never see that bridge at Huy again . . .

1945

DEFEAT!

'Better an end with terror, than terror without end.'

Popular German Saying, 1945

ONE

'Stille Nacht . . . Heilige Nacht . . . Alles ruht, alles schläft . . . Nur das . . .'

Kuno von Dodenburg smiled weakly. The Amis loved the old German Christmas carol, in spite of their hatred of their 'Kraut' prisoners – and in spite of the fact that Christmas was over and it was already January, 1945.

He stared out of the window of the dirty hut which was now his home, together with two hundred other 'Category Black' prisoners – men captured after the recent Battle of the Bulge who belonged to the SS, the paras and other formations regarded by the Allies as particularly dangerous.

It had stopped snowing, but even the white mantle of snow could do nothing to make this POW camp beautiful. Camp Black, as the Amis called the place, was typical of the scores of such places which dotted Eastern Belgium now that the great offensive westwards had been defeated; several acres of hard-packed earth, which turned to thick mud when the rains came, shaped in the form of a hexagon by high, triple-wire fences. These six-metre-high fences were guarded by white-helmeted MPs – 'snowdrops', the prisoners called them contemptuously – armed with sawn-off shotguns or machine-guns. In between the lines of wire were fierce German shepherds, trained by their handlers to go not for the throat of any would-be escaper, but for his genitals. The Americans, von Dodenburg reflected, couldn't be accused of treating their prisoners with kid gloves.

For a week now, ever since the Amis had ambushed what was left of SS Assault Regiment Wotan and brought him as prisoner to this remote camp, he and the others of the 'Blacks' who were prepared to fight on had scoured the place trying to find a way out.

Von Dodenburg frowned, wondering if the rest of his beaten regiment had managed to make it back to the Reich after the ambush. There had been so many greenbeaks among them, and so few old heads. Still, maybe Schulze had managed to escape – and if anyone could lead the survivors home, it would be that big Hamburg rogue.

He dismissed Wotan from his mind for the time being and concentrated on the task at hand.

By now it was pretty clear what was going to be the fate of most of the 'Blacks'. Right from the very first day, after he had recovered from the terrible beating he had received at the hands of his first captors, he had known that the mere fact that he belonged to the Armed SS meant trouble – big trouble. He had heard his captors mutter darkly about 'war crimes', 'concentration camps', 'special courts', and he could see from the look of naked hatred in their eyes that they meant what they said. This wasn't just the customary intimidation that all armies used on newly captured troops to make them reveal military secrets, strategic objectives and so on. This was the real thing. The Amis hated the Armed SS with a passion – and he, von Dodenburg, and all other surviving SS officers, were going to have to pay. There was no doubt of that.

Almost at once he had decided that he had to escape before he could be transferred to a permanent camp further into Belgium. He had heard from comrades before his capture that the best time to escape was right at the beginning, when one was interned in a temporary camp. Accordingly, he had sought around among his fellow prisoners for kindred spirits – men who realized, like himself, that it was now or never.

Soon he made contact with a hard bunch of veterans. There was Hartung, a one-eyed officer accused of having shot British prisoners in 1940; Grimm of the Hitler Youth, also accused of having shot prisoners, this time Canadian;

Degenhardt of the Seventeenth SS Panzergrenadier Division, who was being held on behalf of the French, accused of war crimes allegedly committed in Lorraine. And half a dozen more – men who had nothing to lose and everything to gain from escaping now, before the machinery of Allied justice caught up with them.

Already, on the second night, after the Ami MPs under their leader Big Red, a great hulking NCO with a broken nose and bad little eyes, had worked him over yet again with their fists, boots and pickaxe handles, he had started to survey the possibilities of escape. That night, still burning with the pain and humiliation of the beating, he had stayed awake. When the arc-lights along the wire had been turned on he had attempted to judge their depths and positions by the shadows they cast. In the silence of the long, freezing cold hut, broken only by the snores of his fellow prisoners, he had crouched at the window, timing the sentries on their beat and trying to ascertain whether they changed routine towards dawn, when they would be tired and careless after a long night's duty.

That morning, with the snow still falling, he met the others in the cover of the latrines.

'The wire's out,' Hartung reported. 'We've no tools to tackle it with. And do any of you fancy those hounds out there? You'd be singing tenor in zero comma nothing seconds.'

Von Dodenburg, as senior officer present, looked at Grimm. 'You had the gate. What did you find out?'

'It's pretty tough, sir. The sentries are very alert, for Amis,' he added contemptuously. 'But there might be something we could do with that little wooden shack between the inner and outer ring of the wire to the right of the gate. But how we'd get to it through that first fence, I can't imagine.'

Von Dodenburg sucked his teeth thoughtfully, then said, 'I've been thinking of that, too.' Raising his voice, he addressed the men, formally, almost as if he were back at Wotan, briefing his officers before an attack. 'As you all know, the first principle of any battle is to attack the enemy at his weakest point. Now in my opinion, the second and third line of wire is the Amis' weakest point. Why?' He answered his own question. 'Because their front line is secure and they're not particularly concerned about what's behind it. Now what's their front line?' Again he answered his own question. 'It's that ten metres or so of open ground which has to be crossed before you reach the first line of wire – and naturally the first line of wire itself, patrolled and surveyed by sentries. Once we're through the first line of wire, there's nothing to stop us save the dogs – and I'm sure that a hairy-arsed bunch of old heads like you won't be stopped by a couple of lovable little doggies.'

The men crouched in the stinking latrine laughed hoarsely.

'So how do we get through that first line of defence, the Amis' front line, gentlemen? I'll tell you. We'll tunnel through it.'

There was a groan of disappointment from the others. Grimm cursed. 'Shit, Obersturm, we'll be here till 1985 if we try to tunnel out! Where are we gonna get the tools from for a start?'

Von Dodenburg was unperturbed. He smiled. 'But we're not going to tunnel under the ground, but over it.'

At first the men looked at him as if he were crazy. Then he explained what he intended, and the angry looks on their rough, bearded faces changed to expressions of delight. He knew then that he had convinced them.

Today was the day – and the beautiful thick layer of snow was still there, the vital element in his escape plan. Soon it would be dark, and then all ten of them would make their attempt, all of them – save Degenhardt, the paratrooper – SS officers like himself. Von Dodenburg knew it was going to be tough. One hundred kilometres in the depths of winter through enemy-held territory, with only limited food to keep them going and the thin Ami overalls they had been given on admittance to the camp to protect them from the icy wind. He sucked his bottom teeth. Why even try? Why not let events take their course? Germany was defeated. Sooner or later he would end up in another POW camp just like this and be punished, guilty or not, for the simple fact of having belonged to the SS. Already he and his comrades of the SS had agreed that the Armed SS would be the excuse all 'good' Germans would put forward for the crimes of the Third Reich.

'The alibi of the German nation – that's what we're gonna be, gentlemen,' Hartung had announced cynically only the day before. 'Everything will be laid at our door. Believe you me, once the war's over there'll be Germans by the hundred thousand who will rush to the doors of the conquerors to tell them just what swine the SS were – how they butchered babies, made soap out of Jews and burnt and raped their way through Russia and the East. But not *them*. Oh, no – they were the *good* Germans.'

Von Dodenburg suddenly felt a sense of new resolve. Whatever happened, he wanted out of this damned camp. Let the future take care of itself.

Now the hours of lights-out were passing quickly. Outside, the wind howled and the snowflakes beat fiercely against the windows of the hut, which was filled with a thick blue fog as the men huddled around the pot-bellied stoves, smoking continuously and as usual talking about food, their major preoccupation these days.

Von Dodenburg was glad of the snow. It would stop the Ami guards from venturing out later on spot-checks. They were notoriously lazy, as it was; the snowstorm would do the rest. But every now and again he could hear the eerie howl of the half-wild German shepherd dogs which patrolled between the fences – and it reminded him again of the danger they faced from the animals. Unlike their masters, the dogs wouldn't be put off by a little bit of snow.

One by one the escapers started to assemble in the icy-cold washroom that lay outside the fierce warmth of von Dodenburg's hut, trembling and stamping their feet as they waited there for lights-out.

Suddenly the light bulbs flickered – once, twice, three times; the signal the Amis always gave when they were about to turn the lights off for the day.

'Five minutes to go,' von Dodenburg snapped. 'Last check.'

Swiftly the officers turned to each other, checking that they hadn't forgotten any of their pathetically small escape kit, and making sure that their comrades had no loose equipment which might betray them by rattling or chinking. Then they passed round a precious tin of black boot polish to cover the white of their faces.

Just then lights went out with dramatic suddenness. Von Dodenburg said a quick prayer and then stole over to the door. 'All right, comrades, happy landings to you all. Let's go!'

He wrenched it open.

The whirling snowflakes hit him in the face, making him stagger under their icy impact. But there was no going back now. He knelt, and taking one last glance at the stark, black outline of the first fence and blur of the hut beyond, began to scoop a tunnel in the snow with the aid of the board that he had wrenched from beneath his bunk. The tunnel had commenced.

Now they had been tunnelling through the snow towards the wire for two hours – though it seemed more like two years to the frozen tunnellers, working two abreast, with behind them two other comrades clearing away the snow they had removed with their boards. They had seriously underestimated the resistance of the snow. On the surface it was powdery and wet, but underneath it was frozen hard as rock and the blunt planks were hopelessly ineffective against it.

Still they laboured on in the freezing white gloom, taking 'observations' regularly by means of a hollow rubber tube which contained a mirror at its top. By turning it round until the darkness was replaced by the brilliant white light reflected from the arc-lamps above the first line of wire, they could make sure they were working in the right direction.

Another thirty minutes passed, with the diggers and snow-removers gasping like ancient asthmatics in the icy, tight confines of the white tunnel. Suddenly Grimm dropped his plank with a curse and a muffled yelp of pain.

'What is it?' asked von Dodenburg, working at his side.

'Hit something hard,' Grimm said, and sucked his hurt fingers. 'Hurts like hell.'

'Let me have a look,' said von Dodenburg, and crawling over Grimm's body, he felt his way forward with his frozen fingers, which were covered by soaked socks serving as a kind of primitive mitten.

They touched something hard and made of stone. 'It's the post – we've hit a fence post!' he exclaimed joyously. 'We're at the first fence! Pass it back. We've reached the first fence . . .'

Now they redoubled their efforts, forgetting von Dodenburg's warning that the Amis might well have sensors or other warning devices attached to the wire or buried near the surface of the earth for just such an eventuality. But luck was on their side. Fifteen minutes later they were under the first line of wire, up and out, and crouched together in the little hut between it and the second line of wire, ready for stage two of their bold escape.

Von Dodenburg ceased blowing on his numb fingers and turned to the others crouched there. As he had guessed, the arc-lights illuminated the fat, heavy snowflakes falling to their front but left everything to the rear in half darkness. 'All right, comrades, so far so good. As I reasoned, the Amis concentrated on their first line of defence and have neglected their second and third.' He raised his finger in warning. 'But we mustn't forget the dogs. They're out there somewhere and we might well bump into one of the beasts. It's a chance we'll have to take.'

So saying, he pulled out the precious bar of Lux toilet soap. The soap had cost him the last item of any value that he possessed: a silver ring which Himmler had given him in '42, inscribed with the motto of the Wotan: '*Death Before Dishonour*'.

'Grab some snow and give yourselves a wash about the face, hands and the hair with this stuff. If we do have the misfortune to bump into one of those damned hounds, they might think we're Amis by the smell. It might just give us enough time to deal with them. All right, get to it, comrades.'

Swiftly the bar of soap, highly perfumed and capable of giving a lather even in this freezing cold, passed from man to man.

Behind the hut in the circle of icy white light, the inner compound continued to sleep in the falling snow, looking almost romantic in its heavy white mantle. But to the front of the escapers, all was dark and silent. It was, von Dodenburg, told himself, a perfect night for an escape.

'All right, comrades,' he hissed, 'let's go – and if we spot one of those hounds, hit the deck and pray!'

Now they doubled to the second line of wire, the only sound their own harsh breathing, and Hartung and Degenhardt set about breaking through it. Their method was primitive, but effective. In the way of POWs the world over, the escapers had been on the look-out for anything which might prove useful, when they had come across a bottle of acid that Big Red's snowdrops used to clear the latrines when they were blocked. Now that self-same acid was being used not to clear away good honest crap, but to burn through the wire of the second fence.

To an anxious von Dodenburg, crouching there in the falling snow, the noise the acid made as it burnt its way through the wire seemed deafeningly loud, almost like some gigantic frying-pan filled with sizzling salt-bacon chunks and potatoes. But behind them at the first fence, visible through the flying snow in the burning white light of the arc-lamps, no one stirred. It looked as if the MPs had hit the hay for tonight.

A wire snapped, and another – and another. Degenhardt and Hartung grunted and pulled hard. An instant later they had made a hole in the wire big enough for a man to slip through. 'Quick,' von Dodenburg hissed, 'let's go!'

The men crouching in the flying snow needed no urging. Swiftly they passed through, one by one, and doubled towards the third and final wire fence. To their right, the long line of buildings which housed Big Red's snowdrops lay silent. Tonight not even the local Belgie girls, whom the MPs lured to their bunks with nylons and Hershey bars, had ventured out.

'All right,' von Dodenburg said, 'Degenhardt, Hartung – get to it. We're almost—'

He stopped short, the small hairs at the back of his neck standing erect with sudden fear. There was no mistaking that sound: it was the soft *pad-pad* of a dog stalking through the snow. One of the half-wild German shepherds was coming in their direction!

Suddenly there it was, looming up out of the snowstorm, an ugly brown beast, its fur powdered with snow like a layer of icing sugar. It stopped and sniffed the air. Von Dodenburg hoped against hope that it hadn't seen them. Suddenly it lowered its head, great yellow teeth bared. It had seen them all right.

'In three devils' name,' Degenhardt began to moan, but von Dodenburg cut him short with a laconic, '*Shut up!*' Gently he stole forward, keeping his movements deliberately slow so as not to alarm the dog too soon.

The dog gave a low growl, the long ears sloping back against the wolfish skull. It would start to bark at any moment. Von Dodenburg could wait no longer. He lunged forward and struck lucky, catching the hound's jaw first time. His hands clamped down desperately and stiffled the dog's first warning bark.

Frantically the beast wriggled in his grasp, twisting and turning its eighty-pound bulk in a desperate bid to free itself. It ripped a paw cruelly across von Dodenburg's sweat-lathered face. Blood splattered everywhere. Von Dodenburg yelped with pain, as the dog went down on its haunches and started to drag him through the snow. 'Get his eggs, Degenhardt,' he gasped through gritted teeth. 'That'll stop him . . . *Quick!*'

Degenhardt darted forward, thrust his hand underneath the dog's belly as it crouched there in the snow, and grabbed the animal's sexual organs. He squeezed hard. Suddenly the animal was prostrate with pain. Grimm didn't hesitate. He brought down his plank with a thud on the animal's skull. Its body arched with the terrible pain and von Dodenburg hung on desperately to prevent it barking. 'For God's sake, do it, Grimm!' he urged.

Grimm took a deep breath and brought the plank down a second time, with all his strength. Something snapped. The dog tore itself free. But in the very instant it opened its jaws to bark, the life went from it and it rolled over on its side, dead at last.

Hastily they heaped snow over the dog's carcase and stole on to the next fence, von Dodenburg rubbing snow into the burning wound on his cheek. Five minutes later they were through the last fence, unobserved. In another ten the storm had swallowed them up for good.

Camp Black would see them no more. They were on their way back to their war-torn homeland.

It was unearthly cold, the icy wind racing mercilessly across the snowy waste of Eastern Belgium, lashing millions of razor-sharp particles of snow against their sunken, emaciated faces. Icicles, garishly white, hung from their nostrils. Hoar frost powdered their eyebrows, making them look like old men. Only the iron discipline of the SS kept them going as they stumbled forward across the never-ending plain, shoulders bent, their breath fogging the air around their faces in small clouds.

They had been walking for three days now, dodging the few US troops to be found in the backwoods areas, living from hand to mouth, raiding the farmers' potato and turnip fields and eating the frozen roots raw, combing abandoned cottages for the least scrap of anything edible – but somehow surviving. Now at last they were reaching territory where they might find help from the loyal civilians. One hour before, they had crossed the frozen river which, until the year 1919, had formed the boundary between Belgium and Germany. Here the locals had once been German, still spoke that tongue, and were generally pro-German. At least, so the weary men hoped, as they hobbled, heads bent, across that howling waste.

Grimm had managed to keep himself going for hours now by summoning up delightful memories of good meals he had eaten as a boy, occasionally giggling crazily to himself and licking his cracked, frozen lips as, in his imagination, his plump-bosomed, white-haired old mother thrust yet another delectable, steaming dish under his nose, to assail his twitching nostrils.

Suddenly his nostrils really *did* twitch. He stopped and raised his head to the falling snow, sniffing the icy air like an animal scenting its prey. There was no mistaking it. Somewhere, someone was cooking food!

His lean stomach rumbled noisily. Twin streams of saliva escaped from the sides of his mouth and ran down his skinny, unshaven chin. He caught himself from falling just in time.

'Von Dodenburg,' he croaked hoarsely. 'Comrades! I smell *food!*'

They stopped and stared at him stupidly, swaying dangerously with exhaustion.

'Where? *Where?*' the others cried, their stomachs doing back-flips at the very thought.

Like a bunch of idiots, they stood there in the falling

snow, sniffing the air and surveying the white wasteland, their eyes roaming over every dip, every snowy hillock, every path of firs, until finally Degenhardt spotted it: a thin stream of blue smoke driven furiously into the whirling snow by the wind, but unmistakable all the same. 'Group of pines, ten o'clock,' he cried, as precisely as if he were back in command of his green devils, the paras. 'See it?'

All their eyes focused on the spot, stomachs suddenly rumbling greedily.

'What are we waiting for?' Hartung cried eagerly, and began to stumble forward.

Von Dodenburg restrained him just in time. 'Hold it, Hartung,' he hissed. 'We don't know who's out there, do we? Let's treat this as a minor tactical problem. We'll split up and come in from both flanks. Degenhardt, you take the right. I'll take the left. We've got our sticks,' he indicated the lengths of wood that most of them carried to support them as they ploughed through the deep snow. 'But if whoever's out there is armed, forget it. We'll steal away like thieves in the night. Come on, let's move out!'

Cautiously, the two little groups of men plodded through the deep snow, battling their way forward against the howling, merciless wind. As they drew closer to the firs, von Dodenburg could see that there had been severe fighting here the previous month. What he had taken for hillocks from far off were burnt-out tanks, both German and American, and shattered half-tracks, mercifully covered by snow.

At the head of his group he pushed his way into the firs, the smell of cooking quite distinct now, and thrust himself through the dense undergrowth. Now the desire to break into a run and get at that food was almost overwhelming; yet at the same time von Dodenburg was restrained by the strange atmosphere of this place. There was something awesome, brooding, even eerie about it.

They crossed a little glade. To their right was a frozen tableau of bodies, friend and foe, heaped indiscriminately together and partly covered by snow, through which poked a bloody stump, a frozen hand, a severed head, the sightless eyes staring at the intruders as if in warning.

A moment later, the first group broke through the trees and stared down at the scene before them in the little valley. It was filled with the wrecked vehicles of what might well have been one of Wotan's columns, caught in the first stages of the great drive west by enemy fighter-bombers. In the middle of a circle of wrecked half-tracks, still filled with ghastly, frozen corpses, crouched a small group of men, tarpaulins strung above them to keep off the snow. A fire was burning, and each man was frying a large hunk of meat on a bayonet above the crackling, spitting flames.

'Holy strawsack,' Grimm breathed. 'I can die happy. They're cooking real, genuine *meat!*'

Von Dodenburg wiped the back of his hand across his wet lips and tried to control the urgent rumbling of his stomach.

There were six of them crouched there, huddled in blankets, towels wrapped around their heads for warmth. He couldn't tell from their uniforms whether they were friend or foe, but evidently they were armed. However, the escapers numbered ten in all; and while they cooked, the strangers had placed their weapons in the shelter of the nearest wrecked half-tracks. If von Dodenburg's men could move quickly enough in their present exhausted state, they could take them. But they mustn't give the men down there a chance to get to their weapons; otherwise there would be a massacre.

Holding his finger to his lips for silence, von Dodenburg indicated by dumb show that the two groups should approach the little camp silently, rushing the men down there as soon as they heard the first noise made by the intruders. They nodded their understanding, and set off, the howl of the wind deadening any sound of their approach. Stealthily they slipped and slithered down the snowy slope to the little camp, their gazes fixed almost hypnotically on the men squatting around their fire, their whole attention concentrated on the frying meat that gave off such a delicious odour . . .

They were less than ten metres away, when one of the group of six turned his head slowly, alerted by some noise or other they had made, and stared at the intruders quite incuriously; his fat, well-fed face unmoved, a dull, almost vacant look in his eyes. Slowly he put down his meat and waited for the escapers to respond.

Suddenly von Dodenburg felt a cold finger of fear trace its way down his spine. There was something strange, very strange, about these men, who now turned slowly to stare at the escapers; something animal and uncanny and very frightening. He raised his stick in warning. But none of them made any attempt to reach for the weapons piled close by under the protection of the shattered half-track. Instead, they just remained seated there on the leather cushions they had taken from the vehicles, roasting their meat, for all the world like a bunch of picnickers on a summer's day in peacetime.

Grimm looked at von Dodenburg, puzzled. 'What do you make of them, von Dodenburg?'

Before Kuno could answer, the one nearest them spoke.

'You like something to eat, gentlemen?' He spoke the German of East Prussia, oddly accented, but German all the same. 'We've got plenty more where this came from.'

The escapers' eyes lit up. Degenhardt chortled. '*Plenty more?* Did you hear that, comrades?' Excited beyond all control now, forgetting the strange, eerie appearance of these Germans lost out here in the white wilderness, they stumbled and slithered the rest of the way into the little camp.

Von Dodenburg trailed after the rest, somehow apprehensive, though why he didn't know. Obviously these men must have been cut off from the rest of the army during the great retreat eastwards in the first two weeks of January, 1945. Now, somehow, they were living off the land, making their way back to Germany on their own. Yet . . .

The East Prussian had now risen to his feet, after first

carefully balancing the bayonet skewered through the meat on a stone near to the fire. He walked through the snow to one of the shattered half-tracks, its rear covered by a tarpaulin, while the others stared after him, a sudden look of wild greed in their hitherto dull eyes.

'I expect you're very hungry, gentlemen,' continued the East Prussian, for all the world like some genial host in a rural inn, wetting his guests' appetite for the feast to come. 'But don't worry; my comrades and I will make sure you get plenty to eat, won't we, boys?'

'Yes,' the others mumbled, eyes fixed on their leader, but hands still busy turning the meat, so that it sizzled and dripped great gobs of fat into the flames, growing golden-brown and appetizingly crisp.

The East Prussian chuckled to himself and picked up a chisel and a hammer, of the kind used to knock in track-pins in the Panzerkorps.

Von Dodenburg frowned, his hunger suddenly vanished now. What did the man need a chisel and hammer for? he wondered. But the other escapers had no such thoughts. Their starved faces were animated now by almost unbearable anticipation, their eyes glittering feverishly, following every move the East Prussian made as he prepared to lift up the tarpaulin.

'Let's see what we can do in the way of a nice, tender piece for each of you, *meine Herren*. I'll do my best – though I can't promise you one hundred per cent satisfaction, naturally. You know the way things are in wartime.' Again, he chuckled in that strange way of his.

Von Dodenburg felt the small hairs at the back of his neck stand erect. Now he knew instinctively that something terrible had happened in this remote snow-bound glade. He swallowed hard and waited for the shock that *had* to come.

The East Prussian threw up the tarpaulin with a flourish and, taking the chisel in his left hand, prepared to use the hammer on it. The escapers crowded forward. He raised the hammer and brought it down hard. Von Dodenburg could hear the chisel rasp on bone. Red tears of blood dripped to the snow. The East Prussian brought down his arm yet once again, the powerful muscles of his back rippling, even through the blanket that covered his shoulder.

Suddenly von Dodenburg gasped with horror as he saw for the first time the source of their 'meat': a wizened middle-aged face, yellow teeth set in a desperate grin for all eternity. *The East Prussian was hammering off the leg of a corpse . . .*

'But they're *cannibals!*' he had exclaimed in outraged horror. 'They've been living off the dead bodies of their comrades for days now, perhaps even weeks . . . You can't—'

But even as he protested, he knew that he had lost them. Almost immediately they had squatted down alongside the blanketed ghouls, picking up abandoned bayonets and setting down to the ghastly business of roasting their 'meat', as the East Prussian proudly bore the naked yellow leg, neatly severed at the thigh, towards the crackling fire.

'*Comrades!*' Von Dodenburg made one last desperate plea. Then, his emaciated body racked by sobs, he fled to the bushes, unable to stand that terrible sight any longer.

For a while that ultimate horror – the sight of his comrades wolfing half-roasted human flesh, the fat trickling down their bearded chins, laughing and chatting, as if they were at some regimental smoker in happier times – had turned him slightly mad. He had seized one of the machine-pistols belonging to the ghouls, threatened to shoot them all there and then, before bursting into tears and staggering away into the howling wilderness, shoulders heaving with great sobs. But finally that bitter cold and the gnawing hunger at the pit of his stomach had brought him to his senses, and he realized with a biting sense of loss that he was alone.

For the first time in nearly six years of war he was without comrades to succour, or to succour *him*. Now, in this great waste of the Ardennes, where the battle which had decided Germany's fate had been fought weeks before, which had echoed to the crack of rifles, the boom of the cannon, the rumble of tracks, the commands, the cries, the pleas of hundreds of thousands of men in khaki and field-grey fighting the greatest battle of World War Two, there seemed nothing but a great, echoing, rushing silence.

Reluctantly von Dodenburg forced himself to begin the ghastly task of searching the snow-covered corpses all around him for the life-saving food he so desperately needed. Finally, after clawing his way through a pile of dead troopers, frozen upright by the icy cold and looking like rotting cabbage-stumps in some winter-abandoned allotment, he found a few crumbs of bread and the gnawed end of a frozen sausage. Without a second thought for the death all around him, he had wolfed it down, feeling the life-giving warmth surging through his emaciated, pain-racked body.

It was then that a single shot rang out, sending up a spurt of snow at his feet, echoing and re-echoing back and forth in the ring of white-clad hills which surrounded him.

In an instant, von Dodenburg was the professional soldier once more, his momentary madness dispelled by the sudden danger. He crouched in the snow, machine-pistol at the ready, surveying the white hills for the first sight of the enemy.

His emaciated, dirty face contorted into a harsh grimace. No doubt it would be some fat Ami rear échélon stallion, out to get himself a souvenir to take back to that New World of theirs – that land which had never heard a shot fired in anger, in which no single wall had shuddered under the blast of bombs, no single pane of glass had been shattered by shrapnel . . .

'Friend,' he whispered, talking to himself now in the manner of all lonely men, 'you've picked the wrong man for your little games.' His finger curled around the trigger of the gun with that well-remembered, expert movement. Although he couldn't see the enemy the advantage was on his side. He knew the Amis by now. It was their style to wait for their Army Air Corps, for their tanks, for their artillery before they attacked. But now it was different. It was man against man. He raised his head cautiously and cupping his free hand around his mouth, cried in English, 'Come on, you American bastard. I'm ready for you!'

His words echoed and re-echoed around the circle of white hills, but there was no answer. Von Dodenburg frowned. 'Am I going crazy?' he asked. 'Did I dream that someone fired at me? He stared down at his feet. No, he hadn't dreamt it. There was the hole the lone bullet had drilled into the snow.

Suddenly he grew angry, his frail, starved body racked by on overwhelming, burning rage. He rose to his feet, exposing himself fully. 'My name is von Dodenburg,' he cried to the hills, skinny chest thrust out proudly. 'Colonel von Dodenburg of SS Assault Regiment Wotan! Whoever you are, and wherever you are, if you want me, come and get me!' He lowered the machine-pistol. 'Well, what are you waiting for?' he screamed, almost hysterical now, little drops of spittle spurting from his lips. *'Come on, you bastards, kill me if you dare!'*

Nothing happened. He might have been completely alone on the face of the earth. Around him, all was silent. The snowy waste was deserted.

Von Dodenburg bit his cracked, snow-burnt lip. He was fantasizing. There had been no shot. He had imagined the hole in the snow. He was going crazy, turned mad by the snow, starvation, and the strain of this terrible march through the snow-bound wilderness. That was it. He must find help at once. Immediately.

Dropping the machine-pistol, he staggered forward, babbling to himself, moaning occasionally, a mad flood of pictures racing across his mind, a whole crazed newsreel of the last six years, screaming now, he blundered through the firs, stumbling over the logs felled during the great offensive. Somehow he clambered to his feet again and carried on, driven by an unreasoning, overwhelming fear that if he didn't keep going, he would never find the help he needed so desperately.

He stepped on a log. Halfway across, it buckled and turned slippery. He tried to keep his balance, waving his arms furiously. To no avail. His legs went from beneath him. He found himself slipping, sliding down a gully, a white wake of snow flying up behind him. He hit a rock with his face and yelled out loud. Something struck his head. The pain shot through him with electric suddenness. Almost as suddenly the madness vanished and he was aware of the agony of his burning head and the danger of his position here, wedged in a tight gully, body half-covered in snow, the firs towering above him.

The machine-pistol! Where was his damned machine-pistol?

Above him, the branches parted. He flashed a look upwards. A little man in green civilian clothes was standing there, staring down at him, hunting rifle clasped defiantly at his hip. A moment later the branches parted again and another civilian appeared, older this time, with a shotgun in his hands. His face too was set in a look of defiance, hate and fear.

'Who are you?' von Dodenburg asked, sitting up, the bark of the tree rough and solid behind his back. 'What do you want from me?'

'They told us about you,' the little man answered, eyes intent, speaking in that strange German of the border area, with its French-sounding intonation. 'You're a big noise in the SS. A colonel, the Amis said. You broke out of one of their camps. You can't deny it. Look at those letters painted on your uniform. "PW" – that means prisoner of war.'

Von Dodenburg forced a smile, though he had never felt less like smiling. He knew he had to disarm these two fools. Still, at least they spoke his language. Nearly half a century before they had been born in Imperial Germany;

they *were* German. They were his own people! 'You're right, friend,' he said, deliberately keeping his voice low and his tone conversational. 'I am indeed Colonel von Dodenburg of the Armed SS, and I have escaped from an Ami POW camp.' He stretched out one hand slowly. 'Perhaps you could help me out of the mess I'm in. It's good to be among friends, at—'

The words died on his lips. The older man raised his shot-gun threateningly. 'Don't move!' he barked. 'Stay where you are. The Americans will be here soon. But don't you dare move, or it'll be the worse for you.'

Von Dodenburg swallowed hard and dropped his arm slowly. 'But what have you against me?' he asked. 'You are as German as I am. We are fellow-countrymen.'

The little man dared a look at his companion, keeping his finger on the trigger as he did so. 'He's right there, Peter,' he said. 'We served the Kaiser once, too, at Verdun and on the Somme and in the Argonne towards the end, you know . . .'

The older man shook his head, his face set and determined. 'We're not his kind of German, Otto,' he said through gritted teeth. 'No – we're not like those murdering swines of the SS. We know what kind of soldiers they are, murdering little children and raping women, and worse . . . No, Otto, we were never like that . . .' He swung the shotgun round threateningly, tears suddenly running down his honest peasant face. 'Never. *Never!*'

Suddenly von Dodenburg recalled Hartung's bitter words: '*The alibi of the German nation, that's what we'll be, comrades*' – and he was filled with a burning, all-consuming rage at the injustice of it all.

'What the hell do you mean, you old fool?' he yelled up at the two civilians. 'Do you know what it was like out there in Russia? Do you think we were there for the shitting glory, the medals, the parades? No – we were fighting our arses off for you: for fat-gutted civilians like you, who could sit at home around their warm fires, with their beer and sausage, rubbing their full bellies, fucking their wives, stroking their children and going to church on Sunday full of fake, pious sanctity!' Von Dodenburg's face contorted with wolfish fanaticism. 'What do you know of our war – the way we fought and died? *For you*, for two fat, moralizing peasant pigs, scared of their own shadows!'

Suddenly he managed to scramble to his feet, and stood swaying there in the gully, staring up at them a look of utter contempt on his flushed, crazed face. 'All right, then, peasants – shoot me if you dare! Come on! Have done with it! The Amis will probably give you a couple of cans of corned beef as a reward for shooting the notorious SS Colonel von Dodenburg.' He grabbed hold of the nearest bough, his mouth contorted in a bitter smile. 'Well, what are you waiting for, you hypocrites? *Shoot!* Think back to '40 when we first came, you didn't deliver lectures then, did you? Oh no!' He tested the bough; it would bear his weight. 'You welcomed us with flowers and Heil Hitlers and treated us like liberators.' He grunted and reached up. 'We weren't the black devils of the SS, then. Then we were the German comrades who had delivered you from the foreign yoke—'

'No!' the older man shrieked. *'Don't move any further! Stay where you are!'*

But now von Dodenburg was beyond all caring; he listened no longer, carried away by the burning injustice of it all. 'Did you hiss us when our battalions marched through St Vith . . . Eupen . . . Malmedy?* Naturally you didn't. Oh no, my fat peasant friends, you—'

The older man jerked the trigger of his shotgun, carried away by fear and anger. At that range he couldn't miss. It erupted violently in his podgy, work-worn hands. The blast exploded in von Dodenburg's face, the impact at such short distance whirling him round.

Bone splintered. Blood splattered the snow in thick, red gobs. The urine of fear and shock flooded von Dodenburg's trousers, as his slug-riddled body was flung against the wall of snow. Helplessly, trying to fight off the red mist that

* Former German towns, now Belgian.

threatened to engulf him at any moment, von Dodenburg slithered back into the gully. The last thing he saw was the tear-stained face of the man who had shot him as he dropped the shotgun from his nerveless fingers; then he blacked out. Colonel Kuno von Dodenburg, the last commander of SS Assault Regiment Wotan, had fought – and lost – his last battle . . .

ENVOI

It is now nearly forty years since the trial of ex-Colonel von Dodenburg, held by the Americans at the former German concentration camp of Dachau. At the time it was something of a *cause célèbre*, and raised violent emotions in both Europe and America. Among his former friends and foes, there were those who thought that he had been framed; that just like Peiper, Dietrich and all the rest of the SS *prominenz* who were tried with him, he had been accused of 'war crimes' in order to salve the conscience of the rest of the German people and allow them to get on with the business of achieving the 'economic miracle' and of making Germany safe for something called 'Western democracy'. Soon it would become the Federal Republic of Germany; to be followed almost immediately by the creation of the German Democratic Republic, created by the equally loyal and industrious subjects of the Russian conquerors in the eastern half of the divided country.

On April 10th, 1946, Von Dodenburg had been sentenced to death for war crimes. But the outburst of violent rioting that occurred in Southern Germany at this verdict was conveniently (for the American occupiers) silenced almost immediately by his astonishing escape during a thunderstorm, only days before he was due to die by hanging. The US Army censors clamped a total ban on the newly-licensed German newspapers, and Eisenhower secretly ordered that no attempt should be made to find the fugitive; it would be better that way. Already it was known to US Intelligence that the SS had organized an escape-route for wanted SS criminals known as the 'B-B Line' which took the fugitives from Bolzano to Bari in Southern Italy, where they were shipped to South America, there presumably to rot in the tropical jungles of Brazil or

Bolivia. As Eisenhower remarked to his chief-of-staff the morning that the great escape was reported to him at his HQ in Frankfurt's IG Farben skyscraper, 'Let the bastard run. That way we can sweep him under the carpet. For all I'm concerned, he can drink himself to death in one of those goddam greaser banana republics.'

But Kuno von Dodenburg hadn't been abducted by the mysterious SS escape organization known as the 'Spider'; nor was he fated to drink himself to death in one of those Central American republics, whose tinpot dictators so admired the late Adolf Hitler and granted asylum to those of his Black Band still on the run from the '*gringos*'.

Kuno von Dodenburg's escape from Landsberg Prison had been engineered by one man only: ex-Sergeant-Major Schulze, the big Hamburger, who had survived those last terrible five months of war in the East and had emerged from the débâcle of May 1945 unscathed. Sick to death of the fighting and determined never to take a weapon in his big, capable hands again, he hadn't forgotten his old CO – even in the heady atmosphere of Hamburg's flourishing black market, of which he had become for a short while the uncrowned king. Not even the brothel, which he ran so successfully – where, naturally, he delighted in 'checking out' every new girl – could distract him from his sworn task of freeing his beloved ex-colonel from execution.

Now nearly three months had passed since Schulze had slung an exhausted von Dodenburg over his shoulder like a mere babe and scrambled up that rope ladder, with the whistles shrilling and the cries of alarm growing ever fainter behind him. For a month he had hidden his ex-CO in his brothel, presided over by the 'Belgian Mare', who had nursed the gravely ill von Dodenburg back to health with loving care.

One day soon after, a beaming Schulze had entered his sick room with a completely naked, giggling blonde, all of fifteen years old. 'Sir,' he had barked, snapping to attention as in the old days, that same cheeky grin on his broad face that von Dodenburg remembered from the first time they had met in what seemed another age now. 'Storm-man Schulze reporting, sir, all present and correct. Beg permission to offer you lunch, sir. Never been done, tight as a drum, straight from the country, with the straw still sticking out of her arse.'

'What do you mean, Schulze?' von Dodenburg had stuttered, sitting bolt upright in his bed.

'You're cured, sir, that's what I mean. Thought you might like this delicate little tit-bit to celebrate. Better than all the Belgian Mare's hot broths. And I can swear on a stack of Bibles that this little filly ain't been ridden by any of our noble occupiers, have you, my little cheetah?'

The girl simply giggled.

Thereafter Kuno von Dodenburg's health had improved rapidly. He had grown strong again. His skinny frame had started to fill out, and the scars that now marked his face for ever no longer seemed to be so prominent – all thanks to Schulze's mighty efforts on the black market. Slowly von Dodenburg became restless, wandering nervously around the house when none of the Belgian Mare's guests in khaki with their damned coffee-beans and bars of milk chocolate were present. In the end, Schulze had cornered him and asked with all the brisk realism of his newly-acquired status as a big businessman, 'Sir, what *are* we going to do with you?'

'What do you mean?'

'Well, sir, the way I see it, there'd be a lot of the lads from the old Wotan who would have given their right arms to spend the rest of their lives in a whorehouse with as much to eat and sup as they wanted. But not you.'

'But they're long dead,' von Dodenburg reminded the ex-sergeant-major softly.

Schulze didn't seem to hear. 'So, sir, I think we ought to set you off across the frontier. It's the only way.'

'You mean south?'

Schulze nodded.

Twenty-four hours later, von Dodenburg had made his decision; he would try to start a new life.

Now the two of them marched up the lush mountain slopes that marked the frontier between Bavaria and Austria marked by the debris of a war already fading from the memory.

At midday Schulze called a halt. In the silence, broken only by the lazy hum of the bumble bees in the bright red flowers which filled the drainage ditches on both sides of the lane, they ate sandwiches and sipped cold tea in the shade of a Royal Tiger, metallic holes skewered in its side, indicating how it had met its end over a year before.

Von Dodenburg was in a talkative mood. The knowledge that he would soon be leaving his native country for good put him in a strangely reflective frame of mind. Sipping from his bottle of cold peppermint tea, he wandered round the huge tank, noting the fading divisional sign – a springing greyhound. 'The Greyhounds, Schulze,' he commented. 'They were with us when we fought at Aachen in '44.'

'A long time ago, sir,' Schulze said, his mouth full of bread and sausage.

'Yes, a long time ago, as you say.' Von Dodenburg paused in his aimless inspection, bronzed face scarred, no longer so handsome or so confident as it had been in the good days. 'And bad times . . . Yet, you know, Schulze, they were somehow good, too. We had a sense of importance then, of doing something purposeful. Remember all those young greenbeaks? How they use to flock to Wotan, almost fighting for the honour of being shipped off to Russia or some other God-forsaken spot to have their turnips shot off?' His sombre face flushed suddenly with the memory, his eyes sparkling with momentary enthusiasm.

Schulze paused in mid-bite, the sweat running down his broad, honest red face. 'Shall I tell you something, sir? Straight from the liver?' He pointed his half-eaten sandwich at von Dodenburg like a weapon. 'I had my fun in the war – the whores, the larks, the sauce, the good pals and all the rest of it. But I paid my price for them in blood and misery.

We all did in Wotan. The butcher's bill came pretty damn high, I can say that . . . Remember that old Sergeant Gierig, of the First Battalion? On the December 15th, 1944, just before the offensive started, he told me that if he bought it, I could have his leather jacket. So what happens as soon as he copped one and croaked? I'll tell yer. The first thing I said was, "Where's the shitting leather jacket?" I didn't ask how he died or anything. All I was concerned about was that jacket. That's the way we all were *then*. Heartless. Because our lives were worth about as much as that heap of shit over there in the meadow.' He paused and finished his sandwich in one angry gulp. 'We lost the war, sir. It's all over now.' He looked at his CO, standing in the dark shadow cast by the tank. 'And in a way I'm glad that we lost it.'

For what seemed a long time the two of them faced each other on the Bavarian meadow, frozen into sudden stillness. A profound emotional change seemed to have come over them, destroying all that six years of war had built up: that feeling of comradeship, the jokes shared, the hard times, the good times, the whores, the booze-ups, that sense of utter dependence upon one another that was unlike any other human relationship on this earth. Then Kuno von Dodenburg shook his head, blinking in the sun like a man waking up from a very deep sleep. The past was dead. The man squatting on his haunches in front of him was a virtual stranger. Wordlessly, he turned and started walking up to the peak which marked the frontier with Italy and the beginning of a new life. Schulze hesitated and then, with a shrug, he followed.

Two hours later they reached their destination, the line of half-buried stones that formed the frontier. Down below, the night shadows were beginning to slide into the valley. Faintly, the two men could hear the melodic tinkle of the cowbells on the high pasture. Otherwise all was silent.

'Well, Schulze, this is the end of a very long road.' Von

Dodenburg hesitated and made a last attempt. 'You can still change your mind, you big rogue,' he said, 'and come with me.'

Schulze shook his head. 'No, sir. I don't want to come with you.' He stuck out his hand.

For a moment von Dodenburg didn't take it. Instead he pointed to the darkening valley below. 'That down there, Schulze, that corrupt, new, conquered Germany, isn't worth dying for. You know that, don't you?'

Schulze shrugged, avoiding his former CO's eye for the first time since they had known each other. 'You might be right, sir, I suppose. But one day there might be a Germany down there worth *living* for, don't you think?'

Kuno von Dodenburg's scarred face hardened. In stony silence, he took Schulze's hand and pressed it for the last time. But without warmth. Silently he swung round and walked the last few paces to the peak, his head full of the harsh stamp of many boots and that brave, bold marching song of so long ago:

'Clear the street, the SS marches,
The storm-columns stand at the ready.
They will take the road
From tyranny to freedom.
So we are all ready to give our all,
As did our fathers before us.
Let death be our battle companion,
We are the Black Band . . .'

And then he was over the peak, leaving Schulze to the future, gone for ever.

SS Assault Regiment Wotan was dead at last.

bienvenue à Pa[...]

Bonjour ! Je m'appe[...]
Le photographe, là-ha[...]ère Martin, il a 10 ans.
Tous les deux, nous so[...]s à Paris.
C'est la capitale de la France.
C'est aussi la ville la plus visitée au monde.
Tu veux savoir pourquoi ?
Alors, suis-nous ! On va s'amuser à la découvrir.
Tu vas voir, elle est extraordinaire !

Et pour faciliter ta lecture,
les mots compliqués, surlignés en rose,
sont expliqués dans le lexique p. 59.

Quelques repères...

Il y en a des choses à voir et à faire à Paris. Voici déjà un plan pour mieux te repérer. Maintenant, on peut y aller.

La Villette
Montmartre
18e
17e
19e
Canal Saint-Martin
Moulin-Rouge
8e
9e
Buttes-Chaumont
Opéra
Centre Pompidou
10e
Haussmann
Bd Haussmann
Concorde
2e
20e
Louvre
3e
1er
Notre-Dame
11e
Père Lachaise
4e
Bastille
Assemblée Nationale
6e
Orsay
la Seine
5e
12e
Parc du Luxembourg
Jardin des plantes
Bois de Vincennes
Tour Montparnasse
13e
14e
Chinatown

Paname

Il y a longtemps Paris ne s'appelait pas Paris. On lui a aussi donné plusieurs surnoms. Regardons cela de plus près !

JEU *Bon, pour ne pas faire trop simple quand même, les noms et les légendes ont été mélangés. Sauras-tu les remettre en ordre ?*

LA VILLE LUMIÈRE

A

LUTÈCE

B

PANAME

C

Ce drôle de nom apparaît au début du 20e siècle. Sans doute parce que, à cette période, de nombreux Parisiens portaient un chapeau de paille appelé **"panama"**. *Il avait été mis à la mode par des ouvriers pour se protéger du soleil alors qu'ils creusaient un tunnel au... Panama (en Amérique centrale).*

Cette expression date du 17e siècle. Tout simplement parce que Paris a été la première ville à installer des **lampadaires** *dans toutes les rues. À cette époque, ce n'était pas pour faire joli, mais pour repérer dans la nuit les nombreux brigands qui allaient et venaient dans Paris.*

La ville portait ce nom en – 50 avant Jésus-Christ. Les Romains avaient alors envahi la Gaule (l'ancien nom de la France). Le nom de Paris est apparu en 310, en souvenir des tout premiers habitants, les **Parisii**.

Alors, tu as trouvé ? On dit aussi que Paris est la capitale de la mode, de la gastronomie et même la plus belle ville du monde.

Escargot rigolo

Paris, c'est grand, et depuis longtemps. Alors, en 1860, pour mieux se repérer et s'organiser, la ville a été découpée en 20 arrondissements (des sortes de grands quartiers). C'est encore vrai aujourd'hui.

Regarde sur le dessin, ils s'enroulent en forme d'escargot autour de la Seine et du centre de la ville. Quand tu te promènes, observe bien les plaques de rues. Elles indiquent toujours l'arrondissement dans lequel tu te trouves.

JEU *Suis les indices pour savoir dans quel arrondissement se situe Martin ?*

- *La Seine n'y passe pas*
- *C'est un arrondissement à 2 chiffres*
- *Il est plus petit que le 17e*
- *Il est au nord du 5e*
- *Il ne touche pas au 12e*

La Seine

La Seine, c'est notre fleuve. Elle traverse le centre de Paris sur 13 km et sépare la ville en deux : **la rive droite** (au nord de la Seine) et **la rive gauche** (au sud). Heureusement, **37 ponts** permettent de passer d'un côté à l'autre.

Paris en scène

C'est **autour de la Seine** que la ville de Paris s'est construite il y a très très longtemps. Car, un fleuve, c'était bien pratique pour se déplacer et faire circuler les marchandises. Et c'est sur **l'île de la Cité** que les premiers habitants ont bâti leur maison, parce que la Seine permettait aussi de se protéger des ennemis. Depuis, quel succès ! Il suffit de compter les monuments qui bordent la Seine. Une grande partie de l'histoire de Paris s'y raconte.

JEU

TROCADÉRO, MUSÉE D'ORSAY, NOTRE-DAME, GRAND PALAIS, CONCIERGERIE, TOUR EIFFEL, LOUVRE, INVALIDES

Retrouve dans la grille tous ces monuments situés près de la Seine.

G	T	O	U	O	T	R	E	D
R	A	N	R	N	S	U	M	A
C	O	D	E	I	E	E	T	M
L	N	P	I	F	F	D	R	E
O	C	A	N	V	E	O	O	C
U	I	L	A	A	L	R	S	A
V	E	S	I	L	■	■	A	D
R	R	G	E	I	■	■	Y	E
E	E	I	R	D	E	S	O	R

*Comme dans l'exemple, les mots peuvent se lire dans tous les sens, mais ATTENTION, chaque lettre ne sert qu'**une seule** fois.*

Pour découvrir Paris depuis la Seine, rien ne vaut une balade en bateau-mouche. Nous, on adore ! Attention, ces bateaux ne volent pas. On leur a tout simplement donné ce nom car, à l'origine, ils étaient fabriqués dans le quartier de la Mouche à Lyon.

JEU

La Seine abrite trois îles : **l'île Saint-Louis, l'île de la Cité** *(où se trouve Notre-Dame de Paris) et une troisième qui est souvent oubliée :* **l'île aux Cygnes.**
Bien qu'elle mesure seulement 11 mètres de large, elle est cependant réputée pour sa version miniature d'une célèbre statue. Devines-tu laquelle ?

1
La statue de Neptune
(Dieu de la mer)

Car il y a très longtemps la mer arrivait jusqu'à Paris.

2
La statue de Tintin

Parce que le roi Louis XIV, à 5 ans, adorait déjà la bande-dessinée

3
La statue de la Liberté

En hommage à Auguste Bartholdi, le créateur français de la statue de la Liberté, à New York.

Qui l'eût cru ?

Il arrive que le niveau d'eau de la Seine monte très haut. On dit alors qu'elle est en crue, et elle peut parfois inonder les quais de Paris. Pour la surveiller, les Parisiens observent la statue du zouave, pont de l'Alma. En temps normal, ses pieds sont au sec. Quand ils sont dans l'eau, c'est qu'il y a une crue. En 1910, lors de la dernière plus grande crue, le zouave avait de l'eau jusqu'aux épaules !

Notre-Dame de Paris

Ce nom te dit quelque chose ? Évidemment. C'est le titre d'un roman du **grand écrivain français, Victor Hugo.** Il raconte l'aventure d'une gitane, *Esmeralda*. L'histoire se passe autour de la cathédrale Notre-Dame de Paris, au 15e siècle.

Mais tu connais sans doute encore mieux le dessin animé qui s'en inspire et met en scène le personnage de **Quasimodo, "le bossu de Notre-Dame".**

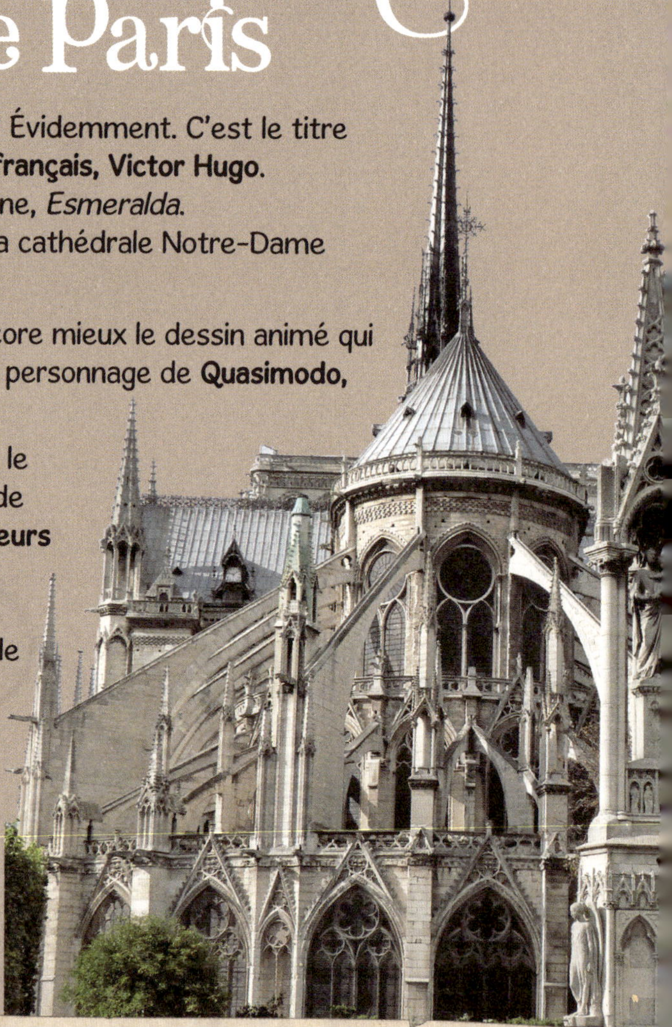

Notre-Dame est le monument le plus visité de France, et donc de Paris ! Avec **13 millions de visiteurs chaque année,** elle vole même la vedette à la tour Eiffel. Il faut dire que cette cathédrale de style gothique est tout simplement magnifique.

C'est en 1163 que l'évêque de Paris, Maurice de Sully, *se lance dans cette grande aventure : construire à Paris une cathédrale à la hauteur de la capitale de la France. Un immense chantier qui va durer* **environ 300 ans !** *Des sculpteurs, des tailleurs de pierre, des charpentiers, des maçons sont venus de toute la France pour y travailler.*

Le résultat est impressionnant : du haut de ses **90 mètres,** *Notre-Dame de Paris domine toute l'île de la Cité.*

Dessine d'effrayants visages à ces gargouilles.

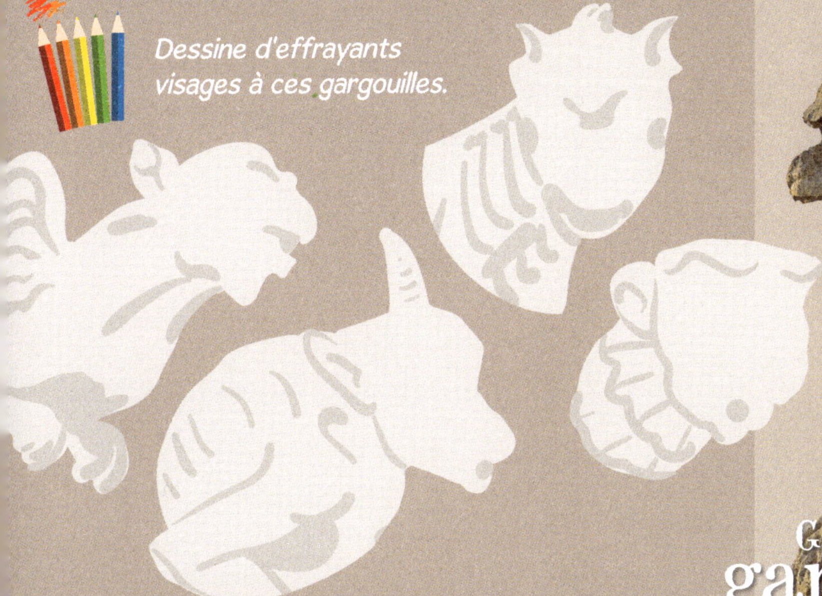

Gare aux gargouilles

En levant bien la tête, tu vas découvrir de drôles de statues. Ce sont les gargouilles. Elles servent à évacuer l'eau de pluie des gouttières et, comme elles dépassent dans le vide, cela empêche de noircir les murs de la cathédrale.

En tout cas, les sculpteurs se sont bien amusés, car les statues représentent des animaux ou des personnages un peu étranges. Parfois, ils font même presque peur !

Emmanuel le bourdon

La tour sud (celle de droite quand tu es face à la cathédrale) renferme un énorme bourdon. C'est le nom que l'on donne à une grosse cloche à son grave. Celle-ci **pèse 13 tonnes.** On l'appelle aussi "Emmanuel". Elle sonne pour les grandes fêtes comme Noël ou Pâques.

JEU *Termine les 2 dernières cloches en suivant la suite logique.*

Bon appétit !

Si tu aimes bien manger, tu vas être servi.
Notre ville est surtout connue pour ses brasseries aux décors traditionnels. Pour en profiter, fais une pause au "Bouillon" Chartier. Cette brasserie est ouverte depuis 1896 ! Tu vas nous dire, c'est quoi le "Bouillon" ? C'était le nom que l'on donnait au 19e siècle aux restaurants qui proposaient aux ouvriers un plat de viande et un bouillon à petit prix. Aujourd'hui, chez Chartier, c'est encore très bon marché (la soupe est à 1 euro). Ton addition sera même calculée directement au crayon, sur ta nappe en papier. Nous, ça nous amuse.

Garçon !

C'est une image immanquable de la vie parisienne : le garçon de café. Ce serveur, qui parcourt des kilomètres dans une journée, se remarque à sa tenue noir et blanc très stylée.

JEU

*Peux-tu aider Martin à choisir un menu à 15 euros **exactement** ?*

ENTRÉES
POTAGE DU JOUR MAISON 1,00
AVOCAT SAUCE CREVETTES 2,50
POIREAUX VINAIGRETTE 3,50

PLATS
STEAK HACHÉ FRITES 8,50
BOUDIN NOIR PURÉE MAISON 9,00
SPAGHETTIS BOLOGNAISE 8,50

FROMAGES
CAMEMBERT 2,50
FROMAGE DE CHÈVRE 2,50

DESSERT
ANANAS FRAIS 4,00
CHOU CHANTILLY 3,50
CRÈME DE MARRON VANILLÉE 3,00

Sur le zinc

Attention, il faut prononcer "zingue". Mais que signifie ce mot un peu dingue ? Le zinc est un métal mais, dans le langage populaire, il désigne le comptoir d'un bar recouvert de ce métal (même si en fait les comptoirs sont souvent en étain). On en trouve plein dans les bistrots parisiens.

Au Petit Zinc, 18 rue de Moscou

JEU

À midi, c'est la course ici !
Peux-tu aider cette serveuse à terminer ses additions ?

Le Louvre Au palais des merveilles

Un musée dans un palais de rois.

Avant d'être un musée, le Louvre était un château fort bâti pour défendre Paris. Plus tard, François 1er en a fait une immense et magnifique résidence pour les rois de France. Après la Révolution (1789-1799), le Louvre est transformé en musée. En le visitant, n'oublie pas que tu te promènes dans un palais !

Une pyramide de verre

Non, elle ne vient pas d'Égypte. Elle a été créée par *Ieoh Ming Pei*, un architecte d'origine chinoise, pour mieux situer le Louvre et l'entrée du musée. La nuit, avec ses centaines de losanges et rectangles de verre, elle ressemble à un grand diamant brillant.

JEU

En effectuant le petit calcul ci-dessous, tu découvriras la date de création de la Pyramide du Louvre.

Le résultat de chaque case correspond à l'addition des 2 cases du dessous.

La Victoire de Samothrace

Cette magnifique statue de marbre date de l'Antiquité grecque.
Elle a été découverte sur l'île de Samothrace, (d'où son nom).
Lorsqu'on l'a retrouvée, elle avait déjà perdu sa tête. Dommage !
Elle représente Niké, la déesse messagère de la victoire.

35 000 œuvres !

Peintures, sculptures, balades en Grèce et en Égypte... Depuis l'Antiquité jusqu'en 1848, tu peux parcourir une très grande partie de l'histoire de l'art. Et surtout admirer de fabuleux chefs-d'œuvre. Tu en connais certainement déjà quelques-uns.
Le Louvre, c'est un sacré programme de visites. Il faudra sans doute que tu y reviennes plusieurs fois. Cela tombe bien, l'entrée est gratuite pour toi.

JEU

Que de monde autour de la star du musée ! Difficile d'apercevoir cette fameuse jeune femme peinte par **Léonard de Vinci**. *Mais à propos, connais-tu le nom de ce célèbre tableau ?*

la ☐ ☐ ☐ ☐ ☐ ☐ ☐

N — la 3ème lettre avant la fin

O — après le J

O — au milieu

C — entre les O

E — à la fin

D — entre le N et le E

J — la 1ère lettre

Une idée bienvenue*

> * Bien vu Monsieur Bienvenüe !
> On dit que c'est le « papa » du métro parisien. C'est lui qui a imaginé le premier réseau. Normal donc qu'une station porte son nom à Montparnasse.

Le métro parisien existe depuis 1900.
Aujourd'hui, 14 lignes et 217 km de réseaux te transportent dans les quatre coins de Paris. Mais avant, quel chantier ! Imagine qu'il a fallu percer de gigantesques tunnels et retirer du sous-sol des tonnes et des tonnes de terre. On a même creusé sous la Seine. Les ouvriers qui l'ont fait ne sont plus là, mais ils pourraient être fiers : plus de 4 millions de voyageurs utilisent le métro chaque jour.

JEU

Trouve le meilleur trajet pour aller de la ***gare Montparnasse*** *au* ***musée du Louvre****.*

Sais-tu pourquoi les quais de métro sont recouverts de carrelage blanc ?

Tout simplement parce que, en 1900, l'éclairage y était trop faible (impossible de lire son journal). Du coup, on a choisi le blanc pour faire ressortir la lumière.

Trop beau le métro !

Vers 1900, à l'époque de l'Art nouveau*, l'architecte **Hector Guimard** a imaginé la décoration des entrées de stations de métro. Les plus belles, avec leur verrière, font penser à des libellules. On en trouve encore deux à Paris : une à la station **Porte Dauphine,** l'autre à la station **Abbesses.**

Comme sur l'exemple, imagine à ton tour d'autres décors de style Art nouveau.

*
Hector Guimard était un représentant de l'Art nouveau.

Ce style s'inspire de la nature. Ses modèles sont des fleurs, des feuilles, des animaux... C'est un art décoratif souvent composé de lignes courbes.

Regarde bien cette entrée de station de métro, c'est comme si le mot « métropolitain » était porté par deux tiges de fleurs !

La tour Eiffel

La tour Eiffel est la construction la plus haute de la capitale. On la voit de presque partout. Elle est aussi la vraie star de Paris. Chaque année, **7 millions de visiteurs** s'y pressent pour monter au sommet de la ville.
Petit tour autour de cette incroyable Tour.

Il a gagné !

1889. Cent ans après la Révolution française, Paris organise une **immense exposition** où sont invités les pays du monde entier. Chacun d'entre eux peut présenter ses réalisations ou ses inventions.

À Paris, trois années plus tôt, **on lance un grand concours** pour savoir quelle œuvre va représenter la France. Et le vainqueur, parmi 700 projets, est l'ingénieur Gustave Eiffel (et son équipe). Son idée ? Une immense tour de fer !

Un grand « savoir-fer »

Commencée en 1887, la Tour, qui prend le nom de son inventeur, est construite en 2 ans, 2 mois et 5 jours. Pour cela, on a dû assembler 15 000 pièces de fer et utiliser 2,5 millions de rivets enfoncés au marteau, manuellement. Un vrai travail de précision et d'acrobatie.

Tous les 7 ans, la tour Eiffel se refait une beauté. Il faut une année et 60 tonnes de peinture pour la recouvrir des pieds à la tête.

Là-haut, par beau temps, tu peux voir jusqu'à 50 kilomètres à la ronde.

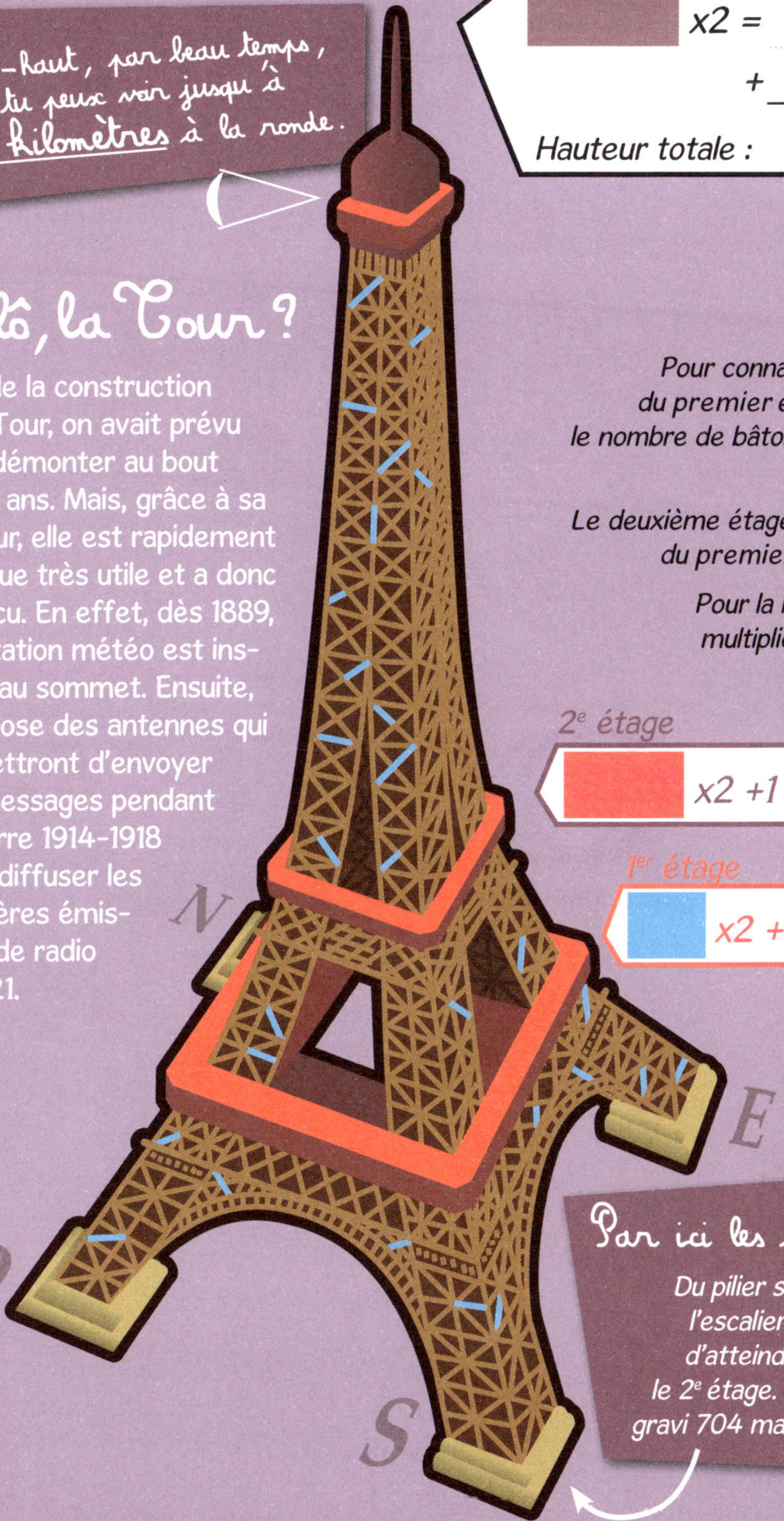

Allô, la Tour ?

Lors de la construction de la Tour, on avait prévu de la démonter au bout de 20 ans. Mais, grâce à sa hauteur, elle est rapidement devenue très utile et a donc survécu. En effet, dès 1889, une station météo est installée au sommet. Ensuite, on y pose des antennes qui permettront d'envoyer des messages pendant la guerre 1914-1918 et de diffuser les premières émissions de radio en 1921.

x2 =

\+ 94

Hauteur totale : m

JEU

Pour connaître la hauteur du premier étage, multiplie le nombre de bâtons bleus par 2, puis ajoute 1.

Le deuxième étage fait le double du premier, plus 1 mètre.

Pour la hauteur totale, multiplie encore par 2 et ajoute 94.

2e étage

x2 +1 = m

1er étage

x2 +1 = m

Par ici les sportifs !

Du pilier sud démarre l'escalier qui permet d'atteindre le 1er puis le 2e étage. Là, tu auras gravi 704 marches. Ouf !

Une place en or !

Place au luxe !

Ici, place Vendôme, tu vas trouver tous les prestigieux magasins de bijoux : **Chaumet, Boucheron, Cartier, Van Cleef & Arpels...** Ces grands noms de la joaillerie font briller cette place entourée de multiples hôtels particuliers datant du 18e siècle.

Elle accueille d'autres célèbres habitants : **le Ritz** (un fameux hôtel 5 étoiles, au n° 15) et **le ministère de la Justice** (au n° 11) ont élu domicile ici.
Au centre, une colonne immanquable de 44 mètres de haut : la colonne Vendôme. C'est Napoléon 1er qui la fit construire pour commémorer la bataille d'Austerlitz.

Bien sûr, c'est lui qui se trouve en haut de la colonne.

JEU

Les noms de ces quatre pierres précieuses ont été mélangés. Sauras-tu les replacer ?

la Mode

C'est sûr, Paris est la capitale de la mode. Les grandes maisons de **haute couture** sont installées ici depuis longtemps. La haute couture, ce sont les vêtements de luxe créés par de grands couturiers. Ils sont très doués. Chaque année, pour chaque grande saison (automne-hiver et printemps-été), ils imaginent une collection de nouveaux modèles qui vont déterminer la mode à venir. **Yves Saint-Laurent, Dior, Hermès, Jean-Paul Gaultier**... Ces grands noms de la mode font connaître la France dans le monde entier.

JEU

A C E H L N O

En suivant le code de ces silhouettes, tu découvriras le nom d'une célèbre créatrice qui a marqué l'histoire de la mode en France.

Et pour les futur(e)s stylistes !
1900, 1930, 1950, 1960, 1970, 1980, 2013
Essaie de retrouver la bonne année sous chaque silhouette.
(tu peux demander de l'aide à papa ou maman !)

Le Pari(s) du baron Haussmann

Nous sommes en 1850. La population de Paris augmente rapidement, les quartiers vieillissent et des épidémies apparaissent. Il faut faire quelque chose. Napoléon III décide de faire appel au **baron Haussmann**. Celui-ci se presse de transformer et d'embellir Paris. En fait, il démolit tout.

D'abord, il remplace **20 000 bâtiments insalubres** par des nouveaux, plus modernes. Il fait aussi percer de très grands boulevards. En te promenant du côté du boulevard des Capucines, par exemple, tu peux encore observer le résultat de cet immense chantier.

Le baron Haussmann a maintenant un boulevard qui porte son nom. Il se trouve à la fois dans le 8e et le 9e arrondissement.

JEU

Trouveras-tu les dix chats cachés dans cette image ?

Géants, les magasins !

Question magasins, Paris, c'est un paradis. D'autant que certains sont vraiment très grands. C'est grâce à **Monsieur Boucicaut**. En 1852, il a eu l'idée d'agrandir (énormément !) une boutique de mercerie, **le Bon Marché**. Il venait d'inventer le plus grand magasin du monde. Évidemment, d'autres ont eu envie de l'imiter. Quelques années plus tard, **la Samaritaine, le BHV, le Printemps, les Galeries Lafayette** ouvrent sur les boulevards parisiens. Ces immenses magasins de vêtements, de parfums, d'articles pour la maison existent toujours aujourd'hui. Avec leurs magnifiques décorations, ce sont aussi de vrais monuments.

Les belles Galeries Lafayette du boulevard Haussmann

JEU *Trouve les 3 ours qui n'ont pas leur jumeau.*

À Noël, les vitrines de ces magasins deviennent féeriques !

C'est pour rire !

Paris, c'est le royaume des théâtres. On en compte environ 200. Pour se distraire, les Parisiens aiment bien se rendre dans les **cafés-théâtres**. Ce sont de toutes petites salles où l'on assiste à des sketchs et des spectacles comiques.

Et puis, il y a le **théâtre de boulevard**. Il désigne des pièces qui veulent d'abord divertir les spectateurs. Elles enchaînent des quiproquos pour s'amuser de nos petits tracas. Au 19e siècle, ce genre de théâtre se jouait boulevard du Temple, puis sur les Grands Boulevards. Son nom, théâtre de boulevard, vient de là.

JEU

Découvre en déchiffrant ce code un des plus célèbres auteurs de théâtre de boulevard.

en haut de l'affiche !

Tous les jours, à Paris, des dizaines de concerts sont proposés. Il y en a pour tous les styles musicaux. Évidemment, la ville est remplie de salles de spectacles. Mais il y en a une un peu à part. Elle s'appelle l'Olympia. On dit que c'est un music-hall mythique.

Il est tellement réputé que l'on ne dit pas chanter à l'Olympia mais "faire l'Olympia". **Les Beatles, Jacques Brel, Édith Piaf, les Rolling Stones** ou encore **Lady Gaga** ont, par exemple, fait l'Olympia.

Souvent, les artistes y font leurs adieux.

JEU *Si tu regardes seulement les traits roses, tu découvriras une célèbre chanson d' Édith Piaf.*

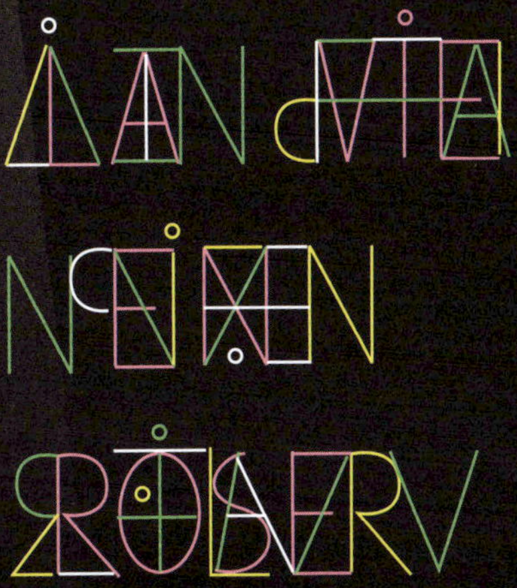

LE SAVAIS-TU ?

Celle que l'on surnommait "la Môme Piaf" à ses débuts, a souvent fait l'Olympia. La petite histoire raconte que, pour aider le music-hall, elle donna la recette de plusieurs de ses concerts.

Merci pour les raccourcis !

Au début des années 1800, une belle invention voit le jour à Paris : **les passages couverts**.
Les passages couverts ? Ce sont un peu les galeries commerciales du 19e siècle. Percés à travers les immeubles, ils offraient de vrais raccourcis pour passer d'un boulevard à l'autre. Et les Parisiens étaient bien contents de pouvoir flâner au calme, à l'abri du mauvais temps, et à l'écart des rues boueuses. Dans ces petites rues coiffées de verrières, ils pouvaient profiter de toutes sortes de boutiques : des librairies, des épiceries, des bijouteries, des caves à vin... Les passages étaient même éclairés et chauffés au gaz.

JEU

Mais que peut bien dire cette jeune femme ? Remplace chaque lettre par celle qui la précède dans l'alphabet. B=A, C=B,...

DF DIBQFBV FUBJU-JM
HBMFSJF WJWJFOOF PV
QBTTBHF KPVGGSPZ ?

Jusqu'au milieu du 19e siècle, Paris comptait environ cent cinquante passages. Il en reste une vingtaine aujourd'hui. Ce sont de vrais trésors d'architecture. À ne pas manquer, ***la galerie Vivienne et le passage Jouffroy****.*

En avant la musique

Vers 1860, l'empereur **Napoléon III** lance un grand concours. Il veut pour Paris le plus magnifique des opéras. C'est un jeune architecte inconnu, **Charles Garnier**, qui l'emporte. On comprend pourquoi. L'Opéra, que l'on appelle aussi le palais Garnier, est un chef-d'œuvre ! Sa façade, avec ses sculptures décoratives, ses mosaïques, et ses dorures, domine tout un quartier.
Même si tu n'assistes pas à une représentation, ne manque pas une visite de l'intérieur. Tu rentres dans un palais de marbre et d'or.

Haut en couleur

*Dans la salle de spectacle à l'italienne, lève bien la tête. Le plafond est une gigantesque peinture de l'artiste **Marc Chagall**. Sur cette fresque, Chagall a recherché quelle couleur correspondait le mieux à telle ou telle musique ou compositeur. Le bleu, par exemple, représente "La Flûte enchantée" de Mozart.*

Un peu à la manière de Chagall, dessine ce que tu ressens en écoutant ta musique préférée.

de la Grande Arche au Louvre

Départ quartier de la Défense. Ici, se dresse la Grande Arche. Elle a été inaugurée en 1989 pour célébrer le bicentenaire de la Révolution française. Son architecte voulait créer un “arc de triomphe moderne”. Le résultat est grandiose : un immense cube de marbre et d’acier de **110 mètres de côté**. De là, on a une vue imprenable sur l’Histoire. Les monuments et les siècles se suivent **sur une ligne droite de 8 km.** De la Grande Arche à la pyramide du Louvre, en passant par les Champs-Élysées, c’est un véritable défilé !

JEU

Belle perspective, les silhouettes se superposent ! Associe la bonne couleur à chacune d’elles.

l'Obélisque de la Concorde

C'est le plus vieux monument de Paris. Et pourtant, il n'a pas été construit ici. Il se trouvait à l'entrée d'un **temple, en Égypte**, il y a plus de 3 000 ans.

Et puis, au début du 19e siècle, un Français, ***Champollion***, découvre le secret des hiéroglyphes*. En remerciement, l'Égypte offre cette grande colonne en forme d'aiguille à la France.

Un énorme cadeau qui trône au centre de la place de la Concorde depuis 1836.

* Les **hiéroglyphes** sont des écritures utilisées par les Égyptiens au temps des pharaons. Ils étaient composés de petites images ou de symboles.

JEU

Sais-tu de quelle ville d'Égypte vient l'Obélisque ? Pour le savoir, lis de haut en bas les lettres cachées parmi les hiéroglyphes.

aux Champs-Élysées

Tout le monde te le dira, les Champs-Élysées, c'est **"la plus belle avenue du monde".**

Difficile à imaginer aujourd'hui, mais jusqu'au 18e siècle, il y avait bien là des **vrais champs** !

Aujourd'hui, personne ne quitterait Paris sans avoir remonté cette avenue de 2 km qui relie la place de la Concorde à l'Arc de Triomphe. Si tu joues au Monopoly, tu dois aussi savoir que c'est l'une des avenues les plus chères de la capitale. Ce sont donc surtout des entreprises, des grands magasins, des cafés, des cinémas, des banques qui se sont établis ici.

De grands rendez-vous

Le **défilé militaire du 14 Juillet,** jour de notre fête nationale, se déroule ici chaque année. Et, depuis 1975, la dernière étape du **Tour de France cycliste** se termine sur les Champs-Élysées.

JEU

Que dit cette femme à son mari ?
1=A, 2=B, 3=C...

5 14 3 15 18 5 4 9 24

2 15 21 20 9 17 21 5 19

5 20 10 ' 1 18 18 5 20 5...

Sucreries de Paris

Miam, miam,
ça a l'air bon par ici.
C'est normal, on va
maintenant te faire
découvrir nos gourmandises.
Il faut aussi savoir
que dans notre ville,
les pâtissiers et les boulangers
sont souvent des as.

les macarons

Ça, c'est trop bon les macarons ! Ces petits gâteaux ronds moelleux, à base de pâte d'amandes, de blancs d'œufs et de sucre, se plaisent bien dans notre ville. Il y en a pour tous les goûts et de toutes les couleurs. À Paris, tu peux te rendre chez **Ladurée** ou **Pierre Hermé.** Ce sont les princes du macaron.

les glaces Berthillon

Si tu te promènes du côté de l'île Saint-Louis, n'hésite pas à faire une pause chez le glacier Berthillon. Il est installé depuis 1954. Vanille, noisette, caramel au beurre salé, mais aussi pains d'épices ou lavande...
Ici, les parfums s'éclatent.

le Paris-Brest

En 1910, le pâtissier Louis Durand a eu une idée amusante : créer un gâteau **en forme de roue de vélo.** Il voulait célébrer la course cycliste Paris-Brest-Paris. Depuis, cette pâtisserie a fait son chemin.

le palais du Président

Depuis 1873, le palais de l'Élysée est **la résidence du président de la République française.** Il se trouve exactement au 55, de la rue du Faubourg Saint-Honoré, dans le 8e arrondissement, tout près des Champs-Élysées. Le président, qui est élu pour 5 ans, a son bureau au premier étage, en plein milieu du palais. Il peut aussi, s'il le souhaite, habiter à l'Élysée. De toute façon, il ne manque pas de place : cette grande maison compte 365 pièces.

Bien sûr, le palais est habituellement fermé au public, sauf lors des Journées du patrimoine en septembre. Ce week-end-là, il ouvre ses portes et son parc à tous les visiteurs.

Les présidents de la 5e République

DE GAULLE
POMPIDOU
GISCARD-D'ESTAING
MITTERRAND
CHIRAC
SARKOZY
HOLLANDE

JEU

Sais-tu ce qui est organisé pour choisir le président français ? Inscris les noms des présidents dans la grille pour le savoir.

L'Assemblée nationale

Depuis longtemps, les grandes décisions politiques de la France se prennent à Paris. Et notamment à l'Assemblée nationale. C'est ici, dans un grand bâtiment appelé le **Palais-Bourbon**, que se réunissent les députés. Ce sont eux qui votent pour ou contre les lois proposées par le gouvernement. Ils sont exactement 577 et sont élus pour 5 ans. Chaque député représente une circonscription, c'est-à-dire un petit territoire de la France. Près de chez toi, il y a donc un député qui a été élu par les habitants.

*Les députés se réunissent dans une salle en demi-cercle appelée **l'hémicycle**. Lors de leurs discussions, comme ils ne sont pas toujours tous d'accord, c'est parfois très très animé.*

JEU

Repère les 5 anomalies

ASSEMBLÉE NATIONALE

L'Assemblée nationale est aussi une petite ville de 3 000 habitants avec son bureau de poste, sa buvette, son coiffeur. Pratique pour les députés et tous les gens qui travaillent ici.

La Seine

Le pont Alexandre III, les cadenas d'amour du pont des Arts et la statue de la Liberté sur l'île aux Cygnes.

l'Arc de Triomphe

L'invité incontournable des promenades parisiennes.

Paris n'oublie pas de laisser aux artistes de l'espace sur ses murs, c'est le street art !

Se prendre pour un roi au jardin des Tuileries.

Dans le quartier de la Mouzaïa, on se sent comme dans un village.

Ici, je suis perchée sur une œuvre d'art : les fameuses colonnes de Buren, dans la cour du Palais-Royal. Quand je vous dis que Paris est un chef-d'œuvre !

Les bouquinistes sont présents le long des quais depuis plus de 300 ans !

Au musée Grévin, tu peux rencontrer les plus grandes stars françaises et internationales. Elles sont en cire mais on les croirait vivantes !

Avec ses airs de temple japonais, la Pagode (7e arr.) est aussi un cinéma.

Orsay, un musée dans une gare

Avant d'être un musée, Orsay était une gare qui reliait les villes situées au sud-ouest de Paris. Et puis, elle est devenue trop petite. Mais elle était tellement jolie avec ses airs de palais, que l'on a décidé de la transformer pour exposer des œuvres d'art allant de 1848 à 1914. Dans ce musée, on a même conservé les horloges de l'époque. Sur la façade côté Seine, tu peux aussi t'amuser à découvrir les noms des villes que la gare desservait.

Impressionnant !

Le musée d'Orsay, mais aussi le musée **Marmottan** *sont réputés pour leurs tableaux de grands peintres* ***impressionnistes.***

Ces artistes du 19e siècle préféraient peindre l'impression qu'ils ressentaient devant un paysage plutôt que la réalité. Ils s'exprimaient par petites touches de couleur.

Renoir, Manet, Monet *sont des impressionnistes français connus dans le monde entier.*

Voici un détail de **Impression, soleil levant*,** *de Claude Monet.*

C'est ce tableau qui a donné son nom à l'impressionnisme.

À ton tour d'imaginer un coucher de soleil avec des petites touches de couleur.

** Tu peux découvrir ce tableau en entier au musée Marmottan.*

La Maison de Molière

Non, ce n'est pas ici qu'habitait Molière, l'un des plus grands auteurs français. C'est le surnom que l'on donne à une très grande et ancienne troupe de théâtre, **la "Comédie-Française"**. C'est le roi Louis XIV qui l'a créée en 1680, car il aimait beaucoup le théâtre.

Depuis plus de trois siècles, la Comédie-Française interprète des pièces du théâtre français, et notamment celles de Molière. Pour lui rendre hommage, la Comédie-Française est donc aussi appelée "la Maison de Molière".

Molière 1662-1673

(de son vrai nom Jean-Baptiste Poquelin)

Les pièces de théâtre de Molière sont des comédies. Leur but est de divertir ou de faire rire. Elles montrent de façon comique les défauts et les excès des hommes de son époque.

Dans *L'Avare*, par exemple, il présente un homme qui ne veut absolument rien dépenser. Aujourd'hui encore, c'est très drôle.

JEU

Voici une scène de L'Avare, une pièce de Molière. Redonne la bonne réplique à chaque personnage.

le Centre Pompidou

Le 31 janvier 1977, les Parisiens découvrent dans leur ville une grande construction un peu bizarre. Elle ressemble à un Meccano géant. Ce bâtiment est en fait un immense lieu d'art moderne appelé le Centre Pompidou. On le surnomme aussi **Beaubourg**. À l'intérieur, c'est un vrai bonheur : il y a un musée, une bibliothèque, des salles d'exposition et de cinéma, et même un espace exprès pour les enfants !

Le Centre Pompidou porte le nom de Georges Pompidou, le Président de la France de 1969 à 1974. C'est lui qui a eu l'idée de le faire construire. Hélas, il est mort avant que le bâtiment ne soit terminé.

Dans ce bâtiment, rien n'est caché. Déjà, il est transparent. Et ses gros tuyaux multicolores ne sont pas là que pour décorer. Ils ont chacun un rôle. ***L'électricité passe dans les tuyaux jaunes, l'air dans les bleus et l'eau dans les verts. Le rouge, c'est pour la circulation*** *(les escaliers, les ascenseurs).*

À la belle fontaine

Juste à côté du Centre Pompidou, tu peux découvrir une fontaine vraiment pas comme les autres. 16 sculptures étonnantes, animées par des jets d'eau y ont été installées. Chacune d'entre elles évoque les œuvres musicales d'un grand compositeur russe, **Igor Stravinski**.

C'est un couple d'artistes qui les a imaginées en 1983 : **Jean Tinguely** et **Niki de Saint Phalle**. Ils ont sans doute voulu rendre la musique visible et encore plus merveilleuse. Jean Tinguely a créé les sculptures qui ressemblent à des machines métalliques. Celles de sa femme ont des formes plus rondes, colorées et gaies.

JEU

Retrouve ces 4 œuvres de Niki de Saint Phalle dans la fontaine Stravinski.

Comme sur le cœur, imagine les jets d'eau sur les sculptures.

Elles décorent Paris

les fontaines de Sir Wallace

Une petite soif ?
Pars à la recherche d'une fontaine Wallace.
Elles datent de la fin du 19e siècle.
À cette époque, l'eau courante et potable n'était pas répandue.
En 1875, un monsieur anglais très riche, *Sir Wallace*, va alors offrir des dizaines de "fontaines à boire" aux Parisiens.
Construites en fonte, elles étaient peintes en vert pour se fondre dans le paysage.
Les plus jolies sont ornées de quatre cariatides (des statues de femmes).
Aujourd'hui, on compte encore plus de 100 fontaines Wallace dans Paris.

JEU

Sais-tu que chacune des cariatides des fontaines Wallace représente une qualité ?

Pour les connaître, suis le code couleur.

A	B	C	É	H	I	L
M	N	O	P	R	S	T

la
la
la
la

les colonnes de Monsieur Morris

Nous sommes au 19e siècle. Monsieur Gabriel Morris est un imprimeur spécialisé dans les affiches de spectacles. En 1868, il obtient un accord de la Ville de Paris pour construire 450 colonnes en fonte de 6,50 m de haut. Ces colonnes deviennent rapidement un beau moyen pour faire la publicité des théâtres.

À l'origine, elles permettaient aussi de ranger les balais et les pelles destinés au nettoyage des rues. Maintenant, elles font la publicité des films, et parfois, elles tournent !

JEU

7 erreurs se sont cachées entre ces deux anciennes affiches de spectacles.

Montmartre un village éternel

Grimpe maintenant avec nous jusqu'à la butte Montmartre. C'est vrai, il faut escalader un petit peu pour arriver au sommet de cette colline. Mais une fois là-haut, on est récompensé : Paris se transforme en village !

Eh oui, au 19e siècle, la butte Montmartre était couverte de jardins, de vignes et des moulins tournaient au vent. Aujourd'hui, même si elle est devenue très touristique, elle a gardé son air de campagne. Rue Saint-Vincent, les vignes continuent même de pousser.

JEU

Ouvre l'œil ! 7 erreurs se sont cachées entre ces deux scènes.

Paris des Artistes

Au 19e siècle, de nombreux peintres et poètes sont venus habiter sur la butte Montmartre. Ils menaient une vie de bohème. C'est-à-dire qu'ils vivaient tranquillement sans se soucier du lendemain.

Sacré-Cœur

Après la tour Eiffel, voici l'autre star de notre ville. Les gens disent qu'elle ressemble à un énorme chou à la crème. En fait, c'est une basilique, à savoir une grande église distinguée par le pape. Elle s'élève au-dessus de Paris depuis 1914. Lors de sa construction, on voulait qu'elle soit visible de partout. Pari réussi. C'est grâce à sa hauteur mais aussi sa blancheur. Le Sacré-Cœur est construit avec de la pierre de Château-Landon, qui a la bonne idée de blanchir en vieillissant !

Un sacré coup d'œil ! Une fois à l'intérieur de la basilique, monte jusqu'à son dôme. Tu auras l'une des plus belles vues sur Paris.

JEU

Un peu d'exercice !
Si tu montes à pied au sommet de la butte Montmartre,
tu vas escalader ____ marches,
____ mètres de dénivelé
et ____ mètres
de distance.

Additionne les chiffres par couleur.

8
2
12
50
25
12
25
20
12
25
150
25

Sinon, tu peux gravir la pente en funiculaire et en 1 minute 30. C'est amusant aussi.

le Moulin-Rouge

Ça tourne toujours !

Bienvenue dans le plus célèbre cabaret du monde ! Un cabaret ? C'est un endroit où l'on peut dîner tout en savourant un spectacle. Attention, celui-ci n'est pas comme les autres. Il est ouvert au pied de la butte Montmartre depuis 1889 ! Dès son ouverture, c'était un lieu incroyable avec sa piste de danse gigantesque et ses miroirs partout. Ce qui a fait et fait encore le succès du Moulin-Rouge, c'est une danse fameuse : **le french cancan.** Autour d'une musique joyeuse et très rythmée, les danseuses font le grand écart, lèvent leurs jambes le plus haut possible, et (chut !), soulèvent leurs jupons.

Miam le Croque-Monsieur

C'est un peu la vedette des bistrots. Il serait apparu pour la première fois vers 1910 dans un café parisien. Selon la légende, il doit son nom à un patron de bistrot dont certains disaient qu'il était un ogre. Un jour, alors qu'il n'avait plus de baguette, il servit un sandwich au pain de mie. Étonné, un des ses clients lui demanda ce qu'il y avait à l'intérieur. Pour blaguer, le patron lui répondit : "de la viande de monsieur, évidemment !".

La recette (pour 1 croque-monsieur)

❶ Prends une tranche de pain de mie et recouvre-la avec la tranche de jambon pliée en deux. ❷ Dépose le gruyère râpé. ❸ Recouvre de la deuxième tranche de pain. ❹ Dans une poêle (avec l'aide d'un adulte), fais fondre le beurre sans qu'il noircisse. ❺ Dépose ensuite le croque dans la poêle, laisse-le dorer doucement de chaque côté.

et hop ! tu n'as plus qu'à te régaler !
Tu peux accompagner ton croque d'une salade verte.

PAS DE JALOUX ! *Et pour faire un croque-madame, il suffit d'ajouter un œuf au plat sur ton croque-monsieur.*

Auguste Rodin

Né à Paris en 1840, Auguste Rodin
est l'un des plus grands sculpteurs français.
Dès l'enfance, **il est fasciné par le dessin.**
À 15 ans, il découvre la sculpture, puis il se passionne
pour le corps humain qu'il observe attentivement.
C'est pourquoi ses figures humaines ont **beaucoup de force et d'expression.**
L'hôtel Biron, où il vécut, est devenu un musée.
Tu peux y découvrir un grand nombre de ses
œuvres, dont *Le Baiser*.

Le Penseur, *sa sculpture la plus célèbre, médite en plein air dans le parc de l'hôtel Biron. À l'origine, cette statue faisait 70 cm de haut et devait faire partie d'une gigantesque porte. Mais Rodin a finalement choisi d'en faire une œuvre isolée, de 1 m 80. Ce jeu va t'expliquer les étapes de la création d'une telle sculpture.*

JEU

Numérote les étapes dans le bon ordre, puis associe-les à la statue correspondante.

- ◯ *Le modèle est fondu en* *<u>bronze</u>.*
- ◯ *Le sculpteur recherche et crée des modèles en* *<u>terre cuite</u>.*
- ◯ *Le modèle choisi est réalisé en* *<u>plâtre</u> à taille réelle.*

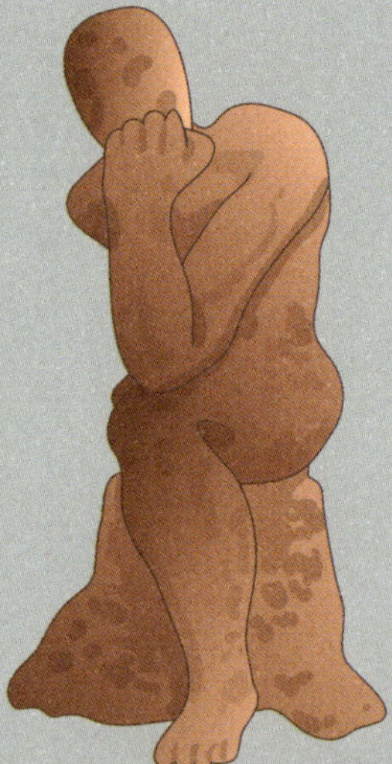

La science amusante

JEU

Si tu veux jouer au petit chimiste ou devenir un grand scientifique, prends le chemin de **la Cité des Sciences et de l'Industrie** ou du **Palais de la Découverte**. On y découvre la science en s'amusant et on participe à plein d'expériences étonnantes.

Dans ces deux lieux décidément incroyables, tu pourras voyager dans l'espace, te prendre pour une fourmi, faire la course avec un squelette ou comprendre des logiques mathématiques.

Normalement, il n'y a pas d'évaluation ni d'interro surprise à la sortie !

Prêt pour une petite expérience dans ta cuisine ? Suis les étapes et observe...

Ce qu'il te faut...

Étape 1

Verse un peu de lait dans l'assiette.

Étape 2

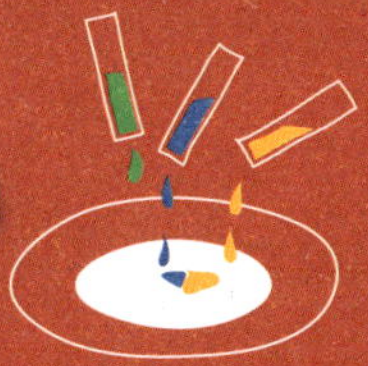

Fais tomber quelques gouttes de couleur au centre.

Étape 3

Trempe le coton-tige dans le produit vaisselle, plonge-le au centre des taches de couleur et admire...

Magique ? Non, chimique !

Pauline fait l'expérience de l'électrostatique au Palais de la Découverte. Dessine ses cheveux dressés sur sa tête !

JEU

Le joli mur végétal du musée

Bienvenue au Quai Branly

Afrique, Amériques, Asie, Océanie. C'est parti pour un voyage aux quatre coins de la Terre. Voici le musée du quai Branly. Son nom vient du lieu où il est construit (au bord de la Seine, tout près de la tour Eiffel).

Parmi les 3 000 objets exposés, tu vas, par exemple, découvrir des masques du monde entier. Ils ne servent pas forcément à se déguiser. Ce sont des objets d'art qui te permettent de comprendre les rites ou les traditions des pays lointains.

Au fil de ta visite, tu verras que ces masques ont chacun une fonction précise : guérir des maladies, aider à trouver de la nourriture, célébrer des mariages ou chasser le mauvais esprit après la mort.

Ces masques du ***Sri Lanka*** *aux yeux exorbités n'ont pas l'air très très gentils !*

Bien au contraire ! On les utilise pour repousser le Mal (lorsqu'on est malade, par exemple).

Le Sri Lanka est un pays situé au sud de l'Inde.

Imagine, à ton tour, un masque le plus féroce possible pour faire fuir les forces du Mal !

le monde à Paris

La Grande Mosquée de Paris

Tout au long du 20e siècle, et encore aujourd'hui, des millions d'étrangers sont venus à Paris pour trouver un travail ou une vie meilleure.

C'est pourquoi, en te promenant dans certains quartiers parisiens, tu as parfois l'impression de te balader **à travers le monde.** Dans le 13e arrondissement, tu peux parcourir le plus grand quartier chinois d'Europe. On l'appelle **Chinatown.** Un peu plus au nord, celui de la **Goutte d'Or** t'emmènerait presque en Afrique. Dans le 5e arrondissement, les musulmans prient dans la plus grande mosquée de France.

Bon voyage !

JEU

À quelle région du monde peux-tu associer ces objets, aperçus à Paris ?

Maghreb

Afrique noire

Chine

Russie

Promenons-nous dans les bois...

Non, il n'y a pas que des boulevards et des monuments à Paris. C'est même une ville très verte. On y compte plus de 400 parcs et jardins. Pour respirer, pédaler, ramer, ou pique-niquer, il y a le choix. Tu pourras aussi te retrouver nez à nez avec plein d'animaux.

Aujourd'hui, nous sommes au jardin du Luxembourg. On peut y faire du poney, du tennis, ou même voir Guignol. Mais ce que l'on préfère avec ma sœur, c'est louer de petits bateaux que l'on pousse avec un long bâton. Ils existent depuis 1881 !

C'est ici, dans le Palais du Luxembourg que se réunissent les sénateurs.

JEU

Qui a envoyé son bateau le plus loin ? Celui de Martin a du rouge et du bleu mais n'a pas de blanc. Celui de Pauline a la même coque que celle de Martin, et il n'a pas de vert.

JEU

Remets cette scène dans l'ordre.

Dans le bois de Vincennes ou le bois de Boulogne, c'est comme si tu étais dans une forêt. Là, le chêne est roi. Pauline et moi, on adore le Jardin d'acclimatation du bois de Boulogne : les miroirs déformants, la barque sur la Rivière enchantée...

Et puis les zoos, oui, à Paris ! Celui de Vincennes vient de faire peau neuve et celui du Jardin des plantes est tout simplement le plus vieux du monde ! Papa, lui, préfère flâner parmi les sculptures du jardin des Tuileries.

Tout près du bois, le château fort de Vincennes, avec son énorme de Donjon (50 mètres de haut !), est l'un des plus grands et mieux conservés d'Europe. Visite très conseillée.

La tour Montparnasse

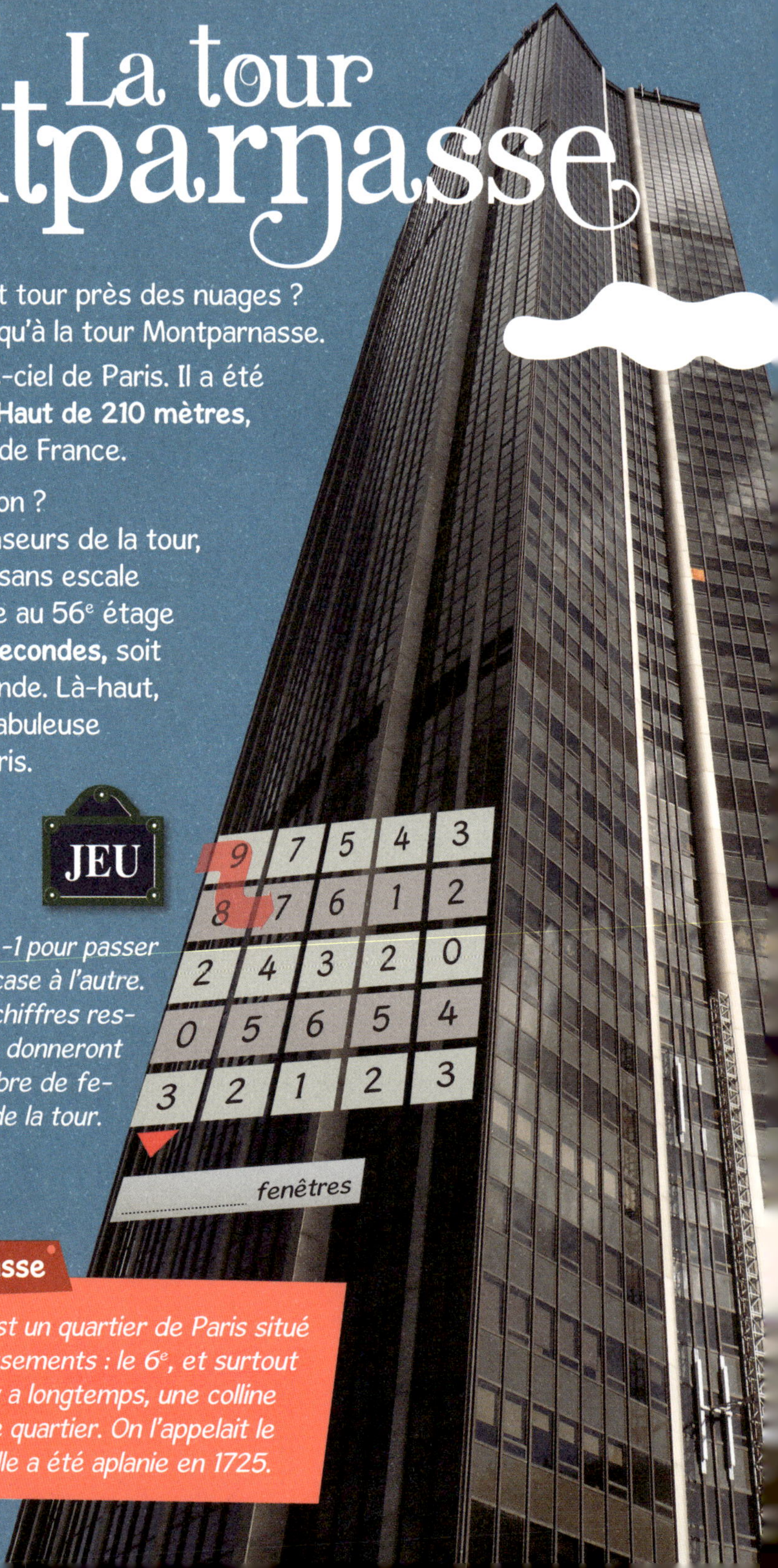

Ça te dirait un petit tour près des nuages ? Alors suis-nous jusqu'à la tour Montparnasse.

C'est le seul gratte-ciel de Paris. Il a été construit en 1973. **Haut de 210 mètres,** il est le plus grand de France.

Prêt pour l'ascension ? Parmi les 25 ascenseurs de la tour, le plus rapide relie sans escale le rez-de-chaussée au 56e étage **en seulement 38 secondes,** soit 6 mètres par seconde. Là-haut, tu auras une vue fabuleuse à 360° sur tout Paris.

JEU

+1 ou -1 pour passer d'une case à l'autre. Les chiffres restants te donneront le nombre de fenêtres de la tour.

9	7	5	4	3
8	7	6	1	2
2	4	3	2	0
0	5	6	5	4
3	2	1	2	3

.... fenêtres

Le mont Parnasse

Montparnasse est un quartier de Paris situé sur trois arrondissements : le 6e, et surtout le 14e et le 15e. Il y a longtemps, une colline se trouvait dans ce quartier. On l'appelait le "mont Parnasse". Elle a été aplanie en 1725.

les dessous de Paris

Il y en a des choses surprenantes dans le sous-sol de notre ville. On peut même les visiter. Allez, suis-moi !

les égouts

Se promener dans des égouts ? Beurk. Mais non, tu vas voir, c'est intéressant. Ici, sous terre, on récupère les eaux usées des habitations pour les diriger vers des stations de nettoyage. C'est comme une ville sous la ville. **Chaque rue de Paris a un égout à son nom.** Il y a même les numéros des immeubles pour se repérer en cas de problème. 300 égoutiers veillent sur ce labyrinthe de 2 500 km. C'est un métier qui, souvent, se transmet de père en fils.

JEU *Cet égoutier s'est perdu, peux-tu l'aider à retrouver son chemin ?*

les catacombes

Depuis la fin du 18e siècle, des milliers de crânes et de tibias s'entassent dans ces carrières souterraines.

À l'époque, il n'y avait plus de place dans les cimetières ; on a alors décidé de transférer tous les ossements des siècles passés dans ce lieu. Ceux de ***Jean de La Fontaine*** *se trouveraient ici. Alors, t'es cap pour la visite ? Même pas peur !*

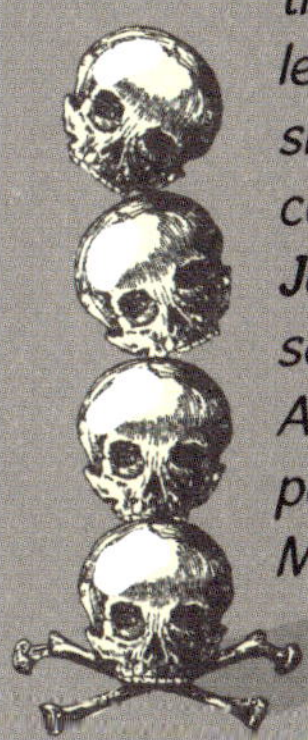

le château de Versailles

Depuis 1979, le château de Versailles est classé au patrimoine mondial de l'Unesco.

Nous voici à 20 km de Paris, mais cela vaut le détour. Le château de Versailles est l'un des plus grands et magnifiques palais du monde. C'est le roi **Louis XIV** qui l'a fait construire à partir des années 1660. Il avait beaucoup de goût pour la gloire et le luxe.

La galerie des Glaces

Imaginé par l'architecte Le Vau, le château s'étend sur 67 000 m^2 et comprend plus de 2 000 pièces, dont la très célèbre **galerie des Glaces.**
Cette salle éblouissante, longue de 73 mètres, est revêtue de 357 miroirs ! Le décor n'a pas changé et, comme les visiteurs de Louis XIV, tu seras forcément impressionné.

Qui a dit que j'aimais le luxe ?

JEU

Connais-tu l'autre nom que l'on donnait au roi Louis XIV ? Tu le découvriras en suivant le parcours fléché.

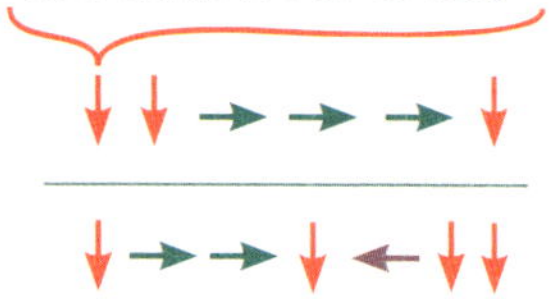

Départ

L	B	A	U	D	V	O
E	-	R	O	E	R	N
G	A	L	I	A	A	B
L	O	E	-	S	O	C
A	R	R	A	E	L	H
C	A	I	A	I	T	A
E	S	E	A	L	E	A

Roland-Garros

Sur terre...

Nous, on adore le tennis.
À Paris, on a de la chance. Tous les ans, on peut assister à l'un des quatre plus importants tournois du monde.
C'est un tournoi du *Grand Chelem* (les autres sont à New York, Londres et Melbourne en Australie). Dans notre ville, les plus grands joueurs s'affrontent au stade **Roland-Garros**. Ici, ils jouent sur des courts en **terre battue**. Elle a une belle couleur orange, car elle est recouverte d'une fine couche de briques réduites en poudre. Cette couche aide à mieux voir la balle et permet aux joueurs de glisser pour la rattraper. Bien joué !

...et dans les airs

Roland Garros était un aviateur français. En 1913, il fut le premier à traverser la Méditerranée en avion. Le stade de tennis porte son nom en souvenir de lui.

JEU

Non, l'avion de Roland-Garros n'était pas une poussette ! Relie les points pour savoir à quoi ressemblait vraiment cet engin.

le canal Saint-martin

Nous, on aime bien se promener le long de ce canal. Ce qui est amusant, c'est de grimper sur une passerelle et de regarder les bateaux ou les péniches remonter le canal jusqu'à la Villette. Ils partent du port de Paris *(ce n'est pas une blague)*, le bassin de l'Arsenal. Ensuite, ils doivent parcourir 4,5 km, franchir 25 mètres de dénivelé et passer 9 **écluses**.

C'est quoi exactement les écluses ?

Ce sont des sortes de petits barrages où l'on change la hauteur de l'eau. Comme ça, les bateaux peuvent passer d'un niveau à l'autre.

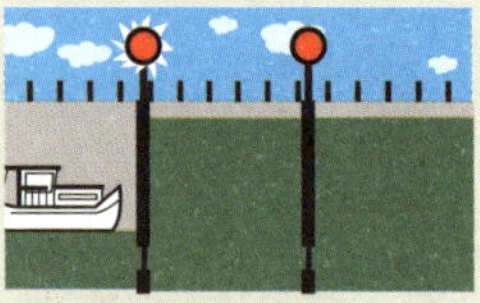

Le bateau demande l'ouverture des vannes.

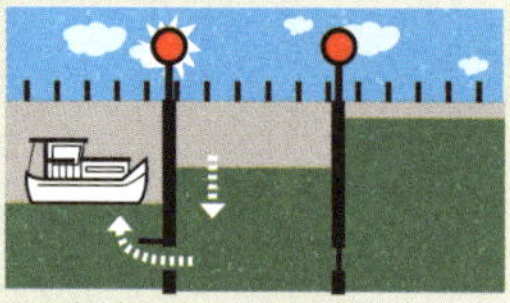

La 1re vanne s'ouvre. L'eau passe.

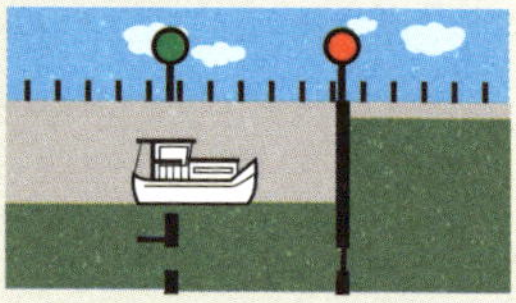

Dès que les niveaux d'eau s'égalisent, le bateau traverse.

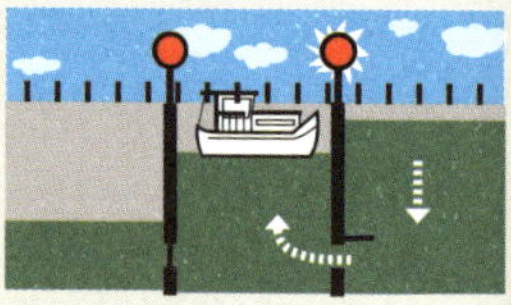

La 1re vanne se referme. La 2e vanne s'ouvre.

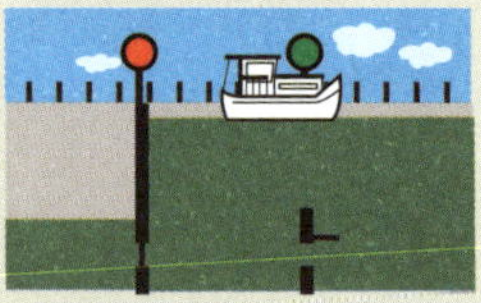

Les niveaux d'eau s'égalisent, le bateau traverse.

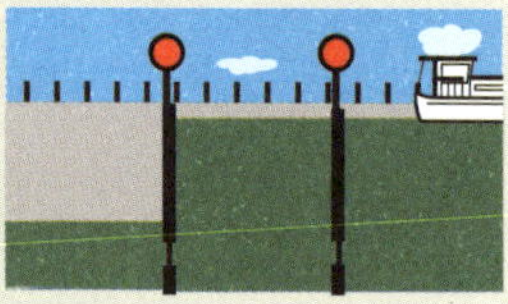

La 2e vanne se referme.

Arrêt sur image

Paris a servi de décor à des centaines de films. Certains, même très anciens, sont devenus célébrissimes. Par exemple, ***Les enfants du Paradis*** ou ***l'Hôtel du Nord***, des chefs-d'œuvres sortis au cinéma lorsque ton papi et ta mamie étaient encore bébés !

HÔTEL DU NORD (1938)

*Le film se déroule dans ce petit hôtel, au bord du canal Saint-Martin. La scène la plus célèbre a lieu sur une passerelle, juste à côté. L'actrice principale y prononce une réplique devenue historique : **"Atmosphère, atmosphère... est-ce que j'ai une gueule d'atmosphère ?"***

Aujourd'hui, l'Hôtel du Nord existe toujours, mais il est devenu un restaurant. Sa façade donne encore l'impression d'être à l'époque du film.

JEU

Voici l'actrice principale de ces deux grands films français. N'oublie pas son nom, c'est une vraie légende !

A E L R T Y

Rébus & Quiz

1

Comment appelle-t-on les fameux bateaux qui naviguent sur la Seine :

1 - les bateaux-libellule
2 - les bateaux-crapauds
3 - les bateaux-mouches

2 *On peut y voir des spectacles.*

3 *Mon préféré...*

4

L'équipe de foot de Paris s'appelle le PSG pour :

1 - Paris Sans Grenouille
2 - Paris Saint-Germain
3 - Passe Siffle et Gagne

5

Sous quel nom est connu Jean-Baptiste Poquelin :

1 - François Mitterrand
2 - Gustave Eiffel
3 - Molière

Le petit lexique

Antiquité
La plus ancienne période des civilisations. Elle s'étend du début de l'Histoire, jusqu'à la chute de l'Empire romain (vers 476 après Jésus-Christ).

À l'italienne
Une salle de théâtre à l'italienne est une salle à la forme arrondie. Elle est organisée sur plusieurs étages disposant de balcons.

Bataille d'Austerlitz
Elle s'est déroulée en 1805 dans l'actuelle République tchèque. Napoléon 1er la gagna.

Chef-d'œuvre
Une réalisation, une œuvre remarquable, parfaite.

Dénivelé
Une différence de niveau.

Épidémie
Une maladie qui touche, en même temps et au même endroit, un très grand nombre de personnes.

Electrostatique :
C'est l'étude de l'électricité statique. L'électricité statique est la force qu'amène un objet chargé d'électricité sur un autre objet ou sur un corps.

Étain
Un métal un peu gris, facile à modeler.

Flâner
Prendre son temps, se promener sans se presser.

Ingénieur
De formation scientifique, c'est une personne qui dirige des travaux et fait des recherches.

Insalubre
Malsain, mauvais pour la santé.

Joaillerie
L'art de fabriquer des bijoux avec des matières précieuses (or, argent).

Music-hall
Une salle de spectacles de variétés.

Mercerie
Un magasin d'accessoires de couture, fils, boutons, rubans...

Mosquée :
Lieu de prière des musulmans.

Musulman :
Une personne qui pratique la religion de Mahomet, l'Islam.

Mythique
Fabuleux, légendaire.

Patrimoine mondial de l'Unesco
Pour faire connaître et préserver les sites culturels ou naturels de très grande importance dans le monde, l'Unesco (Organisation des Nations unies pour l'éducation, les sciences et la culture) a établi une liste qui compte aujourd'hui plus de 900 lieux. En France, par exemple, le Mont-Saint-Michel et le château de Versailles sont classés dans cette liste.

Antiquité

Quiproquo
Un malentendu, prendre une chose ou une personne pour une autre.

Réplique
Au théâtre, c'est une phrase, un texte qu'un comédien dit en réponse à un autre personnage.

Rivet
Une sorte de clou.

Rite : coutume, habitude

Style gothique
Un style d'architecture très répandu entre le 12e et le 16e siècle, notamment pour construire les cathédrales. Il se distingue par ses jolies voûtes et ses grandes fenêtres.

Verrière
Un grand plafond de verre.

Zouave
Un soldat de l'ancienne armée française d'Afrique.

Music-hall

Réponses

Page 6 :
La Ville Lumière : B
Paname : A
Lutèce : C

Page 7 :
Martin est dans le 10e arrondissement.

Page 9 :
3 - C'est la statue de la Liberté.

Page 11 :

Page 8 :

G	T	O	U	O	T	R	E	D
R	A	N	R	N	S	U	M	A
C	O	D	E	I	E	E	T	M
L	N	P	I	F	F	D	R	E
O	C	A	N	V	E	O	O	C
U	I	L	A	A	L	R	S	A
V	E	S	I	L	■	■	A	D
R	R	G	E	I	■	■	Y	E
E	E	I	R	D	E	S	O	R

Page 14 :
La Pyramide date de 1989

Pour fêter le bicentenaire (200 ans) de la Révolution Française.

		19	89	
		40	49	
	15	25	24	
5	10	15	9	
2	3	7	8	1

Page 15 :
La Joconde.
Elle reçoit 15000 visiteurs par jour !

Page 12 :
Par exemple :

potage du jour	1,00
spaghettis bolognaise	8,50
camembert	2,50
crème de marron vanillée	3,00
	15,00

Page 19 :
1er étage : 57 mètres
2e étage : 115 mètres
Hauteur totale : 324 mètres

Page 16 :

Page 20 :
- Diamant
- Rubis
- Émeraude
- Saphir

Page 13 :

Page 21 :
Coco Chanel

Page 22 :

Page 23 :

Page 28 :

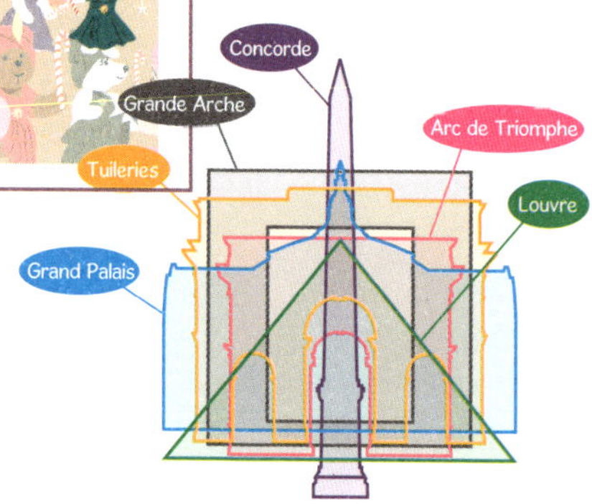

Page 26 :
CE CHAPEAU ÉTAIT-IL GALERIE VIVIENNE OU PASSAGE JOUFFROY ?

Page 24 :
FEYDEAU

Page 25 :
LA VIE EN ROSE

Page 29 :
LOUXOR

Page 30 :
ENCORE DIX BOUTIQUES ET J'ARRÊTE...

Page 32 :
des ÉLECTIONS !

D**E**
GAU**L**LE
MITT**E**RRAND
GIS**C**ARD-D'ES**T**AING
CH**I**RAC
POMPID**O**U
HOLLA**N**DE
SARKOZY

Page 33 :

Page 37 :

Page 39 :

Page 40 :

- BONTÉ
- SIMPLICITÉ
- CHARITÉ
- SOBRIETÉ

Page 41 :

Page 42 :

Page 43 :

222 marches
36 mètres de dénivelé
108 mètres de distance

Page 49 :

Page 46 :

Page 50 :

Martin a envoyé son bateau plus loin.

Page 51 :

Page 52 :

La tour Montparnasse compte **7200** fenêtres.

Page 53 :

Page 54 :

Le Roi-Soleil

Page 57 :

ARLETTY

Page 58 :

1 - Les bateaux-mouches
2 - Le Moulin-Rouge (Moule-Un-Roue-Jeu) et l'Olympia (Eau-l'Un-Pie-A)
3 - Macaron à la vanille (Mât-K-Rond-A-Lave-A-Nid-Yeux)
4 - Paris Saint-Germain
5 - Molière

Dans la même collection :

LE MONDE ARABE
LE MAROC
LA TURQUIE
L'ESPAGNE
L'ITALIE
LE PORTUGAL
L'ANGLETERRE
NEW YORK
PARIS FOR KIDS
(Version anglaise)
NANTES
LA VENDÉE

Du même auteur :
LES GUIDES DE CONVERSATION
DES ENFANTS

LA CUISINE
DES ENFANTS

Auteurs : Stéphanie et Hugues Bioret, Julie Godefroy

Illustrations : Stéphanie Bioret, Julie Godefroy

Crédits photographiques : Fotolia - iStock - Rémi Jouan *Opéra de Paris (p 27)* - Nicolas Sanchez *Horloge et Musée d'Orsay (p 36)* - Stéphanie et Hugues Bioret

Remerciements : M. Fabien de Sylvestre (*illustration Paris XVIIe siècle*), Bouillon Chartier (groupe Gérard Joulie), Domitille Bioret, Guy Bioret, nos petits "testeurs" de jeux, Martin, Angèle et Jules.

CONTACT :
tél. 06 13 54 19 80
bonhommedechemin@orange.fr
www.bonhommedechemin.fr

Malgré le soin apporté à la conception et au contenu de cet ouvrage, celui-ci est tributaire des changements et des évolutions. N'hésitez pas à nous faire part de vos remarques. Les suggestions sont aussi les bienvenues.

Conforme à la loi n°49956 du 16 juillet 1949 sur les publications destinées à la jeunesse

ISBN : 979-10-92714-01-2

Impression Groupe Lussaud (85)
Imprimé sur papier PEFC

Achevé d'imprimer en juillet 2014

Dépôt légal : février 2014

PEFC
PEFC/10-31-1658
PROMOUVOIR LA GESTION DURABLE DE LA FORÊT

IMPRIM'VERT®